A CELTIC

TAPESTRY

Livia Ellis	Elle J Rossi
Hunter S Jones	Miranda Stork
Laura De Luca	Carolyn Wolfe
Elodie Parkes	Tara S Wood

A Celtic Tapestry

Livia Ellis, Elle J Rossi, Hunter S Jones, Miranda Stork, Laura de Luca, Carolyn Wolfe, Elodie Parkes, Tara S Wood

ISBN-13: 978-0-9575757-0-7

Moon Rose
Publishing

STORIES

Chapter One

Somebody is going to die tonight.

"Oh, lucky me. It's Josie. I see you've joined the living."

I stop and squint into the dark interior of Wolfie's, where I tend bar five nights a week and sometimes on Sunday. Annoyance wraps its prickly arms around me, instantly changing my mood from thoughtful to combative. Perhaps the cocky bartender has a death wish. So what if I'm a little late tonight and didn't show up for work last night? I don't have to explain my reasons or whereabouts to this knob. At least I'm here now. Sore, but here. As for the living part, I can't really claim to be completely alive—not in the human sense of the word—but no chance will I be sharing that bit of juice with the tool behind the bar. The less he knows the better. Same goes for most of the general population.

Ignorance is bliss. Especially this time of year. Ostara—the Spring Equinox—is one of only two times a year when light equals dark. When the secluded lore creatures come out of hiding to wreak havoc on the innocent. When daywalkers and nightwalkers co-exist for a full twenty-four hours. A recipe for disaster, also known as: My Busiest Season.

Even now, I'm scanning the crowd, alert and ready to protect. Humans are so unassuming, so blasé when it comes to their safety. In their defense, they don't know what lurks around the dark corners at night. I do, and it isn't pretty.

I'm Josie Hawk.

I'm a killer. Literally. Technically I'm classified as a Huntress (even though I'm only a half-breed), but the ultimate outcome of any given hunt is death. Be it by hand or weapon — I prefer blades with blinged-out handles. It isn't easy, but it's who I am. My father taught me how to hunt and how to live. My mother, God rest her soul, taught me how to love fiercely. But then she died and took most of that love with her. The fierce part I kept though. I hold it close, like a baby clutches a blanket, security in the purest sense. If I'm fierce, I'm alive. If I'm alive, I can hunt. And if I can hunt, I can protect the people of my city.

To most, I'm just another bartender in another bar. Friendly enough, even if a little off with my over the top opinions and fashion choices. I don't mind being off. I suppose some killers might prefer to blend, become part of the scenery. Not me. I prefer to be the brightest flower in the bunch. The red rose stashed in a white bouquet. The lone neon sign on the dark street.

As I sashay by in my zombie stompers and ripped fishnets, I try hard not to limp from my recently injured ankle, because let's face it, limping totally ruins the whole sashay effect.

But I can't be that flashy all the time. Not when I'm hunting. The time between last call and dawn, I become part of the shadows, part of the night. I spend so many hours there, it's no wonder I prefer the spotlight in my off time.

It's a little quiet in Wolfie's tonight, and that has the fine hairs on my arms standing on end. A quiet country-western bar is like a hamburger joint with no fries. I quickly note the lack of a band. Must be running late. Not cool. I'll need to make a phone call and get a replacement if they don't show up soon. For the life of me, I can't remember who I had scheduled to play tonight. I did schedule someone, didn't I? This whole Ostara business has my mind muddled and I don't like it.

"Nice outfit, by the way," Tool Boy says before averting his attention to a rag and the bar, rubbing the pungent cleanser in circles and then wiping it away.

My squint turns into an eye roll and I know I'll never be able to stop the words that are only a breath away from tumbling out of my mouth. I have the habit of throwing sarcasm more often than a pitcher throws a ball in the World Series. A smile tugs at the corners of my mouth while I run my finger across the gleaming oak.

"Yeah, go ahead and polish your wood, Wes." I arch a brow. "You're really good at it." His eyes widen and I know I've hit a mark. I'm not usually this combative with him. Maybe now he'll back off. Personally, I rather like tonight's attire. After waking from the longest stretch of sleep I've had in six months, I took an even longer shower before carefully choosing my ensemble. I paired a white tee embellished with ropey chains with a black tutu. Chances are, the chains will come in handy at some point in the night. The glittery earrings I'd added as a pick-me-up. Anything to add some sparkle to my dark world.

Wes mumbles *"bitch"* under his breath and quickly turns away. I couldn't care less and don't even bother to reprimand him. The small crowd in the bar whoops with laughter, encouraging the caustic banter.

Attention seeker that I am, I drop my messenger bag, hop up on the bar, curtsy to the crowd and tip my black cowboy hat to a snarling Wes, who practically has smoke coming out of his ears.

After the last bit of applause echoes and fades, I allow a man in jeans and flannel to help me off the bar. Even though I catch him looking up my skirt and frowning when he sees the frilly bloomers beneath rather than the anticipated skin, I blow him a kiss and offer him my hat. He winks, takes the hat and puts it on his head, pulling it low over his brow. The exchange with Wes flees my mind quicker than a deer sprinting into the woods. He really isn't worth the effort.

A current ripples through the air. No one notices but me. Something about this Ostara is different, though I can't quite put my finger on what has caused the shift. Somehow the nasties are seeping through the cracks two days earlier than they should be. This does not bode well. How many times do I have to beg the Assembly—the governing council of all lore—to form a committee to negotiate a peaceful alliance between the light and dark creatures? I've busted my ass to make it happen, trying to prove to the Assembly that I can lead the troops. I want to lead. I need to lead. An answer has not been forthcoming. Their silence—scratch that—their *negligence* to let me do what needs to be done to protect my city, to protect people like this friendly just-wants-to-enjoy-his-beer-and-have-a-good-time cowboy, eats at my gut like a pack of starved and snarling wolves.

I grab my bag off the stool and head to the back of the bar, smiling to the patrons as I walk by. Recognizing a few regulars seated at the corner table near the soundboard, I force myself to take a few moments to chitchat. Typically, I enjoy talking to people.

Tonight, I can't seem to focus on the conversation for any length of time without eyeing the door for lethal beings. It's exhausting, but with the help of these friendly people, I somehow manage to forget about the incident from two nights ago—the one that kept me away from Wolfie's. I even manage to forget about the pain in my ankle and the hours I'd missed while my body recuperated. I am home again.

I love this place. Not just Wofie's, but this entire city. From the autographed memorabilia adorning the walls of this dark bar, to the Elvis impersonator on the corner of Broadway and Fourth, to the random guitar player on every other corner. Nope. This isn't Vegas. It's Nashville, baby. All the way. Music, lights, and really great people. My people. I took a vow to protect the innocent many years ago, and the only way I'll break that promise is if I get myself killed. I'm not dead yet, at least half of me isn't, though I've come close to total lights-out plenty of times.

Being Friday night, I stash my gear under the bar and take a deep breath, readying myself. Though there are only a few people in the bar now, within the hour the place will be packed and Wes and I will have our hands full. I pull my bright red hair into a low pony, and my eyes zero in on the stage again. A quick glance at the clock has me really pissed off that the band hasn't shown up yet.

Normally, live music plays from noon to two a.m., with band changes every four hours or so. Just now, Alan Jackson is crooning from the overhead speakers and that's just not good enough. The empty stage reminds me of a ghost town. The platform sits right next to the front door, placed there for space as well as attracting the people off the streets. The entire front wall of Wolfie's, and every other bar in Nashville, consists of windows. Cheapest marketing out there. And another reason we keep the door open.

Unfortunately, the vamps in the area also consider an open door their invitation in. As long as they keep their fangs to themselves, I'm cool with them. Only once have I had to take someone out back, so to speak. One of us returned. The other? Let's just say, ash happens and leave it at that.

Damn. I should know what's up with the band, or lack thereof. I'm supposed to be in charge. Truth is, I'm part owner of this place. Sage Larson, my best friend and the nicest vampire you'll ever come across, has the other fifty percent stake in Wolfie's. I love that girl. It has nothing to do with the fact we're practically mirror images—except she's a skinny mini with dainty fangs and I'm . . . we'll just say not so skinny and very unfanged. Our connection runs deep for many reasons, but mainly because I know I can trust her and—most importantly—she'll never leave me.

Not to mention the fact that she forgave me for breaking her brother's heart. Just thinking of Keller gives me the tingles. The good and bad kind. But that's history, and history is where Keller will stay even though my body still craves his bite. Technically Sage and Keller aren't related, but the same sire turned them, and their sibling bond is stronger than if they had shared a womb. Sometimes I'm jealous of their closeness. Most of the time, I'm just happy Sage has a brother who would do anything for her. Anything at all.

"Where's the band, Wes?" He ignores me and continues stocking the beer cooler as I give him my angry laser stare, minus the laser.

"Wes!"

"Don't know," he says over his shoulder, not daring to make eye contact.

I guess he's decided I won this particular battle. Yay, me. Having crashed for a solid day has me feeling a little lost in my own world. I can't even remember which band I had scheduled to play tonight. Normally, those details are stored in my brain, which tends to be more organized than any notepad or computer system I've ever attempted to use. But not tonight. Even though I'd won, that last hunt really whooped my ass. My brain is throbbing just as much as my blasted ankle. I hate not being in prime condition. But I can't let my ankle or a killer headache keep me from hunting tonight. I need to be on the streets.

Nasties certainly will be.

Which leads me back to my current issue. The fact that none of the band members have shown up yet gives me a queasy feeling. Musicians in this city are not only talented but very reliable. My instincts tell me something is wrong—like maybe they're not here because they're dead—but that could just be me trying to get my bearings back. The fog of sleep still has me under its spell. If I were full Huntress, I wouldn't sleep at all. But since I'm half human, I need to refuel my energy every now and then.

No band equals loss of revenue. Big time. I close my eyes and lean back against the bar, propping my boot up on a low shelf. The need for more sleep threatens to pull me under, and if it wouldn't smear my eyeliner, I'd rub the sandpaper from beneath my lids. Popping one eye open and then the other, I bite my lip as an idea takes form. I can fix this. I'll just hook up the karaoke equipment. Wes's newly shined bar is about to get boot-scuffed. Like peanut butter and jelly, karaoke and bar dancing are always better together.

I drop my boot to the floor and cringe as sparks of pain shoot up my leg. I transfer all my weight to my right foot. That shifter had really done a number when he'd sunk his canines into my leg. I smile to myself. He paid for it with his life. The smile quickly fades as dark thoughts creep in. Just because that particular beast is dead doesn't mean the teenage boy he'd sold drugs to won't find someone else to buy from. Another corner. Another dealer. Innocence forever gone with the purchase of one little package. I don't like it. Not in my city. I plant both feet firmly on the ground and crack my neck. The next dealer will have to die, too. They all will. One by one.

I shake my head to clear the last bit of sleep fog and turn to the small crowd sitting in the back of the bar. "Karaoke in twenty. Who's ready to show off their pipes?"

"*Aye*, I'd like to," a rumbling lilt answers in my ear. Goosebumps instantly cover every square inch of skin on my body. I know that voice. I feel his breath on my neck and I don't know whether to run or fight.

Four deep breaths and several mental pep talks later, I turn to face a history that is doomed to repeat itself. "Hello, Keller."

Chapter Two

Just like in one of those really obnoxious romantic movies, the voices grow muffled and everything around me slows down. I know it's not really happening, and I feel like a total sap-ass jerk, but the imaginary tunnel obscures everything but the man in front of me. Keller O'Leary. His dark and dangerous looks, his three-week-overdue-for-a-cut hair, his two-day beard, his jet-black eyes. Eyes that have always seen too much. Eyes that probe until I feel as if he can see inside my soul. He wants to own me, still. I can tell. He doesn't even try to hide it from me. I wasn't ready for his intensity last time. Considering my heart is tumbling through my lava-hot blood in the direction of the floor, I know I'm not ready for him now either.

I never will be.

He demands everything without ever speaking a word.

"What are you doing here?" I ask. I shove past, ignoring the electric jolt I get when my shoulder brushes against his arm. It's always been that way. Such explosive passion should not exist between two beings. It's not safe. He's not safe.

He grips my elbow and I immediately throw up my walls and fortify them with gumption and determination. This time will be different. "If you're looking for Sage," I say, "she's not here."

Keller smiles, slow and wide. His eyes offer a hint of laughter, and already my walls start to crack. Right now they're just surface cracks, tiny little microscopic fissures, but it won't take long for him to obliterate my entire foundation. I'm so weak around him and I can't stand it.

"*Aye*," he says. "I know. She'll be in later. I'm here to play, Josie."

As if. "Well, I'm not a toy. And I have work to do." Except I want to be his toy in a really bad way. If only he could learn how to keep things light.

He laughs. His dark gaze scans the crowd and I wonder what he's up to. He knows I'm a Huntress. That it's my job to keep tabs on my patrons. Not his. That's one of the reasons we broke up. As a matter of fact, that reason sits at the tippy top of a very long list.

"As much as I'd love that," Keller says. "I donnae' have the time. My band mates are unloading the gear now. We'll be set up in a half hour tops."

Whoa. What? "Band mates?" Regardless of how sexy those words sound coming from his Irish mouth… Uh, uh. Not gonna happen. Keller has always loved music, but I'd thought drumming was just a hobby. Conveniently—*not*—an image of him shirtless, his lean muscles slick with sweat as he drives the beat of the music is way too easy to conjure. I realize I want to see him play and that just burns my bloomers. I thought I was over him. Out of sight, out of mind has never worked, so why the hell I thought seeing him again wouldn't affect me had been an ignorant assumption on my part. And here I pride myself on actually having brains. Said brains are now mush.

Keller leans his elbows against the bar, striking a pose that is meant to be casual. It's not. His back is straight, his jaw tight. "I thought Sage would have told you." He shrugs. "I joined a band. We were in the area and she said we could play tonight. I guess you had an open slot." Reaching for my hair, he slides his thumb along my cheek before wrapping a curling strand around his finger. "How incredibly fortunate."

For him, maybe. "No." I pull my hair away. "Sage did not tell me." I'm going to kill her. I'm not stupid. I know a setup when I see one. This is a big one. Epic. But business is business and if Keller's band mates are anything like him, they'll rock it tonight. He never does anything halfway. Never. "Fine. Whatever."

"Things are heating up outside, Josie. You need to be careful."

Though I know what he's talking about, I don't take the bait and I definitely don't appreciate the stern tone of his voice. "Of course it's heating up." I give him my best duh look. "Winter's over."

He narrows his eyes. "You know what I mean."

I tilt my head. "Do I?"

I scan the crowd and spot a dressed-to-kill sorceress perched on the end of the bar. Strappy sandals snake halfway up her bare legs. Her skirt is so short, any slight bend on her part will expose more than I'd ever care to see. Her hair is sleek yet tousled; blood red lips frame her enchanting smile. Already two cowboys are making their way over to her. I'll have to watch her closely. Make sure she keeps her magick contained. I sneak a look at Keller to see if he's noticed her. If he has, I can't tell. Not with him staring at me like a starving vampire. Oh, wait... Right. Vampires are always starving for one thing or another.

"What's the name of your band?" I ask absently to quell the sizzling tension. "I'll make an announcement." I shift so I can see the sorceress better.

Keller leans in, skims a knuckle over my jaw to draw my attention back to him. "Crimson Beat."

Hello, dramatic eye roll. "You have got to be kidding." He nods his head toward the front of Wolfie's. I turn just as the rest of the band walks through the door, and I know Keller isn't kidding at all. Vampires. Every last one of them. Strong, lean and sexy as hell. I turn back to Keller, narrow my eyes and jab my finger into his chest. "No trouble. Do you understand me?"

He wraps his hand around my finger, brings it to his lips for a kiss. I jerk away, but not before my breath catches in my throat. He notices, runs a fang across his lower lip.

"*Aye*, love. I understand. I'll tell the boys to keep their fangs to themselves. Though I cannae' say the same for myself."

Before I can respond, Keller pushes off the bar and makes his way to the stage. As if on cue, someone hits the stage lights, illuminating Keller in a bright, tinted blue halo. I'm not fooled. Keller is about as far from being an angel as I am from being a saint.

The night went better than I expected. Crimson Beat rocked the house, playing a mix of country and rock. They even threw in a couple of Celtic jigs in honor of Ostara and managed to make them sound contemporary. Wolfie's was packed for hours. Sage had finally made an appearance, but I didn't have the time to grill her. We were too busy. Instead, I recruited her to help out behind the bar while I made sure the lore in attendance stayed on the up and up. Not an easy task in general, and the pull of Ostara made it even more difficult.

Thankfully, I was able to keep the peace in Wolfie's with only a handful of scuffles and evictions, and had only been mildly distracted by Keller's show. Whatever. Very distracted, but it didn't keep me from doing my job. No matter how freaking hot he looks rocking a drum solo. Whether I wanted it or not—that would be a big fat not—he insisted on playing the role of security during his breaks. I swear Keller's full name must be Keller Irritate-The-Hell-Out-Of-Josie O'Leary.

Now the band is packing it up. I usher the last of the patrons out the door. I feel Keller's stare from across the room and ignore it. I head upstairs to prepare for the night and run into Sage, who is more than a little frazzled. Nervous energy buzzes around her like a swarm of killer bees.

"What gives, Sagey Sage?"

A blush spreads across her cheeks. Unusual for a vampire to show so much emotion, but Sage and I are close and she can't hide her feelings from me.

She brushes her bangs to the side. Wide grey eyes stare at me. "I'm sorry, Jose. Keller was sort of in the area, and I just think —"

"Don't go there," I say, waving my hand in front of her face. "Keller and I can't be together."

She stomps and crosses her arms over her chest. "Yes, you can. And you should. You know it just as well as I do." She narrows her eyes. "You're just being stubborn."

I lift a brow. Sage isn't usually this aggressive. "It's not a matter of being stubborn." I sigh and close my eyes briefly, collecting my thoughts. "Look. I know you think your brother and I are meant to be, but it's not going to happen. After a while, all the head-butting causes a relentless headache." It's true. Keller thinks I need someone by my side to protect me day and night, namely him. I can't stand it. I'm strong on my own. Always have been. Except when it comes to him, but I'm not going there again. I'm not.

I slide my hand down Sage's arm. "I'm sorry. I've got to get out there. I have a feeling this night is gonna be hella bad."

Sage smiles, but it doesn't reach her eyes. "Be careful."

"Always am."

"No, you're not. You take unnecessary risks and one day those risks are going to bite you in the ass."

I laugh to lighten the mood. I know she's right. It's already happened. But every time my ass has been in trouble, I manage to get myself out. Maybe not unscathed, but out. That's why the lack of support from the Assembly bothers me so much. I have a lot to give. The fact that they don't see it…screw it. "I'll be careful. Promise."

Sage huffs and stomps down the stairs. Again, the sense that something more is at play here tugs at my mind, like an idea, a memory, just out of reach. I shake my head and focus.

Gathering my blades and strapping them to my body soothes my inner turmoil. Each weapon has its place. I can do this with my eyes closed, but I don't. Tonight is not a night to relax. Urgency settles over me like a scratchy blanket, and I make quick work of arming myself. I've learned many ways to conceal over the years. Two blades strapped to each ankle, hidden beneath my tall boots. Three blades holstered around each thigh, hidden beneath the layers of tulle on my tutu. I tuck a couple more into my waistband and head downstairs.

Other than Wes and Sage, Wolfie's is empty now. My heart hurts a little that Keller left without saying goodbye. *Yeah, yeah.* I know my thoughts contradict themselves. It is what it is. I can't blame Keller for his fast exit. I hadn't been very welcoming, and had probably told him to leave at least a dozen times throughout the night. Still.

Out of the corner of my eye, I see Sage watching me with a curious and knowing look. I hitch my chin up and plaster a smile on my face.

"I'm out," I say.

"Typical. Why is it you never help clean up?" This from Wes.

Sage elbows him in the ribs, yet I'm the target of his venomous stare.

I bat my eyelashes, unaffected. "That's what you're paid for." Further discussion is not needed, though I hear him grumbling behind me.

I step into the night and suck in a deep breath. I catch a whiff of the budding promise of cherry blossoms and breathe deeply. A sure sign of spring. Too bad that isn't the only scent drifting on the breeze. Death taints the air of Nashville. By sunrise, the odor will be pungent. Humans will dismiss it as pollution. In a way, they are right. Pollution in the form of nasties.

One more breath dictates my direction. Tonight, I head south.

I meld with the shadows, gaze flicking side to side. Festive banners decorate the sidewalks and storefronts, announcing tomorrow's big Ostara street party. A party that will leave some grieving for something they'll never be able to fully comprehend. I'll do my best to keep the numbers of fatalities down.

My hearing is acute. Whispers to my left. Heavy breathing to my right. I turn, note the source of the panting and move on. Just two lovers sharing a heated kiss. If I warn them the streets are unsafe, they'll only laugh. Like I said, ignorance, bliss, and all that shit.

The whispering though, takes on a heated edge. I creep around the corner, careful to stay hidden. Five males are huddled around a body. An unmoving body. I unsheathe two blades and step into the light, drawing their attention. I suck in a surprised breath. All eyes are on me now and I desperately want to rub mine. This can't be real. Not much surprises me anymore. These killers have just made that statement a fallacy. How could they? I glance at the dead man. His throat is torn wide-open, blood pooling around him. "What have you done?" I ask the assailants, but my eyes zero in on one of them, nailing him with a gaze so intense I'm surprised he doesn't burst into flames.

"It's not what you think, Josie."

But it is. It so is. Even though my mind screams the denial, the evidence is laid out before me. I crouch into fighting stance as my target steps forward. Sage is going to hate me. I can't help that. All five members of Crimson Beat are about to die.

"You promised, Keller." My voice is shaky.

Keller shakes his head. "*Aye*. That promise is kept. We found him like this." The other vampires nod, step forward as if they can protect Keller from me.

I want to believe them, but the blonde one has blood on his hands, under his nails, and the others are acting strange, fidgety. To me, that equals guilty. Guilty of what has yet to be determined.

The ground begins to shake. Very bad timing. I shake my head disapprovingly at the vampires, crouch lower and distribute my weight. The vamps do the same. Three red-scaled demons squeeze through a crack in the asphalt. Menace oozes from their auras. Hot air wheezes out of their nostrils, fetid and thick. I don't have a choice but to give Keller and his band mates the benefit of the doubt. For now.

One demon snarls low in his throat and lunges at me. I hold my ground, slam my blade into his gut and pull up. He screams and lashes out with sharpened claws. With a curse, I pull my arm back, but the damage is done. I've got a major injury, but at least this demon is dead.

Only two more to go.

My arm hurts like a bitch, burning, throbbing, and my breathing grows shallow with the pain. Instinct kicks in. Swinging around, I jump over the tail of another demon, listing to the side.

Keller rushes to me and closes his hand over my gaping wound. "I told you to be careful," he snaps. He quickly brings his hunger—if not his anger—under control, but not before his eyes flash red at the scent and sight of my blood. I curse loudly this time, my words directed at Keller rather than any of the demons. Damn him for distracting me. If he hadn't been here, this wouldn't have happened. Now he sees me as weak again. The crux of our debates.

Pulling me close, Keller lifts my arm to his mouth and sucks out the poison. I sway. Not from the pain, but from the pleasure. He licks the wound and it closes up tight. A boost of renewed energy surges through me. Again, damn him.

"I've got this," I tell him and yank my arm away. He merely lifts a brow as his vampire friends kill the last two demons by wrenching their heads off. But they aren't the last. The night is young.

Chapter Three

Unfortunately, for the rest of the night, I've got five bodyguards. Lucian, Matthew, Alex, Grant, and Keller. I'll admit they are badass fighters, and *maybe* they hadn't killed that man in the alley, but I don't trust them. Especially not Keller. He's acting all weird and shit, more possessive and protective than he's ever been. And if he stands any closer to me, he'll swallow me whole. At this point, I'd rather be eaten alive by a shifter.

I can't breathe with all his crowding. But having the assistance of these vamps has helped to keep the streets of Nashville semi-safe, so I'll deal with the Keller-induced claustrophobia. This is what I've been asking the Assembly for. Draw up an agreement for the light and dark lore, and let me put a team in place to enforce it. Not that Keller would be on said team, but maybe someone like him.

Rules, laws, whatever the hell the Assembly wants to call it… All beings need to be held accountable for their actions. This free-for-all method of mayhem doesn't work. Everyone wielding their powers without care for the damage they cause, and the curtains of obscurity they rip apart in the process, only leads to more fear and destruction. Eventually the lore will no longer be considered fairy tales and figments of human imagination. Is that what the Assembly wants? I had never considered that as an option. Now I have to consider that they might. My gut sours at the thought.

The first colors of dawn eventually leak over the horizon. I wait for the vampires to react to the sun. They don't. I start to ask, but then remember that Ostara allows them to walk in full light without being affected. I can't imagine what it's like to have to live in the dark all the time, never seeing the light of day, never feeling the warmth of the sun. No wonder so many of the lore consider this one-day holiday the equivalent of being reborn.

I watch as the vampires, Keller excluded, tilt their faces toward the sky and let the heat of the sun wash over them. Keller doesn't have time for the sun. He's too busy watching my back.

I'm exhausted, sweaty, and bloody. So many kills tonight. I never predicted Ostara would be this bad. Stalking shifters, destructive trolls, witches, warlocks, a phoenix hell-bent on arson, shadowed creatures I've never seen before… Why don't we add confusion into the pot and call it one hell of a clusterfuck, shall we? Hitting the shower is first on my to-do list. I turn to Keller. "You've got some explaining to do," I say quietly, not wanting to interrupt the blissful moment his friends are having. I haven't forgotten about the dead man in the alley, but I have come to the conclusion that Keller and his friends are innocent of the murder. If those demons hadn't popped up when they had, I may have temporarily lost my mind and *ashed* five blameless vampires. I shudder. "I assume you're not leaving town today?" Assumptions do not equal hope. Not even close. I'm glad I settled that with myself.

Keller shoves his hands into the back pockets of his jeans. His t-shirt stretches tight against his flat stomach. I drag my gaze to his when he chuckles. "Aye. I'll be in town for a bit," he says without committing or admitting to anything. That irks me more than it should. He turns to the members of Crimson Beat and tells them he'll catch up with them later. When he turns back to me, his eyes are liquid pools of simmering emotion. "I'll walk you home."

I shake my head. "No, thanks. I'm good."

"Stop being stubborn."

"You and your sister need to trash that word, okay?" I don't wait for an answer, just barrel on. Keller, once again, is the source of my anger and frustration. "I'm not being stubborn. This is me. Take it or leave it."

He smiles and I realize my error. I back up. Keller follows, stalking me like this is a game of cat and mouse. It's not a game. But my heart rattles around in my chest. Damn it, I'm excited. A good hunt always spins my adrenaline out of control. That I'm the hunted this time makes no difference. In fact, it only exacerbates the situation.

I turn and sprint, my boots pounding the pavement as I gain speed and the buildings pass by in a blur. Two blocks down, I glance over my shoulder, but Keller isn't there. This chase is over before it even starts. Relief and disappointment battle for first place in the emotion challenge. Neither is the victor. There is no winner in this war I've waged against Keller. Only losers. Two of them.

I slow as my apartment building comes in sight and hide my smile by biting the inside of my cheek. Hard. Keller didn't disappear after all. He's sporting a sexy half-grin and I know he knows I'm happy to see him. Not all of me. Just a few parts of me. I don't think he cares.

I completely ignore him and walk up the stairs. I turn the key in the lock, shove my door open and leave it that way. I will have that shower. What Keller does is up to him. Like I said, I'm weak where he's concerned. My body craves his kiss so badly I'm shaking. I fumble with the shower knobs. A strong hand covers mine and turns the hot water on. I silently remove all the blades from my body, set them aside and then step into the shower, boots and all. I'm a total vamp junkie and I know it. Thankfully, my addiction is exclusive.

Husky laughter mixes with steam, enveloping me in heat. The hot water eases the strain of my sore muscles. I lay my cheek against the cool tile, enjoying the contrast of temperature. My eyes are closed, but I know he's about to join me and I can't stop my breath from hitching. I hear the slide of his zipper, the pull of jeans over skin. I smell his strength—it's everywhere—and I shiver. Strong and familiar arms slide around my waist and Keller pulls me to him. I lean against him and don't move. He kisses the top of my head and something about the tenderness of the moment has tears sliding down my cheeks.

Keller turns me around and lifts me off my feet. I can't look at him. He doesn't demand that I do. I feel cool lips on mine, and I sigh. That is enough for him. He kisses me now, slow, sensual. Panic stirs in my soul, but Keller shushes me with his consuming embrace. Setting me back on my feet, he slowly undresses me, exposing more than the flesh of my body. Still, my eyes are closed. This only adds to the sensations, allowing me to focus on the way his hands feel against my skin.

I'm naked now.

I'm freezing.

I'm on fire.

I'm so confused. I want what can never be. What I won't allow. If I'm with Keller, I have to be who he wants me to be, not who I truly am. But I can take this moment in time. And this time *will* be the last. It has to be. Finally I open my eyes and lift my face. Keller stares down at me. He rocks my core. I reach up and trace the hard lines of his face. He doesn't move, just waits for me to finish my exploration. His body is so hard, so perfect, so addicting, so dangerous. I grab his neck and yank him down for a kiss. This moment will have to last me for eternity. I'm going to make the most of it. I'm going to show him how *un*-weak I am.

I'm ravenous, fusing my mouth to his, my tongue dancing across his teeth until I feel him smile. A playful nip before his tongue grazes mine, and it's all over. I arch against him. He slides his hands down my back and over my ass to lift me up so I can lock my legs around his waist. Like the hot water and the cool tiles, his hard body feels amazing against my softer one. Keller has always said how much he likes my curves. Those words ring true as skilled hands travel over every inch of body. Gentle one moment, rough and demanding the next. Keller reads me so well. He always has. How he knows just what I want, and how I want it—he increases my need to feel him inside me. And just like that, he glides in with one smooth push. I still. He stills. I feel him throbbing against me, a mirror echo of the pounding of my heart.

I begin to move and Keller matches me thrust for thrust. With my back pressed against the shower wall, water sluices over us like the most extravagant of waterfalls, instead of the crappy shower with poor water pressure that it truly is. Keller's ability to turn the most ordinary into something fantastical almost makes up for our differences. Almost. I bite my lip and shut down my brain.

Keller cradles my face in his hands. "We're good together, Josie. We belong together. How can you not see that?"

How can I argue when every move he makes doubles my pleasure? "Shhh," I say against his lips. "Don't talk." Talking will only turn into arguing. I don't want to argue. I want to feel. I want to escape into a world where only Keller and I exist. Where our differences no longer matter.

A moan tears from my lips when Keller moves from my mouth to my neck, one fang grazing the tender flesh just below my ear. I know what's coming. I should stop him, but I can't. I don't want to. My body becomes frantic, writhing against him as he pounds into me.

"Aye, that's it. Say yes." Keller licks my ear. "Tell me you want it as badly as I do."

His whisper nearly causes me to climax. I squeeze my legs, pulling him deeper.

He moves his mouth to the other side, torturing, tormenting, demanding that I respond. I shake my head, unwilling to admit not only how much I want his bite, but also how much I want him.

Keller slows to languid strokes that are no less demanding. "It's okay," he croons in that sexy accent that always affects me in the most basic way. "I already know."

The only answer I give is a slight tilt of my head, exposing the full length of my neck. Keller smiles against my throat, drags his lips across my skin. I sigh. He pierces. I scream as ecstasy courses through my entire body like a tidal wave hell bent on destruction. Keller tenses, moans, consumes my blood as if it's a gift from the gods. Ambrosia. My climax hits hard. He continues to drink, drawing out my orgasm until at last and all too soon his body tenses. A growl erupts, breaking past his lips just as he licks his bite closed. That simple act has me moaning. So intimate. So delicious.

The water grows cold. Without a word, Keller shuts off the shower and carries me to the bed where he proceeds to lick every drop of moisture off of me. My body responds in ways that I never thought possible. Maybe he's right. Even if I can't be with him, maybe I belong to him. Body and soul.

Chapter Four

When I wake, Keller is gone. My heart feels as empty as the bed, like a wolf craving its mate. I ignore the tug of longing, swing my legs around and plant my feet on solid ground. I'm thankful he's not here. Being alone gives me at least a few moments to collect my thoughts and decide on a course of action. I'm not like most girls. I don't feel used. If anything, I used him.

Didn't I?

I really don't know anymore.

One thing I do know is that Keller is in town for a reason, and it's not to play music or to satiate my wanton desires. I've learned to listen to my gut, and my gut is screaming he's here for another reason entirely—has been screaming since he'd snuck up behind me in the bar. I'm just a side note. An important one, but a side note nonetheless.

As I dress, I realize Sage is probably in on this in a bigger way than I had initially thought. That hurts. I've always trusted her. We've always trusted each other. Never once have I questioned that. It bothers me that I'm questioning it now and I wonder who's to blame for that.

I stab my feet into a pair of black leggings, drag a bright pink long-sleeved tee over my head and drop onto the bed to pull on a pair of black cowboy boots. Thoughts of betrayal creep in, and any lingering pleasure my body feels from Keller's touch gives way to tightening muscles. I stretch my neck to one side and then the other, but the kinks remain. A painful reminder of what I have to do.

On most days, I've got my make-up application down to five minutes. Today takes only three. Running a comb through my hair, I decide to reserve judgment on Sage. I won't know what she knows until I ask her. Which is something I plan to do—I glance at the clock—in the next fifteen minutes. I retrieve my blades from the bathroom and swear I only stare at the shower for a second. But that's all it takes to start the flashbacks to this morning. The phrase *'damn Keller'* is permanently perched on my tongue these days.

The streets are already crowded and it's barely noon. The sounds of country music and jovial people surround me. Normally the infectious vibe would have me dancing in the streets right along with the other partiers. Today is a day for celebration, after all. Bright colored streamers decorate the light poles. Local actors are dressed in festive costumes, representing country music legends of past and present. The tourists eat it up, taking advantage of a plethora of photo-ops.

What their cameras won't catch are the lurkers, the nasties that walk amongst the innocents. I see them though. They know I'm watching. Some take a wide berth; others offer me a wicked smile. A couple of djinns with genetic issues flick their poisonous serpent tongues out at me, forcing me to sidestep out of the way. One giant troll dressed in grungy overalls crouches in front of me and tries to get me to make eye contact with his third eye. Instant death. Only a newbie would fall for that trick. Other than that, they seem to be behaving. That won't last. I need to hurry. I've got to get this conversation with Sage out of the way and then get on the streets. I shove through the growing crowd as politely as I can.

My neck tingles with warning.

I turn, but if someone is watching me, I can't tell who. I clench my fists at my sides to keep my itchy fingers from rubbing my neck. No way am I giving the creep the satisfaction. Instead, I opt for scratching the back of my head with my middle finger and just keep walking. Childish, but a personal victory nonetheless.

Sage is hard at work behind the bar at Wolfie's. The place is slammed, patrons vying for the last few spots of standing room only. Doesn't matter. I need answers and I doubt Keller will give them to me.

Sage sees me and offers a weak smile, while perfectly pouring a tall one from the tap, angling it just enough to keep the beer head to a minimum. She slides the glass down the bar to a customer. I wedge between two cowboys. "I need to talk to you," I call to Sage.

Her mouth pulls down in a frown. "Now? Kinda busy here." She offers her palm in a what-can-I-do gesture.

Not buying it. "Two minutes. That's all I need."

Sage sighs and wipes her hands on the rag she has tucked in her back pocket. After telling another bartender she'll be back, Sage crawls under the bar door and walks over to me. "What's up?"

This isn't the ideal spot to hold a conversation, especially not one as important as this one, but I don't have a choice. More people are filing in and it would take too much time to fight the crowd to have a private discussion in the office upstairs. Taking a deep breath, I whisper in Sage's ear. "Truth," I say. "Why is Keller here?"

She stiffens, then slowly lets out a breath. Her eyes find mine and I know she won't lie. She'll never lie to me, and I feel guilty that I'd ever thought it. "The Assembly sent him."

My face heats as if I've been slapped. "Why?" I ask, though I think I already know.

Her shoulders slump a little. "To form a team to negotiate a peaceful alliance between the light and dark lore."

Forget the virtual face slap. Someone just stuck a dagger in my heart, and twisted it in good and tight too. She knows this is what I want for myself. I blink several times and look past a guilt-stricken Sage out to the crowded street. Tendrils of black smoke rise from the sidewalk like crooked fingers beckoning a weak soul. I'm not weak, damn it. I'm not. And I'm not about to let someone else take credit for all the hard work I put in convincing the Assembly in the first place.

The crowd roars their approval as if the smoke is all part of the show. Before I can figure out what it is, the smoke curls into itself and disappears. Whatever it is, it can't be good.

Time is ticking. I've always known that Ostara would be the prime time to get the document signed. The Spring Equinox gives a slight advantage to the light creatures because after midnight, the scales are tipped to the side of light until the Fall Equinox. That the

Assembly sent an outsider into my city rather than make me the lead has jealousy sitting like a fiery rock in the pit of my stomach.

Sage grabs my hand and squeezes. "I'm so sorry, Josie."

I withdraw my hand from her grasp. "So am I."

"Please," she implores. "Talk to Keller. He'll explain everything."

I shake my head, already heading toward the door. "There's nothing he can say."

I know what I need to do.

Cross—my current arch nemesis and someone I've vowed to destroy—lives on the outskirts of Nashville. His home is not what one would think a drug lord vampire would reside in. It's a modest ranch in need of fresh paint with half-dead shrubs lining the perimeter. I've never been on the inside, though I've been invited on more than one occasion. Today will be a day of firsts.

If all goes well, this will also be a day of lasts. The *last* damn time the Assembly doubts me. *I* will get Cross to agree to sign this treaty. No matter what it takes. Once he does, my hope is that other dark lore will sign, too—albeit begrudgingly, I'm sure. Cross is a leader. Not a good one, if you ask me, but leaders come in all sorts.

"State your business," says one of the drug lord's vamp security guards flanking the front door. Their all-black attire makes their pale, stark faces look even closer to death. That's the way

Cross likes them. Just this side of zombie. How he manages it is beyond me, other than keeping the blood supply to a minimum. And by minimum I mean almost non-existent.

I relax my stance. I've tangled with them and their brethren on numerous occasions. They know who I am, but I can play nice when I have to. The comforting weight of my daggers reassures me that I'm ready should this strategy fail.

"Just visiting, fellas," I say with a toothy smile. "Do me a fave and tell your boss I'd like to speak with him."

They laugh as if they share an inside joke. "You want to speak to Cross?"

Hmm…could swear that's what I just said. I nod. "Yes, please." The word please tastes rotten on my tongue. I keep smiling anyway.

The smile is not returned. The vamps have a silent conversation with each other courtesy of telepathy. I know this because I see the air between them crinkle slightly, like a handmade fan a child makes in art class. Only instead of paper, this fan is made from air frequencies.

Being still doesn't suit me. Energy swirls beneath my skin, ready for action. I bite my tongue and wait it out. Reacting to their lack of urgency will not serve my purpose. Still, I swear the sun will set and rise again before they either let me in or deny my request.

My tongue is bleeding now and I swallow. Blood just tastes like blood to me. Always has. I wonder what it tastes like to Keller. *Damn.* I've gone somewhere I don't need to go. I know it's not really fair to label what he's done as betrayal, considering I never told him I wanted to be the leader. I never told him anything other than a hundred different versions of back off. Either way, it's now clearer than ever that Keller has no place in my life. I wish my heart felt the same way.

Someone sniffs. I look up. The vamps' eyes are wide, electric. They scent my blood. Dangerous, dangerous territory I'm skirting here. I keep my mouth locked tight and breathe through my nose to keep the blood scent contained as much as possible.

My head starts to pulse. I recognize the pain for what it is and curse my stupidity. Drinking my blood always temporarily opens a connection between Keller and I. I'd forgotten that until now. I feel his soft mental push sorting, sifting, trying to locate me. No doubt he's spoken to Sage and knows I know. I slam that door closed and do my best to wait patiently for this door to open.

At last, it does.

I step over the threshold and the door bangs shut behind me. Locks click into place. I pretend not to notice even as doubts finagle their way into my mind. Meeting with Cross alone is not the wisest idea I've ever had. He's killed more than I have. But anger propelled me to this place and I have to see it through, or die trying. Preferably the former, please and thank you.

I find Cross lounging on a leather sofa, three women draped over his body in an opulent room befitting a king. The outward appearance of his home is nothing more than a smokescreen. For the first time—*ever*—I stifle the eye roll. His pale hair is cropped short. Ice-blue eyes study me before he offers a wisp of a smile.

"To what do I owe this pleasure, Ms. Hawk?" The three strumpets don't spare me a glance. Perhaps Cross has them under persuasion. That wouldn't surprise me in the least. Though in all honesty, I can see why they're attracted to him. He is rather striking in a very lethal kind of way. Ancient power practically radiates from his pores.

I wet my lips. "I have a business matter to discuss with you." He doesn't offer me a seat but I take one anyway. I may be scared out of my gourd, but I don't have to act like it. I lean back in the armless chair as if I'm in a good friend's home.

Cross arches a brow and slowly drags his gaze from my face to my toes and up again, assessing, gauging, calculating. "What is it you propose?"

His tone is nice enough. But those eyes… "Yeah, about that. Any chance we can speak privately? They," I tilt my head toward the women, "are a bit distracting."

"Are they?"

"Very."

"Maybe you'd be less distracted if you joined us?" His lips curve into a full-out, wicked smile.

Now I'm annoyed. "Look. If all you're going to do is answer me with questions, this is a waste of my time." It was a big mistake coming here. Cross won't help me. Even if it will benefit him. Not that he'll ever know. We'll never get past phase one if he keeps rocking the bullshit vibe.

Cross stands quickly and sends his threesome crashing to the floor. They giggle and I gag. *Get a life already.*

They scurry away and I wonder if they heard me. Then I realize their master's demeanor has completely changed and apparently, they are a lot wiser than I am.

"I'm wasting your time?"

Lucky, lucky me. Another question. But I keep my mouth shut.

White-hot pain explodes behind my eyes. I clench my teeth and bear down so as not to expose my pain to Cross. I have no doubt he'll take advantage of it. Keller's subtle mental push has turned into an all-out war. I start to sweat with the effort to keep him out of my thoughts. This is what I get for getting caught up in the moment. For getting lost in the meadow of sexual euphoria. One hell of a brain violation.

Cross cocks his head and I wonder if he senses Keller in his territory even though it's just a mental connection from miles away. He crooks his finger at me. My body rises out of the chair before I realize I'm moving. I grit my teeth and regain control. He narrows his eyes and my feet move of their own accord. Things are about to get ugly up in here and I wonder if I should let Keller in. If I should let him help me. But isn't that admitting I need help? That he's been right all along. thinking I can't do this on my own? Screw it. I'm so not going down like this.

"Knock it off, Cross," I order through clenched teeth.

His only response is the whisper of a brutal laugh.

I reach for my blades with both hands. The leather grips are just the incentive I need to break Cross's hold. I plant my feet and assume the stance. Keller pushes harder. My head may very well explode. I swear, fighting two vamps—these particular vamps—was not on today's agenda.

Cross *tsks*. "So now you plan to attack me in my own home? What a pity." He closes the distance between us in zero seconds flat. His hand is around my throat and my feet aren't touching the floor anymore. I kick and nail him in the shin. He doesn't flinch. When I said ancient power, I literally meant *ancient* power.

With a quick one-two, I stab him with both knives, one between his ribs and one in the kidney. He barely moves and that's just so he can squeeze my neck tighter. The pain in my head recedes and I feel Cross's choke hold more than ever. Keller is giving up. I know I can reach him before he disappears. I don't, and I wonder if I'll live to regret it. Keller and Sage are right. I am stubborn.

"Shall we talk about this *business* first, Ms. Hawk? Or shall I just kill you now?"

Not sure how to answer that one. I manage to wheeze out one weak word before he crushes the light right out of me. "Keller." If Keller's still there, I don't feel him. I send a mental apology anyway. I've been wrong. So very wrong.

Though I was right about one thing. This is a day of lasts. My last breath.

Chapter Five

Soft fingers graze my cheek. *Keller.* I struggle through the webs of unconsciousness until I can manage to open my eyes. My gaze flicks all around like I'm a panicked rabbit. Now I wish I would have stayed asleep. Keller's familiar and comforting touch is gone, had probably never been there. Just a mind trick I played on myself.

A lone bulb offers the only source of light. It flickers constantly. Through the bars of my jail I make out other shadows. The Huntress in me responds to their sickening negativity. My mind grows frantic as I search for an escape route that isn't there. These aren't friends. These are the lowest ranks of Cross's security. They're starving, on the cusp of death, and I am their only chance to keep mortality temporarily at bay.

Keys jangle and menacing growls echo off the cold walls of my prison. So much for showing the Assembly what I'm made of. How I ever thought proving my worth to them was the most important thing in my life is beyond me. What a fool I've been.

The shadows draw closer with slow and tortured steps. Even the smallest movements cause them pain. Their agonizing bellowing sounds hollow and eerie, echoing like a broken record. My heart sinks like an anchor at sea. I'll never laugh with Sage again. I'll never again get the opportunity to feel Keller's embrace. At least Sage knows how I feel about her. I've never hidden my love from her. Keller, on the other hand, will never know that he is— scratch that—*was* my one and only.

Though I can't see outside, the pull of the moon calls to me and dread churns noxiously in the pit of my stomach. Midnight is only minutes away. I pray those minutes will pass quickly. Once the bells toll twelve times, most of the lore will have to retreat again. My city will go back to normal—as normal as it's ever been—and my one hope is that Keller will stick around and take care of my people.

"*Aye.* I can do that, Josie," says an almost inaudible whisper.

I whip around and jump to my feet. He's here. How, I don't know, but he is. I move to rush into Keller's arms. He stops me with a look and places his finger to his lips.

Hungry moans sound behind me. I turn. Five pair of red eyes stare back at me. Only me. They don't know Keller's there. *Hello, advantage.* I smile to myself and inch away from the bars until I feel Keller's chest against my back. His strength is staggering, and for the first time, I'm one hundred percent happy he is with me. I need him. Not just to keep me alive today, but I need him in my life.

Keller squeezes my shoulder and kisses the top of my head. I think he already knows. Doesn't matter. It's important to me that he hears me speak the words.

More flickering from the blasted light. I wish it would burn out already and shroud us in darkness. One vamp inserts the key into the lock. He struggles to turn it. I'm sure he'll figure it out soon enough.

Keller lifts my shirt up from behind. I stiffen against him. He can't seriously be considering sex at a time like this? Cold metal slides against my skin and I realize he's arming me. A whisper of a laugh caresses my cheek. I'd forgotten to keep my mental walls up. I don't care. Where he's concerned, the walls have permanently crumbled.

Likewise.

Keller? I swear I just heard you in my head.

Aye.

Never before have I been able to hear him speak to me like this. *Will it always be this way?*

If we keep the blood connection strong, it will.

I nod. *Why haven't I heard you before?*

You didn't want to. Things are different now.

Very different. In the past I've known he can read my thoughts after his bite, but I never thought I'd be able to hear his. The new level of intimacy is staggering. The cell door swings open with a screech. *I need to tell you something.*

It's okay. I already know. Keller backs up.

I follow, giving the perception of retreat. Thank goodness this is a big cell. *I want to say it, Keller.*

Aye, love. I'm listening.

I slide my right hand around to my back and grip the blade handle. I take a deep breath. This is huge for me. *I need you. I always have. Always will.*

He strokes the back of my neck with his thumb and I shiver. *I'm not leaving again, Josie. Never again.*

Keller's words touch me deeply. If we were alone, I'd show him just how much. A distorted and hungry whimper reminds me there's a chance we might not live long enough to celebrate the incredible shift in our relationship. The vamps are sluggish but dangerous. There's so much more to say to Keller but time has run out.

For now.

I'm taking a big risk, but there's something I need to do. To seal the deal, so to speak. I give the vamps my back and kiss Keller soundly. Before I grow too intoxicated from the flavor of his lips, I pull back and shake my head to sober up. "Let's do this." I don't bother whispering.

"*Aye*," he says just before he slams his blade into the closest vamp. I take the next one, kicking him in the gut. He doubles over. They are starved and have little energy. It almost seems too easy. I bring my knee up and connect with his head. The vamp falls over backward with a grunt. Straddling him, I plunge my blade through his heart. He immediately turns to ash.

"Behind you," Keller calls.

Adrenaline rips through my blood. I jump to my feet and swivel on my heel to face the starving vampire. Eyes so black they seem like nothing more than bottomless pits bore into me, sizing me up like I'm the prime rib at an all-you-can-eat buffet. He smiles and drool drips from his fangs.

I shudder. "Gross."

Another vamp drops behind me and I wait to hear the sizzle that sounds right before he disintegrates. I'm not disappointed. Keller is lethal.

My vamp lunges. I barely dodge his grasp. This one is stronger and faster than the others. I run behind him and jam my knife in his ribs. I shove him forward. Instead of falling, he swings around and grabs my elbow. With a grunt, I try to yank my arm out of his bony clutches. His grip tightens and he drags me to him like he's reeling in the catch of the day.

So much for easy.

His sharp nails dig into my skin as he whips me around and pulls me close. He stinks. Bad. The pungent odor of rotting vamp makes me want to hurl. I hear his excited gasp and realize my arm is bleeding. I kick hard, ramming him in the knee with the heel of my boot. The scent of my blood has made him crazy strong and my kicking has no effect. He sniffs my neck like I'm a dog in heat and he's the would-be mate. I kick again.

I see Keller out of the corner of my eye, but don't dare call out. He's got his hands full in an all-out scrapping match.

I throw a hard elbow and am rewarded with the sound of cracking ribs. My vamp howls in pain, but maintains his hold and cranks my head back,

Keller roars, I hear a sizzle and then silence. The next thing I know, Keller is standing directly in front of me.

"Don't move," he says. I know he means it, but...

I start to argue, but then a feel a scrape along my neck and force my body to go dead still. A burning sensation creeps along my skin and I know I am a second away from being bitten.

Oh, hell no.

No vamp, save Keller, has ever bitten me and I'm sick at the thought that this nasty being's fangs will violate me in that way. This is not my first vamp fight. Not by a long shot. I've had my share of close calls, but have always managed to evade the fangs.

The vamp inhales against my neck. Keller cocks his head and clenches his fists. Sweat slides down my cheek. My sweat. One wrong move and this vamp will snap my neck.

And then another scrape of his fangs as if the wretched vampire is savoring his last meal. Now I'm pissed and if Keller thinks I'm going to stand here and let this happen, he's got a lot to learn about me.

I look Keller straight in the eye. Having heard every last thought in my head, he smiles.

Before I can act, two razor-sharp teeth prick my neck. The vamp follows that up with a soggy lick. Keller's eyes burn bright.

He nods once and I use all my strength to duck. Keller drives his fist into the blood-starved jerk's larynx. The vamp staggers back, dragging me with him. I reach around and pull my blade out of his back just as he topples over. We land hard and the breath is knocked out of me. Stars flicker over my vision, but I suck it up and get to my knees. Keller is a blur of motion. With one swoop, he slices clean through my captor's wrist, severing his hold.

"Ash-hole!" I yell before plunging the knife straight through his heart.

Breathless, I do what I've wanted to do since I first opened my eyes. I rush into Keller's arms and hold tight. We steal those moments and I lock them up tight in my heart where they will stay forever. My head is tucked beneath Keller's chin. He strokes a hand over my hair, and I feel the rumble of his chest when he speaks.

"Are you all right?"

I take a deep breath. "Yeah. My neck feels like it's being eaten by acid, but I'll be fine."

Keller tilts my head to the side. "It's not deep. The burning will ease up in a minute or two."

I tuck my head again. I like being wrapped in his arms. "Your bite never burns like this."

He doesn't say anything at first, but I know he's smiling. "I'd like to say it's because we're meant for each other. Sadly, that's not the case. He burned you because poison spreads poison."

No further explanation is needed. I know exactly what he means. Whether it was Cross's fault or not, these vamps were toxic through and through.

"Ready to get that treaty signed?"

I look up at him, eyes wide. "Seriously?"

Keller smiles. "Absolutely."

"Yeah. I'm so ready." Of course, the flickering light chooses that moment to burn out. Keller grabs my hand and tugs me forward. I follow blindly. He has my complete trust.

"Stairs," he says.

"Got it." I lift my feet and we take the steps two at a time. A church bell chimes in the distance. *Midnight.* "You think there's time?" Another chime. *Dong.*

"I do. However long it takes."

I love Keller's confidence. With my dagger in one hand, we reach the top and burst through the door. *Dong.* Cross is waiting for us. He's not alone. The two thugs he'd had guarding his door upon my arrival are standing front and center.

Time slows down as we work our way through Cross's security team. These are stronger than the vamps downstairs, but Keller and I are very motivated. We make an unstoppable team. Not to mention, I'm flying higher than the moon right now and ready to take on the world. Within seconds we skewer the guards like pigs over an open fire. Confetti made of ash floats around the room. I sneeze.

More guards rush in and my confidence starts to waver.

"Stop!" Cross's order does not go unnoticed. His power is undeniable. Everyone obeys, including Keller and I, but we do it for different reasons.

With Keller by my side, Cross's persuasion tactics don't work on me. I'll have to figure that one out later. The bell chimes two more times and I realize it won't chime again for another hour. My shoulders slump. We're too late.

It's never too late to do what's right.

I study Cross to see if he also heard Keller. If he did, he doesn't have a tell. Cross takes a seat and assumes an unimpressed stance. I beg to differ on that. He gestures to the couch across from him. We step over ashes and take a seat.

"Speak."

I lift my brow at the order. Keller squeezes my knee. I look over and he shakes his head. As concisely as I can, I lay out the details of the treaty. Cross leans forward, steeples his fingers and listens, nodding occasionally.

When I'm done, I sit back and let out a huff of breath.

Cross shakes his head. "There's nothing in this for me. The answer is no. Show yourselves out." Cross stands and moves to the bar. He pours two fingers of scotch and tosses it back in one swallow.

Not cool. I'll leave on my own terms. "Nothing in it for you?" My blood is simmering. "How about we let you live if you sign it? I'd say that's something." Whether I can back that statement up is yet to be seen. Right now I can't bring myself to care.

Cross smiles, all sinister-like. "I'll live anyway, and we both know it."

Keller clears his throat. "You see, that's where you're wrong." His voice is eerily calm. "I'm here to represent the Assembly. I have their authority to dole out punishments as I see fit. The way I see it, you have two choices here. You can either listen to Josie, sign this treaty, and then pack your bags and move your operation out of Nashville, or you can die in this house when I burn it to the ground. Had you signed two minutes ago, we wouldn't be having this conversation. Now there are no other options for you."

Cross stiffens. He pours another drink, but this time only swirls it around in the glass.

"Perhaps, Ms. Hawk," he says with a tilt of his head, "you can tell me more about this treaty."

I'm in shock, but I manage to keep my expression bland. If — scratch that—when we get out of here, I'm going to jump Keller the first chance I get.

I answer his questions even though I know he's only stalling for time. Cross isn't stupid. No doubt he's already figured out which city to taint next. Keller doesn't speak again until I'm finished.

He rises. I stand with him.

"Sign it." Keller's order surprises me. Cross is older and stronger, but in this moment, Keller takes on the superior role.

Working on behalf of the Assembly holds clout in every corner of the world. I'm so proud to be standing next to Keller, I can't help but smile.

Cross waves his hand in the air. One of his vamp cronies brings him a pen. He signs the sheet of paper Keller had brought. How long he's had it with him? Doesn't matter. The deed is done and Nashville will be safer. Cross will still deal drugs, I'm sure of it, but this is a start. At least he'll be out of my town.

Outside, I breathe in the chilly air. Keller wraps his arms around me and we begin the trek back to my apartment. Keller makes a phone call to the head of the Assembly to tell them about the treaty. I ignore the twinges of jealousy. I'll get over it. As long as I'm on the team and can help protect the innocents, that's what really matters.

Once inside we head for the shower at the same time. Keller turns on the water while I undress. Both completely nude, we step under the water and Keller pulls me against him, flesh to flesh. This is better than déjà vu. Ostara has faded and offered a brand new day.

"You made this happen, Josie."

I sigh and lean against him. Only a short time ago, I had told myself the Assembly's approval meant nothing to me. That isn't true. It still does, but it isn't the most important thing in my life anymore. "You're wrong. *We* made this happen."

"The Assembly agrees with you." Keller turns me in his arms. "We're both leading this team from today forth."

I can't hold back my cheek-splitting smile. I swallow past the lump in my throat and blink back tears, unable to form words.

Keller cradles my face in his hands. "We're a team, Josephine Hawk. And I, for one, like the sound of that."

I shrug shyly. "Yeah. I kinda do, too."

He lifts both brows. "Kinda?"

I roll my eyes. "Take what you can get, Irish."

Keller lifts my chin with his finger, leans down and kisses me long and hard. I'm breathless when he breaks away. "I'll take your heart, Josie."

I nod. "You already have it." And I'm totally okay with that.

Chapter One

Ireland 1952

The day had been warm, at least warm for Ireland in the spring, but the night would be cool. Not that Sorcha minded. She'd worked hard since sunup making preparations for the beginning of summer. Beltane was approaching. The waning gibbous moon hung low in the sky. Bathing in its cool white light would not only refresh her body, but it would sooth her soul and her nervous mind. In seven nights summer would arrive. She would no longer be a maiden. Assuming the promise Nature had made her was fulfilled. Her home in the west of Ireland wasn't exactly overflowing with available men. In seven nights so many mysteries would be solved, provided a man made himself available to her. Although she'd never admit it, she was just a touch nervous. Truth was, she was a thirty-five year old virgin and had long ago gotten used to sleeping solo.

She stepped from the prim stone cottage with its tightly thatched roof, on the edge of the lough where she had lived all of her life. The house rested in a glade surrounded by ash, oak and apple trees. The house itself was unremarkable, but the gardens which surrounded it were of note. Extensive and well-tended, the gardens were not just a thing of beauty. The gardens were so much more. Every flower, herb, and plant served a purpose. But some things were simply more potent if grown outside of the confines of the cottage walls.

It was on this night, with the moon hanging heavily in the sky, Sorcha set out to gather whatever she might come across. When she'd stepped beyond the stones that marked the circular boundary of power that enclosed the house, she looked up at the moon. Her clothing felt sticky, restrictive, and unnatural. A barrier between her body and nature. Without fear of discovery, or any misplaced sense of modesty, she set her basket on the ground and stripped off the layers of clothing that she felt bundled up in. When her clothes were in a neat pile and her skin was bare to the air, and to nature as a whole, she was finally able to embrace the moon.

On her bare skin, the moonlight was a luscious caress. Her clothes had made her grumpy and incapable of enjoying the brisk night air which was, in its own way, another gift from nature. Like the herbs she had come out to cut in the moonlight. Although her purpose was to fill her basket, that didn't mean she couldn't go down to the lough and wash before she got to work.

At the banks of the lough, Sorcha dropped her basket, took out the small sliver of soap she'd purposefully brought with her and stepped into the water. Her hands reached up to her hair as she gathered it into a knot and stuck it in place with a twig. The moon bathed her skin as the water washed her feet. She reached up to the moon, letting her back arch as she stretched, and spread her legs just a little. Her personal greeting to the spirit of the moon. She pulled herself a little taller, and then let her arms drop as she bent forward at the waist. Stretching and moving her body in the night air under the gaze of the moon was as invigorating as a spring rain.

When her salutation to the moon was completed, she carefully placed one foot after the other as she waded into the water. When the water was at her thighs, she spread her legs just enough for the surface of the moving water to brush the black hair covering her sex. That slight whisper of a touch was more tantalizing than a pawing ever could be. She took the sliver of soap, lathered a thick layer of suds between her hands, and then ran them over body.

She watched the moon as it gazed down at her. With a sigh, she asked the moon for a favor. A small favor. She needed a man. A handsome man with deep blue eyes and black Irish hair. Charming with a nice body wouldn't hurt. Smart was always good. Musical? Why not? If she was making a list of her perfect man he would definitely be musical. And like to play cards. Perhaps enjoy cooking. But that might be a push. With a shrug of her shoulders, she gave the moon a saucy wink and blew it a kiss. Not the most powerful love spell in the world, but it might be enough to hook a man for a night.

Every month since she'd discovered the joy of bathing under the moonlight, she could be found wading in the spring. Her body was ready to be touched. With every cycle of the moon, the draw to seek out a lover became more and more pronounced. She wasn't ready to become a mother, but she was ready to start exploring the glory of her body. Part of that exploration was learning what made her body hum in delight and anticipation. Coming to the lough had been part of that awakening. Like all sprites, the spirit of the lough was a creature of nature. One that responded to the cycles of the moon as much as she did. When the moon was full and round, they were both desirous of the touch of another that responded to their respective needs.

The sprite of the lough swirled around her feet, then wrapped around her legs like a silky ribbon. "Hello, Feenie," she sighed as she deepened her stretch. Her legs spread a little wider; the lips of her sex came into contact with the water. An invitation for the sprite to slide up just a bit more. She'd been coming to the lough in search of more than just bathing for some time.

There was something about the way Feenie slid up her body that made her tremble and sigh. The first time the sprite had slipped up her legs, she'd giggled as it tickled her. The next time it didn't tickle as much as it made her purr. Since that first time, every time she returned the sprite moved up her legs just a touch more. The last time, the sprite had wrapped around her totally like an extra layer of shimmering blue skin. The ripples and waves of the water had brought her within reach of her first orgasm. But the touch hadn't been quite enough. She wanted more, but Feenie wouldn't give it to her. Feenie had left her trembling with desire as she gurgled and splashed away. Sorcha had smacked the water with her hand in frustration. A futile action. Teasing and playing was the way of sprites.

This time was different yet again. When the silky sprite's formless body wrapped around hers, soft tendrils slipped between her thighs and massaged her sex in the most tantalizing manner. This was new. This was what she'd begged for the last time she'd come down to the spring. She sighed a little as she spread her legs to a wide V. The movement spread her cunt lips wide open. Her arms and hips moved as she gyrated around the touch of the sprite.

Like a ribbon of silk, a tendril of the sprite's form flicked and stroked at her sex. The water bubbled and vibrated between her thighs. An uninhibited cry of pure delight came from between her lips as a jet of water aimed directly at her clitoris shot out of the stream. The pummeling from the stream was unrelenting as it flicked and shot around her opening sex. When she was ready to fall into the water, Feenie took on more substantial form and gripped her from behind. Watery hands grasped her breasts as silky fingers plucked and pulled at her nipples. Another jet of water rose from the stream and began pulsating against her anus. For once, Feenie was going to finish what she started.

Sorcha leaned back into the sprite as the rippling water refused to relent, and pushed her to a splendid orgasm. She splashed and cried out as the rapidly pulsating water became slippery silky tendrils once again, licking and rolling gently around the bud of her clitoris. When sighs replaced cries, the watery form of Feenie cascaded down from her body, but continued to swirl around her. She knelt down, the water coming up to her chin. The feel of the water sprite swimming around her was bliss.

"That was lovely," she told the lough as her hands moved through the water. "That was truly divine. Thank you for bringing me so much pleasure."

In the moonlight, she could see before her eyes a face of perfect proportions in the surface of the water. The face rose up and became a shimmering head, surrounded by a mane of rippling tendrils of watery hair. It was, for certain, a beautiful face. Clear as crystal, and reflecting the moonlight. The wet mouth with full lips and liquid tongue touched hers. Her lips parted as the slick, watery tongue swirled around the inside of her mouth. The watery hands and arms rose from beneath the surface and reached for her hair.

Sorcha could not speak the sprite's language, but she understood her. She let Feenie release the twig that held her hair. When it was free from the knot at the top of her head, she let it tumble down into the water. She dipped her head back into the water and let her hair be massaged by the sprite. Watery hands massaged her breasts, which broke the surface of the water like two perfect islands, as the water combed through her hair. Between her knees, there was a gentle flicking and caressing that was a sensuous tease. Another orgasm began the slow build-up to release.

Had Feenie not jerked her suddenly, almost as if by surprise, for certain she would have been crying out in pleasure and ecstasy moments later. But the sprite had. And it was odd. They were alone and she knew they were alone. Feenie would know better than her if there was a danger in the water. So Sorcha trusted the sprite. She did not resist when Feenie's current pulled her to a deeper pool and hid her amongst the rocks. For certain, the water was the safest place for her to be if there was danger. Feenie could protect her without any doubt, as long as she remained within the water sprite's domain.

Nothing would dare touch her in the water. Which was why she was very still when she heard at last the sound of a man running quickly towards them. Feenie held fast to her in the water as a splashing interrupted the silence of her night. A dome of water, that she suspected looked like any other boulder protruding from the water in the moonlight, was cast over her head. Through the haze of the water, Sorcha watched silently, as a man whose hair was white in the moonlight threw himself under the water.

Where he stayed. She didn't dare say a word, but she did wonder if he was still underwater or if he'd swam down the shore. There was, for certain, something odd about the man. What it was, she couldn't quite tell. Feenie's protection dulled her senses.

The sound of horses' hooves caught her attention. They came at a pace from just over the hills and stopped at the banks of the lough. Sorcha doubted the riders had the courtesy to ask Emer, spirit of the valley, for permission to cross her land, so they had stopped for another reason. She didn't have to be even marginally intelligent to figure out that reason more than likely had something to do with the man who had yet to resurface.

The men on horseback spoke amongst themselves. They were too far away from her to be understood. Eventually they moved along. When they were well and gone, the man resurfaced from the water. He climbed out onto the banks and turned back. "Thank you for hiding me, spirit of the lough,". "Although superficially you might assume I am the bad guy, in reality we are all creatures of nature just trying to get by in this world. So I thank you again. I do appreciate the suggestion. I'll find the copse of trees and ask the spirit to hide me in her branches."

He trotted off in the direction of the woods. Feenie released her, but not before taking her down the shore as close to the door of the cottage as possible. Feenie practically threw Sorcha out of the stream with the nudge she gave her, to the circle of stones that surrounded the house. Her basket, which was left on the bank, followed her out of the water. "I get it. Go home." Nothing that wasn't invited could enter through the ring of stones. Except mortals. They can go pretty much anywhere they want to go, simply because they have no concept of the fact there are some places they shouldn't go.

Sorcha picked up her basket and walked the hundred or so paces to the circle of stones. As she crossed the line, she knew she wasn't alone. Something had had been here. But there was no sense of menace, so she continued. Her feet reached the path approaching the house. On either side grew thistle, rosemary, chamomile, thyme and the rest of their innocuous herbal cousins. Most of what was grown had been planted generations earlier, and refreshed with the seeds from the previous season the following spring. Everything in the garden had its season, purpose and place in nature. What didn't grow in her garden, she gathered from the forests, hills, and sea which lay just beyond the next valley.

On that moon-filled night, hiding under the fragrant branches of a basil plant, was a cat. A black cat with eyes as blue as the Irish Sea, that watched the girl as she walked in the moonlight. The cat had wandered into the valley a few nights earlier. In the ring of protection surrounding the pretty witch's home, he'd found a level of peace and calm he'd longed for since his journey had begun. A deep purr came from his core as she passed. For a brief moment, she stopped and looked around, spying him. Sorcha scratched him under the chin, and then continued on her way. The touch of her fingers under his chin made him shiver a little as his fur stood up on end. This is what the girl did to him. She made him purr.

Chapter Two

Sorcha had been born in the cottage. She was fairly certain she would die in the cottage. Someday, hopefully a long way away, she would turn the cottage over to a girl. The girl who would one day replace her in the coven. A maid, a mother and a crone. An unending line of women. Their lineage stretched back to a time before the gods had left the land. There was an energy attached to the land, which drew women who possessed an extraordinary ability to commune with nature to make it their home. As it had been for generations, going so far back in time that local lore surrounding the house on the lough had named the occupant of the house "witch". It wasn't an inaccurate description, but perhaps a bit sensationalized for Sorcha.

With the death of the crone, she had been promoted from the maid to the mother. The mother of the coven, her Aunt Fionnuala, was now the crone. As much as Sorcha loved and as much as she embraced being a maiden witch, she was ready for a man long before Orla died. Being a maid in a coven was a rather a misleading title. It just meant she was the youngest and a virgin. Get a long lived witch as the crone, and a maid could linger in a lonely bed for a long time. She needed a man to help her pass the threshold from maiden to mother. The problem was, she hadn't found the right man and the reality was she just had a couple of nights to find him.

With a sigh, she took her basket and headed away from the lake to her home. Her Aunt Fionnuala and Aoife, who would become the maid of the coven, would be coming for dinner. When she reached the small outcropping of trees which stood between her and home, the air felt different. Cooler than it should be with the shadows darker and deeper than even the setting sun justified. Sorcha stopped out of curiosity when common sense told her to move, and move quickly. There was magic in the outcropping that wasn't normally there. And silence. Nothing moved. No energy pulsed. It was if the very life force of the trees, the creatures that lived among them and the very earth itself had been dampened.

"Belle?" she called the name of the sprite that lived in the trees.

"She's hiding," a male voice said.

"Who's there?" She jumped, dropping her basket. She felt nothing coming from the direction of his voice. Nothing at all. Which was impossible. There was no beating heart thumping quietly in her ear, the energy of an aura wasn't tickling the back of her neck, no random thoughts slipped into her mind unbidden. It was as if a shield was in place. A powerful shield.

"I'm here. I'm not a threat." A man stepped forward from behind two trees. A young man. Probably not more than twenty or twenty-two. It wasn't that his face was so beautiful, nor his black hair with its soft curls, or even his eyes which were the color of the ocean that caught her attention. It wasn't that his clothing was torn, filthy and bloody and his arm had been wrapped in a makeshift sling. It was the harp case he carried on his back and the staff he held. Taller than him and slim. Oak. She didn't move, but stood staring at him. "You're a druid. A young druid. But still a druid."

"Yes," he said, smiling at her, leaning against his staff.

"This is a valley of witches. There is no place for you here."

"Please." He held out a hand to her. "I've lost most of my power. I've been chased for a very long time. I'm trying to get to my family, but the hunter that's after me keeps cutting me off. I need your help. I was hoping to just hide in your valley, heal and be on my way in time, but those riders scared the piss out of me last night and I need you." His words slipped over his tongue to her ears on a satin ribbon. "Please."

"Very well." With a sigh and a jerk of her head, she relented. Not that she'd put up much of a fight. Druid or not, the young man was injured. "You can stay tonight. Tomorrow you're on your way again."

"I'll take what I can get." He followed her as she made her way into the house.

Sorcha could see Aunt Fionnuala and Aoife gathering herbs in the garden when she returned with her basket of cuttings and the druid in tow.

"Sorcha." Fionnuala looked up. "What's the matter? Why are you bringing home stray druids?"

"He's hurt. A hunter is after him."

Fionnuala rose from the patch of marigolds she'd been tending. "You wouldn't know anything about a group of riders all infused with the holy spirit of their bloody god I felt pass through the valley last night?"

"I might," the druid suggested.

"What's your name?" Sorcha questioned.

"Cormac."

"Well, Cormac the Druid," Fionnuala sighed. "What did you do, to get a bunch of hunters on your tail? Most druids I've met in my time tend to lay low. Not draw the attention of those who have taken an unbreakable vow to flush out anyone that doesn't worship their bloody god."

"They caught me out at a pub in Boston. I've been running for a long time. I figured I might stand a chance coming home to Ireland."

"Why were you in Boston?" Aoife quizzed.

"I'm a doctoral student," he explained. "I was there to study."

"They do like us Irish in America," Fionnuala nodded. "And the other way around."

Sorcha's ears picked up a sound in the distance. *Horses.* "Did you...?"

"I hear them," Fionnuala stated.

"Horses?" Aoife added. "I hear horses."

"Horses," Cormac laughed. "Who rides horses anymore?"

"People that are smart enough to know in the rural backcountry they can maneuver better on four legs than four wheels," Sorcha explained.

"Please," Cormac pleaded. "I can't run anymore. I don't know that I can even transform into a cat and turn myself back. I had a hard go of it this morning. I very nearly didn't return to my form."

"Into the house," Sorcha ordered. "Move."

When the four were behind their bolted door, Sorcha, Fionnuala, and Aoife threw up additional charms.

"You stay here," Fionnuala ordered Aoife and Sorcha as she swept her cape over her shoulders. As the oldest of the three, Fionnuala was the most powerful. Her magic was tested, and the well of strength she had to draw from had been dug one spell at a time during her long life. Sorcha watched from the window as her aunt took to air and circled around above before disappearing into the night sky. The three left behind waited in silence.

What felt like an eternity, but was in reality not even half an hour later, the door blew open and in flew Fionnuala in the form of a raven. Sorcha quickly closed and bolted the door behind her. When she transformed back into the tall, older woman, who wore her silver hair wrapped in a crown around her head, she looked grim. With a flick she removed her cape and hung it on a peg next to the door, as if it were an ordinary cape and not one infused with great magic.

"I think I pushed them off the trail," Fionnuala said. "What I'd like to know, is how they are tracking you so easily? So. Any thoughts? Something pop to mind?"

"I don't know. I don't. If I could figure it out, believe me, I would try to be rid of it. My old master thinks they've marked me somehow, but I can't seem to find the spot on my body."

Fionnuala hummed for a moment then went to the door. "Fenton!" she called to the woods. "Fenton, show yourself and I'll give you a treat." She left the door open before returning to her basket of cuttings and withdrawing a bundle of mistletoe. "Take this." She shoved the bundle at Cormac and instantly he looked healthier.

"Thank you," he sighed. "I've lost my knife."

"You really are in trouble," Aoife snorted.

"What to do with you is the question," Sorcha mumbled as she put the kettle on the fire.

"Make him take a bath?" Aoife suggested, sniffing the air.

A throat clearing at the door caught their attention. "You promised me a treat?"

"Fenton," Fionnuala said. "Look at the druid. Is there an enchantment on him?"

Fenton looked at Cormac. "Yes. My treat?"

Cormac made a face. "A leprechaun?"

"Druid." Fenton made a face like a bug had flown in his mouth at Cormac.

"He's quite harmless," Sorcha smeared a large hunk of brown bread with strawberry jam. "I have his pot of gold. He's also quite useful on occasion."

"What is the enchantment?" Fionnuala asked. "Leprechaun? Elf? Selkie?"

Fenton scrunched up his nose. "Looks like a witch's spell to me. It's not very powerful, but it does sort of buzz. I was wondering what that flickering through the bushes was last night. Thought it might be a pixie. Check his skin. He probably has a mark on him."

Sorcha handed the leprechaun a plate with the slice of jam-covered bread. With a deep intake of breath, she opened her third eye and gave Cormac a good look. Then she laughed. She knew what the enchantment was, and who had put it on the significantly weakened druid. It was a love charm and she was the witch that had sent it out into the world in search of a man. A man with blue eyes and black hair with a gift for music. Life truly was funny, and the moon had an excellent sense of humor.

"Cup of tea?" Fenton hummed. "Please? I'll tell you another secret."

"What's the secret?" Aoife questioned.

"Someone's coming." Fenton gobbled his bread. "Riders approaching. Four. There's a hunter with them. He's got a magical googaa. Sort of makes me feel a bit ill."

"Give him a cup of tea," Fionnuala told Aoife, putting an apron on over her dress and smoothing her hair. "I'm going outside to have a sniff around."

"What about me?" Cormac demanded, looking around. For the first time, he noted the house as it appeared on the outside couldn't possibly be as spacious as it appeared on the inside. Although it was hardly a palace, it was certainly comfortable.

"Just sit and be quiet," Sorcha hissed as she slid an apron over her dress and tidied her hair. When she was in the guise of a simple country woman, she took a stoneware jar from above the hearth. From it she drew a handful of flour and tossed it over him with a muttered word.

He sneezed and convulsed involuntarily. "Care to explain?" he exclaimed as he dusted the flour, which only served to coat the shambles of his mucky clothing in a filmy paste.

"Just be quiet and don't move," Sorcha ordered.

"Today just keeps on getting better and better," he mumbled as he ran his hand through his hair, fairly certain the combination of dirt and magical flour made it stand up nearly straight.

Sorcha tried to suppress a laugh, but was failing. His eyes went to her and she returned his gaze. There was still a drop of desire in their brown depths, but it was smothered down by her curiosity and poorly concealed mirth at his current situation. *Witches*, he laughed in the confines of his brain. He wasn't sure at that moment if he'd be safer with the hunters outside.

"Fenton," Fionnuala snapped, stepping past him into the kitchen. "Go hide in the bushes. We may need you to be Connor. Will you do that?"

"Will you make me sausages AND potatoes?"

"When they've gone I'll make you some sausages and potatoes. There might be pie."

"Pie! I'll do it." Fenton scrambled away from the door, which Fionnuala closed behind him.

When there was a knock at the door, Sorcha went to open it. Sure enough, on the other side was the hunter that had chased Cormac on a zigzag across three continents and nearly had him. Stupidity, overconfidence, and arrogance had brought him back home to Ireland and to the tidy kitchen in the stone house. He was so far from his home in Dublin. His lovely home just outside the gates of Trinity College where his father and uncles were professors. His home where his family had lived for generations. He was the next in a never-ending line of druids. And he'd gone and gotten himself nearly nabbed by a hunter and under the control of a coven of witches. Genius.

"Sir," Fionnuala said with a cold professionalism. "Why do you call at my door at this late hour? Do you require a midwife or nurse?"

The hunter stepped forward, uninvited into the home as if he were a proprietor, followed by the three men that flanked him. "Search it," the man ordered.

As if on cue, Aoife screamed and Sorcha flew to the girl, enveloping her in her arms. Aoife was hardly the timid creature she appeared to be, and begged the men not to harm them as they were poor women without a man to protect them.

He sat in his chair and watched the scene unfold around him, aware that he seemed to be invisible to the men that searched the home.

The three men that searched the rooms returned and called the all clear without bothering to go upstairs to the second floor. They seemed to not notice it existed.

"Have you seen a man?" The hunter asked with an assumption of authority.

The women cowered together. "There are no men here," Fionnuala whimpered. "Just us poor women and this girl who is but a maid. Please don't hurt us." The three wailed in sync. He had to bite his lower lip to stop himself from laughing. *Witches.* These hunters were clearly no geniuses, which said what about him.

"Will you stop with your incessant wailing?" the hunter demanded. "I'm not going to hurt you, you silly women. Now answer me; have you seen a man?"

The three women looked at each other, shaking their heads. "No," Fionnuala answered with a shrug.

"Nor I," Sorcha claimed. "The last man I saw was Martin O'Grady when he called for a tea to ease his woman's aches."

"How goes she?" Fionnuala asked conversationally.

"The babes are already heavy," Sorcha said with a concerned sigh. "She'll deliver any moment now, and in truth I worry for her."

"As do I," Fionnuala said with a sage nod. "She's thin hipped...."

"You," the hunter turned to Aoife, cutting off Fionnuala and Sorcha nattering about the business of midwifery. "Have you seen a man?"

Aoife looked down to her hands as her eyelashes fluttered.

"Aoife?" Sorcha said the girl's name sternly. "Have you seen a man?"

Aoife began to cry as she buried her face in her hands.

"What man have you seen?" Fionnuala demanded gently.

"Was he pale of face with eyes of blue?" the hunter questioned. "Taller than me, carrying a staff and a harp?"

"No," Aoife cried. "You don't understand."

"What don't we understand?" Sorcha insisted.

"I love him!" Aoife cried into her apron. "I didn't mean for things to go so far, but you don't understand..."

Not even on the stages of London and New York had he seen such a performance. It was the best pantomime he'd ever seen.

"What do you mean *go so far*?" Fionnuala repeated, with a tone of a woman that understood all too well what *go so far* meant.

"Who is this man?" Sorcha prodded.

"Does he have the look of this man?" The hunter held a rather unflattering picture of him up and shoved it in the girl's face.

"I don't know that man," Aoife cried, and shook her head.

"Who, Aoife? Answer me now," Fionnuala insisted.

"Connor," Aoife sighed.

"Connor?" Sorcha gasped. "You have been forbidden from seeing him. His only interest in you is your pretty face and sweet form. He'll only leave you with tears and a baby."

Again, as if this play had been acted out a thousand times before, there was a knock at the door.

One of the hunter's men jerked the door open, and on the other side stood Fenton the leprechaun wearing the illusion of a young man.

"Who the devil are you?" the hunter demanded.

"Connor," Fenton said with a bow as he doffed his hat — perhaps a touch too theatrically. Leprechauns. Cormac nearly snorted out loud.

"Connor," Aoife sighed as she ran to Fenton's waiting arms. "I'm so sorry, my love, but I had to tell them. They knew I'd been with a man."

"I shall protect you, my love," Fenton said with a flourish of one arm, as the other swept Aoife against him so he could gaze longingly into her eyes.

"Tell me you haven't deflowered our Aoife?" Sorcha wept as she rung her hands. "We are poor women and have nothing to offer a man but her pretty face and her chastity. Whatever shall we do?"

"Aoife," Fenton fell to his knee. "I am a wealthy landowner and could have my pick of all the girls in the county, but it is you I want." Fenton raised one hand to the sky. "You! And you alone, my love! You will make my days complete." He dropped his head to his chest. "I beg you. No, implore you, say you'll have me."

Sorcha moved to speak, but was silenced by Fenton hamming it up and continuing his scene. "For it is you, and you alone, that has shown me the life of Ireland' s most notorious rake is shallow, and only through my love for you will I truly find redemption. Say you'll be my wife, or I shall go and fling myself into the ocean." Fenton bowed his head to his chest as he waited for Aoife to respond.

"Yes," Aoife exclaimed, clasping her hands together as Fenton rose from his knee. "I will be your wife."

"Oh happy day," Sorcha cheered as she came forward.

"Aoife, may you live happily ever after," Fionnuala said, completing the drama.

Cormac wanted to applaud, toss coins, and stomp his foot into the floorboards. Fenton had overdone it, but the women had been magnificent.

"We're done here," the hunter said with an annoyed grunt.

"No," Fionnuala said warmly. "You must stay and raise a glass to their happiness."

"Yes you must," Sorcha insisted.

"Please," Aoife gushed as her pink cheeks flushed and she held Fenton's hands in her own.

"I insist," Fenton added.

"One drink won't hurt," one of the hunter's men murmured.

"For their happiness," another seconded.

Sorcha placed glasses on the table while Fionnuala pulled a bottle out of a cupboard. "My wildflower wine," Fionnuala said, uncorking the bottle of honey-colored liquor. "The recipe has been in my family for generations."

Clearly, the drama hadn't played itself out. Were he truly watching the play on a stage in London, the crowd would be shouting to warn the men who had been hunting him not to drink the wine. He knew that was how the hunt for him was going to end. Fionnuala had promised him she would send the hunters off in the wrong direction.

"To the bride and groom." The hunter raised his glass to drink along with everyone else in the room, including the women and Fenton. "Very fine. My compliments."

"You're kind. As you know, we are poor women, but we do well selling our little concoction — which is what we assumed you were here for before terrorizing us."

"Would you sell me a bottle?" The hunter asked, looking down into his glass

"I'll sell you two," Sorcha said with a saleswoman's smile. "It was a very good year for wildflower wine. A drink a day will ward off all manner of agues, rheumatisms, fevers...." By the time she was finished with her sales pitch, Sorcha had sold four bottles to each man, and Aoife was filling the men's glasses for the third time. He noted that the women and Fenton had barely touched their own glasses after the first sip.

"You gentlemen seem very tired," Fionnuala yawned. The hunter yawned broadly at the suggestion.

"Very tired," Sorcha said soothingly. "Very, very tired. Exhausted even."

"Clearly you need a rest," Fionnuala stated. "Somewhere far, far away."

"Somewhere exotic," Aoife concurred. "You'll want to go to Italy?" She looked to the older women.

"Farther I think," Fionnuala suggested. "Greece."

"What about Japan?" Aoife offered. "I've always wanted to go to Japan. Or China. Or India. Or Persia." Aoife had the travel bug whether she knew it or not.

"Persia." The hunter nodded as he looked into the liquor the color of sunshine in his glass. "Yes. Persia. Harems of women. It's been a long time since I've had a woman. Chasing damnable druids around the world. The whole lot of them. Shape-shifters, witches, immortals..."

"You should go to Persia," Fionnuala said warmly. "You're bored with hunting. It's frustrating and dangerous."

"It's dangerous," agreed one of the hunters with him. His voice was dreamy and thick. "I want to be a cobbler. Not a hunter."

"Then you should be a cobbler," Aoife said smoothly. "Go to Italy. Learn your trade. Forget about druids and hunting. Shoes are such a lovely thing."

By the time the three women were finished, the hunters were walking out the door in search of Persia, a master cobbler, a wife and a new life. Each had promised to have a sip and only a sip of the wine she'd sold them for all the coin they had in their purses but enough to get them to their destinations. When Fionnuala closed the door behind the men she bolted it shut. "They're gone," Sorcha sighed.

"My sausages?" Fenton requested, back in the form of a leprechaun again. "And potatoes. Don't forget the potatoes. And the pie. I want some pie. And I got the googaa. It was in one of their packs."

"What was it?" Sorcha questioned.

"One of those." Fenton held up two fingers and made a cross. "Had some powerful juju in it."

"What did you do with it?" Fionnuala asked.

"Tossed it to Feenie," Fenton laughed. "She gave it a cleanse. It's clean now."

"You did put it back in his pack?" Sorcha questioned.

"'Not dumb," Fenton grumbled. "Put it back."

"It'll take him half a year to run out of wine," Fionnuala examined the bandage on Cormac's arm before cutting it away with her knife. "Then another few months for his senses to return to him. I suggest you be somewhere else this time next year."

"I will be." Cormac looked to where Sorcha stood. He winced as the elder of the three examined his arm with the delicacy of a field surgeon in the middle of a battle.

"It's just a sprain," Sorcha said. "Bad sprain, but you'll heal quickly now that you're here."

"For now, I need rest and food. Please will you help me? When I'm at my full strength I'm powerful. I can control the weather as if I made it, I can read the stars...Whatever you want."

"Whatever I want?" Sorcha confirmed.

"Whatever you want," he confirmed. The look that passed between the two older women made him wonder if he wouldn't regret not placing a caveat on the offer.

"Fair enough," Sorcha said. "Aoife. Get the table set for the four of us. Apparently I have a guest for the next few nights." She looked at Cormac. "You come with me."

She led him through the house and up the steps to the bathroom. With a flick of her hand, she turned the hot water on and let it fill the stoppered bath.

"Please tell me this is for me," Cormac sighed.

"This is for you. You need a bath," Sorcha sniffed "You stink. I'm not used to men and their men-smells in my home. If you leave the toilet seat up, I'll boot you out myself."

"Please. Don't hold back," Cormac retorted. "Any idea what you want from me?"

"You can stay until you're healed. When the Beltane fires burn, you walk through the flames with me. I need a man and you're a man. If you're half as powerful as you seem to think you are, then you'll suit my needs."

"I…" Cormac stuttered. "I didn't think…"

"You said whatever I want. That's what I want." She went to the cupboard and removed a black cube. "Scrub yourself with this."

"Which is?" He took the black cube and sniffed.

"Soap with volcanic ash and clay," Sorcha said. "It'll get the smell off you."

"Can you help me?" He tugged at his shirt. "My shoulder is better, but I'm actually still in a lot of pain."

"I'll give you something more for the pain after you've bathed." She helped him undress. "I have a rub I can put on your shoulder." The men ill with fever, injured, damaged or dying she'd seen undressed somehow were different from this one. Nature had promised to deliver a man to her before the Beltane fires. Nature always kept her promises.

Chapter Three

After Aoife and Fionnuala left, Sorcha sat in front of the fire in the living room as Cormac knocked around in the spare bedroom he'd been offered by his hostess. How had he ended up in the west of Ireland in a witch's house? How? He knew in a practical way what had happened, but the druid in him didn't believe it was simply a coincidence that he landed on the doorstep of a witch that needed a man to pluck her like a flower a week before Beltane. It was just too perfect a coming together of energies to be a coincidence.

What he did not want was to become a father. Which was what would happen. That was pretty much a guarantee. Sorcha was probably a lovely woman. A bit older than him, but very pretty. These things were not the issue. He did not want to be tied to back country Ireland by virtue of the child he'd put to the witch.

They needed to have a conversation.

He found her in the living room in front of the fireplace. She was pretty. That was for certain.

"Can we talk?" he asked, finding a seat in one of the two overstuffed chairs.

"Of course," she said. "Just so you know, before she left, Fionnuala and I put some wards and protections up around the house. Fenton is also out there keeping watch. I've had a chat with the sprite of the lough. We'll know if your hunter comes close."

"I truly appreciate that," he said. "This is hard to broach, but…" He paused.

"You don't want to go through the fire with me."

"I'm sorry, but I don't. I do want to go through the fire to remove the mark the hunter put on me, but I'm not ready to be a husband, and I'm certainly not ready to be a father."

She studied him. Her eyes were a deep brown and her smile mirthful. "I don't have any interest in making you my husband. Not even a little. I need you for just a little bit of time, then you are free to go as you will."

"I don't want to be a father," he said. "I'm still just a student."

"Cormac," she said. "Maybe I'm not being very clear. When we're done, I want you to go and never come back. Unless you're fundamentally stupid, once the mark is off of you, the hunter won't be able to track you down again. You're a druid. I'm not certain what you did to catch that hunter's eye, but I suspect you weren't being as discreet as you could be."

"You mean that? I really can just go? Because I've already missed a lot of school."

"You really can just go. I need a man in my life like I need a third leg."

"Are you a lesbian?"

She laughed lightly. "No. I don't know. I don't think so. I've just been a maid for so long that I've rather given up on the idea of a man in my life. I did love Orla very much, but even for a witch she lived a very long life. I'm actually the second maid of the coven. The woman that was the maid before me went to be mother of another coven long ago."

"I just don't want to be tied down."

"How old are you?"

"Twenty-four."

"What are you studying?"

"Philosophy."

"Of course you are," she said. "Druids. It was that, botany or astronomy."

"How old are you?"

"Thirty-five."

"Really?"

"You don't need to sound so shocked," she laughed. "I don't look that old."

"No. Actually, you're really pretty," he said.

"Thank you. I promise, Cormac. In two weeks you can just forget you ever met me."

"I'm sorry. I'm just not ready to be a father."

"Cormac. You're very young and very sweet. You've just had a terrible fright. I've never really left the valley, but I know there are some terrifying things out in the world. I'm not certain what it is you find out there, but there is nothing now or ever tying you here."

"I really appreciate that," he sighed.

"Just so we're clear, this goes both ways. Do not come back here in ten years when you've grown up a little and start to think you have some responsibility to me or my child. Because that's really what this is about. isn't it?"

"Yes."

"Rest assured. my life will be easier with just one baby to look after rather than two." She rose from the floor. "I'm going to bed."

"Can I sleep with you?" he asked quickly.

"What?" Sorcha laughed loudly.

"Can I sleep with you?" he repeated the question. "I'm serious. Look, you are asking me to be physically intimate with you, maybe being a bit familiar with each other might help."

"Physically intimate? Cormac, you are adorable."

"What do you want me to say? Plough you like a field? I understand I'm not at my best, but I was raised better than that."

"Physically intimate is better," she laughed.

"You want me to do that to you in front of a group of trouping fae, and I'm sure a fair number of other witnesses. I think building a bit of intimacy in advance might not be a bad thing."

"Cormac," she said gently. "Are you a virgin?"

"I..." That was the one question he did not want her to ask. "Maybe."

"It's sort of a yes or no question."

"Yes. Okay? Happy? I'm a twenty-four year old virgin. I just – honestly I just never found the right moment. My master told me to wait. That there was power in my first time..." his words faltered.

"Being physically intimate?" Sorcha offered helpfully.

"Yes. And I just never imagined it would be..." again his words faltered.

"With a witch that was pretty much a stranger to you in a public rite?"

"Well... yeah. I mean. I don't want to be pushy, but I'm sort of worried I might get nervous and have a problem. You know – a man problem."

Sorcha smiled and held out a hand. "I'm new at this too. Maybe a little intimacy building might help both of us."

Cormac took her hand and rose to his feet. He was taller than her by nearly half a head. He bent down to kiss her, and was surprised when her fingers reached behind his head, drawing his lips to hers. He took her mouth with a novice's eagerness to learn. The tingle of pleasure the pressure of her lips was creating down his body equaled the thrill he'd experienced as he'd spied her from the shadows taking pleasure with the spirit of the lough.

He pulled back and saw the tilt of her smile as she looked him fearlessly in his eyes. The invitation to continue was in the dark depths, but he knew he could only go so far. So he was to be careful with her. Being run off or worse would be bad for him at that moment. As it stood he was broke, without a set of his own clothing and quite possibly still being hunted. The display of removing the hunters had been impressive, but who was to say they wouldn't wake up in the morning with hangovers, angry they'd been duped by a bunch of clever women.

His trousers were uncomfortably tight as he bent over her and pressed his mouth to hers. Her tongue sought his as her strong arms wrapped around his neck, pulling him closer. Taking her hand in his, he pressed it against his aching cock through the linen fabric of his breeches. When she didn't shrink away or cower, but rather took the initiative and started to explore, his balls ached and his cock throbbed.

"Come," she ordered, taking his hand. "Let's go to the bed. It's a good place to intimacy build."

"Are you teasing me?"

"Just a little."

He followed as she led him up the steps, and past the door to the bedroom he'd been given, to her room. She faltered slightly before he took over again. He'd told the truth that he was a virgin.

That didn't mean he was wholly without experience. Odd as it seemed, it was possible he was actually more experienced than Sorcha.

He sat on the bed and pulled her next to him. Kissing seemed to be a good place to start. Kissing lead to touching which moved on to more touching and finally to laying back against the pillows. Quick as he could with his arm still aching from the shoulder sprain, he pulled his clothes off. Sorcha looked at his bare body. "You don't have any wards or shields on your body."

"No," he answered. "Not yet. Maybe before I leave you could brew an ink for me? Something powerful?"

"I will," she offered. "I'll do that for you. It will be my gift to you."

"Thank you," he said climbing on the bed. His fingers crept down her cotton nightgown, gathering the fabric as they moved until her damp sex was exposed to the night. She closed her eyes as she bent her knees letting them flop open to the sides. Her akimbo knees pressed into the mattress as his fingers wound their way through the slippery wet curls of her bush down into the slick folds of her vulva.

With her nightgown bunched around her waist he went exploring. He placed his hands on her feet then slid them upwards until he brushed the firmness of her thighs, the smoothness of her hips and the pert roundness of her breasts finishing with a flourish as he pulled her nightdress over her head letting it fly to the floor.

The room was dark but for the light from the moon. His eyesight was attuned to the dark and he saw her in the night shadows stretched before him. "You're very pretty," he sighed. "Do you know how pretty you are?"

"No," she said. "But I'm so much more than pretty."

"You are." He pushed her legs apart until they lay spread against the bed. "You smell like summer." His nose nuzzled the damp brown curls that shielded her sex from his eyes. With his tongue he ran a line from one end of her slit to the other. The involuntary twitch of her body with accompanying gasp made him grin. "And you taste like honey." It was obvious Sorcha knew the technical side of what happened between a man and a woman, but not the sensual side.

He leaned back against his heels and gazed down at her. As he took one of his long fingers and stroked it down her slit, inching deeper with each pass, her legs moved restlessly against the mattress. Her hips tilted upward encouraging him to work harder and faster, as her hand came down on his pressing it against her. He gave her lips a little pinch as he leaned forward and kissed her.

"Sweetheart," he murmered, smiling at her. There was nothing quite like an eager beginner to make his work more pleasant. "Can you just let me be in charge right now? I know what I'm doing."

"I thought you were a virgin," she whispered.

"I am," he replied. "But that doesn't mean I've gone without female attention."

"I'll bet all of those perky college girls like you," she grumbled. "Your eyes are so pretty."

"You like my eyes?" He kissed her neck.

"Yes," Sorcha sighed. She released his hand, letting him continue. To assure he would be able to proceed uninterrupted, he took her hands and placed them behind her head. Her pink tipped nipples thrust upwards, tempting him to distraction from the task at hand. He returned his finger to her sensitive flesh, running it around the rim in smaller circles each pass until it slid effortlessly into her opening.

She was snug and hot around him, her clenching muscles threatening to take his finger off. Her hips twitched involuntarily encouraging him to stroke her. Sorcha was definitely not the woman for a man that was insecure in his own ability to please. She growled with displeasure when he removed his finger, then purred with delight when he inserted two. He slid them out then plunged them back inside as the pad of his thumb pressed against the hard nub of her clit.

Her climax was growing. He could feel it in the movements of her body, the rapidness of her breath and the speed of her blood coursing through her veins. Her passage closed around him, pulling him deeper. His own desire thudding inside of him was pressed down - at least momentarily. Her pleasure was his primary goal – at least at that moment. In time he would find his own release, but not before he brought her to the climax she so wanted.

"More," she whispered, moving against his fingers. He withdrew his fingers, widening them gently as they gradually slid out. Before she could protest he lowered his mouth to her wet sex, breathing in the heady aroma of her desire. With his fingers he parted her labia and slipped his tongue into the top of her cleft, drawing a line through her cream then returning to the bundle of nerves of her clitoris. Beginning gently, he swirled his tongue as one finger returned to her passage. When she had her fingers in his hair, he lashed at her with his tongue. Sorcha shuddered and trembled as she cried out, her orgasm energizing her body. While her body recovered he cupped his hand against her sex, squeezing as her muscles convulsed.

"Marvelous," Sorcha sighed, laying back against the pillows. "What's next?"

"This is really only just the beginning." A wicked smile brushed his lips. Before he could kiss her, she slipped off the bed and out of his arms. Her bedroom was warm. Or maybe she was warm. Either way, she needed some air. She went to the window which was a series of diamond cut pieces of murky glass bonded together with strips of lead. With a yank, she tugged it open. The moon was nearly overhead. Milky white and pure, the moon kept the time for her. It was the moons cycles that mattered. In seven nights the moon would be full. There would be no more waiting.

As Sorcha crawled into her bed between the cool sheets, her body ached with a longing she didn't know would ever be satiated. Sighing, Sorcha raised her head, throttled her pillow, then let it drop again. Cormac fell into her arms as she opened them to him. Seven nights. When the dirt was washed away, he turned out to be quite handsome. But then again, what could be more handsome than an Irish man with deep blue eyes, black hair, and that milky white skin? Nothing.

She lay back on top of her bed and listened to the sound of the wind in the trees, lulled by the familiar rustling as their limbs twined together. Sounds of the night floated in through the window along with the breeze. When she'd crawled out of her bed that morning, she hadn't wondered what a man in her arms would be like. As she lay back in her bed with, Cormac's hand on her thigh, wishing she could just let him ease the ache that threatened to make her scream in frustration, she knew what would happen in seven nights. A bit of intimacy building in advance had in fact been an excellent idea.

Chapter Four

Their final morning together. The sky was a bright blue and the sun was warm, promising an early summer. Already the roses were blooming like it was June. The appearance of the world was perfect, but Sorcha could not shake the feeling of unease that had gripped her as the end of her time with Cormac approached. She sought the source of it and found none. She sought signs that the hunter was returning for Cormac. Unless he was very clever, he had not doubled back. She opened all of the windows. Her broom swept out the last remnants of the spring that had been too hard and had lasted too long out the door. Outside on the lines were crisp white linens snapping in the breeze. The people of the valley had been hauling wood and branches to the fairy ring hidden in the trees just beyond the line of her property, to build up the makings of what would become the Beltane fire that night.

Sorcha felt the tingle of Cormac's approach on the back of her neck long before his lips touched her sweaty skin.

"Come with me," he whispered, taking her hand and tugging on it.

"I'm busy." She stopped her sweeping and wiped a hand across her forehead. "Tonight is the night. I have so much to do and time is running."

"I want you." He bit her earlobe as he stood behind her. "You need a rest. Time to take a break."

"I do not need a break," she countered. "You're just bored. You've done nothing but rest, read and thumb your cock all week."

"I love it when you're direct." His arms wrapped around her from behind. "Come thumb my cock for me."

"Can you be quick?"

"I can," he insisted, taking her by the hand and leading her to the bedroom.

When the door was closed he came up behind her, and released her hair from its chignon one pin at a time. The mass of chestnut hair tumbled down her back. When he left he would take a lock of it with him, just to be certain he'd never forget the way it smelled of the chamomile water she rinsed it in and the sunshine she let it dry in. The mass of brown locks were lifted to his nose, and he inhaled deeply as he rubbed the silken stuff to his cheek. Each hand took a rope of hair which slipped through his hands until it cascaded down her back.

He sat on the bed with Sorcha standing between his thighs. His hands moved under her skirts they roamed over the smooth, firm skin of her thighs, hips and ass. He cupped her sex in one hand, letting one finger then two slip inside the slick wet lips of her pussy. When he fluttered his fingers she bent her knees slightly, letting her legs spread. One long finger entered her followed by a second, which he kept absolutely still as he pressed his palm against the hard nib of her clit. If she wanted release she'd have to work for it, which she did. She rubbed against the palm of his hand, bringing herself closer and closer to her peak. When he felt her inner muscles tremble he removed his hand. A cry of anger at being denied came from Sorcha's lips. As she pressed her warm forehead to his, he pulled her skirts up, exposing the mound of soft brown curls at the apex of her thighs. Warm day or not, Sorcha rarely wore undergarments and never wore a bra.

"Do you want me to worship you?" he asked, teasing her a little. Her skin smelled of the violet soap she'd always made for herself, of her sweat and sex. He knew he was leaving. She'd made that clear enough and had said nothing to even him that she wanted him to stay, but at that moment in time all he could think about was the woman standing before him with the thatch of damp curls begging for his attention.

He dipped his head and blew gently on her wet hair. She moaned and spread her thighs farther, giving him access to her sex. He gazed at her waiting cunt slick and ready for him. She took the folds of her dress from his hands, giving him freedom to touch her. One finger slipped between her lips coating itself in her cream. He withdrew it and placed it in his mouth, sucking on the taste of her. With his hands free he wrapped them around the backs of her thighs, sliding them up until they were stopped by the crease where her ass and legs met. He pushed her forward so her hard nub would be exposed to him. Finally he dipped his mouth to her exposed sex and his tongue explored her wet labia.

She hooked a leg over his shoulder exposing more of herself to him. Petal soft folds of her flesh, pink as roses glistening with dew, opened before him. He breathed in the scent of her sex, relishing the lingering sweetness of her still intact virginity. His expert tongue licked and sucked, swirling around her clit. Just when she was about to climax he moved his tongue off her hard little nub and moved his mouth lower. Penetrating her with his tongue, he drove himself in and out of her, alternating between shallow and deep and occasionally with a twist. She moaned at the sensation and her supporting leg went boneless. In a single move he switched places with her on the bed. When she lay back he draped her other thigh over his shoulder and pressed his face against her. He lapped at her clit, gently circling it with his tongue before taking it into his mouth and sucking. Again, when she was close to climaxing he pulled away from her, eliciting a moan of disapproval.

"Why do you always stop?" She slammed her fists into the mattress. He ignored her protests, knowing full well she enjoyed the slow torment as much as he did. He took one finger and ran it the length of her creamy slit drawing her natural lubricant lower. When he reached the small pucker of her rim he stopped. Sorcha sighed, and he felt a small shiver of pleasure that he'd finally gotten the reaction of an uninitiated virgin out of her.

"Do you know what we can do here?" he asked as he began a gentle yet insistent massage with his thumb. Sorcha shook her head no but didn't ask him to stop or protest. He inserted his finger just up to the first joint. When she gasped a small gasp and her eyes sparkled with anticipation he knew he could continue.

"Will you show me?" she demanded annoyance, frustration, arousal and anticipation mingling in her words.

"Don't be so impatient," he laughed at her. "You are wanton."

"A woman knowing what she wants doesn't make her wanton," Sorcha retorted, stiffening. Cormac sensed dangerous terrain approaching and quickly moved clear.

"Of course not, sweetheart," he cooed, laying the two of them on the bed, stretching their bodies out. On the comfortable bed which had become his, he moved the skirts of Sorcha's dress out of the way so he could have access to her sex. Without hesitation or pulling back, he pleasured her thoroughly.

Her tongue slipped in his mouth, tangling with his. He pressed her back on the bed, hoping she understood that on occasion he liked to be in charge of his own seductions. Leaning over her, with his arm cradling her neck, he continued to stroke and pinch the folds of her labia occasionally slipping a finger then two inside. She trembled around his hand, her arms grasping him behind the head and pulling his mouth to hers. With a back arching cry she shuddered and climaxed, falling back against the curve of his arm when she was satiated.

"That was lovely," she sighed, kissing him and moving to get up. "Not exactly quick, but still very nice."

"I'm so happy you appreciate my efforts," he announced, dragging her back down on the bed. "We're not done."

Sorcha let her fingers creep inside of the trousers he wore slowly inching their way to his already stiff and ready cock. He leaned back and put his arms behind his head, perfectly content to be the object rather than the moderator of what was to come. Both of them had learned a great deal in their days together.

She released his cock and he watched as her hand slid up and down the long shaft, stopping on occasion to toy with the slit in the tip or to squeeze hard or gently. Sorcha had made a great study of his cock and what it took to pleasure him. In one move she took him in her mouth, sucking hard and vigorously enough to make him gasp. That was new. When he was still accommodating himself to the delicious onslaught of her mouth, a second surprise came in the form of her hand reaching between his ass cheeks. A finger rather indelicately pushed inside his unprepared hole drowning him in a world of sensation. She forced her finger deeper past the ring of muscle as her mouth laved and sucked at his balls, drawing them in one at a time. His back arched, forcing her finger in deeper. She took him into her mouth as deep as he would go while adding a second finger to thrust up his anus. He cried out like he didn't know he was still capable of doing as a climax the likes of which he had never imagined exploded out of him.

"Sorcha," he exhaled as she returned to the curve of his arm.

"Did you like that?" She leaned over him and studied his face.

"Yes." He pulled her mouth to his, letting the kiss linger before he moved his mouth to her neck.

"I need to finish my chores," she muttered not moving.

"How did you know to do that?" he asked pressing his lips to her hair. "With your fingers."

"You did it to me," she replied. "I liked it and I figured you'd like the same."

"I did," he laughed.

"I have a lot to do," she said, pulling herself reluctantly from the bed.

He stared at her as she adjusted her skirts and smoothed her hair, retying it into its tidy chignon. "Stay in bed with me. Please. It's our last day together."

"I'm trying not to think about that," she admitted, turning to him with a pin in her mouth. The pin was removed from her mouth and tucked into her hair. "I don't want to think about you going. I'm sorry. I just don't."

"Do you want me to stay?"

"That isn't what we agreed. We agreed that when the deed was done, that you would go. You have no obligation to me after tonight. I will brew up the ink for you so that you can have a shield tattooed on your body. That will take a few days."

"So I'll stay a few more days," he suggested, holding her hand.

"Just a few more days," she replied. "Any more and we both might start saying and doing things we'll regret."

Sorcha found Fenton sitting at the edge of the ring of power that circled her cottage. The feelings of unease and anxiety that had been only momentarily suppressed when she was in Cormac's arms returned the moment she stepped beyond the ring. All of the negative emotions which had been building in her boiled over like an unwatched pot.

"What is it?" she asked the leprechaun. "What is it that we feel?"

"Somebody's coming," Fenton whispered.

"Who?" she wondered. "Is it the hunter?"

"I don't know," Fenton muttered. "But it's coming."

"I need Fionnuala," she stated. "Will you run for her for me?"

"No. I'm sorry, Sorcha, but no. You've taken my pot of gold from me. Outside the line I'm vulnerable. There's something out there and I won't willingly stretch my neck out, even for you."

"Okay. You know I'll give you your pot of gold back one day," she added.

"I know you will," he said. "You know I don't mind so much that you're the one that has it. You're real good to me. Cormac's not so bad either. Is he going to be sticking around? Because he's got that glow about him. Like a lad in love."

"It's not real, Fenton. It's just whatever it is that pulled us together working its magic on him. In time it'll pass. I won't have him stuck here with me and a child when he comes out of the stupor."

"Maybe he wants to be stuck here. I'm not exactly unhappy."

"You funny thing you, Fenton," she laughed. She bent down and kissed him on the forehead. "I'm going for Fionnuala. Tell

Cormac something is out there and not to leave the circle until I've returned."

"I'll tell him. You be careful."

"I'm the scariest thing in the forest, Fenton. Don't worry about me."

She walked for perhaps a mile, more than half the distance between her cottage and Fionnuala's when it happened.

The hunter and his party circled Sorcha with their ring of torches. A new member had since joined them. A woman. It only took one look from Sorcha for her to know the woman was not only a witch, but one that often called forth demons. As they circled her a ring of fire formed on the ground. There was little magic that could be used by those without ability that would have any effect on her, but being encircled by flames was one of them. She couldn't break free of it on her own. She needed help from the outside of the circle.

"The druid," the hunter shouted from his place of safety outside the ring of fire. "Where is the druid?"

"Druids aren't for real," she lied. "They're just men in stories." Thirty men and more surrounded her.

"Where did he go?" the hunter demanded, grabbing her by the arm.

"I don't know," she cried, falling to the ground in a heap. "Please. I'm so frightened! I'm just a defenseless girl. Please don't hurt me!" She wept and wailed as she appealed to the captors circled around her.

"Not going to work on me twice. Where's the druid?"

"I don't know what you mean." She cowered as she looked up at him, her arm raised as if she expected him to strike her. "Please, there's been a mistake."

"Bind her hands, her eyes and mouth," the woman who rode with the hunter told him. "I can make her talk, but not here. I need some privacy and my things."

"Fine," the hunter responded with a curt nod of his head. One of his men was given the order. She was dragged up from the ground and bound in such a way as to inhibit her ability to perform even the simplest of spells. Although she was blinded by the black cloth over her eyes, she could feel her body being hoisted up into a horse. A rider took a place behind her and held her fast to him.

She was dragged from outside to inside. If she didn't think the smell could get worse, it did. Without being able to see or breathe properly, her instinct to gag was nearly overpowering. Finally she was stood in the middle of a room. The sound of falling sand circled her.

"Remove the bindings," the woman who rode with the hunter commanded.

When the blind came off her eyes she surveyed her surroundings, trying to imagine where she could be. She looked at the woman very closely for the first time, and saw one of her own. Whoever she was, she was a powerful witch and willing to sell her services for a fee. Like the three witches of the valley. But unlike them, she was willing to harm one of her own kind and even kill.

That made her a practitioner of the black, where the three of the valley only delved into the white.

The black witch stared at her from beyond the ring of salt. The one thing her prison provided her was with the safety of avoiding direct contact with the woman on the other side. Sorcha couldn't step out of the ring without it being broken, but neither could the other woman step into it without breaking it.

"We're going to make a deal," the black witch explained. "You're going to give the hunter the druid." She was on the other side of the salt barrier.

"The druid isn't mine to give. The druid belongs to himself."

"He's your man," the dark witch stated.

"No. He's not."

"I can smell him on you," the dark witch retorted. "He's your man."

"Call him to you," the hunter ordered.

"I don't have a hook in him," she declared. "I'm sorry to disappoint the two of you, but you're wrong. He's long gone."

"What happened to your Connor?" the hunter laughed. "Damned fool I was... where's the druid?"

"Gone," she lied. "Healed and sent away, loaded down with protections made by my hands and covered with my monthly blood for him."

The dark witch sniffed the air. "You stink of him. But you're still a virgin."

"Yes," she retorted. "He's smarter than you give him credit for and now he's stronger than you can imagine. You'll never catch him."

"We don't need to," the dark witch snapped. "He'll come for you."

"Doubtful. He's gone. He didn't want to be bound to me and he left.

The dark witch turned to the hunter. "Go. Check the cottage."

"He's not there," the hunter cursed. "I've watched the place for days. He's not there."

"He is there," the dark witch confirmed. "She's hidden him from you."

"Prove me wrong," the hunter demanded. "I tell you he's not there."

"Get your thugs to watch her." The dark witch turned with a click of her heels and walked to the door "The druid is somewhere near."

The hunter followed the witch, leaving Sorcha alone in the small room, lit by a small window at the top of the wall.

She looked up as a swallow flew in and perched on the high window sill. "It's okay," she whispered. "They can't seem to sense you."

The swallow floated down to the ground, then transformed into Cormac. In his hand he held his staff.

"You need to go," she told him.

"No." Cormac stepped across the salt barrier as if it wasn't there. "We have a deal. I've been a very patient and a very good boy all week. We have plans tonight."

"You need to go," she repeated. "I'll get another man. There are always stragglers that are pulled in by the fire."

"No. I'm staying. You're not getting rid of me that easily." He stepped back over the salt line.

"Free me now," she demanded.

"No." Cormac leaned over the salt and tipped up her face with a finger under her chin. "We can't let your jailers know I've been here. Trust me that I know what I'm doing." He kissed her quickly then let her go.

"You know what you're doing? Are you serious? Do you remember a week ago? The whole being chased and hiding thing?"

"I'm a lot stronger now."

Without hesitation he bent down and placed his lips to hers. His lips were soft and his breath was warm as she reached up to meet him. When he broke away his eyes held hers. "I love you, and I will get you out of here. If you'll have me, I'll be yours."

She wrapped her arms around his neck and pressed her body to his, as he held her while she cried. He separated from her reluctantly with more promises and kisses. When he had gone through the window as he had entered, she saw him completely as the man he was. She knew she'd never look at him as anything other than a man again.

Chapter Five

The day marched on and nightfall drew near while she paced around her circle, waiting for rescue.

To her disappointment, the door opened and the hunter walked in with the dark witch. Disappointment turned to shock, when the two were followed by Cormac who had his staff pointed at them.

"Move, witch." Cormac gave the dark witch a nudge.

"I'll find you," the dark witch purred. "I will, and you will regret it."

"I'm shaking," Cormac laughed, clearly not shaking. "You weren't smart enough to avoid a non-magical trap and I should be worried? I'm not."

"When I get you..."

"You're going to what?" Cormac demanded.

The dark witch plucked at the rope of braided mistletoe around her throat and yelped in pain as it sent lightning bolts to her fingers. They traveled down her body and left her in a twitching heap on the floor.

"I told you not to touch that," Cormac sighed. "Dumb witch." With that, Cormac hit the hunter over the head with his staff. He went down like a dropped sack of flour.

Sorcha gasped. The Cormac that stood before her was not the delightful and sweet young man she'd been tumbling around with for the past few days. In his place was a powerful druid that had taken control of the situation. "What did you do?"

"I outsmarted them," he said. "Not really very hard to do."

"Are you going to set me free?" she asked with a smile. "Before they wake up?"

"They're out for hours. I'll be back in the morning to deal with them. You and I have an appointment to keep first. But first..." He looked down at the ring of salt. "While I have you where I want you..." he chuckled a little. "Convenient trick by the way. Next time I need you to stand still and listen to me, I'm just going to buy a bag of salt."

"Cormac!" she snapped. "Let me out."

He raised a finger. "I'm not leaving. You're not going to make me leave. I've fallen in love with you and I'm staying."

"You only think you're in love with me," she sighed. "I think the enchantment you're under... well, I think I might have accidently cast a love spell and you were the first man it hit. When you walk through the fire it'll be gone. It might take a few days or even a few weeks for it to pass, but it will. You don't want to be stuck here with me and a baby. You want to go home. I know you do. You want to finish your studies and bury yourself in your Plato."

"Actually I'm more interested in Pythagoras, but I do like Plato. I love you. That's not going to pass."

"It will."

"It won't."

"Will you please let me out?"

"First I need something from you." He smiled at her.

"Cormac, please," she exclaimed.

"We're fine for the moment. Fionnuala has the hunter's men glamoured, and Fenton has his shillelagh ready in case someone needs to have the belligerence knocked out of them. Not really very bright, your leprechaun, but he is loyal to you."

"Fionnuala?"

"Of course, sweetheart. You think I don't know when I need help? She's a clever old bird. I do understand that this has all been a bit uncomfortable for you, but truth be told Fionnuala and I have had the time of our lives this afternoon," he said, stepping closer but not over the line of salt. "I want something from you." He stared into her eyes.

"What?" She'd wanted to feel what it was like to be vulnerable, truly vulnerable with him for as long as she'd shared a bed with him, and at last she had her opportunity.

"What will you give me for your freedom?" he questioned.

"Whatever you want," she pleaded, actually meaning it. "I'll give you everything. I love you."

"I know you do, sweetheart," he replied. "Just as I love you."

"You don't. It's not real."

"It is," he claimed. "But I need to convince you I really want you to be mine. So I'm going to leave. I'll be gone with these two in the morning. When I return, you'll know that I really love you." With a kick from his boot he broke the circle, setting her free. As she stepped past him, he picked up the dark witch in his arms and dumped her in the middle of the salt circle.

"You don't love me," she insisted.

"Come," Cormac ordered. "We need to hurry. The Beltane fires wait for no witch or druid."

Chapter Six

Out on the street, Sorcha realized she'd been kept captive in the old public house that had shut down with the death of the old man who owned it.

"They kept me locked in the pub?" she snorted.

Cormac grabbed her hand. "There is too much female power in this valley. You need a druid or two here. Tip the balance back to somewhere in the middle. What kind of respectable small Irish town doesn't at least have a pub? Bloody disgrace, that is."

"Killiven doesn't need a pub."

"Two tea shops. No pub. No wonder you had to cast a love spell to get a man. Your coven has mentally castrated the men of this town. Hold tight."

A moment later Sorcha felt herself flying through the air. Cormac, who was still himself and also a bird, carried her along in his spell. They circled over the town, over the lough, and finally the forest as the last rays of sunlight slipped out of the sky. Below them a fire burned. Cleansing and bright. Warm and welcoming. Lines of livestock were already being moved through the ring as dancers moved in a circle.

They spiraled down and landed just outside the ring of her property on their own feet.

"I want to do that again," she sighed. "That's marvelous."

"Just wait until I take you horseback riding," he stated. "And don't you dare say anything about how I don't love you and it's all a spell." He took her by the hand and they walked together to the fairy ring.

The last of the cattle and sheep were being pushed through as they approached the ring of stones that marked the boundary between the mundane world and the gateway to Tír na nÓg. The gateway glowed red from the light of the fire. Without stopping, they walked directly to the edge of the fire. The heat coming off the flames was intense. But as they stepped into the fire it was cool. The flames were like a sheer curtain providing a small amount of privacy.

Sorcha looked at Cormac. The love spell wrapped around his heart fluttered away like a butterfly. That was sorted. The only thing left was to take care of her.

Cormac kissed her, grabbing her roughly as his hands probed her body with the casual arrogance of ownership. "I still love you." He nipped at her ear. Cormac was not shy about the fact that he wanted her. He pressed his tongue into her mouth as he licked and twirled, while his fingers grasped the fabric of the smock dress she wore. In a single, practiced move, he slipped the dress off over her head and tossed it to the side. The mixture of rough clothing over hard body, and smooth hands brushing over her bare skin cooled by the air made her tingle.

A low moan came from Cormac's throat as she ripped open the buttons on his trousers and freed his full thick cock from its confines. His erection continued to throb and he shifted, trying to encourage her to touch him. Hard and long, it jerked as if trying to reach for her itching for her touch. His shaft pulsed against her abdomen as he pulled her tightly to him. Sorcha pushed back, her palms against the cotton of his t-shirt. She looked him up and down as she had a thousand times. Cormac was a perfect specimen of masculine sexuality and he was hers to do with as she wanted. A thrilling sense of feminine power shot through her at the thought of being in control of all that masculine energy. It had always made her horny to think of all that power between her legs and the command she had over it.

His t-shirt was pulled off over his head and discarded in the same direction as her dress. Her nipples tightened and heat pooled between her thighs at the sight of his bare muscled chest and abdomen. His shoulders were wide and his biceps like twined ropes. His hands shifted, slipping over the mounds of her breasts. He stroked a finger along the full weight of one breast, sending zinging pleasurable sensations through her. His light touch circled her nipple, stroked across it, then traveled to the other nipple. With a quick pinch and a twist, he silently asked her if she wanted it rough.

Cormac enjoyed mixing up their exploits as much as she did. Their romps would vary depending mostly on her mood. He was always up for anything and never afraid to let her know what he wanted. Whether she wanted to be a sultry, wanton minx enjoying the ride of her life, a goddess to be worshiped, or a slut that needed to be screwed, Cormac gave her what she desired. Her unspoken answer to his question came in the form of her teeth nipping at his bottom lip as she kissed him. While she ran her mouth over his face and raked her hands into his hair, he got his jeans past his hips and let them slide over his knees to the floor. He kicked his shoes along with the rest of his clothing off, while Sorcha slid against him, stroking his arousal.

She didn't protest as they sank to the ground, and he nudged her hips, telling her without speaking what he wanted. When she was on her hands and knees, she sunk down to her elbows, pressing her bottom up to him. Sorcha arched her back in anticipation, pushing her glistening sex to him and exposing herself totally. She was ready. He was the right man.

Her blood pumped heavily through her veins as heat suffused every inch of her. She bit her lip to keep from screaming in frustration when he fingered the folds of her sex; stretching, pulling and exploring while avoiding the knot of nerve endings at the apex of her want. She pushed back to meet him, but he wanted to make her suffer a little. He held back, placing only the tip of his cock at her entrance, letting it move in and out with the rhythm of his heartbeat.

"Tell me what you want," Cormac demanded as he wrapped her hair around his hand and wrist, pulling with an exquisite firmness.

"You," she gasped as the tip of his cock stroked her swollen sex.

"What do you want me to do?" His hands reached around her and plucked at her nipples.

"Take me," she ordered.

Gradually, bit by bit he eased himself inside of her. He forced the tip deeper then withdrew causing her to moan at the denial of pleasure, controlling how much of him he gave to her. His fingers clamped around her waist in a tight, biting grip and stopped her from taking all of him inside at will. The feel of his cock sliding into her heat made his gentle torment an excruciating test of wills for her. She wanted to press back against him and take him in all at once, but the strength with which he held her prevented her from filling her cunt with his cock. In one swift and unexpected move he entered her with the full stiff length of his cock, until it pressed against her inner walls and his balls kissed her swollen pussy lips. She shifted on him and felt her hot inner channel contract around his rigid length, wrapping around it like a tight glove.

Her inner muscles relaxed and contracted, coaxing him deeper inside while the walls of her cunt closed around his solid cock like the grip of a hand. One moment the tip of his cock would be teasing her entrance, then the next her swollen pussy lips were kissing the smooth skin of his balls. Her back bowed as she shoved her ass upward inviting him to have her as completely as possible. One finger slipped up to the first joint into the tight pucker of her anus. Just enough to tease and enhance her pleasure.

Her cunt sheathed him and held tight like a vice which folded around his immense cock, feeling every inch of his thick member penetrating her. He buried himself as deeply as he could go and stopped, just holding her against him. Together they paused to fully enjoy the range of sensations which coursed through their bodies. The only sounds in the fire were the heavy sighs of passion reaching its apex and the rapid breathing of exertion.

Cormac resumed his effort by rapidly pulling out, followed by a powerful thrust with him buried inside her. He repeated the movement, bringing both of them closer to climax. His balls brushed against her hard clit, causing her to tremble with pleasure at every fleeting touch. She groaned at the liquid intoxication of sensations that invaded her. The friction of his thrusting against her tight inner walls sent her senses into overload.

Sorcha felt the potential energy of her orgasm coil low in her core. She was so close and Cormac was not going to deny her. Her breathing was ragged as her cheek rested against the swirling ash, while her ass pressed upward to meet the stroke of his cock with a thrust of her hips. He pumped his hips and she felt him all the way to her core. She lifted and moved to match his thrusts, feeling every inch of his prick as it stroked along her sensitive, dripping channel. Her body ached for release, but her pussy cried out for more, harder, faster and deeper.

The feeling of inevitability that told her there was no more prolonging the exquisite ecstasy of being denied came over her as her climax blossomed out of her core like ripples on a smooth surface of water. A vibration of sensation rippled through her as she let go and came. There was no stopping the intense climax once it had begun, not that Sorcha would have denied herself the intense pleasure for anything. She cried out his name as her back arched like a kitten's and her ass thrust up to his cock, as the rippling sensation radiated through her in wave after wave of pleasure.

When the last wave washed over her, he came at her hard, strong and hungrily, placing his hands on her hips and grinding into her. He moaned and sputtered, telling her what he wanted to do to her while his hips jerked forward in a sexual staccato as he sought his own release. With a cry of pure pleasure, Cormac pulled her up, planting her wet, spent sex against his cock as hot jets of cum emptied into her.

Her entire body shivered, then moaned with disappointment when Cormac slid out of her with a wet pop. He stood from where he'd knelt behind her and stretched his body. A hand was held out for her that she accepted. Cormac helped her from the ground and stood her before him. He cupped his hand behind her hair and around the back of her neck as he stared into her face.

"I love you," he murmured. "It's done. Let's go home."

In a beat of her heart they were once again taking to the air. Moments later they landed on their feet in front of the kitchen door.

Sorcha gasped as Cormac lifted her from her feet into his arms. The door popped open and he carried Sorcha over the threshold. "I still love you," he restated as he carried her through the house, up the stairs, and to the bedroom. When they stepped into the room, the candles which had been spread out came to life. "Fenton is actually a pretty good little leprechaun," he conceded. "At least he got the candles right. I'm honestly not certain why there are clumps of dead leaves on the bed, but he certainly gets top marks for effort."

"They're his gold," Sorcha said with a smile. "Not his real gold, I have that, but his illusion. Put me on the bed."

He laid her down and the bed glowed gold. The thousand little dead brown leaves became infused with illusionary magic. Cormac lay down next to her. "Still love you," he sighed as he kissed her. He stroked her cheek, her arm, and her hip as they lay side by side. At some point in the night she drifted off to sleep. In the morning, just as she knew he would be, he was gone.

Chapter Seven

After Sorcha bathed until her skin pruned, and Fionnuala with Aoife had helped her wash her hair, she slid her arms into a crisp nightdress which had once been hers more years ago than she could believe. She opened the window to her bedroom and stared out over the lough drenched in the light of the waning moon.

"What are you thinking?" her Aunt Fionnuala asked from behind her.

"I love him. I can't believe it. I love him. He's just a boy, but I love him."

"Cormac is young, but he is not a boy. A daughter will come from your love."

"It wasn't real. I told you."

"You told me. But I am hard pressed to believe a druid as powerful as Cormac would be taken in by a *wink at the moon* love spell. You'd need something a lot more powerful than that to get him around your finger. He'll return to you."

"When?" she retorted.

"In time."

Chapter Eight

Their lives took on the same predictable pattern it had had before Cormac had crashed into their world. Sorcha tended the garden with Fionnuala and Aoife. Fenton lounged around in the sun and tended to his patch of shamrocks. They drifted into a casual ease. Sorcha knew days after that night she carried a child. Preparations were made and time marched on.

It was during the days before Samhain that she wandered into town to see if there was anything for her at the post office. Hard as it was to let Cormac go, she'd done her best to remove him from her system. Hard to do as his child tapped her little foot against her ribs. The last holdout of hope was that he might write her. Hence the weekly trip to the post office.

She was showing. That was obvious based on the way her dresses didn't fit anymore. The walk did her good. Fionnuala had practically moved in and Aoife was around constantly. The town was mostly the same. One main street filled with small traders and two tea shops. And a pub.

"Odd." She stopped in front of the old pub that had closed down years earlier. The exterior was getting a fresh coat of paint. A van with a delivery of tables and chairs was being unloaded. Cormac was right. There was a very strong female energy in the town. A pub was just so masculine.

Just as she was going to continue on to the post office she was stopped by the sound of her name.

"Cormac?" she laughed as she watched him cross the street.

He took her in his arms and squeezed her. "Missed you," he whispered in her ear. "Still love you. Your witchcraft never really worked on me, you know." His hand slipped into her coat and onto the curve of her belly. "I've moved to Killiven. This valley needs some druids. Too many witches."

"You bought the pub?" she exclaimed.

"My brother Padraig and I bought the pub. Our father thinks we're crazy, but we think he's just a little jealous. Let's be honest – what druid wouldn't rather spend his days and nights playing music and living in the country?"

"What about school?"

"Plan change," he answered. "I'm going to be a father and a business owner. I've also fallen in love with this grumpy little witch. So – do you want to meet my brother?"

"Yes."

"Are you going to let me move in with you, or do I have to keep on sharing the apartment over the pub with my brother?"

"You can move in with me." She reached up and kissed him on the cheek. "I didn't think you'd come back."

"I'm back. And I'm never going away again."

Chapter One

Warm and warmer, the fire and her face, hot and glowing from the incense that flowed from the cauldron as it hung heavily over an open fire. The herbs lent an almost narcotic atmosphere to the group ritual celebrating Midsummer. She sat quietly blushing as she thought about the fire vision she had just witnessed. The vision still held her body in thrall. Danie felt the urgent longings that the male counterpart in her vision had aroused in her. He was very male, with tousled black hair worn long, down to his shoulders. It framed a strong, beautiful face, for it was too pretty to be called handsome, with eyes the color of new spring grass. Added to this was a golden-tanned, muscular body that she had seen helpless and completely aroused. Danie leaned back, eyes closed, recalling every detail.

He lay deep in the woods, his breath shuddering from his body itself, unable to move. Hovering over his head was incense smoke, misty and smelling of herbs and opiates. The scent pulling at his loins with primal lust, desire, need, at the same time wreathing his mind, scattering his thoughts in disarray, he couldn't think...not clearly... could only breathe in the heady smoke and feel his body react strongly to the drugged scent, swirling all around him.

He was a prisoner in his own skin, more than he was when he was trapped back in the dungeons, in the ...where was that now... had he been trapped? Just when was that? He could not think...but feel, oh yes, he could feel. He felt urgings, longings and an impossible ache. Maxfield felt as if his body was betraying him, leaving the trappings of his civilized self behind and entering a dark place where nothing of civilization remained.

From out of the woods, a woman appeared. She was unclothed and fair skinned with black eyes that swallowed light as they drew in his gaze. Her waist length black hair, was a tease as she walked, first showing her bare breasts then hiding them from view. Finally she stood over him, the wind playing with her hair in such a fashion that she was completely exposed, yet completely at ease. She smiled wickedly at him lying helpless on the ground before her.

Max was inflamed. He watched her with a mixture of horror and relief as she kneeled down beside him and began to lightly caress him. She stroked his stomach, his legs, then his sensitive inner thigh, at the same time her eyes told him that she was a nightmare. Max knew he should recoil at her touch, not long for it, not beg for it.

The smoke above his head began to coil like a snake, his body was wrapped with a terrible urgency, he had to have her, had to, would do anything if she would just let him have her. His body arched and his head fell back as she touched him, stroked him and prepared for him to enter her. Max, eyes closed as he whimpered, felt her descend until she was almost upon him and then disappear into thin air.

Max cried out in frustration, and lay there trying to catch his breath as the smoke finally began to clear.

"Come back," was the only thing he could think of for the next hour.

It was sunrise before he finally regained control of his body and got up, seeking relief in the icy pond nearby.

Wet, but still unsatisfied, he sat down on the bank and tried to gather his wits.

Aileann had found him.

Coming back to herself, Danie's mind was filled with questions.

Who was this man, and who was this dangerous siren Aileann that he was so drawn yet repulsed by? And more importantly, who was he to her, at this time and place? An ancestor? A mate in her future? Or just a whim of the night air, teasing her and making her long for a dream lover?

Danie shook her head in order to clear away these questions, then sat up straight and began to join in the humming that was happening around the fire. By raising energy with tonal sounds, and hums, the group was readying itself to raise a cone of power to end the evening's ritual celebration.

She hummed and her whole body buzzed as the power rose into the night air, taking their Midsummer wishes, desires and needs to the stars.

The Circle was then closed and the group all said a very tired good night to each other, mostly leaving the group in couples; though they did not all start out that way.

Midsummer had a way of bringing people together. Danie walked away from the doused fire, alone but still buzzing, wishing for the dream lover in her vision.

She looked up at the stars, feeling the connection to the sky. Danie closed her eyes and listened to the sounds of the forest all around her. She could hear the gentle buzz of the locusts and the snapping of twigs as if from a small animal stirring. These gentle noises meant that life unseen was happening all around her. This was such a magical place, this old growth forest in the heart of Virginia. It had spoken to each of the members of her coven the very first time they visited this National Park. It had everything they needed, cabins, a dining hall, restrooms, and a huge pit for their bonfire to be made safely. This park had all the comforts needed for a rustic romp in the woods. Yet there was more here, much more. It had the feel of connection to all things wild. The forest, which was protected by the government, had developed its own ecosystem, undamaged by the hand of man. Magic lived here, wild woodland magic, the kind that opens the heart and mind, the kind that reaches into the hidden places within you and gives voice to your deepest longings. Walking back to her cabin, the night air whispering around her, Danie began thinking of the man in her vision and of how he was having a very different and unpleasant experience in his forest. Maxfield's frustration and fear plagued her even now. As she got ready for bed, Danie felt that she could hear voices in the wind outside, telling her secrets that she was unable to decipher. That night she dreamed....

He was there, alone in the forest, afraid and desperately unhappy that he had been found and had to escape Aileann's grip again! Danie found herself there, a shadow in the dream, following him, watching over him like a bereft lover. She who was fair, with short pixie hair and fleet of foot, found it easy to track him. Danie even knew his name, it was Maxfield Blade and he was the son of a Dark Magician. He did not follow his father's interest though, and disdained the Black Arts. His father, Tomax Blade, was not to be so easily dismissed and had sent a siren of the

night to coax Max back into the fold. He knew Maxfield had an unusual
power. A power that Max was terrified to use. A power Tomax was
desperate to control.

Danie woke up with visions of the dream still clouding her
mind. She felt hot, yet her body was drenched in a cold sweat.
Danie began to wonder if this dream was not actually a vision of
some kind. This was the time of year when the veil was thin, and
portals could be opened to other dimensions. Danie began to
wonder to herself,

Could Max belong to another world, concurrent with her
own? Perhaps another dimension, or even a world of magic likened
to the land of Faery? This question burned in her mind along with
the main question of, who was Max to her? Why did she know his
story? Why shadow him as if she would be his protector? Danie
had no idea, but was determined to find out the answers to her
questions.

ॐ ॐ ॐ

Clumsily, she crawled out of bed and left her cabin, walking
to the public rest area where she had left her clothes for the
Midsummer ritual this morning. She needed to get washed and
dressed and to clear her head of those fantastic dream images!

Showered and attired she joined her coven for breakfast and
decided she should speak about this to Michael, their High Priest.
He was a good friend and had always encouraged members to
speak openly with him, about anything.

The opening ritual of Midsummer was a drumming circle at dawn. To Danie, beating her drum and gazing at the awakening sky, the drum beats felt like the heartbeat of the forest sending its greeting to the Sun.

After the drumming, the High Priest Michael and the High Priestess Michelle, led the group in song and chant, thanking the God and Goddess for the abundance of this season. They danced inside the circle as the chanting grew louder and louder, the energy building inside each of the coven members as they called out their gratitude to the sky, until their combined energy finally burst out in a group shout of salutation to the Sun. Afterward it was time to ground the energy of the group and so they all walked to the long Viking structured dining hall, to break their fast.

Danie sat down, looking at her breakfast plate full of eggs and toast and wondered if Max had eaten. Would he too be eating now? Did time even run the same where he was? Thoughtfully, before she realized what was happening, she began to understand that he was real. Somewhere in another world, Max was real, scared, and haunted by his father's greed and the siren that held him in her power. Danie knew this, with a knowing that was deeply rooted in her heart. She decided to wait until she had more facts before running to Michael with her visions. She did not know why she wanted to stay silent about it, but something inside her told her she must be patient, and learn.

She finished breakfast, chatting idly with the others, but looking forward to the bonfire they were to have that afternoon, for fire brought visions and she knew she would see her Max again. Maybe even reach out to him.

Later that afternoon, sitting before the fire, Danie breathed in the woodsy smell of mugwort that had been thrown into the flames, in order to enhance the vision quest. Quietly monitoring her own breathing, she began meditating on who she was and about this beautiful group that she belonged to.

She was Danie Grace, Leo born, a child of fire, and the sun, and her golden looks reflected her birthright. Her strawberry blonde hair was cut pixie short, with just a hint of curl. Danie's build was athletic, slim but strong, her legs were powerful (she could out run anyone in her group), and her skin was tanned a deep honey color. Her eyes were cornflower blue, and searching, always searching as if there was something more to see.

She loved her Coven members as family, The Modern Cauldron Coven was a Celtic Wiccan Coven, filled with a group of rugged individuals. Each member had been drawn to the Craft through their searching, through their remembering, that the world was full of magic. It seemed that every one of the members had come to realize that there was much more to this universe than what science dictated. The Modern Cauldron Coven followed the Celtic Traditions, with a bit of their own mix thrown in for good measure, savoring the rich tapestry of Irish and British Lore. They numbered the traditional thirteen, seven woman and six men. The High Priest and High Priestess were a hand fasted couple, terribly in love and in perfect sync as they led the rituals that celebrated and worshipped the God and Goddess.

Now Michael and Michelle, reflected each other in perfect harmony as they danced the circle round, asking Spirit to join them in their quest. Danie breathed in the mugwort, breathed in the wood scent of the fire, and let her body sit perfectly still as she entered into the realm of the astral plane. She knew that she was on a very specific quest, to find Maxfield and to save him. This she must do. Slowly she felt her astral self rise from her body, upward through the mists of the astral plane. She felt a reflex to look down and saw her body still sitting, surrounded by the coven. Turning her thoughts away from her still, silent form, Danie focused her attention on finding Maxfield.

Finally, she found him alone in the woods.

A loud cawing awoke Maxfield from his dreams. In those dreams had been a woman, strange in attire with short reddish-blonde hair and glowing skin. She had been reaching for him. Not like Aileann, not in a dark way, but instead in an almost loving way. It was as if she was trying to help him, but the next thing he knew there was the sound of chanting and she was gone.

The cawing became a cacophony, some poor small beast of the forest had caught their attention. A "murder" of crows was an apt description indeed, for there was black murder in their cries as they circled above and below the tree line at the edge of the forest.

As Maxfield prepared himself for the long trek ahead, he hoped his uncle who had befriended him as a child would give him sanctuary. Hunterson Castle, the home of his Uncle James Hunterson and his cousin Jack, was far over in the next Kingdom. It was, at least a three day long hike from where he was standing, and he was so tired already. Irritated with himself at his inability to focus, Maxfield shook his head to forcefully release himself from the spell of the dream and of the nightmare cries of the crows. Max hurried to retrieve his belongings and food rations that he had stored in a burlap sack, hidden in a hollowed tree trunk. He swung the sack purposefully, as he strode onto the next leg of his journey.

Suddenly Danie's vision shifted, from woodland scene to high mountain fortress.

It was a castle, strong and fierce in its stand against the sky. No banners flew, no flags of any kind. The drawbridge was shut tight, even in daytime- no visitors to this place was allowed. Instinctively Danie could feel that this was a place where no honest joy could be found, just an unhealthy glee of winning at any cost.... Danie tried to clear her head of this terrible vision, but instead of clearing, the focus sharpened until she was in a room with two figures, male and female in a Sorcerous meeting of the minds.

"So you found him, Aileann, good, good, keep a close watch on my whelp. Do not let him go too long without uh... stirring the pot. I think you understand my meaning."

Tomax Blade gave a knowing leer at the dark haired woman before him. Aileann smiled knowingly. "Yes, Tomax, the 'pot' has been stirred and... disappointed, I should think." She smiled at the memory of Maxfield calling out to her in a desperate plea. She had him now, by the...

Tomax interrupted her thoughts, with the question she had been waiting for. "Where is he going?"

"I could not discern that, Tomax, his thoughts were a bit preoccupied" Her smile showed teeth. She had no intention of letting Tomax know his son's destination. Knowledge was power and the fact that Maxfield was running to the estranged brother of Tomax, whom he hated, was deliciously rich in power. Besides, Tomax might become so enraged that he may just order her to pull Maxfield back by magical means, and that would not suit her, not at all. The son was far more powerful than the

father and she meant to drain and use that power for her own ends. Let this fool think she worked for him; Aileann worked for herself.

Eyes downcast over her wine, she let those thoughts dissipate lest he catch a whiff of what she had in mind. Instead she delicately sipped the wine and pretended to be interested in what Tomax had to say. After all, at one time Tomax was her lover. Though he did not have the same beauty of his son, he was still fiercely handsome, hiding his cruelty with ease. His muscular build had never run to fat and he was as trim and fit as ever. She remembered well the man's strong dark charms that nearly matched her own and his rough house play at love suited her just fine until he got too rough. The last time they had lain together, it had taken days of spell work to bring her bruised and abused body back to its glowing good health. It was then that she had cautiously decided to let him end the affair, leaving plenty of room for a partnership of sorts.

She listened now, with only half an ear, as Tomax was pondering where in the land his son might run to. Never guessing the lad would run to his closest kin. For Tomax had deceived his brother and murdered his wife, out of jealousy, and they were declared deadly enemies when Maxfied was still a small boy. James had even changed his name from Blade to Hunterson, after their mother's maiden name. Sir James Hunterson, along with his only son, Jack, had left the kingdom in dark anger and severed all ties of kinship. Aileann knew the Hunterson family as a self-righteous bunch, disdaining the black arts with such conviction that any who practiced on their land would be imprisoned. But magic they possessed in full measure, just as Tomax did, and they were artful in its practice.

She had made sure that Maxfield had been able to escape from his father's dungeon after she had whispered in his ear at night while he was asleep, all the information he needed to seek sanctuary in his uncle's home.

Aileann liked her prey full of hope and the promise of freedom; it made the chase more thrilling.

Danie was awakened from this vision by Michael. The coven members were gathered around her, each with terribly worried looks on their faces.

"You've been out of reach for hours, Danie," Michael said, shaking her gently to make sure she was fully awake.

Danie felt like she needed another shower after the filth she had been privy to in her vision. Oh, how dirty she felt. Looking around at all those she loved staring at her in bewilderment, and fearful for her welfare, Danie decided it was time to come clean and tell them all that her visions entailed. Danie now knew she would need all their wisdom and magic in order to rescue Maxfield, and this she was determined to do.

Chapter Two

After Danie had finished telling everyone about her dreams and visions, with only a few interruptions for clarification, everyone was silent for a moment. Then Allison, the cheerful redhead of the group whose gift was card divination, questioned Danie.

"So, you believe you are tapping into another dimension, Danie?"

"Yes, I really do, it is all very real," Danie replied eagerly, she very much wanted the group to believe her.

Gina, whose gift was mythological research and spell writing, spoke up next.

"Danie, could you be tapping into an ancient past connected to this place?"

"No, no, it was not here, it was not of this world, it was far away!" Danie almost shouted, they were not getting the immediacy of this situation. Something had to be done right away and here they were questioning the validity of her visions.

Chelsea, the oldest woman in the coven and a very sensitive empath, smiled understandingly at Danie's frustration.

"No, Danie, we are not questioning the validity of what you saw, but perhaps there are a few different ways to interpret it?"

"I don't think so, Chelsea. I saw a man, being pursued by sorcery, and betrayed by his own Dad. He needs our help, what other interpretations are there?" Danie argued, hoping for them to see the need to find a solution to Maxfield's problem.

"Honey, there are many ways to interpret a vision. It could be about your own journey, or maybe it is about your feelings for your family, or some other message from beyond the veil. We need to talk about what your visions really mean, and not necessarily do anything but learn from them," Chelsea finished, looking around at the group to see what they thought.

Danie was about to argue back, but then Michael finally spoke, " Danie, let's say it is all just as real as you say. That there is a man being dogged by a sorceress, and trying to escape his fate with his father. Okay, what in the world do you think we can do about it?"

"Rescue him, damnit!" Danie said, "What good are all our gifts if we cannot actually do something for someone in trouble?" Danie jumped up from her chair and began pacing around the room. Her movement became frantic as she tried desperately to think of some way to convince them to help Max.

Michelle, Michael's hand fasted mate and ever the diplomat, stepped in. "Okay, Danie. I do believe our gifts are very valuable. I also believe that as a Coven we are strong and have helped each other and our planet a great deal. I'm not diminishing who we are or how special the magic of this group is. However, having said that, other than astral travel, none of us have ventured into another dimension. This is going to take much thought, and lots of research."

Mitchell finally broke the silence that had fallen after Michelle's statement. He was an adept who had been traveling on the astral planes since he was a small boy, "Actually, Michelle, research may not help us since this is out of our experience. We need to actually talk to Max, and I think I know how to do it."

Finally, thought Danie, *now we are getting somewhere*.

"What are you thinking, Mitch?" asked Michelle.

"Well, maybe by hitch hiking a ride on Danie's vision? We could get a fire going, throw on some mugwort, and Danie can try to consciously reach this guy Max!"

"Maxfield, Mitch, his name is Maxfield, and I have no idea how to even attempt this," Danie said uncertainly.

"Well, Hon," said Chelsea, "There is just one way to find out!"

The fire was built high as each of the thirteen coven members drew the circle round, creating a protective barrier enclosed in the sacred space. Each had a handful of mugwort to throw onto the fire, stating their intentions for this ritual. First Michael stood with his arms raised and stated firmly, "Here in this hour I do ask thee Divine ones, for the safe journey of your son and daughter. Let their mission bring success. So will it be!"

Next his wife, Michelle, raised her arms, and stated, "I ask for courage and strength for these two travelers. So will it be! " She threw her handful of mugwort into the fire.

Then Chelsea, who was one of the elders of the group, came and stood before the flame. She raised her arms and stated, "May the connection be made across the barriers of time and space. May the travelers learn what they need to learn and stay safe in your protection. So will it be!" Her mugwort burned brightly as it hit the flames.

One by one, came the rest of the coven, Allison, Richard, the male elder of the group, Candice, Michelle's sister, Bryant, Michael's cousin, Tina and Terry, twins in mood and magic, that had been best friends of Michael's for years, as well as the married couple Pam and Greg, newly welcomed to the group last summer. Each asking for safe journey and safe return for Danie and Mitchell.

Then Mitchell stepped before the flame, and with arms raised, and stated 'I ask thee for the strength and endurance to reach this sister world and be successful in our purpose, so will it be!" He then looked into the flame as if looking for answers and tossed the mugwort deep into the heart of the fire.

Finally it was Danie's turn, She walked up to the flame, and though her voice wavered her will did not. Arms raised, she said, "I ask my Lord and Lady to please help and guide us on our journey to save this man from deadly danger. I ask this with all my heart. So will it be! " She tossed her mugwort high into the flames, then sat down in the center of the circle beside Mitchell and held his hand. Slowly the coven members circled and chanted as they prepared to go into a vision trance that would take them on their journey.

Then Michael and Michelle both chanted together, "We ask our Lord and Lady, and the powers of Earth, Air, Fire and Water to join us here and speed these two travelers on their journey. May they be safe, may they be strong, may they succeed, and may they return home safely." The rest of the Coven then repeated the chant.

"May they be safe, may they be strong, may they succeed, may they return home safely."

This chant was repeated over and over. Danie and Mitchell felt their astral selves leave their bodies. Together, they were transported along the astral plane into another world.

Slowly, Danie saw the familiar landscape of her visions, the area was still wooded but different. In the distance, she could see a grand castle, banners fluttering in the breeze. A drastic contrast to the gloomy fortress belonging to Maxfield's father, this was a thing of beauty, glowing brightly of white stone and crystal, in the strong sunlight of the day.

Suddenly she felt a presence beside her. Mitchell was here, he had joined her and the comfort of his presence was almost overwhelming. Not needing to communicate, Danie narrowed her focus in an effort to find Maxfield. There, down at the edge of the woodland, strode Max. He looked very much worse for wear, with his back pack slung heavily on his back and hunched over by the weight of both the pack and his hunger. She could tell that his destination was to the castle and could also see that he would not make it before nightfall. It was too far and he was too tired. How she wished she could pick him up in her arms and carry him there, or back home, anywhere to keep him safe! She felt Mitchell's reaction to her strong feelings toward Max, but she could not help the way her heart longed for this strange, sad man.

"Maxfield!" Danie called out as loud as she could, hoping he would hear her.

Max started at the sound of her voice, looking around in a wary fashion. He immediately began to run, thinking this was just another dark denizen from his father's arsenal.

Then she heard Mitchell's voice, booming out loudly, "Maxfield Blade, stop right now, we come in peace!"

At the masculine tone, Max stopped abruptly. His father only had sent female wraiths to torment him. What kind of magic was this?

He abruptly halted and looked around him, finally staring up at the sky. He then asked, "I hear you, spirits, what do you want with me?"

It was Danie who answered, terribly relieved they had gotten through.

"We are not spirits, Max, but flesh and blood like yourself, only we come from..." Here she hesitated, not sure what to say.

Mitchell finished her sentence by adding, "We come from a sister world of yours, traveling the astral to contact you here in your world."

They were coming into view now, appearing before Max in a transparent fashion. Max looked from one to the other in confusion. He felt shaken and not convinced of this "sister world." Perhaps his father was using a different tact this time, to bring him to heel.

Peering at them closely, Max queried, "I ask again, spirits, or whatever you claim to be...what have you to do with me?"

"Maxfield, look at me, you know me, I am Danie from your dreams. Please listen to my voice, you must remember," Danie pleaded with him. She knew they had to get through to him in order for him to accept their help.

He looked closer, and realized this was indeed the beautiful woman who had appeared in his dream.

"Danie, you are... real?" Maxfield stuttered, unable to cope with his dream vision suddenly appearing to him in broad daylight.

"Real as can be, and I really want to help you, Max!" Danie answered, delighted that he knew her.

"Help me?" Max asked, feeling overwhelmed that she had come all this way just for him.

Mitch spoke up, "Max, Danie saw your plight, and knows about your father and his plans." Mitch stopped speaking as he saw Max back up at the mention of his father.

"You know my father, do you?" Maxfield thundered at them "Begone foul beings, and never return. I am not to be be-spelled by the likes of you!" Max turned and ran forward toward the castle.

Danie's outrage at his unjust accusation spurred her into action. She appeared before Max, and shouted, "Look you moron, Mitch and I and our whole coven have gone to a great of trouble to help you. I will be damned if you order us away like errant school children!" Danie stopped speaking and almost smiled at Maxfield's surprised expression.

"Maxfield," Mitchell said in a more conciliatory tone, as he joined Danie in confronting Max. "Danie and I want to help. Look you are the one who came to Danie in her dreams and visions. That contact must be for a reason and now we need to figure out just how we can save you from your Father's tricks."

"'Tricks' is too small a word for my father's misdeeds towards me and everyone who crosses him. 'Tricks' does not cover the amount of cruelty and anguish he visits upon anyone who gets in his way."

Maxfield decided to trust these spirits. After all who else had come to aid him? He would take help wherever he could get it. Besides, beautiful Danie had called him a moron, and this he needed to disprove immediately.

"I'm sorry, Danie, I am used to my father forcing his dangerous messengers on me in order to force me back to his dungeon. A moron I may be, but not a fool to not accept help when it is offered." He smiled warmly at Danie, hoping to be forgiven.

Danie smiled back, which warmed more than Maxfield's heart, and he just stood there grinning back until Mitchell spoke up.

"Well, okay then, let's get down to the business of getting you the help you need. Danie said that you have magical powers that your Dad wants to use, is that true?"

Turning his gaze to Mitchell, Max answered tightly, "Yes, my 'Dad' as you call him, wants to use my power to open portals in order to defeat his enemies."

"Wait, what? You can open portals to other worlds?" Danie asked. The realization dawned on her that his power was what had enabled them to reach each other through their visions. She was so lost in thought that she almost missed his next question.

"Yes, Danie. Wait, why is your name Danie? That is a male's name in our world." Max asked her.

Danie laughed at his confusion. "Danie is short for Danielle, I just prefer the nickname that's all!"

"Oh, well I would prefer to call you 'Danielle' rather than some lad's name, if that is alright with you," Max said softly.

Mitch could not believe that they were flirting instead of figuring out what to do. He impatiently interrupted Max and said, "Max, this is all very nice but our time here is limited, what exactly is your power?"

"Oh, sorry." Max smiled sheepishly. "I am a Worlds Crafter, I can create portals to other worlds or to other places in my world through my word craft."

"Well then, why haven't you used your power to create a portal to get you the hell out of here?" Mitch asked impatiently, punching his hand into his fist for emphasis.

Maxfield answered him softly, "I cannot. I dare not use any magic at all. Not even to perform a simple fire spell, because that would call my Father directly to me. He and his minions are far stronger than I. Besides, it takes a great deal of energy and willpower to create such a powerful spell as opening a portal and my strength is far diminished."

Mitch interrupted him to ask, "Why is that? I thought you were such a powerful wizard, or whatever?"

Maxfield bristled a bit at Mitch's tone but answered truthfully, "My father half-starved me in his dungeon and I have not recovered. I simply could not hope to open a portal in my condition. I am simply not strong enough."

"I didn't realize...Your own father starved you?" Mitch asked, visibly moved by Maxfield's plight. Before Max could answer, Danie spoke up,

"We can help you, Max, we have a whole coven full of magic!"

Danie felt a strong tingling down her spine; an early warning sign that her physical body was in danger. She looked over at Mitchell, and noticed a flickering in his appearance. They had stayed too long.

Mitchell quickly asked the question that had haunted him since Danie first spoke of Maxfield and his plight. "Maxfield, what is the name of this world?"

Max looked surprised that Mitchell did not already have this knowledge. He folded his arms and looked at Mitch with sudden suspicion. Then slowly asked, "How did you come to my world without the knowledge of its name?"

Sensing Maxfield's distrust, Mitch shrugged and answered with complete honesty, "No clue, Max. Danie just seemed to be able to direct us here as soon as we entered the astral plane."

Maxfield looked over at Danie with profound respect, and whispered to himself, "Did she indeed?" Lost in thought, he simply gazed at Danie.

Danie, acutely embarrassed, shook her head and said, "Mitchell is exaggerating my importance. He is a powerful witch and we had the help of our whole coven to send us here." Danie smiled shyly as she viewed Maxfield's bemused expression.

Mitchell interrupted impatiently, "Maxfield, you have still not answered my question. What is the name of your world?"

Max shook himself mentally and tore his gaze from Danie, long enough to look at Mitch and answer him directly, "Somerwynd."

"Somerwynd, how beautiful!" Danie spoke in an awed whisper. "And we came here in the heart of Midsummer, there has to be some connection."

Mitchell and Maxfield nodded at her logic.

Danie gasped as she felt a terrible tug. Seeing Mitch's pained expression, she knew they had to get back to their bodies immediately.

"We have to go now, Max, but please, please come to me in my dre..."

Danie's sentence was cut off as she disappeared completely from Maxfield's sight.

As Danie and Mitch awoke in their own world, they saw the coven members all gathered around them, each with a terribly worried look on their faces.

"You would not wake up, we were so afraid we would lose you! How could you be so stupid as to stay so long?" Michelle, eyes wide with fear, shouted at them with just a hint of hysteria in her voice.

Blinking tiredly, feeling extremely cold despite the warm fire in front of him, Mitch just murmured, "He's real, it's all real."

Danie nodded in agreement and added, "He's real and really scared. Oh, I told you it was all true!" Danie smiled happily in spite of her extreme fatigue and the desperate chill she felt in all of her bones. Moving closer to the fire she stared intently into it, determined to reconnect with Max.

"Oh no you don't, Danie, my girl," Chelsea chided her and dragged her to her feet. "Have you lost your mind? You know better than to do another vision quest on top of what you just went through. Have you forgotten all the training I gave you?"

"But Chelsea, we were so close, I just want to finish..." Danie stopped speaking as she was forcibly dragged by Chelsea toward the dining hall.

"Food and bed are next on the agenda, time enough tomorrow to figure out what we are going to do," Chelsea said putting an end to their argument.

Meanwhile, Michael spoke softly to Mitchell, "So now what?" Michael asked.

"So we help him." Mitch answered.

"How in the hell do we do that?" Michael asked, looking directly into Mitch's eyes.

"No clue," Mitch answered.

Chapter Three

Aileann felt something astir in the ether. She lifted her face to look at the sky, as if sniffing at the wind. "Yes," she hissed softly to herself, "There it is, a whiff of interloper magic." Eyes flashing, she moved to action. Outside interference at this stage of her plans, would not be tolerated. She decided to up her timetable and pay another visit to her favorite prey.

❧ ❧ ❧

Maxfield was still recovering from his visit with the spirits. Not spirits, he corrected himself mentally, but flesh and blood travelers, coming a long way to what? Rescue him?

He shook his head, but somehow Danie still clung there, tangled in his thoughts. That such a beauty would take notice and take wing to come to him and she looked...enticing.

He smiled as he remembered her short hair, curling flirtatiously around her face. Then his concentration centered itself on her slender body, curving in all the right places. He had to admit, her astral image was sexy as hell. Even more so because she was just so eager to help him. She seemed completely unaware of the spell her image was weaving as she offered their assistance. He smiled weakly now. How kind of them to offer assistance but it would be of no help. His father was too strong and only his Uncle could offer him the help that he needed. Still, he was connected to them in a way he did not understand. It was very tempting to take them up on their tantalizing offer of help.

His mind was still on Danie and her sparkling eyes, when he felt the air shiver. He felt as if a sinister presence was standing behind him. As he spun around, there stood Aileann. She was beautiful, terrible, and so very near. This was more than his already aroused body could take. She wasn't Danie but she wasn't bad...well, yes she was, but...

Aileann sensed his weakening and felt his desire, but was a bit put off that his thoughts were not for her alone...who was this new witch, and how dare she work her wiles on prey that was already taken? Shaking off her irritation, she smiled a perfectly filthy smile at Max and beckoned him closer.

Danie woke up terrified, having seen in her dreams Aileann's attack on Max. She struggled to contain the urge to go to him right away. She was still exhausted from their last little astral jaunt, and she could not go it alone in any case. She sat up in her bed, shaking with fear that was quickly burning into rage...

Aileann pulled Max into her arms. Her kiss fueled the fire that Danie had started and he felt his resistance drain completely away. This kiss, this was what he needed, what he wanted, so damn him and damn her and even damn Danie for causing his body's disarray.

He took the kiss deeper, completely seduced by Aileann, and knew he had to have her now — right now. Aileann, skilled at this dance, pulled away. She lightly touched his face smoothing back his hair, making him want, making him wait. Her subtle touch sizzled and taught his body what it meant to burn.

Sensing his growing discomfort, Aileann laughed softly, wickedly, and began to gently caress his shoulders. She opened his shirt so that he could feel the cool air mixing with his heightened sensitivity at her touch. She felt his shudder, and knew now that he would be hers. While still standing from him, she let him hold her waist, as much to steady him from falling as it was to hold onto her. She bent her head and softly, expertly, traced her tongue down his chest, licking and kissing with a sucking motion. Then she paused, giving him time to experience the sensation before gently pulling on the cord that opened his trousers. Maxfield groaned as her tongue found its target.

The thunder of horse hooves pounding the dirt gave Aileann pause just long enough to allow Maxfield to jerk away from her. He quickly tried to recover his pants along with his senses, before the soldiers arrived. For soldiers they would be.

Viciously angry, but aware she could not dare to be caught, Aileann quietly disappeared, leaving Max to stand awkwardly alone to face his uncles' border guard.

The Guard rode swiftly up to where Max was standing, regarding him with wary curiosity, as he stood there in front of them and swayed. Max's mind was clearing, now that the spell Aileann had woven around him was shredded along with his dignity, and he could not bear to look up at the soldiers' sneering faces.

He did look up however, when his cousin Jack Hunterson called him by name.

"Maxfield Blade, cousin, is that you?"

"Yup," Maxfield managed, before passing out at Jack's feet.

Danie let her rage burn through her as she studied on what to do. Now that Aileann was on to them, this was going to make another astral projection visit dangerous, if not impossible. Fighting tears of frustration, Danie tried to focus on a way for them to communicate with each other, without alerting Aileann. Putting that aside for the moment, Danie tried instead to formulate a plan about what she would say to Maxfield the next time they did meet. Max was a Worlds Crafter, but how did that work? How could she get him to do what he feared most- using his magical ability? Somehow, she had to convince him to teach them how he opened portals, and then to let the coven help him do it! First she had to talk to her Coven mates on how best to reach Max again. They had to fly under Aileann's radar, so maybe she could come into his dreams consciously and they could chat.

She laughed at herself. Here she was determined to save Max when she had no idea of how to visit him in his world. This was next level stuff and her Coven had yet to expand their knowledge or their skill into this area. *Oh well*, she thought, *no time like the present*.

It was Mitchell who ended up convincing the group of the need to help Max, and he knew just how to do it, kind of. The idea was that Danie had the vision craft powers and the strong connection to Maxfield. This was no small talent. If she could consciously have a waking dream, and be able to remember every detail of their conversation in order to convey Maxfield's message to the group, this might actually work. Maybe.

Max woke up and instinctively reached for his backpack. It was gone! So were the woods. He woke fully and realized that he was in a bed, a soft, luxurious bed and covered with a woolen blanket. He was warm, he was alive and he was going back to sleep, he thought drowsily, letting his head fall back onto what seemed to be a mountain of pillows.

When next he woke, he smelled food and the rich aroma of strong tea. Before his brain realized what was happening, Max's body was up and out of bed, searching for his breakfast. He barely noticed he was wearing a night-shirt of gold brocade, nor the richness of the hardwood floor under his feet as he went unerringly down the winding stairway and into his Uncle's dining room.

His uncle James was sitting at the table, already laid out for the morning meal. He looked unsurprised as his hungry nephew gave him a shy smile, then wandered in and sat down across from him.

"I knew the scent of breakfast cooking would rouse you from your slumber," Uncle James said with a smile.

Max replied, "Thank you uncle, I am starving."

As James looked at Maxfield, he realized that this was all too true a statement. Max was far too thin and looked, even after his deep sleep, haunted and fatigued. Max helped himself to the feast before him of porridge and pancakes, scrambled eggs, thick toast, and tea. Lots of wonderful, richly scented tea.

They ate in silence for a few moments before James spoke. "You look as if you have been taken ill, Max. What is ailing you, son?"

Max looked up and swallowed nosily as he tried to figure out how to explain his father's ultimate betrayal of family by locking him in the dungeon. Suddenly, the words just tumbled out, how his father had first tried to persuade, then bully Max to join together to defeat his Father's enemies. When Maxfield refused, his father had him beaten, then thrown in the dungeon and half starved, in order to break his will.

His uncle listened with a clenched jaw, his eyes widening as he heard how often his nephew was beaten. Rage warred with guilt as he realized that he long ago should have taken Max to live with him, instead of leaving him to the savagery of his brother. As Max filled him in on the long years of loneliness and hardship he had endured living in his father's castle, James silently began to formulate a plan of red, bloody revenge.

Max spent the next few days getting to know his cousin Jack again and filling up on delicious food, drink and warm welcome from his family. At night he would sit in, while his uncle laid plans to fortify his castle with powerful wards. Everyone knew that Tomax would be coming for his son, and that the battle which was to be waged would be a powerful, bloody and dangerous one.

Finally, one night soon after he arrived, Jack asked him about the Spirit Mages who had visited him.

"I have not seen nor heard from them since," Max answered Jack's question cautiously. He knew how much help was needed and wished with all his heart he could conjure up the help that Danie and her friend had offered. He knew it would not take long for his father to learn his whereabouts, especially since Aileann had seen whose soldiers were riding *toward them, before she disappeared. Max had already explained Aileann's hold on him to his Uncle and cousin, and was surprised to learn that she was once his father's lover too. That did not sit easily on his stomach.*

"Well, we shall just have to save ourselves then, without your spirit mage's help," Jack said in a reassuring manner to Max. Although he was far from feeling reassured himself. Jack was a year younger than Max, slender in build, with ginger hair and blue eyes. He was as handsome as he was handy, with either a blade or a song, whichever was needed at the moment.

Jack and Max had instantly renewed their kinship for each other, and had been working on a spell song to defeat Tomax. With Max's powerful magic, and Jack's magical gift of music and rhyme, they were hopeful that they could win the day. At least that is what they said to each other. Secretly no one in the castle, including Max's uncle James, were at all sure of any kind of victory.

The Modern Cauldron Coven had been desperately trying to reach Maxfield, having no way to tell if he had actually reached the safety of his uncle's castle. Each time Danie and Mitchell tried to reach out to him, they found themselves hitting a wall of magic that instantly defeated their skills. Danie went to bed that evening with a heavy heart and mind, wondering if they were already too late to save Max.

"Hey Max, didn't you say you saw this woman Mage in your dreams?" Jack asked while they were both at the dinner table, eating their fill and more of the sumptuous stew and freshly baked bread.

Max answered between mouthfuls, "Yes, I did. Her name, by the way, is Danielle and she is beautiful. So beautiful that I just could not believe the woman in my dreams was real, but she was, and now..." Maxfield stopped talking, and looked so discouraged that Jack spoke the first thing that was on his mind.

"So dream her back up then!" Jack stated boldly, looking at Max.

"Aww, Jack, don't you think I have tried? She is not there, just a wall."

Max pushed his second helping of stew away from him in disgust. He was angry that his gift had failed him so completely where Danie was concerned. Especially since they needed her and her coven's help so badly!

"A wall? A wall, oh of course! Max, you are hitting our own castle's wards!" Jack jumped up excitedly. "Listen, I can spell-sing you past the wards, I know just how to do that," Jack boasted.

"Umm, won't that be dangerous? Those wards are there for a reason," Max argued, but was actually getting excited about the idea of seeing Danie again, if only to say goodbye.

"You won't need to be there long, just to build a connection, then you can use each other as conduits. You know, fuse your energy with hers," Jack said, sitting back down and leaning over to Max in earnest, completely dismissing the idea of danger. "Besides, Max," Jack said soberly, "Without their help we may not make it anyway."

Together they each took a piece of bread and chewed thoughtfully, wondering how many meals like this they would have together before the final battle with his father.

"You're right. Jack, let's do it." Maxfield said, grabbing his bowl and began eating with renewed fervor. He needed all his strength to try and reach Danie.

ℵ ℵ ℵ

"Danie, Danielle, awaken, I am here."

Danie was deep in sleep, and was at first unsure of what she was hearing. Then suddenly Max appeared before her in her dream, standing in a white tunic and breeches, his hair cut and combed and his eyes snapping with anticipation.

"Maxfield, you're here!" Danie squealed overjoyed to see him standing there looking so much stronger than the last time she had seen him. "Where have you been, Max? We, the coven and I, have been trying to reach you for days."

Max moved closer to Danie, drinking her in, so afraid that this would be the last time they would meet and needing her so much it hurt. How had she captured his heart so completely?

He realized she was waiting for him to answer her question and quickly spoke up, "Danielle, I have been trying to reach you too. I had not been able to get past my Uncle's protective wards until now. My cousin helped me and…well it's a long story but we are preparing for battle and I just wanted to see you again," Max hesitated not knowing if he should tell her of his feelings, then finished by stating instead his need for her help.

"Oh, Max, I am so glad your Uncle is helping you, and of course we will do everything in our power to save you from your father."

Danie's words came out in a rush as she explained what the coven had planned.

"Mitch has an idea that we, the coven, can join our energies with yours, using me as a conduit. Then we can send the entire energy of the coven to you when you need us to."

Danie stopped talking and stood silently for a moment, trying to gauge his reaction to her words.

"Great minds think alike," Maxfield quipped, terribly pleased that all parties involved were on the same page. "My cousin Jack and I thought of the same thing."

"So the next question is, how do we do it?" Danie asked, wondering if she was strong enough to help him, then dismissing her fear. She was determined to rescue Max, no matter what.

Max was really not sure of how to proceed. He had never actually fused his magic with an Other Worlder before and did not know, despite his earlier bravado, if it could be done. Usually the people involved had to touch, and dream figures simply had no power to do that. Before he could speak of his doubts, Danie reached out and clasped his hand.

"The coven is strong, Max, we have a lot of talented people who can…" Here she paused because she was not exactly sure what they could do, but then continued on with conviction, "…help you defeat your father, I am sure of it!"

Her eyes looked deeply into his, begging him without words to believe in her. Maxfield looked into the depths of her beautiful blue eyes, sparkling with unshed tears and was about to answer her, when suddenly he realized that a miracle of magic had just occurred. Needing desperately to confirm this, Max asked simply, "Danielle, will you hold me?"

Danie could only imagine how frightened Max must be, and her heart wanted to weep at his simple request.

She let go of his hand and circled her arms around him, trying to convey in her tender hug all the feelings that she had stored up for him. She needed him to feel all her compassion, her need, and her understanding of his plight. Most of all she needed him to understand her resolve to bring him safely through this ordeal.

Max felt her energy combine with his, blending with his blood and bone, reaching into his heart, his soul, and he reveled in the abandon he felt at such power. She completed him, she rang in him like a bell, causing tempests to storm through him as he and Danie connected. Max badly needed to take this to the next level. Slowly he lowered his face to hers until their lips barely touched. The contact was almost too much for them to bear, as the kiss deepened, driving them both to want more, need more, demand more...

Suddenly, Maxfield felt a strong tug and could hear Jack's voice in the back of his mind. Damn, he had stayed too long and it would take at least a day to recover his strength. Slowly he lifted his lips from Danie's, and saw in her eyes the need to go further.

"Danielle, I have to go now," He said softly.

At Danie's sharp cry of denial, Maxfield smiled weakly and said, "But we have already begun the process of fusing our energies, and it will not take too much more effort until we are completely in sync with each other."

Longing for another kiss, her body overheated, her mind tried to concentrate on what he was saying.

"This will work then?" Danie asked. Maxfield nodded and said firmly, "Tomorrow night we begin." then disappeared from her dream like smoke.

Danie awoke with a start, with her lips swollen from their passionate kiss and tears running down her cheeks. Slowly, rhythmically, she breathed in and out, struggling to get her body under control, and clear her mind. Finally, she felt enough in control to leap off the bed and wake the others. It was time to put their plan in motion!

Chapter Four

Aileann finally had to admit defeat. The wards that Max's uncle had cast around his castle were too strong for her powers. Now, when Max should have been deeply in her power, he was instead safe within the castle's walls. Too late she realized her mistake of sending him to his uncle. James had not been as fierce a magician in the old days, and she had not counted on such a powerful defense. Now she had to tell Tomax where to find his son. Tomax would not be pleased and would see through any lie she tried to speak. He had told her to find his son, and had been surprised when she could not. This 'new information' she had about Max would be seen for what it was—an attempt at betrayal.

$\mathcal{S}\quad\mathcal{S}\quad\mathcal{S}$

"And I was able to touch her, Uncle. This means that our idea of building a conduit between the worlds can work!" Maxfield exclaimed. He had spent the last hour explaining his dream journey to his uncle. His uncle had listened patiently, only interrupting to clarify a point or two.

Now he spoke, "Maxfield, this is excellent. We will work with the Other-Worlder energy to bring your father down." He looked at Maxfield to see how this affected him. James understood that Max going against his own father, no matter what he had done, was a painful matter.

"Good. I want nothing more than to see that tyrant vanquished!" Maxfield said, his eyes filled with fire. James, satisfied that Maxfield would feel no remorse, went on to say, "Agreed, Max. I too want nothing more than to see my brother defeated and his reign of terror at an end. It is interesting that you said that you could touch this woman, Danielle, in your dreams. She too must have your power to open portals, else even with your great power, this could never have happened."

Maxfield's eyes widened as he realized that this had to be true, Danielle was a Worlds Crafter like himself. That is how they connected; she was able to reach out to him in his world and he in hers. He had finally met a woman as powerful as himself. His Uncle interrupted Maxfield's train of thought by saying, "And one more thing Max, it is to be hoped that we are successful in vanquishing your father. Still, and I say this not to scare you but to make your position here very clear, you are in great danger from your father's enemies. Your father has created great discord throughout our many kingdoms and all those harmed by your father will want to take revenge on his son."

"But, Uncle, I have done nothing to them." It was clear that Maxfield had not thought of this and was unprepared for the violent future that he had ahead of him, here in his world.

"I will, of course stand with you against your enemies, Max. You are as a son to me and my forces are yours. Still, we may be at war for many years."

Maxfield looked at his Uncle, grateful beyond words for what this man of peace was willing to risk for his sake. "Uncle, I am overcome with thanks to you for your offer. How I wish you had been my father, how different my life would have been! But now, in my love for you, I cannot risk losing you or embroiling you and my cousin in war after war for my sake."

As his uncle sought to reassure him, Max remained adamant. "No, Uncle, I will leave here after we vanquish my father and not return."

"Max, you must think this through, where will you go?" James asked quietly, not at all happy at this turn of the conversation. He wanted Max here with them, regardless of the cost.

"I do not yet know, Uncle. But first things first, we must defeat my father," Max said quietly, his heart deeply troubled but his mind sharp with the need to stop his father no matter what.

Danie explained to her coven mates over breakfast what had happened to her in her dream. "He really believes that we can do it; create a doorway in which we can send him our energy. I am to be the conduit. Isn't this perfect?" Danie gushed.

It was Mitch that spoke up first. "Well, Danie, it's a start. Now that we know you can communicate with Max, we have to get up to speed on how to create a cone of power with so much energy it can travel from our world to another. This is something we have never even thought of attempting." Mitchell looked at the others, who had remained silent throughout Danie's explanation.

Michael spoke up saying softly, "We could all be in danger if we do this thing."

Danie's eyes widened in fear, "If? What do you mean if, Michael? Maxfield needs us!"

Chelsea snapped at Danie, "He is a stranger to us though, it is not like he is one of us. Should we risk everything for this man whom most of us have never even met? Be reasonable, Danie, this is a very serious matter."

At Danie's stricken look, Michelle spoke up and out to the group. "Yes, this is dangerous. Yes, this is new. And yes, Maxfield is not known to us all. But we have been called by fate and by the Gods at this time when the veil is thin between our worlds to help someone in grave danger. We cannot turn our backs on him now. I will not, and I ask you to stand with me and see this thing through." The group stayed silent, pondering her words. When no one spoke, Michelle continued, "What is our magic for if not to help others in need? Is our power just for ourselves? I believe we came to this moment for a reason, that our powers are meant to serve a higher purpose, to help others. I do not believe that it is a coincidence that Danie and Maxfield found each other at the time when his need was greatest. I say that this was meant to be, and I for one will stand with Danie, and fight for him." Michelle radiated strength of purpose, and it was easy to see in this moment why she had become their High Priestess. It was obvious to everyone in that room that she had been born to lead.

Michael looked at his beloved, and then into each individual's face. He loved these people, they were family and he was going to ask them to risk everything. "I concur with Michelle, I say we fight for Maxfield. Who is with us?"

Danie held her breath, hoping that her friends would decide to stand and face the danger. She knew that she wanted this for terribly selfish reasons, but she loved Max, truly loved him and could not bear to see him defeated and imprisoned, or worse.

One by one, each coven member raised their hand.

Mitchell said, "I am with you, Danie. But damn, girl! Couldn't you find a boyfriend in this world? Did you have to go to such an extreme just to find a guy?"

His attempt at levity created nervous laughter throughout the group. Danie had tears in her eyes, as she hugged Mitchell. "Thank you, Mitch, thank all of you so much!"

Michelle smiled at Michael, brimming with pride over their wonderful coven mates, as the group fell into planning their next move.

That night, as Danie went to bed, she could hardly sleep for the excitement of seeing Maxfield again. She needed to tell him that they were all with him and ready to send their magic to him as soon as he said the word. Finally, after quieting her mind through meditation, Danie slept. Immediately he was there…

"Danie, Danielle, I am here," Maxfield greeted her. Danie ran into his arms, and told him everything that had happened today; that the group had chosen to stand with him, no matter what. Maxfield was thrilled to hear this, but hesitant to ask his next question.

He had been thinking all day of what his uncle had said about him not being safe in his own world. The answer had come to him as if he had always known the solution. He wanted to be with Danielle, in her world. Now that the moment was there, he hardly knew how to ask her if she would help him cross through the portal to join her coven.

"Danielle, I am so grateful to your coven for their faith in my cause and their help. It is not only me that they are saving, but many. My father has destroyed kingdom after kingdom in my world, sowing hate and discontent wherever his armies go. He has to be stopped and I am so grateful beyond words that you all are going to help me."

Not knowing how to ask what he so needed to ask, Maxfield hesitated. Danie could see something was wrong and urged him to speak his mind. "Max, what is it? I feel your energy is so nervous, so...unquiet, please let me help," Danie said softly, holding his hand in hers. Max spoke quietly, hoping he was not asking too much of her, "My uncle, James, has pointed out to me something that I should have realized from the start. You, Danie, are a Worlds Crafter too. We reached out to each other because we both have the same power." He stopped talking and waited to see how Danie would digest this information.

"I was wondering about that, Max, because today at breakfast our High Priestess said that all this happened for a reason, that this was fate. I knew that there was a connection between us, although I hardly think that I am a Worlds Crafter..."

Maxfield interrupted her because he had to make her see that she had the power. She had to know that she could bring him into her world. "Danielle, you need to trust me. I know without a doubt that you have my magical gift. Actually, I am in great need of your gift because I have to escape from my world. You see, my father's enemies will come for me. After my father is defeated, there will be no place in my world where I will be safe." Maxfield closed his eyes, trying to muster the strength to ask his next question. " I was hoping that perhaps you and your coven mates would let me join you in your world. I have many gifts to offer the coven, and many things I could teach..."

Danie interrupted him by flying into his arms. "Oh, Max, I am so glad. I wanted so badly to ask you to come to my world to join me, but I didn't have the nerve. Yes, please, please come and be with me in my world!"

Maxfield was dumbfounded at her reaction. He had expected hesitancy and yet here was overwhelming acceptance. He was humbled by her giving nature.

"Thank you, Danie," Maxfield said quietly, looking deeply into her eyes. Then he added briskly, "Okay, so now we prepare ourselves for the battle ahead and for my journey to my new home." He smiled at Danie.

"I am ready." Danie asserted, and together they touched hands, sharing and synchronizing their energy fields. They both knew how much work was ahead of them, but now they were committed not only to winning the day, but to each other as well.

🌀 🌀 🌀

Aileann's face burned from the vicious slap that Tomax had delivered to her after hearing the news of his son's whereabouts. "I should have killed my brother when I had the chance!" he shouted, slamming about the dining room, breaking precious crystal-ware in his towering rage. "I will take them all down now, and my son will beg for my mercy *before this is through. And so will you, Aileann, and so will you." With those parting words, Tomax began the task of going to war upon his brother and his son.*

Bloody in body, a torn and wounded messenger arrived at the Hunterson castle gates with one message before he died. Tomax was coming.

That night, Maxfield appeared to Danie one last time for a brief moment. "Danielle, my father's armies are on the move. They will be here in the morning. Are you ready?"

Danie gave him a brilliant smile, and said with a conviction she was far from feeling, "Yes, Max, we are ready."

As he disappeared, Danie awoke, and leapt out of bed to tell the others that the hour they had prepared for had finally come. As she moved from cabin to cabin, awaking her coven mates, she prayed with all her heart that they and Max would survive the day.

The wards held for the first two assaults from his father's army. But the army was not the real danger, and they all knew it. It was the magic of Tomax that they had to defeat. Everyone in the castle could feel the weight of a powerful, deadly storm brewing and heading their way. Max, his uncle, and cousin all made final preparations for the fateful battle ahead.

The Modern Cauldron had gathered in a circle, surrounding a towering bonfire burning with tremendous power. Its flames reached hungrily to greet the sky, as if reaching for its Father, the Sun. Smoke weaved its way throughout the circle, stinging the eyes of the coven until tears were streaming from their eyes. Still they stood steadfast, drawing in the fire energy, and combining all their individual energies to create a gigantic cone of power. Drawing from the earth, envisioning the sun's rays coming down and touching the circle, the coven hummed. They hummed until their bodies were buzzing. Together they created a cone of light, love and courage to save their friends. It would be used to banish the darkness that now shrouded the Hunterson's beautiful castle. Slowly the cone grew in power. Michelle and Michael focused its center directly over Danie's head. Danie used every ounce of energy she had to envision this cone passing from this world into Maxfield's, and becoming a super battery of power for Max to use to defeat his enemies. They hummed, and the buzzing became an almost intolerable sound building and building until finally it was shaped by Danie's vision into a blade of power for Maxfield to wield against his father.

☙ ☙ ☙

Tomax and Aileann had arrived with the storm and the magical battle had begun in earnest. Maxfield was exhausted, they had been battling for hours and their battered energies were no match for his father and his minions. He had lost hope of Danie's group being able to break through the barrier in time to save them, and his will faltered. Aileann smiled triumphantly at Maxfield's devastated face and beckoned to him.

"Maxfield, give yourself to me and together we can defeat your father. Your friends are not coming. They are too weak and too far away. I am here for you, Max. Remember Maxfield, how good we are together. Remember how my touch can make you burn. I can help you defeat your father. I alone can help you. Come to me, Max, come..."

Her crooning insinuated itself into his mind, already clouded with despair. He swayed a bit, but then Jack's voice rang out. "Maxfield, no, don't listen to her, I know in my heart that we can still win the day, have faith in your friends, Max, have faith in Danie."

At the mention of Danie's name, Max envisioned her bright beauty, her shining courage and those eyes of hers sparkling with love. He repelled Aileann's advances using his memory of Danie as a shield against her dark arts. Maxfield felt a surge in the ether, something was coming, something bright, something really big. He gasped, as his right hand felt a sudden shock of electricity. Into his hand a glowing sword appeared. It was of such excellence as he had never seen before. Power surged up his arm, enveloping his body and burst out of him like the sun's rays, pouring energy into every man, woman and child of the castle. It gave to each of them the much needed strength to overcome the darkness that was Tomax.

Tomax, for the first time, felt fear. This sword was like nothing he had ever witnessed before, and its power was ever growing. He used his dark magic with all of his force, to strike the sword from Max's hand.

The Coven felt the might of Tomax Blade's power. Wind ripped through the circle with a fierceness that threatened to tear their hands apart. Still they held fast. Rain came in torrents, soaking them with water so cold, it burned. They held fast, still humming loudly all through the wildness of the storm. Danie, soaked and freezing, held onto her vision of Maxfield and his sword — directing the coven's energy to feed it power.

As the coven was battered mercilessly by the power of Tomax's black magic, suddenly the flames of the fire expanded, grew white hot, and a shape began to appear inside the center. It was a deep blue heart, beautiful to behold. It gave each coven member a sense of well-being and conviction. They now held a true knowledge that victory over the darkness would be theirs. Danie saw the blue heart in her vision, and thanking the Gods, she envisioned herself standing with Max and handing him this heart.

૎ ૎ ૎

Max felt Danie beside him, felt her warmth, courage, and love as she presented to him the blue heart of the flame. He held now in his right hand the sword, in his left hand the blue heart. Max knew at that moment they would win the day. As Danie's form faded, Max raced toward his father, easily defeating the poor fools who stepped into his path. Tomax looked at the battle rage in his son's face, and the victory light that danced in Maxfield's eyes, and knew his day was done even before he felt the glowing sword pierce his heart.

As Tomax fell, the heart spun up and away from Maxfield's hand and floated to the ceiling of the castle, filling every inch of the fortress with its deep blue light. Tomax's army fell back in terror, and screamed as the rays hit them and they were destroyed, each one dispersing like the shadow beings they were.

Only Aileann was left, but even her magic could not save her. Her form was fading as the light filled the room with white magic, more powerful than any magic she had ever known. As Max watched, Aileann screamed a curse at the light, and was vanquished.

Together, as one voice, the residents of Hunterson castle cheered their victory.

೪ ೪ ೪

The rain was gone, the wind was warm, and the fire was out. Each member of the coven sat exhausted yet triumphant, with Danie standing in the middle of the circle, her face to the sky with tears of gratitude streaming from her eyes. Max, at last, was safe.

Tomorrow, they would bring him home. Danie walked silently with the others, sleep paramount on her mind, and a powerful joy filled her heart. They had done it, she and her beautiful coven mates had joined forces with Max and saved him and all the others. Not bad for a day's work.

Then a shadow of fear reached her heart. What if now that his father was defeated, Max wanted to stay in his world? Danie went to sleep with heartbreak on her mind.

That night Max visited Danie in her dreams. He knew he could only stay a short while as he was exhausted after the battle and had only a small reserve of energy left.

"Danielle, we did it!" Maxfield cried out joyfully.

Danie, still unsure of him and what he wanted to do, could not help but smile back. She replied, "Oh Max, I am so happy for you and your family!"

Maxfield felt her reserve and wondered if he was still to be welcomed into her world. He decided to ask outright before his courage deserted him. "So, Danie, what now? Am I to come and live with you and your friends in your world?" He held his breath as Danie hesitated, becoming more afraid by the moment that she had changed her mind.

Danie looked at him, but his face gave no clue as to what he may want from her. Did he want to leave his family and friends now that the danger had passed? Finally she said, "Max, I will understand if you cannot bring yourself to leave your family and friends, now that you finally have a home. Please do not feel obligated to..."

Maxfield interrupted fiercely, "Danie, if you have changed your mind, please speak plainly. I am not a man who is interested in beating around bushes."

"No, Max, I have not changed my mind at all, I...umm...we all want you to come and join us here in our world, nothing has changed!"

Maxfield looked at her wonderingly. "Surely something has changed, because you are neither smiling, nor giving me a great amount of encouragement to come there," Max said softly.

His rebuke finally broke down Danie's reserve, and she cried out to him, "Oh, Max, I want you to come so very badly, but not out of some obligation that you think have to me. I want you to come because that is what you want to do."

Danie felt the bright future she had hoped for slipping through her hands.

"Obligation!" Maxfield laughed, finally realizing that the energy that he felt coming from Danie was fear. She was afraid he was not going to want to come to her world. "I am not coming to you from any sort of obligation, though I do owe you and your coven much, I am coming because I want to be a part of your world."

Danie finally gave Maxfield a real smile, brilliant and captivating as she answered him by leaning over to him and giving him a deep and passionate kiss. The kiss was unfortunately short lived, as Max simply did not have the energy to fight the urges in his body, and at the same time maintain his stay there in her dream. He quickly ended the kiss, with a promise of more to come when they both saw each other on the morrow. As Maxfield faded from her dream, he shouted out,

"Danie, we are all prepared on our end, you know what you need to do!"

Then he was gone, and Danie, smiling, returned to her slumber. She knew that she needed to get a good night's rest before the magical work that was to be done tomorrow.

Max, his uncle, and cousin had sat together long after the victory celebration was over, knowing that Maxfield must leave and yet not being able to say goodbye.

"I am so glad that I had a chance to get to know you both again, I am honored to be a part of your family," Maxfield said in one last toast to his Uncle and to Jack.

"Aww, now cousin, we will see each other again. You and Danielle are powerful magicians, and I know you can find your way back for a visit."

Uncle James nodded his agreement at this son's words and added, "The fates would not be so unkind as to separate us forever, now that we have found each other again. We will see each other again, young Maxfield, count on it."

The toasting over, they knew it was time for sleep. Tomorrow was going to be a very big day.

৯ ৯ ৯

Early the next morning, Danie and her coven stood in their Sacred Circle and began to chant together.

"We open the gates of Somerwynd, where powerful friendships have yet to begin.

We dance and sing the circle round and bring you from where you are bound.

Maxfield, our friend join us here we say, leave Somerwynd and with us do stay.

From Somerwynd to Midsummer's end, come and be with us dear friend.

We ask you to take this leap of faith, as this, your final step do take!"

⅌ ⅌ ⅌

At the same time as they were chanting their song, Max began chanting his.

Max had already said his farewells to his uncle and cousin, feeling the loss of them keenly, despite his cousin's assurance that this new portal could be used to travel between the worlds at will. Max hoped his cousin was telling the truth and not just a pretty lie to make him feel better. He wanted so badly to believe that this was not goodbye and he would see his beloved family again. At the time appointed, Maxfield sang out loudly, accompanied by Jack, who played his harp as never before.

"We open the gates to Midsummer's end, where powerful friendships now begin.

We dance and sing from where we're bound and open the portal to a new world found."

As Max chanted these words, he could feel a massive amount of energy building.

"From Somerwynd to Midsummer's end, I travel to live with my new friends.

I now take my leave of Somerwynd, to live anew at Midsummer's end.

With all my heart I trust in fate, as this last step, I now do take!

֍ ֍ ֍

As Max shouted the ending to his song, so too did Danie and her coven.

A thunderous roar was heard, all but deafening those in both worlds. A blue flash appeared and the portal opened. It was a roiling mass of energy, looking less like a tunnel and more like a rabbit hole, but Max was undaunted. Looking back one last time at his family and friends, Maxfield entered the portal.

As Danie and everyone in the Coven held their breath, Maxfield suddenly appeared in a flash of blue light, right in the middle of their Sacred Circle.

To see Maxfield there in the flesh overwhelmed Danie to such an extent that she stood frozen, incapable of either movement or speech. The happiness she felt was so fragile, she was afraid that it would break and he would be gone.

Sensing her terrible fear, Max walked over to her. His green eyes filled with tears at actually being able to be with her at long last. He slowly drew her shaking body into his arms, and hugged her as if he was never letting go. Her fear evaporated at his touch, and she hugged him back as fiercely as he was hugging her. Together they stood, embracing each other while the rest of the coven members dashed around madly, setting up supper. Everyone was exhausted, and knew that they needed to immediately ground themselves after such an amazing expenditure of energy.

Later, after heavily celebrating Maxfield's arrival, and toasting to being victorious in their defeat of Maxfield's enemies, the rest of the coven said goodnight to Max and Danie and staggered off to sleep.

Finally they were all alone in her cabin, and Danie looked at the man she had lost her heart to. She reached into her mind for a way to open a conversation, but Maxfield had other ideas. He strode over to Danie and grabbed her, claiming her mouth with a kiss of deep and utter longing. As Maxfield slowly deepened the kiss, Danielle's body begin to quiver with an excitement mirroring his own. His lips left hers, only to kiss her neck and travel lower down to the hollow between her breasts. Danie's breath caught as his tongue teased her.

Ever since she had seen him in her vision, she had longed for this moment. The fusion of his energy to hers had felt almost sexual in nature. Now it was finding its release. A release they both needed very badly. The impediment of clothes was quickly dispatched as they desperately fell on to her bed and touched each other, first gently, then with a heightened sense of need. They were at last free to touch, to taste, to revel in what had so long been denied them. Danie arched her back as Maxfield teased her nipples with his tongue. Meanwhile her hands stroked his sensitive inner thigh, rhythmically moving up and down, creating a friction that Maxfield reacted to strongly. He traced his tongue down from her breasts, to her belly, then lower. As his tongue explored her, he found that she was slick with need for him as she wildly arched her back and moaned. He loved her taste, loved the way she moved and gasped at his touch.

As he lifted his head to kiss her, she slipped from his embrace and pushed him gently backward. It was her turn now. She slipped her hands between his legs, smiling at his bemused expression. Clearly he was used to having the upper hand with women. Well, that was about to change, drastically. She touched and tasted him, her tongue darting over his sensitive skin, making him groan in ecstasy. As she skilfully used her tongue and hands to create momentum, he turned rock hard and knew he had to have her right then.

"Danie, enough. Please, I need you now." At his plea, Danie released her grip and moved into his arms. As Maxfield slid inside of her, she shuddered and they began to move rhythmically together, in perfect sync, feeding off each other's energies that served to heighten the experience until it was almost too much to bear. Both reached climax at the same time and slept deeply in each other's arms...

Upon awakening, Danie reached for her lover, and was surprised to only feel an empty space beside her. Quickly getting up and getting dressed, she ran out of the cabin, only to find Michael and Maxfield in deep discussion. Curious, she walked over toward the two men, and was surprised to see a very sheepish expression on Maxfield's face when he saw her. Michael, on the other hand looked suspiciously smug.

"Hi, Danie. Did you sleep well?" Michael asked with a knowing smile. Ignoring Michael, she turned to Maxfield and asked, "Just what were you two talking about, hmm?"

Michael, refusing to be ignored, stepped in and said, "Nothing much, Danie. Maxfield was just asking if I had ever presided over a Handfasting before, and I said ..."

Danie did not wait to hear the rest, she leaped into Maxfield's arms and he held her tight, kissing her soundly.

"So I guess that's a 'yes' then." Michael smirked, as he strode off to gather the others. They had a ceremony to perform.

Chapter One

IRELAND 1170

The pervasive scent of smoke and the sound of shouting jolted Saoirse upright, her hands flinging back the bedcovers in one swift move. Her feet slapped against the cold floor as she tore open the door to stick her head into the hallway. Harsh male voices, along with the noise of booted feet on stone, assaulted her ears. Saoirse tilted her head around the door frame to get a better look at the bodies rushing by in a flurry of panic. She blinked sleepy eyelids and focused as a familiar figure rounded the corner into her view.

"Fergal? What's going on?"

"The damned MacCrohan are at it again!" her brother yelled, jerking to a halt mid-run. "The south pastures are burning, and the crofter's huts have gone up in flames as well! They've taken swords to the cattle, Saoirse! Gods help us, it's a bloodbath!"

Saoirse's jaw set in a hard clench at the rage in her brother's eyes, an angry hiss escaping unbidden through her teeth. "I'm coming."

"No!" Fergal shook his head. "You stay here where you'll be safe. Donal's bringing the women and children into the house. Áthair will not be pleased if he sees you. This is a man's fight, little sister."

"Fergal!"

Her brother's eyes narrowed. "Do as you're told, Saoirse. I'll not be burying you along with the cattle." He didn't stay to listen to her retort and ran off downstairs to join the fight.

Saoirse whirled back into the room, pulling off the linen nightshirt and tossing it to the floor. She dressed in seconds, tugging on a tunic, a pair of soft leather breeches, and lace up boots. A sharp curse slipped past her lips when her fingers caught in the snarls of long blonde hair as she secured it back with a leather tie. Dropping to her hands and knees beside the bed, she reached underneath to pull out a wrapped woolen bundle. She opened the folds with a careful hand and pulled out the longsword, secretly pleased that it was about to have its first taste of battle. Her father would object when he saw it, but what was done was done. She only hoped the smith would not incur too much of her father's wrath for forging it.

She scrambled to her feet and secured the sheath to her body, belting the tunic. Saoirse blew out a calming breath and breached the doorway, ready to earn her place among her brothers and the other Ó'Laighin warriors. If she happened to kill one or two of the bastard MacCrohans in the process, well…that was all the better. Lughnasadh was approaching; it was a good day to spill MacCrohan blood in offering.

Saoirse emerged from the cathair to chaos. Fires raged on every point of the horizon, the thick smoke billowing into the air, tainting it with the taste of ash and death. Her father's warriors were divided; only a few of the MacCrohan straggled behind, still fighting in close combat. The rest had made their retreat. The damage was done. Huts smoldered around the perimeter of the stone ringfort, charred black remains standing stark and barren like skeletons stripped of their flesh. In the outlying fields she could see the corpses of the livestock, mangled and bloody, lying on the soft carpet of green Irish grass. She sent a quick prayer heavenward in hopes that few of her people had met the same fate.

Her hand tightened on the hilt of the longsword as she moved forward to the fray of battle, ready to strike out at any MacCrohan still lurking about. A sharp shout in a familiar voice made her turn, and her eyes latched onto the sight of her middle brother, Carrick, locked in arms with a swarthy MacCrohan interloper. She rushed forward to see the MacCrohan sword arc through the air as Carrick dodged, the strike glancing off his sword arm in a quick slice. He cried out and fell into the dirt, the force knocking the sword from his hand. The MacCrohan laughed and spit, raising his sword for the final blow.

"No!" The sound that emerged from her throat was loud and piercing, and she was rewarded with the surprised widening of the MacCrohan's eyes as her longsword slipped free of the sheath and plunged directly into the soft flesh of his belly. He slumped forward over the end of the blade, the sudden shift in weight too great for her slight frame to hold, and they both crumpled to the ground next to Carrick.

Her brother grunted, clutching at his injured arm, and moved to shove the MacCrohan off the end of her blade with his foot. "Saoirse! What the devil? You'll get yourself killed!" he shouted, pulling her to her feet.

"Are you alright?" she asked, ignoring him. "Can you fight?" The clang of swordplay and the howls of both MacCrohan and Ó'Laighin men were growing fainter. The pounding of horse hooves grew stronger and she could see the grass and dirt flying as more of the MacCrohans retreated.

Carrick grabbed her arm and swiveled her back toward the house. "Go on with ye, lass. This is no place for a woman." He shoved the bloodied sword into her hands, pushing her from him. "Go," he warned, "before Áthair sees you and that thing." Carrick reached for his own sword and took off at a trot toward the retreating line of horses. Her eyes searched the wreckage of burning huts for the rest of her brothers and more of the invaders. She wiped the flat of the blade on her breeches and sheathed it, then headed for the fields, grabbing a discarded blanket on the way.

"Saoirse!" Her father's booming voice cut in over the din of shouts and the crackle of fire, stopping her dead in her tracks. She turned, swallowing hard as the anger in his eyes flared further at the sight of the sword at her hip. Saoirse felt her mouth open to protest, but no sound emerged. The Ó'Laighin's eyes narrowed to points as he jerked his head toward the large stone cathair. "Get inside. Help tend to the injured. We'll talk about this," he inclined his head to her longsword, "later." Her father's lips fell into a deep frown, emphasizing the crags of a battle-weary face. "Send any able man you find out here when you go. There are bodies to bury."

"Yes, Áthair." Saoirse's eyes shot to the ground in deference and her knees locked together as he rolled past her, the scent of earth and spice tickling her nostrils as he passed. The lump in her throat gradually receded, leaving the bitter taste of regret on her tongue. She hated disappointing him.

$$\text{ဒ္ဓ} \quad \text{ဒ္ဓ} \quad \text{ဒ္ဓ}$$

Saoirse felt the weight of her father's heavy and oppressive stare on her shoulders, the force of what was unspoken pinning her feet to the floor.

"Now," the chieftain intoned, "the MacCrohans are getting bolder, crossing over into our lands, taking what they want without fear of reprisal. This must end."

Fergal stepped forward, his face skewed in anger. "Then we take the fight to them!" he exclaimed, shaking his fist. "We make them bleed." Beside Saoirse, Donal and Carrick nodded their assent. "We cannot be caught unaware again, Áthair. Let us surprise them for once!" Shouts of agreement from the assembly rang off the stone walls. Her father held up a hand to silence the room.

"It is simply a fact that we do not possess the manpower necessary to make that effective, Fergal. I would not march you to your deaths, no matter how noble it seems." He sat back in his chair with a heavy sigh, rubbing his hands over the arms in thought. "The MacCrohan himself has approached me in an effort to bring peace. I have a mind to acquiesce."

"You cannot!" Fergal cried, with more shouts of protest bolstering his words. "His promises mean nothing."

The Ó'Laighin's eyes narrowed on his eldest son. "I'll decide what his promises are worth. While there is still breath in my body, I am chief of this clan. Do not be so bold as to overstep me, my son."

Fergal stepped back, chastised. His jaw twitched as he said through clenched teeth, "As you wish, Áthair."

"The MacCrohan has his sights set higher, to the north. I believe he intends to grow his holdings in an effort to quell the Norman invaders. In this, I agree with him. We must keep Henry and his dogs at bay." Murmurs of approval rippled through the crowd. Saoirse knew their unease. Fending off the MacCrohans was one thing; the Normans were a different beast altogether.

Her father cleared his throat and cast a glance over his band of warriors. "His list of demands was small. However, there is one request among them that stands out and holds the promise of a lasting peace. It is this request which has my attention."

A cold wave of fear passed over Saoirse as dread pierced her heart. Her voice trembled. "What does he want, Áthair?"

The shadow of regret on her father's brow was fleeting, but his voice was firm. "You."

The roar of dissent among the crowd was deafening. Her three brothers lurched forward in unison, adding their cries to the din.

"Silence!" her father yelled. All eyes turned to Saoirse.

She wanted nothing more than for the floor to open up and swallow her whole. "Wha-what exactly does he intend?"

"A union between our two clans will go far here in the south," he said. "We are respected, and marriage would solidify our alliance. It would inspire confidence in other clans. We would still retain our lands and autonomy, but we would stand together against any Norman invasion."

"And you mean to sell Saoirse into slavery to do it?" Fergal sneered.

The Ó'Laighin stood and peered down at his son. "You think this pleases me? Giving my only daughter to a man with his reputation?" the chief exclaimed. "It does not. But she is young and strong, and if this is the most distasteful of his demands, I am prepared to pay the price to ensure the safety of my people." His eyes narrowed. "Of *her* people. *Your* people." He eyed the crowd. "Now go. I wish to speak with Saoirse alone."

The crowd scrambled to their feet and departed with a hush of whispers and backward glances. Fergal, Carrick, and Donal were the last to leave. As he passed, Fergal gathered his sister into a fierce hug.

"I don't know what else he intends," Fergal whispered into her ear, "but you be careful, Saoirse. The MacCrohan is not to be trusted, no matter what promises he puts forth." He gave her one last squeeze and left, leaving her alone in the vast space with her father.

She managed to quiet the trembling in her limbs as she cast a glance at her father. "Áthair, I—"

"Believe me when I say it gives me no pleasure in taking this action. But you have left me no choice in the matter, Saoirse." His voice was a quiet rumble. "You've yet to take a husband. I find you in the thick of battle--with a sword no less! I don't know what to do with you! This is your moment to step forward and do something to help your people."

"I have not married because I do not wish to do so," she shot back. "I don't see why I cannot fight alongside my brothers! And please don't say it's because I'm a woman. There are others-"

"They are not you! You are the chief's daughter! Your place is-"

"Wherever you put me, apparently!" Her face was hot, flushed with anger. "You want me to sit idly by and needlepoint my life away while the rest of the people I care about are out there," she jabbed a finger at the door, "doing things that I should be doing! And now you want me to leave here and fulfill my destiny as what? A brood mare for the MacCrohan?" She shook her head. "I cannot." Her spine stiffened in defense as she glared at her father. "I will not."

"Do not make me force your obedience, girl. You know I will. And yes, your place is where I put you. Cast aside your selfishness for once and act like the warrior you think you are. Think of the greater good." The Ó'Laighin drew himself up to tower over her. "If you don't want to be treated like a child, do not act as one." He turned from her and gazed heavenward. "If your mother were here, perhaps she could talk some sense into you. Gods know I fail at every turn when it comes to you."

She couldn't help the quiver of her lip at the mention of her mother. "She wouldn't allow you to do this."

"Perhaps. But she would see reason behind it. And no matter my decision, she would have obeyed."

"No." The whisper was soft on her lips.

"Aye," he said, returning his eyes to her face. "Aye, she would have. Without question. You could have learned much from her." Disappointment clouded his features. "For once, I'm glad she is not here to see how you oppose me."

"Áthair-"

He looked away and waved a hand at her, his shoulders hunched. "Go. It is done. I will send a missive at first light. You will be married to the MacCrohan as soon as it can be arranged. That is final."

Saoirse swallowed a choked sob and ran from the room.

ॐ ॐ ॐ

Saoirse shoved some items in a makeshift pack and made her way down on cat feet, traversing the cathair in silence. Undetected, she slipped past the guards standing sentry and entered the stables. She crept up to Fergal's black stallion, murmuring soft words as she approached. His ears flicked in recognition, and she smiled and patted his neck, offering him an apple. He accepted the gift with a small crunch and she continued to stroke his side as she slung the pack over the saddle.

"Easy there, boy. We're just going for a little ride," she cooed as she grabbed the reins to lead him out the back. She walked him for a few paces until she was satisfied she wasn't seen, and hopped astride. The stallion balked for a moment, used to the weight of his master, but she produced another apple and he quieted, accepting her presence. Saoirse turned him out into the yard and eased him into a quiet trot. She looked back over her shoulder at the cathair in the distance, sorrow warring with anger in her heart. She dug her heels into the horse's side and galloped off into the night.

Chapter Two

The scent of sea spray and salt was heavy in the night air as she came upon the abandoned hut at the sea's edge. Saoirse tethered the stallion, gave him a few more apples from the pack and a quick rubdown, before depositing it inside the door.

Her emotions ran wild within her breast, her mind reeling as the sudden plan she had formulated came into view. She was lost. She could not return home, she now realized. There was nowhere to go. Her absence would be noticed in the morning, and she knew that if she were to seek asylum from another clan, she would promptly be returned to her father.

She needed help. Guidance. With Lughnasadh on the horizon, now was the best time to call upon the gods and try to discern their plans. Surely a new destiny had been decided the moment she chose to leave. There were paths available, fashioned by the gods' own hands. All she had to do was see where they led.

She gathered a pile of driftwood and started a small fire on the sand, careful to keep it from the hut. Clouds shifted above and the moon came into view, illuminating the rocky shore. The moonlight was bright on her face and she smiled. The gods were with her. All would be revealed.

Saoirse opened her arms and began to pray aloud, her voice ringing clear into the night. She prayed for peace and prosperity for her people. The harvest time was near; the season for all that was sown to be reaped. The MacCrohan and his warriors be damned. She would not submit, would not be consigned to the fate her father had decreed. Perhaps the gods would bless her and turn her father's heart around.

A fierce wind kicked up out of nowhere, whipping strands of hair into her face, threatening the burn of her fire. She continued, speaking louder, calling on the benevolence of the gods, asking them to place their hands on her people and her father. The fire sputtered, buffeted by the harsh slaps of salty wind and the mists of the sea blowing in.

"No, no!" she cried, desperately adding a few more pieces of wood, hoping to bolster the flame. As long as it burned, her prayers would be carried to the gods. Thick black smoke began to smolder on the fire and panic seized her heart. *The fire must burn, must stay alive.*

"Please!" she yelled. "Please, I need you to hear me!" The glow of the moon receded as dark clouds rolled in, low rumbles of thunder in the distance. It wasn't working. She ran to the shore, snagging more twigs and handfuls of dry seaweed, anything to throw on to keep the fire from going out. Her hands dug in the damp sand, the grit stabbing underneath her fingernails, the hard rasp scoring her flesh and tearing apart the hope in her soul.

Saoirse's fingers snagged something soft and supple, like a sheath of leather, and she clutched it to her breast, preparing to throw it on and watch it burn.

"Stop!" A deep male voice echoed out into the dark and she turned, wide-eyed, her heart thundering in her ears. "Give that to me!"

The man came into view just as the clouds rolled by on another swift pass, and the moonlight shone down, casting a glow on his body. His naked body.

Neither of them moved. Saoirse's mouth fell agape in shock at his lack of clothing. He dripped, fresh from the sea, tiny droplets accumulating at the fringe of his dark hair to plop to his shoulder and run in a slow trickle down the wide expanse of his bare chest. Her breath caught in her throat as her eyes fixated on the trail of wetness sliding over smooth moonlit skin, over the hard muscle of his upper body. The droplet flowed like a swish of silk down the indentations of his rippled torso, down further until a heated blush suffused her cheeks and she could follow it no more. She averted her gaze to the sky and swallowed, unable to meet his eyes.

He made no move to cover himself. Instead, he gave a fierce shake of his head which sent glistening drops of sea water flying like starlight into the air. Saoirse worked her mouth to speak, but no sound came forth. Her tongue felt dry and thick and she cleared her throat, forcing out a raspy 'eek'.

"Who are you?" she managed.

The heated look he gave her sent shivers of something foreign down to the base of her spine. Even in the dimness of moonlight, she could see the intense blue of his eyes, sparkling back at her like sapphires. His lips parted into a dark smile, revealing a set of strong white teeth.

"I am Ronan."

Ronan. The sound of his name reverberated through her body like a thunderclap and the delicate shivers surged, forcing her to lock her knees to remain upright. Her fingers curled reflexively into the scrap in her hands, and his eyes caught the slight movement, narrowing on her.

"You have something of mine. I want it." His voice rumbled over her like the crash of waves against rocks and she clutched it harder, stepping back to steel her resolve. His stare was pointed and direct. He meant it.

She looked down at her hands to discern what exactly it was that he wanted. Her fingers slid over it, feeling the softness akin to supple leather. She gasped in recognition and the whisper passed from her lips into the air.

"Selkie."

The dark head nodded. "Aye. Selkie."

Before common sense could prevail, she ran to the hut and shut herself inside, stuffing the pelt underneath a loose stone in the floor that had long been a hiding place for childhood trinkets. Her heart pounded as she replaced the stone. He would come for it. She knew this, knew the legends as well as anything. It was the pelt he wanted. No, needed. As long as she held his sealskin, he would remain human, unable to return to the sea and his true form. He was at her mercy. A brief thought froze her in place. What would he do to reclaim it?

The thought heated her blood in a rush, and a sudden reel of questions and answers swirled through her head. Had her prayers been answered? Was this Ronan her gift from the gods? How could he help her change her fate? Was it worth finding out? She placed the pack aside and dug through the old chest in the far corner of the hut. Grabbing what she wanted, she went back to the door with determination. She opened the latch and sent a silent prayer to the gods. Thank you.

His brows shot up in surprise when she threw open the door and shoved the clothes in his hands. "Here," she said on a breath. "Cover yourself."

The smile returned as he bent and dressed in the doorway. Fergal's leftover clothing fit him, albeit a bit snug, but Ronan was taller than her brother and the legs of the breeches ended well above his ankles. He chuckled. "Presentable?"

"Yes." Her breath came out in a rush as she stepped aside and allowed him entry into the hut. She watched as his eyes scanned the tiny interior. *Looking for the hiding place.* She would have to find somewhere safer to secure it when he wasn't looking. Difficult, but not impossible. She was a resourceful woman.

He moved further inside and sat down next to the stone brazier without waiting for an invitation. "The pelt, woman. You know I want it."

"And you'll get it." His stare was unnerving. "After you help me," she added.

She felt the hot sear of his gaze as his eyes flicked over her skin, taking her in from head to toe. "What is it you," he swiped the point of his tongue over his lips, "need of me?"

Saoirse's stomach fluttered under his frank appraisal, the innuendo not lost on her. "My father," she started, "he-he seeks to offer me in marriage to a man I do not want."

The corner of his mouth quirked in amusement. "Then do not marry him."

"I have no choice," she snapped in defiance. "I will not be offered up like a prize to the MacCrohan."

Ronan's spine stiffened in the chair. "MacCrohan?" he hissed. "He seeks to give you to the MacCrohan?"

"You know of him?"

Ronan's voice was like steel. "Aye. I know of him. He is the reason I have left the sea. Like you, he has taken something from me. I intend to retrieve it. By force, if necessary."

With a boldness born of desperation, she moved forward and crouched to kneel in front of him. "I have nothing to offer you," she said, "but I know in my heart that the gods have sent you to me for a reason. And I promise you, if you help me escape this marriage, I will help you take back what the MacCrohan has stolen from you. Only then will I return your pelt to you. You have my word."

His lip curled. "And what is that worth to me? Your promise? You said it yourself; you have nothing to offer me." Her eyes darted to his hand as it came up, caressing her face in a brush of knuckles. Saoirse's breath hitched as she dared to look into his eyes, fierce and focused. "Let me say this - you have more to offer than you think."

She pushed back with a start and set her chin with a warning glare. "You are presumptuous. And far too forward. I am the daughter of a chief, and you think I will lie with you like a common whore?" She gave a haughty sniff. "I think not. I can offer you gold, sir. An amount of your choosing."

"Gold?" He laughed, the sound deep and rich. "What do I need of gold? I am a selkie. We care not for the trappings of the landed." Ronan's voice dropped to a husky whisper. "But to lie with you," his eyes roved her body again with keen interest, "yes, I would gladly accept that as payment. And I assure you, you would find it well worth your time."

"You think highly of yourself, selkie," she scoffed.

"I have yet to hear otherwise."

She stared at him, searching for deception in his face and finding nothing but confidence. No. She couldn't. Could she? "I will lie with no man who is not my husband."

"Then we are at an impasse," he said swiftly, moving to rise. He stepped forward, towering above her. "You leave me no choice but to take what I am after." She paled, wanting to step back from his presence, but her feet would not move. "It is here in this dwelling. I can feel it." He glanced around the hut. "And I will tear it down to the dirt to find it. You can either accept my terms, or," he leaned in to whisper in her ear, "face the consequences. One way or another, little one, I will get what I want."

Saoirse pushed at his chest and gasped as his hand closed around her wrist. "You would take me by force?"

That damnable chuckle sounded in her ears again and he whispered, "It is not force if you submit. And you would, little star, I promise you."

The kiss was swift and commanding, but there was no threat of violence concealed in the movement of his lips. Heat burst on her skin and he swallowed her cry of surprise, gentling his lips to taste hers. As quickly as it had come, it was over and he stepped back, smiling into her eyes. "Oh, yes, réiltín, you would submit."

Saoirse snatched her hand back and stared at her wrist, certain she would find her flesh reddened from the heat of his touch. The fog receded and she narrowed her eyes in affront. "What is it the MacCrohan has of yours that you would stoop to such depths?" she snapped.

"My sister."

"What?" she exclaimed. "Kidnapped?"

"Yes. And Orlaith is not the only one. Several of the females in my colony have gone missing. Orlaith was the last to be taken, and I have discovered that MacCrohan and his men are behind it. What he wants with them, I do not know, but I can only imagine the worst. I intend to find them and bring them home. With their pelts." His eyes sobered and she felt a lump rise in her throat. "They will wither without them. They will not die, but they will live in misery if I cannot return them to the sea. So you see, if I help you, then you must lead me to the MacCrohan and his bastards."

Saoirse staggered back until her legs hit the side of the small bed, forcing her to sit. It was fate, it had to be. The gods had led him to her because of the connection to the MacCrohan. This was truly the path the gods had set before her. To turn away from it...she could not imagine what would happen. The words left her mouth before she could call them back. "I said I would not lie with a man who was not my husband. And that is my vow. If this is what you will take in recompense for my help, then I suggest you...marry me." She stared up at him in question even as the fires of hope flared in her soul. "Marry me, selkie, and I will lie with you. And I will do everything I can to help you find your sister. You have my promise."

He said nothing, and her head reeled with the weight of her words. If she lay with him as husband and wife, there would be no way her father could force her into a union with the MacCrohan. "Please," she said, her voice strained to her own ears. "If we marry, then my father-"

"Can't give you to the MacCrohan," he finished. Ronan's brow furrowed. "Are you a virgin, little one?"

Shocked, she stammered, "I-I don't see what that-"

"Are you a virgin?" he repeated. "If you return home with a husband and the covenant of the marriage bed, will he still force this upon you?"

"No." She shook her head. "My father is an honorable man. If I return with you, he would not. His pride would not allow it. He would not turn me over knowing that I have been with another. He is likely to disown me, but that is a risk I am willing to take. I will not marry the MacCrohan. Ever."

"You are spirited, little star. But you must know this. Once I have my sister and the others, along with their pelts, you will return mine," he flicked his eyes softly, "and I will leave you to return to the sea. Can you accept that?" Ronan's dark head shook with conviction. "As you will not be bound to the MacCrohan, I will not be bound to the land. I have no wish to remain human forever." He moved to stand over her, his hand once again caressing the side of her face. "Humans can be cruel. And it will be known when I leave you. Can you withstand the shame? Because shamed you will be. No decent man will want you, and the men who do will not be worth having."

Tears sprang forth at his words, not because they cut, but because they rang with truth.

"You're torn. You want to marry for love."

Saoirse's voice trembled, despite the heat of the fire. "Are you reading my mind, selkie?"

Ronan smiled in a breathtaking slide of lips as he shook his head. "I'm reading your face. Your notion of love is that of a woman. Love is fluid, like the waves of the sea, writhing and cresting until it reaches the shore and breaks apart into a thousand pieces."

"What are you saying? That love is fruitless, because it can be destroyed?"

He chuckled, the low rumble shooting straight to the base of her spine. "No. I'm saying that like a wave, I can break you apart and make you come undone. It would be worth the shame."

Her breath caught in her throat at the surety behind his words. She bit her lip and nodded in silence. "Yes," she croaked. "I can live with that. The alternative is not an option."

He knelt in front of her and gathered her hands in his. "Then yes, little star, I will marry you. I will marry you and take you to bed as my wife."

She wiped the tears away with the back of her hand, stood, and sniffed. "Then we have an agreement, selkie?"

He smiled and she felt the flutter in her belly again. "Yes, I believe we do."

Chapter Three

Ronan couldn't help the twinge that curled his lip as he watched her rebuild the fire. The night breeze gusted in gentle puffs to stoke the orange flames into the sky. Where she struggled before, it seemed her gods were with her now.

She straightened, dusting the palms of her hands on her breeches before turning toward the dark horse. Her hands were quick and sure as she pulled two lengths of long fabric from one of the saddle packs and turned toward Ronan. She stopped short in front of him, reaching for his hand.

"Now," she began, leading them both toward the fire, "this will have to do. I haven't any other cord." She suppressed a small smile. "I didn't think I'd be getting married on this journey, or I would have packed better." She didn't wait for him to reply before knotting the wool scarves together. "There," she said, arranging the fabric over his wrist, "grab my right hand with yours. And the same with the left." Ronan kept quiet, but did as instructed. She managed to pull the fabric over both their hands. "It's not perfect, but it will do. Now—"

"Just a moment," he interrupted, smiling at the surprise in her eyes. "Am I to know my future wife's name? Or will it be terms of whispered endearment forever?"

She blinked as a blush crept into her cheeks. "Saoirse." Her voice was soft. "It's Saoirse. I am the daughter of the Ó'Laighin."

It must have been the heat from the fire that caused his voice to shake, because he hardly recognized the husky sound of his words. "I am honored, Saoirse."

She smiled in response, her beautiful face glowing in the firelight. Saoirse's eyes darted toward their bound hands and she raised them up in offering. "As this knot is tied, so our lives are now bound." She paused, her eyes finding his. "You are blood of my blood, and bone of my bone. I give you my body, that we two shall be one. I give you my spirit, until our life shall be done."

Her voice was steady as she spoke, and the cheeky squeeze she gave his fingers as she finished started a warmth that spread through his chest. He squeezed back and was pleased to see her lips part on a small gasp. His words found strength as he spoke. "You are blood of my blood, and bone of my bone. I give you my body, that we two shall be one. I give you my spirit, until our life shall be done."

$$\mathcal{S}\mkern-4mu\mathcal{S}\mkern-4mu\mathcal{S}$$

He had spoken the vows like a man with every intention on keeping them, but Saoirse's heart knew otherwise. It didn't matter now. She was married, like it or not. They had taken the vow before the gods, spoken the words and completed the ceremony. All that was left now was… Her eyes lingered on the blanket-covered bed in the corner and she swallowed, glad that her face was turned from him as he set to building the fire in the brazier. Weren't most brides nervous on their wedding night? She picked at the tie on her shirt, unsure of what to do with her hands at the moment. Unbidden tears sprang to her eyes. This was not how she had envisioned it. Shouldn't there be laughter and excitement? A hope for the future? Love? She had none of those things.

Anger tore through her tears and she cursed her father and the MacCrohan. It was their fault she was here, pigeon-holed into this situation. She might have had hope for those things. Now she was resigned to keeping her word and giving her body to a man she did not love. All in exchange for her freedom. Saoirse closed her eyes as her trembling fingers went to work on the ties again, this time able to pull the tiny knot free.

"You should let me assist you."

Her eyes flew open at the sound of Ronan's voice. He watched her with quiet interest as the fire burned in the background, the chill of the room already dissipating. Her hands fell to her sides as he moved forward, filling her field of vision with the wide expanse of his shoulders.

"Are you frightened of me, little star?"

She couldn't manage a verbal response, only shook her head in dissent. Ronan chuckled and brushed the pad of his thumb across her cheekbone, his palm cupping the side of her face.

"Good. I'd much rather you not be afraid. Nervous, I understand." His lashes fluttered. "But fear has no place in my bed. A point in my favor over the MacCrohan, I'd wager."

Saoirse blew out the breath she hadn't realized she'd been holding and stiffened. "I do not fear —"

"No, of course not," he smiled. "You fear little. Not even the scaly clutches of a man such as him." Ronan's fingers captured the loose tie and pulled it completely free. Her lower lip caught between her teeth as he pulled her forward and slid a hand beneath the fabric to rest on the bare skin of her torso. "Soft," he murmured, dipping his head to her lips. "Warm." The press of his lips on hers was drugging with its heat. Nerves snapped to attention, awakened from slumber, her body acutely aware of every patch of bare skin. Aware because now it was alive with sensation at his touch, tingling and ready for more. She stepped closer, breaching the gap between them to collide her chest with his. Saoirse felt his lips ghost into a smile as he pulled back, the dark blue of his eyes glittering in amusement. "She wants," he said on a breath, swooping down again for another kiss. "Good."

At the second pass of his lips, all Saoirse could do was curl her fingers into the corded muscle of his upper arms and hang on under the slow, meticulous assault on her senses. Ronan held her firmly in his grasp, aligning them from chest to thigh as his mouth moved in dragging, hot slides over her flesh. She broke free, gasping for air, resting her forehead on his chest. Everything was a swirl in her mind, overwhelmed with sensory information, and she sagged against him for support.

"Easy, réiltín, I've got you." He turned her toward the bed, easing her down. Long fingers stroked her face as he cooed softly, hushed whispers reaching her ears.

She willed her body to relax, but didn't release her hold on him. "I'm sorry," she whispered. "It's too much...I—"

"Shhh," he said, placing a finger over her lips. "I know. All I ask is that you trust me." Blue eyes bored into hers with intensity. "I promise you, if you trust me, I will take care of you." Ronan's fingers tilted her chin upward. "Can you trust me, Saoirse? Can you open that warrior heart of yours to me?"

She was surprised to hear his hiss of indrawn breath as she leaned up and boldly fused her lips to his. Her answer was well-received. Ronan growled and thrust his hands in her hair, his fingers tangling in the long locks to hold her in place. He kissed her with purpose, not force, she realized. His lips and mouth moved in a determined order, their movements setting off a chain reaction of want and desire that had her gasping again in seconds.

He took her shortness of breath in stride, taking the opportunity to divest himself of his shirt and breeches before covering her body with his. Between the fluttering of her lids and the flickering of the fire's embers, she only saw brief flashes of tanned, smooth skin. The urge to look was quickly overridden by the need to feel as Ronan's long fingers worked their magic wherever they landed. She arched into his touch, her body acclimating to his hardness and doing its best to accommodate it.

She tensed as he worked the shirt over her head, baring her chest to him, but his lips were back on hers before the garment hit the floor, distracting and teasing, focusing her attention. His palms were hot and smooth on her breasts, her sudden gasp swallowed by the thrust of his tongue in her mouth. Saoirse moaned into him and melted into his touch, unable to anchor herself, yet unable to pull away. Ronan was a maelstrom, a squall on the open sea of her soul, pulling her under with each heated caress.

His breath rasped in her ear, his murmured words of encouragement hot and wet, exciting. She opened her mouth to speak and grazed his cheek, the taste of salt and spice on his skin bursting onto her lips. He groaned at the tentative press of her tongue on his flesh and hooked his hands beneath her to rid her of the rest of her clothing.

Her arms wound around his neck of their own accord, pulling him closer, her body seeking out every point of contact. It was the slide of skin on skin, the hard press of flesh on flesh, the yield of soft against firm that had her head thrashing from side to side, her fingers tangling with Ronan's as he urged the last point between them to the juncture of her thighs.

Saoirse's eyes flew open to find his, dark and hungry with pleasure. She felt his fingers, blunt and seeking at her center. She drew in a deep breath and relaxed, allowing him access. Ronan's touch was like fire, searing heat that spread out to her limbs, burning and scorching as it passed. His thumb rubbed in tiny circles over her swollen sex and she cried out, her body tightening in anticipation. He continued for a few moments more with the delicious torture before something larger replaced his fingers.

Ronan bent over her with soothing hands, stroking her legs and hips as he inched forward. Her body gave resistance and she balked, but he hushed her with kisses.

"Relax, little star. I know. I'll go as easy as I can. Hold onto me."

She nodded into his neck and placed her hands around his arms, hanging on for all she was worth. "I'm alright," she whispered. "I trust you, Ronan."

As soon as the words fell from her lips, his fingers tightened on her hips, and his mouth fastened on hers. Ronan's body surged forward, sliding into her with one sharp thrust.

There was a moment of pain, brief and intense. She felt him still within her, as he peppered her face and neck with soft kisses. His hands roamed her body, skipping over her skin with feather-light touches. Fingers and palms caressed every dip and hollow, lighting up nerves along the way. As quickly as it had come, the pain receded, leaving her with a strange fullness and an ache in her belly.

Ronan shifted and she gasped in pleasure, wriggling to get him to move again. He groaned and pressed her hips to the bed, stilling her movements. "Easy, Saoirse. Give it time."

She panted, trailing her fingers along his sweat-slick skin. "Please. I-I need…Oh, Ronan!" she cried. Saoirse panted and bucked against him, needing more of the desperate friction, wanting him to move, to do something, anything which would create more of the sweet fire that was flooding her lower body. She was caught as he moved, trapped beneath the weight of his body, loving the feel of each heated stroke within her.

Ronan moaned, a deep throaty sound that seemed to come from his toes. Her hands reached out to grab on to his hips, clutching with greedy curls of her fingers. She threw her head back and cried out, unable to form words.

"So responsive," he croaked, keeping the pace, "Stay with me, little one." He grabbed for her hands and entwined their fingers, pulling her arms over her head, pinning her in place. In an instinctive gesture, her thighs fell apart and her knees curled up, bracing herself against each snap of his hips.

Over and over, like waves battered against rocks, the swell of pleasure came high and hard, and all she could do was ride out the storm. Ronan continued the relentless pace, the lines of his muscled neck taut under the strain. He murmured low under his breath, in a language she didn't understand. Her body was able to decipher exactly what he meant and she matched each thrust with an arch of her own, causing his eyes to darken and his lip to curl in a feral snarl.

The crest was building, deep inside in places never before touched, and she wanted what lay on the other side. Dark curls fell across his beautiful face as his head dipped low to capture her lips in a biting kiss. At the salty press of his hard lips, the dam of sensation burst, spiraling outward in a quaking torrent of waves as she came.

The cry that was ripped from her throat was unrecognizable to her ears, but he heard it and growled in triumph, thrusting harder to bring her over. He pumped for another few blinding seconds, and then stiffened, baying out her name in a gravelly moan. Slowly he stilled, relaxing against her to bury his face in her neck, continuing to gently kiss and nibble at the tender flesh. She shuddered with tiny aftershocks, her body melting bonelessly into his.

Ronan shifted his weight to the side and withdrew, pulling her into his arms, tightening around her like a protective cocoon. She gave in, snuggling in closer, smiling as he whispered in her ear. The language of the selkies felt soft and lovely on her skin. Idly, she wondered if they would be together long enough to learn it. It was the last thought she had before sleep claimed her.

Chapter Four

"Selkies and the MacCrohan?" The Ó'Laighin's voice was like ice. "This is the story you return with?"

Ronan's hand tightened on hers. "She speaks the truth."

Her father's head whipped around to lock angry eyes on Ronan. "I will deal with you in time. Think you can take my daughter and expect a warm welcome?"

The selkie returned the chief's steely gaze. "I took nothing that was not offered to me willingly."

The Ó'Laighin's eyes widened on his daughter. "Is this true, Saoirse? You have given yourself to this man?"

Saoirse took a deep breath and lifted her chin. "Aye. He has taken what is his by right." She threw the knotted fabric at his feet. "We hand fasted over a Lughnasadh fire. We made a vow to the gods. We are married. I am Ronan's wife."

"You shame me, Saoirse," her father began. "You shame this house and my good name. You do this in defiance. You might as well have spit on your mother's grave, the gods rest her soul. You know-"

"There is no time for this," Ronan interrupted. "Even now the MacCrohan works against us all. I don't know what he wants with the selkies, but he has not stopped, nor do I think he will. He will take everything here for his own design, and if you do not move against him, he will succeed."

"Enough!" The Ó'Laighin roared, "I will not hear-"

The double doors of the assembly room burst open in a clatter, and Carrick and Fergal rushed in with swords drawn.

"Áthair!" Carrick shouted, "The MacCrohan's are back! With greater numbers! We are under attack!"

The Ó'Laighin whirled on his daughter. "Get you to safety. I don't want to find you on this battlefield." He locked eyes with Ronan. "Can you wield a sword?"

"Aye."

"Then find one," her father sniffed. "If you can take my daughter under the cover of darkness, then you can damn sure defend her people in the light of day."

Ronan nodded. He squeezed Saoirse's hand and pressed a kiss to her lips. "Do as he says. Get to safety."

Saoirse's eyes widened. "You?" she said with conviction. "You wish to fight, selkie?"

"The little star is spirited," Ronan chuckled. "Aye." He reached out to tuck an errant gold strand behind her ear before dropping another quick kiss on her mouth. "It appears I am to prove myself. I am adept with a blade. Do not worry. Make no mistake, réiltin. Selkie I may be, but I am no stranger to the desires of man. A man will fight for what is his. A smooth sea never made a skilled mariner."

She had only a second to process his words before her father shoved him toward the doors.

"Out of sight, daughter," he called over his shoulder. "The MacCrohan has shed the last drop of our blood." They were gone, leaving Saoirse with a lump in her throat and an uneasy feeling in her chest. She turned to head back to her room upstairs, but at the last minute turned and headed for the stables. *It wouldn't do to start listening now, would it?*

The fires in the fields raged again, although how they burned was a mystery, the earth already scorched from previous raids. It seemed the MacCrohan was prepared to burn them to dust if needed. She went unseen among the rushing of warriors, their attention claimed by the fields and the myriad of fights across the courtyards. Her sword remained where she had left it, sheathed and tied to Fergal's black stallion. In her father's anger at her return, the horse had yet to be tended.

She grabbed the sheath and strapped it to her body, picking up a discarded practice shield on the way out. It was not optimal, but it was better than nothing. As she emerged from the stables, she could see her father's forces once again driving back the raid. They would hold them off. Her eyes caught a familiar flash of dark hair and she watched as Ronan cut his way through a group of three MacCrohan, hacking and slicing until they lay before him in a bloody heap.

She paused at the sounds of violence, then pressed onward. Her path was cut off by the point of a sword thrust in her face, but she managed to bring up the shield and block the attack. Saoirse dropped to her knees and pulled the sword free, slicing at the dirty bare knees in front of her. A strangled cry escaped her target as he crumpled to the ground, immobilized. She felt nothing but ice in her veins as she raised the tip of the blade and delivered the killing blow, stabbing straight into his heart.

Yanking the blade free, she regained her footing and began to run. "Ronan!" she called out, not registering the sound of hooves behind her.

Ronan's eyes were panicked as they found her and his mouth opened to scream, when the pounding of hooves finally reached her ears. She watched as Ronan's face went from surprise to rage and his body lurched toward her. Seconds later, she felt herself lifted from the ground and slung over the back of a saddle.

She managed to push herself upright and look into the face of her kidnapper. MacCrohan. Saoirse screamed and her hands came up to claw at him, but he was faster, the back of his fist connecting with her jaw in a burst of pain. Ronan's eyes flashed in her vision before everything went dark.

ॐ ॐ ॐ

Ronan scrambled across the field, dragging the bloodied blade behind him. He whirled as a rough hand grabbed at him, pulling back a fist.

"Easy, man!" Saoirse's father yelled, focusing his attention.

"He's taken Saoirse!" he shouted.

"What?"

"The MacCrohan!" Ronan exclaimed. "He's snatched her across the back of his horse. That's why they're leaving! He's gotten what they came for!"

"Bastard!" The Ó'Laighin called out for his sons, who came straggling with blackened blades of their own.

"I'm going after her," Ronan said. "After her and the selkies."

The chief nodded. "We must regroup. I need to see what he has cost me this time. Go. Find my daughter. Keep her safe until we come." He motioned to Fergal. "Get him a mount, now!"

Fergal said nothing, but turned and headed for the stables at a dead run. He returned in seconds with the black stallion and handed the reins to Ronan. "He's fast, but he needs a strong hand, or he'll buck you off in seconds. He's a right ornery bastard, this one."

Ronan strapped the sword to the saddle and swung himself into the seat. The stallion reared, but Ronan pulled tightly on the reins, gaining control of the horse.

"I mean it, selkie. You keep her safe, or I swear by the gods, I'll have your head on my wall." The Ó'Laighin glared up at him.

"I just found her. I'm not about to let her go now." He turned the stallion and dug in his heels and took off.

"Áthair?" Fergal said, confused. "Who is that?"

The Ó'Laighin snorted. "Your brother-in-law."

෪ ෪ ෪

The MacCrohan stronghold was an easy thing to find, slung out on a high outcropping of cliffs overlooking the sea. Ronan dismounted and staked out the horse, taking the sword and sneaking his way in among a narrow stone passage far from the massive front walls. The noise was deafening on the inside, shouting and the clang of metal echoing off stone. Celebratory. Victorious.

Ronan crept to a set of back stairs, leading downward past the great room to what he hoped was the dungeon. Knowing the MacCrohan, it was likely that he had stashed Saoirse and the others here until he had need of them. *Kept like livestock*. Rage clouded his vision. Bastard. He would pay.

It should have surprised him that it wasn't Orlaith or the others that sprang to the forefront of his mind, but Saoirse. Saoirse with her halo of golden hair laid out in tangles on the pillow, her angelic face skewed in passion, her long limbs twined with his, her breathy pleas tugging at his heart. She was artful in her innocence, seductive in her enthusiasm. Awakening her had been a pleasure; he knew it would be, but he hadn't expected to be this enchanted with her. Not once since their coupling had the sealskin entered his mind, nor was the need to have it back clawing at his insides. Instead, his soul yearned for only one thing. Saoirse.

With a fierceness he could not deny, he realized he would have to make a choice. There would be no way he could have both Saoirse and his freedom. He could stay with her as her husband and forsake his ties to the sea, or return and leave behind the one thing his heart clamored for. But could she love him? The only reason they were bound in the first place was the MacCrohan. If he were defeated, then there would be no reason for her to want him any longer. She said herself she could live with the shame if he abandoned her. What if she were the one to choose to leave?

Lost in his thoughts, he didn't hear the scrape of boots behind him, nor did he see the fist flying through the air until it was too late.

Chapter Five

"Put him next to the others. Let him see what he has come for." The MacCrohan's voice filtered in through the small hole in the door, rousing Saoirse. She scrambled to her feet to peek through, and watched as two men thrust Ronan's limp body into the cell across from her and slam the door. Her protest was cut off by the MacCrohan's face filling her vision.

"Pay him no mind, chieftain's daughter. He will not survive to see next light," he sneered. Rheumy eyes raked over her face with a leer. "Do not trouble yourself over him. This should be a happy time for you. Every bride should be happy on her wedding day." He laughed, cruel and taunting.

"I would see you dead first," she spat.

The MacCrohan smiled, revealing a crooked row of ugly yellow teeth. "Keep it up, and you'll get your chance, lovely. It will be a pleasure breaking you."

"Never!" she shot back. His laughter trailed as he walked down the corridor.

"You're wasting your breath," a feminine voice sounded from her left. Saoirse craned her neck to look across at the cell next to Ronan's. "He'll get what he wants from you, or he'll kill you. It's that simple. Heed my words."

"Who are you?" she whispered. From her limited view, she could only see pale skin and dark eyes, and the hint of long black hair. But even from this distance, it finally dawned on her to whom she was speaking. "Orlaith?"

The face nodded. "Yes. How do you know me?"

"I don't. They have just brought in your brother. He's next to you. He followed me here."

"Ronan?" Orlaith's voice was sharp. "What?" Saoirse could see the shake of her head. "How is it possible?"

"It's a story for another time. We have to get out of here. Are you alone in there?"

"No," she said. "There are four of us. The others are sleeping now. They needed rest. His men came for them when they returned from battle. I've been tending their wounds."

"Wounds?" Saoirse gasped. "They're hurt?"

"Nothing that won't heal," Orlaith said grimly. "The MacCrohan and his men are not gentle."

Saoirse paled as her words became clear. If she didn't get them out of here, she would be resigned to the same fate. That would not happen. She would die first, or at least die trying.

The scrape of boot on stone caught her attention and Saoirse looked back down the corridor to see one of the guards headed her way, keys jingling from the belt of his breeches. He stopped short in front of her door and licked his lips.

"The chief's packed himself off to bed for now. Don't suppose he'll take offense iff'n I sample a bit of what's to be passed around anyway."

"Get away from me," Saoirse snarled.

He tutted and shook his filthy head. "Now that's no way to be, now is it? I can offer you a ride like you've never dreamed." He fumbled with keys and her heart sank as she heard the tumble of the lock.

Think, Saoirse, think. She backed up from the door and allowed it to swing open. He ambled inside and her stomach rolled as the stench of his unwashed body permeated the small cell. Her hand came up to the tie on her shirt and she pulled, revealing a large amount of her pale flesh to his view.

"That's more like it," he huffed. "Take it off." She hesitated, and his hand went to the dagger on the other side of his belt. "Take it off, or I'll slice it off you. A little blood isn't going to bother me."

She swallowed and tugged the shirt off, throwing it to the floor. He laughed and came forward, reaching for her with stubby, grimy hands. The second he was in range, she brought her foot up and kicked him squarely in the groin.

"Bitch!" he shouted, doubling over in pain. She rushed at him, knocking him off balance to the ground. Her litheness gave her the edge she needed. She slipped the dagger from his belt and plunged it into the soft expanse of his belly. The resulting gush of blood was warm on her fingers and she pushed harder, grinding the dagger to the hilt.

The guard fumbled for her hands, trying to dislodge them, but to no avail. Saoirse yanked the blade free with a satisfying sucking sound and brought it up to thrust into his exposed throat. He went down hard with a sick gurgle and she staggered back to retch in the corner. She heaved once more and righted herself, grabbing his keys and her discarded shirt.

Fearing another guard could appear at any moment, she shrugged it on in haste and headed across the corridor. She struggled with the keys for a second, the right one finally slipping home on the lock to Ronan's cell. He roused as she entered, confusion and fog ghosting over his eyes.

"Saoirse?"

"There's no time. Your sister and the others are here. We have to get out and get back to Áthair," she said in a rush, helping him to his feet. His hand slipped from her bloody one and his eyes widened.

"Are you hurt?"

"No," she said, pushing him to the door. "He meant to rape me," she nodded her head to the dead man in her cell. "I wasn't about to give up without a fight. Come on."

"Your father is coming. He'll be here with reinforcements. We need to get to the MacCrohan."

She rushed to unlock Orlaith's door and the women tumbled out, Orlaith reaching to embrace her brother. Loud shouts and the roar of voices suddenly kicked up from nowhere, and the sound of men calling to arms was unmistakable.

"He's here!" Ronan's sister shouted. "We must go!"

They barreled up the stairs as a group, spilling out into the middle of the fray. Chaos reigned in a clash of swords and shouting as MacCrohan and Ó'Laighin forces came together in a wall of man and metal. Saoirse caught sight of her father engaged in combat. The rush hit her hard and she snatched up a discarded sword, ready to head into the fight. Ronan grabbed for Orlaith and the others and ushered them into Fergal's waiting arms. Fergal quickly whisked them out a side entrance to waiting horses. She got a brief glimpse of them as they mounted and Carrick appeared, tall and lithe on horseback, turning to lead them to safety.

Fergal followed, but not before kicking up a fallen sword and throwing it to Ronan. "Go!" he shouted. "Carrick will get them home. Stay with Saoirse and the Ó'Laighin!"

Ronan nodded and ran back to her. They fought side by side for several long moments, the bodies of the MacCrohan warriors falling easily under the surprise attack. Saoirse kicked and hacked her way across the common room as the rest of the fighters in the room funneled out into the open for better vantage points.

A loud shout from above made her blood run cold and she looked up to see MacCrohan himself, tousled from sleep, with anger creasing the lines of his craggy face. "No!" he shouted from the balcony. "Cut them down! Every last one!"

The bellow of rage she heard erupt from her father made her turn, and she watched as the Ó'Laighin fought his way to the stairs, intent on heading for his enemy. She ran, leaving Ronan behind to intercept him. The MacCrohan moved, faster than she thought the old man could have moved, reaching to snarl his gnarled fist into her hair. She cried out in pain, the surprise giving the older man time to knock the sword from her hands and drag her back up the stairs.

"Saoirse!" Ronan's howl was a battle cry of stormy wrath, born of blinding seas and deadly riptides, its current spreading out in waves of destruction. She looked up to see the MacCrohan's eyes blow wide with the knowledge of what exactly he had unleashed.

Ronan's blade flew in a flurry of steel, clanging off metal, crunching off bone, shredding anything fleshed in his way. Bodies fell under his blade like a house of cards blown apart by blustering winds as he came. His lip curled in a deadly snarl as the MacCrohan's dagger appeared at her throat, the tip pressing in to pierce her skin. She hissed and jerked, causing the cut to go deeper.

The warning did nothing to dissuade Ronan and he advanced like a man possessed, uncaring of what damage occurred before he made his final move. His bluff called, the MacCrohan shoved her body in front of his like a shield, but Ronan kept coming.

"I'll kill her!" he shouted down at Ronan, panic and desperation tinging the rough timbre of his voice.

Three more men fell under the bloody blade of the maddened selkie as he bounded the stairs two at a time, bellowing, "It will be your head either way, MacCrohan! Dead or alive! But if you kill her, I promise it will be slow!"

Before the chief could form a retort or implement a new diversion tactic, Ronan was on them. He came with the force of a typhoon, swirling devastation and writhing winds, blade high with purpose. Saoirse ducked, wincing as the flat of the dagger sliced through her throat as she went down, and slammed her elbow into the MacCrohan's midsection. The air rushed from his lungs in a hearty wheeze, his grip slipping on her arm as he gasped. She dropped to her knees, tucked her head to her chest and launched herself toward the stairs.

Ronan barked out a last shout of triumph and jumped just as she rolled under his feet. She tumbled down the flight of steps and hit the landing, just in time to see the point of Ronan's blade come down into the middle of the MacCrohan's chest. His scream of "No!" was cut short into nothing more than a sick sputter as blood gushed from his chest and bubbled from his lips. Ronan's shoulder twisted and he drove the blade deeper, pushing through the chief's body to protrude from his back, slamming the MacCrohan to the stone floor. There was a sickening snap of steel as the point hit stone and shattered.

The room went quiet as the MacCrohan wheezed with the death rattle, all attention on Ronan as he pushed back from the body with a sneer. He yanked the blade free with a grunt, wiping a bloody hand across his brow as he descended the few steps, and reached down to hoist Saoirse into his arms. Swords clattered to the floor and a low rumble of awe snaked its way through the remaining MacCrohan warriors. The men parted as they passed, dropping to one knee in deference.

Her father rushed forward to help lower her to her feet, sliding one arm around her waist for support as Ronan did the same on the other side. There was a shuffling of boot on stone as one warrior came forward, unarmed, with a grim countenance.

"You've killed him," the man said. "You've killed my father. I would avenge him."

Ronan snorted. "Then you would perish in your efforts. Is that the legacy you intend to leave? Your father was a cruel man who met the fate he deserved. If you wish to challenge me, do it now while you have your best chance. Because if you wait, it will be painful. Painful and bloody. And you will not defeat me."

The man's jaw set in a hard line as he considered Ronan's words. His eyes flicked from the selkie to Saoirse's father and back again before he dropped with his kin, lowering his eyes to the floor. "What was his is now yours. I will not oppose you."

"Then, it is my right to do as I wish with you?" Ronan asked.

"Aye."

Ronan motioned for the Ó'Laighin to come forward. "You will swear your fealty to this man. I have no use for you. I came for what is mine, and I will return with it. All that you are now belongs to the Ó'Laighin. You are his to deal with as he sees fit. I suggest you take what he offers you and be grateful. I think you will find him to be a better master than your father. Is that clear?"

"It shall be as you wish." The man turned his head and shouted at his kinsman. "Swear to the Ó'Laighin! Swear to him or you will face me!"

Rumbles of "Ó'Laighin!" rippled through the hall and outside, building into a crescendo before descending into silence.

Ronan gathered Saoirse up close to him, moving her toward the doors.

"I'll be taking her back. They're yours now."

The Ó'Laighin nodded. "Aye."

Chapter Six

Ronan wiped the last of the grime from his body and placed the flannel on the bedside table. Saoirse watched the emotion play across his face as he removed his clothing to sit naked on her bed.

"You leave at first light, then?" she asked, her heart turning over in her chest at the anticipation of his answer.

"Aye." The softness in his voice didn't match the tension she saw in his body.

It was inevitable. She knew it would come to this, had agreed to it in exchange for her freedom. Now that she had it, victory tasted hollow. Empty. She blinked back the tears that threatened to spring forth, reminding herself that she was a warrior. Not just a woman. She had offered him her word and now she had to be strong enough to keep it. She went to the chest and opened it, pulling the old pack from within.

"I had it brought up here when we returned," she said in explanation, digging through the bag.

"What?"

She turned and held out the sealskin. "This. Didn't you know it was here?"

He let out a low laugh laced with pain. "Would you believe I didn't?"

"No."

Ronan stood and came toward her, as naked and proud as the night he stepped from the sea, taking the skin from her and placing it without a thought on the table. "I didn't."

"But I thought you knew where it was, if you were close. You said before you could feel it before."

"I can. But my mind has been elsewhere lately."

She blushed. "Oh."

"Aye."

If she didn't say something now, she knew the courage would never return. Even though he had no intention of staying, it would kill her if he left without knowing. "I don't want you to go."

"I know."

"But I know you cannot stay." She shook her head, this time letting the tears come, uncaring if they showed her weakness. Something far greater than embarrassment was at work in her heart at this moment, and she was not about to let it slip away. "So, I will not try to stop you. Our agreement is finished." She lifted her chin. "And I accept the consequences." She moved closer and placed a hand on the hard plane of his chest, relishing his intake of breath at the contact. "But only if you take me to your bed as your wife one last time. Leave me if you will, but leave me with that."

He paused as if to speak, but all that came out was a strangled growl as he hauled her to him and crushed her mouth to his.

"Saoirse." It was a whisper of breath, a sound so low her ears almost missed it.

She wound her arms around his neck, bringing their bodies flush, returning the fierce kiss for all she was worth. If it was only to be one last time, she wanted to etch him into her soul, let every part of him seep into her bones. It would keep her warm on cold nights, light fires in her heart when the loneliness became too much to bear.

Ronan's mouth slanted on hers, hot, wet and insistent. She felt his hands grip and pull, tearing the shirt from her body to fall to the floor in scraps. Saoirse's fingers tangled with his to remove her breeches in one quick pass. Once bare, he turned her in his arms, pushing her down on the bed to cover her with the solidness of his naked body, hard and pulsing with want.

She panted, writhing beneath him, her hands skipping over his skin, soaking in the sensation. His touch was like fire, burning her from the inside out, setting her ablaze with need. This was what she wanted, this frenzy, this fierce expression of emotion, designed to combust and consume. She wanted to be overwhelmed. She needed to be dragged under and crashed against the rocks. Anything less would be hollow, empty.

Emboldened to anchor the memory in her heart, she pushed, letting her hands roam and explore. He relaxed, moaning into her mouth, only to gasp sharply as her fingers curled around the rigid length of his cock. She squeezed, marveling at the dichotomy in textures, soft and hard, like velvet over steel.

"Enough!" he groaned, stilling her hand to press biting kisses over her shoulder and over her breasts. She arched as his mouth fastened over the taut peak of a hardened nipple, her body pooling with liquid fire as he sucked. He lavished it with attention for a few seconds more before sliding down her body to lick at the hollow of her navel, nipping with tiny caresses.

"Ronan!" Her head shook from side to side in wild abandon as he found the center of her being with his mouth, slipping his tongue within the folds of her sex to tease her with its tip. Sweat blossomed on her skin as heat and pleasure suffused her limbs, her nerves alive and quaking with the tremble of desire.

He groaned in approval from between her thighs, his focus attuned to the tiny nub that seemed to be connected to every point on her body. Need spiraled in waves, cascading down with thunderous force, pinning her in place under the weight of the tide.

Her hands carded through his hair, her fingers digging into his scalp, and his breath hitched as a low moan escaped him and vibrated over her greedy flesh. She arched again, helpless under the strain, her body ready to break apart into oblivion. Saoirse cried out as her world splintered under his mouth, the breathless tide finally carrying her home. She quaked beneath him and he kissed his way back up her body, his hot length finding her core and slipping inside on a heated growl.

She hissed at the new sensation, the fullness only adding to the tremors of pleasure. He thrust hard, seating himself to the hilt, and rocked against her. Her hips snapped up to meet his as he began a rhythm, dark and compelling, and gave herself over, clinging to him for purchase.

Ronan slammed into her, stroke after stroke, deep, guttural noises working their way from his throat as he moved. He gripped her hard, holding her to him as if she would drift away, fusing them together. Faster and faster, he drove into her, rocking them both on the bed. One last growl and he was gone, his climax taking him over.

He collapsed against her, sweaty and heavy, murmuring softly in her ear. Her arms twined around him without a thought, her body needing the weight and the contact. She held him like that until his breathing evened when sleep claimed him. Only then did she allow more tears to fall.

Sunlight broke through the window, bathing her face in warmth. Saoirse reached out, feeling only emptiness beside her. He was gone. Her heart lurched in her throat as she sat up and looked around the room. All trace of him was gone.

She shot out of the bed and dressed, hoping she wasn't too late. Maybe there would be time for one last goodbye. No pleading, she had long since reconciled herself to that, but to see him one last time...

The stallion's hooves pounded over the ground, kicking up grass and mud as they galloped. In the distance, she could see the tendrils of smoke on the horizon. Lughnasadh fires. The gods. Her prayers. It was too much to hope for.

As she came closer to the hut, she reined the stallion to a halt, dismounted and started at a dead run, praying she would find what she hoped for. Saoirse ran faster, her feet moving swiftly up the rise and down to the beach. As she crested and saw the frothy caps of the sea, he came into view.

Ronan.

Grass turned to sand, impeding her gait and she slowed, panting. The fire burned; hot and high, bright orange flames flickered skyward like a beacon calling to her. Ronan faced out to the sea, the sealskin clutched tightly in his hand.

"Ronan!"

He turned, his eyes as clear as the sea behind him. "Saoirse."

She stopped short in front of him, the words she carefully mulled over in her mind suddenly gone.

He shook his head, the war in his heart evident in his gaze. "I cannot go. The sea calls to me, but I cannot answer. I cannot leave you." The beginning of a smile quirked at the corner of his lips. "You have bewitched me, little star. I thought I could leave you and go back as if none of this had happened." He sighed. "I realize now that is impossible."

"What are you saying?" Her voice was breathless, hopeful.

"I once told you I would break you apart, but it is you who have broken me. I could never return and be whole." He reached up to caress her cheek. "I love the sea...but I love you more."

Saoirse launched herself at him, throwing her arms around his neck and pressing her lips to his. She pulled back and smiled. "I love you, too. I was prepared to let you go, but I couldn't let you go without saying goodbye."

"There is no goodbye, my love," he said, holding her close. "There is only the future."

"Then you will stay? Stay as my husband?"

"Aye." He grasped her hands in his and placed the sealskin in them. "Forever."

"We can live here," she said in a rush. "Make this place our home by the sea. So you can see it every day, so it will always be a part of you. We can raise our children here. Build a life and a family. Will you do that with me?" Her face broke in a wide smile. "Husband?"

"I would like that very much, wife. But only one thing remains." He looked down at the sealskin and then at the fire. "It must be destroyed." Ronan guided them to the fire's edge, away from the shore. He pressed a long, sweet kiss to her lips. "You are blood of my blood, and bone of my bone. I give you my body, that we two shall be one. I give you my spirit, until our life shall be done."

Saoirse slipped her arm around his waist as they held the sealskin to the fire. She rested her head on his chest and spoke, loud and clear, into the fire. "You are blood of my blood, and bone of my bone. I give you my body, that we two shall be one. I give you my spirit, until our life shall be done."

He pressed a kiss on the top of her head, and together they cast the sealskin into the flames.

Chapter One

Morgan looked around at the saplings he had planted in the spring. They were healthy and strong, he decided. Summer was virtually over and he could see the first signs of autumn around him. He was in tune with the forests, and he smiled as he gazed around. To say Morgan was in love with trees and all the things that grew and lived in forests was an understatement. They were his reason for living.

He ran his hand through his thick dark hair and sat down on a nearby fallen tree. The trunk was still thick where he sat, but it was fragile further along. The tree had fallen from age. This part of the forest that Morgan tended had some of the oldest trees in the country growing within it. Morgan liked to think it was because of him that they achieved such great age. He took out his thermos of coffee and poured himself a cup. A leaf sailed down from a nearby oak. It was a pale, golden-orange color, and it landed at Morgan's feet. He looked up at the vivid blue sky through the canopy of the trees around him.

"Give it another week, and there'll be more leaves falling," he said to the forest, and in answer a soft breeze ruffled the bright leaves of the nearby birch and Morgan's hair.

The breeze flew on through the forest and down into the nearby town. It played with a discarded chocolate biscuit wrapper, pressing the silver and purple paper up against a railing before flowing on. As Ava came down the steps of the town council office it lifted her skirt. It heralded autumn, and yet summer had not been kind that year. Ava would have liked a little more warmth before the end of September, but it didn't seem that was going to happen. It was just over a week to the autumn equinox, and Ava had noticed that already some trees in her garden were beginning to look a little less green and a little more golden.

She sighed, and her sigh was picked up by the soft breeze as it rounded the corner of the building and brushed her shoulder as she entered the car park. It took a tendril of her dark auburn hair, held back by a tortoiseshell comb, and wrapped it around her face. Ava pushed the hair back behind her ear and opened her car door. She threw her bag onto the passenger seat and slid her laptop case along behind it. She sat in her car for a few seconds, just looking out at the row of rose bushes that fringed the car park. The breeze was busy in the high street, where it had gathered speed and was whipping along a plastic bottle that once held spring water with a spritz of lemon.

Ava had driven home by the time the breeze had moved on down the valley to the next town. She opened the front door of her cottage, and after putting her bag and laptop down on the hall table, she shrugged off her jacket and stepped out of her high-heeled shoes.

Ava went straight into her kitchen and filled the kettle to make a cup of tea. As the water boiled for her tea, she ran up the stairs to her bedroom and changed into jeans and a jumper. She padded downstairs in her bare feet carrying a pair of socks, having decided to go for a walk. The meeting had been stressful, and she felt restless. She made her tea, and then sat down on one of the kitchen chairs to pull on her socks and the short boots she wore to walk.

She glanced at the digital clock inset in the glass door of the electric oven, and without drinking the tea she had made she picked up her keys and cell phone. She slipped them into her pocket and closed the cottage door with a small thud.

Ava lived only five minutes from her favorite walk. There was a path that crossed a field and then wound into the woods, and Ava took it. She liked the path through the field especially when the poppies grew wild as it lay fallow, but she didn't classify her favorite walk as such until she was in the woods.

Chapter Two

Morgan didn't feel the cold unless it was frosty, and he had his shirt off as he coppiced a small area of the trees in the forest close to the 'right of way' path. He had driven over from the part of the woods where he had taken his coffee break, and parked his Land Rover on the access lane that ran alongside the small area for coppicing.

He was humming a song that he had heard on the radio as he had driven, and was intent on the young tree before him as he cropped it close to the ground. He was coppicing this section of the ash early because he had been concerned about reports of disease in a forest in the next county.

The woods made the air cooler, and Ava was walking quickly when she saw Morgan. She slowed down as she approached the area of the woods where he worked. Unable to help herself, she stared at him. He was tall and muscled. His thick dark hair fell over his forehead as he worked and Ava slowed her pace a fraction more. She let herself gaze at him. He was very attractive. His waist tapered a little from his muscled chest and his jeans riding low on his hips gave her a view that almost took her breath away.

Ava was lonely if she let herself admit it. She didn't let herself very often because it led to bouts of looking amongst internet dating sites in the hopes that someone would catch her eye. No one ever did, and Ava would close her browser and go in search of a book to read, or a movie to watch.

Ava was passing Morgan when he paused in his task and looked up.

She could see his face and she felt her loneliness keenly then. The man was beautiful. She could see the angle of his jaw and the blue of his eyes quite clearly. She looked away and walked on, feeling a kind of desperation.

Morgan had been surprised when he had seen the young woman. Her hair was a darker shade of some copper beech tree leaves that grew by the side of his house door. He had seen the lightness of her eyes in contrast to her hair and found emotion in them. He watched her slender figure disappear up the path as it wound into the woods. He focused back on the tree stump before him, but felt confused. The woman had given him a prickle of anticipation as she stared at him. It was unfamiliar, and Morgan was uneasy as he continued his task.

He was careful and almost tender as he checked the trees over when he had finished the job. It was mid-afternoon, and Morgan thought he would sit amongst the older trees on the other side of the path and finish the coffee he had with him. He put away his tools and brought the thermos from his Land Rover to sit down amongst the ferns at the foot of a large, old, oak tree. He sighed with pleasure as he felt the bark against his back.

Morgan watched a squirrel run along a branch high up in a tree nearby as he drank the last of his coffee.

Ava had reached the edge of the forest and gone halfway into the old growth that adjoined a smallholding before turning back to walk the way she had come. She would normally have followed the path around where it looped and took her back home through another part of the woods. Ava wanted to see the man again. She was doubling back specifically to see him, and to have another look at this gorgeous man. Ava had to admit he was so lovely it made her sad to think she had no one. She especially had no one like him and she would so like to. She felt another strange wave of sadness.

Morgan had not expected the young woman to come back along the path. He knew that it was a path walkers took, which led away, and through the other side of the woods. Walkers usually followed it without coming back. He saw her as she came around the bend in the path and his heart flipped. It shocked him and he put his coffee cup down to watch her. The path would bring her only half a meter from his feet as he stretched his long, jean clad legs out, leaning against the beautiful oak tree.

Ava had been looking for him, and to find him there at her feet was almost frightening.

She faltered as she walked, and Morgan smiled at her.

"Hi. It's a lovely day for a walk."

Ava stopped, and with her heart thudding, she answered, "Yes, but the woods are always lovely." Her voice was throaty because she wanted Morgan and yet she was afraid. She didn't know how to act around him because he stirred such strong feelings within her.

Morgan liked the sound of her voice. Its softness melted his heart and his eyes darkened at her.

Ava gazed at him. He still wasn't wearing a shirt and as he pushed his hair away from his forehead, she experienced a wave of sexual longing so deep her eyes found the junction of his thighs. Then her stare settled on the bottom of his hard flat stomach where his jeans revealed a fine line of hair. Ava swallowed as she realized how low his jeans were cut.

Morgan felt a growing warmth as he realized she was openly admiring his body.

He grinned at her.

"Do you walk here a lot? I haven't seen you around, and yet I work in the forest often."

Ava relaxed. She had seen the big, black Land Rover with the National Trust logo on it. She smiled at Morgan in response.

"I walk here maybe twice a week. I missed last week because of the rain. The path gets very muddy quickly." She glanced around to the access road where Morgan had parked his vehicle. There were still large patches of mud.

Morgan stood up. "You're right, it does. It's because there's a tendency for the rainwater to stay pooled in places. The ground water table is a little variable in this forest."

Ava watched him as he stood up and stepped closer. She had never felt the kind of sexual attraction she felt right then. Morgan could feel it too. The young woman before him seemed to be radiating need, and he soaked it up. He liked it. He looked at her and he wanted to fold her in his arms and kiss her. It was a good feeling and one he hadn't felt for a long time.

They stared at each other. Morgan thought nothing of being without his shirt. Ava thought only of running her hands along his smooth skin, and perhaps even letting her fingertips follow that little line of fine dark hair that started low on his body and dipped into his jeans.

Chapter Three

Morgan was unwilling to break the spell that seemed to exist between himself and the young woman as they gazed at each other, and he felt the silence laden with sexual need. "My name's Morgan; Morgan Green," he said, and offered Ava his hand to shake.

Ava looked at his hand and then took it as she answered, "Ava; Ava McCartney." She whispered this, because the touch of Morgan's hand did actually give her some kind of jolt. It gave her a fluttery feeling in her stomach and a wetness between her legs. She wanted him so much it showed in her eyes.

Morgan's own eyes seemed to flood with affection as Ava looked into them. Morgan was feeling his need strongly. He couldn't help but notice the shape of her breasts in the soft sweater she wore, and he liked the way her hair fell around her shoulders and down her back. Her eyes were a gray-blue and she had a mouth made for kissing.

They both tried to pull themselves together at the same time.

Ava thought he must think she was bizarre the way she was staring at his body.

Morgan was worried she would see the growing bulge in his jeans and think he was some kind of sexual predator.

He bent and retrieved his thermos and coffee cup. Ava watched this and knew he might be preparing to leave.

"I'll take this to the Land Rover," he said nervously.

Ava nodded silently.

She walked with him, unwilling to lose his presence right then.

Morgan put his things into the back of the car and took his shirt from the seat. He put it on. "I work in the three forests that cross the county. Maybe I will see you again in this one." As he spoke, he desperately wanted to catch hold of Ava and kiss her.

Ava knew they were parting. She knew she may never see him again and it hurt. She looked down at the muddy ground where she stood next to the Land Rover and noticed a tiny patch of new grass growing. When she raised her eyes to Morgan's face, he could see her pain.

He closed his eyes and opened them again, hoping it would be gone from her eyes, but it wasn't. Not knowing how to handle this instant, deep attraction to Ava, Morgan took a deep breath, and opened the door of the Land Rover to get in and drive away. Ava stepped back and smiled sadly. She raised her hand in a little wave, turned, and began to walk down the path home. She heard the Land Rover start and the crunch of the tires as Morgan navigated the access road that led away from the path. It would go deeper into the woods until it abruptly joined the main road that led eventually into town.

Ava felt tearful as she walked quickly home. She didn't see the squirrel as it ran along the branch and jumped to the next tree right in front of her. She didn't notice the patch of nettles at the corner of the path had suddenly produced a last flourish of purple flowers in the late afternoon sun.

She sighed several times, thinking that Morgan was more than likely not single. She asked herself why a man like that wouldn't have a woman in his life. He might even be married she thought, as she crossed the field, and joined the lane where her own cottage was situated.

Morgan was driving along the main road, and would take a turn soon that led to a National Trust depot to pick up a trailer that was needed for the next day. He could still see Ava's eyes as he thought of her, and wished he had arranged to see her again. Morgan wished he had found out if she was single, and turned into the driveway of the depot cursing his own ineptitude. She had taken him by surprise. The whole encounter was surprising. It was strange and lovely. It was dreamlike and addictive. Morgan decided to go back to that part of the forest the next day. Maybe she would walk again. He could easily find something to do there. "Load some of the cut tree wood for a start," he said to himself, as he coupled the trailer to the Land Rover, smiling.

Ava reached her cottage. She dropped her keys and cell phone onto the hall table, and as she took off her boots, she threw them one by one into the corner of the kitchen.

She made a cup of coffee and booted her laptop.

She needed to take her mind off Morgan Green and read the files concerning the awful job she had just been given in her capacity of environmental officer.

Chapter Four

Ava read through all the emails and the proposal from the chemical research company with growing unease. The company had recently bought a smallholding situated alongside one of the nearby forests and a stretch of woodland, which admittedly over the years been left to grow wild because of its size and proximity to the old crown forests.

The chemical research company had put a plan into the council for a laboratory as well as offices to be built on the land, and it involved clearing the woods.

The local community was naturally against the proposal. Several community groups and nearby landowners had formed a committee to try and put a stop to the whole venture. Ava had been engaged to do an environmental impact study in the hopes that there would be flora and fauna found to preclude the chemical research company from doing anything at all. That would be the preference amongst the locals, but Ava thought that at least they might be able to stop the clearing of the woods purchased along with the smallholding.

She had walked some way into them that day, before doubling back to take another look at Morgan Green. Ava smiled. The threatened woods were beautiful. They were wild but it made

them even more breathtaking in her opinion. She had never walked all the way through them but knew that they were adjacent to some other property, as well as the old growth forests that Morgan seemed to take care of. That property was on the ordinance survey maps but she couldn't figure out exactly what it was.

She had another cup of coffee as she planned how she would approach the environmental impact study. She was on a deadline and not just because of the season. The company had powerful allies in the local council and in government. They had promised jobs would follow and according to their brief, the work they would do was not invasive and non-toxic. Ava didn't believe that, and shook her head as she read their replies to the local committee objections. Ava decided that the most important thing to the local community seemed to be to stop the razing of the woods. She loved the forests too, and had used them as sanctuary against the stress of her job for the last few years.

She finally packed her bag with her tablet computer, camera, and her few tools she would need. The sooner she started, the better, she thought. The screening had been done, and now in the space of a week she had to do the preliminary assessment that would hopefully lead to a full-scale assessment, and hold off any development of the land and woods for a long time.

Ava made herself a cold chicken sandwich for dinner and ate it looking out of the conservatory windows at the gathering dusk. She watched a leaf float down from one of the trees at the bottom of her garden and she thought about Morgan Green.

She decided to walk through the same woods the next day at about the same time as she had seen him working there that day.

She would take her work things and if he was not to be seen then she would walk on into the smallholding wood and start some work there.

Ava dreamed about Morgan that night. His face was not exactly clear in the dream but his body was. He held her close against him. In her dream, Ava pressed against Morgan and lifted her face to be kissed. When he bent his head to hers, to kiss her lips, Ava lifted her arms to hold his head to hers, but all she held were leaves. It woke her up.

The sky was gray through her bedroom windows and there was a splatter of raindrops across them. Ava thought about the dream. She would have liked to feel that kiss.

She showered and dressed, all the time thinking about if she would see Morgan working that day.

As she drank some coffee, and then did some chores to pass the time until she would walk into the woods, she came to the conclusion that she might not see him. It was Sunday after all.

Chapter Five

Ava's heart was beating fast as she approached the place where she had seen Morgan. She was almost afraid to look and concentrated on the trodden path that was wet with the continuous mist of rain. The forest sheltered her a little, as the rain was not yet heavy.

Morgan was just finishing loading the logs and cut tree branches into the trailer attached to his Land Rover. There was not much left to do, and he had twice glanced at his cell phone to check the time, in the hope that Ava would walk by before he left the area.

He was clipping the gate up on the trailer as he heard her. She had splashed in a puddle and then crunched a few twigs that remained almost dry when she had tried to avoid the wetter part of the path.

Morgan felt elation as he saw her.

Ava looked up and saw Morgan.

They both smiled. Morgan left the trailer, and began to walk towards Ava, and she went to meet him.

They stood in front of each other about a pace away.

"Ava, I didn't think anyone would walk in the rain," Morgan said, meaning he hoped she would.

"I didn't expect you to be working on a Sunday," Ava replied.

Morgan raised his eyebrows. "You hoped to avoid me?"

She shook her head. "No, no." She stopped because she didn't want to say she hoped to see him.

Morgan's eyes filled with emotion.

"I hoped you would walk again. I enjoyed talking with you yesterday." He gazed into her eyes for a few seconds.

Ava looked at his lips and remembered her dream. She wanted that kiss.

Morgan almost groaned. He felt sure she wanted to kiss him. He wanted her. He couldn't just kiss her, could he?

As they stood close but not close enough, surrounded by beautiful trees, the heavens opened and the trees gave up their role of umbrella. Huge drops fell, splattering around them. Ava tried to get her jacket hood up. It was secured by the backpack she wore and wouldn't move. Morgan grinned, and took her hand.

"Come on," he instructed, and they sprinted to the Land Rover. Morgan opened the back door and helped Ava into the cabin. He got in and closed the door just as the rain got even heavier.

They were both laughing. Morgan ran his hand through his wet hair and it spiked at the front. Ava was trying to take the backpack off so that she could sit on the car seat properly. Morgan began to help her and leaned close. Their faces were almost touching. Ava closed her eyes to savor it. Morgan moved a little and noticed. He gently held her face and kissed her.

He had no idea what to expect, so when she put her arms around his neck to hold his head to hers and began to kiss him back, he felt the kiss all the way to his thighs. She didn't want to stop. The kiss was soft and yet firm and she moved her nose against his. Morgan held her head, his hands in her hair and his eyes closed. He began to trace the seam of her lips with his tongue, and when she opened her mouth to him, the feel of her tongue sliding against his gave him an intense tingle of longing.

They didn't stop kissing each other for a few moments. One kiss led into another and they trailed their fingertips along each other's face. They held each other, clasping handfuls of hair, and then to catch their breath they rested their cheeks against each other's.

Morgan kissed down Ava's neck. He moved aside her jacket collar to kiss further down her neck and sucked the tiniest bit at the soft part where it met her shoulder. Ava made a little sound of pleasure, and moved to him, wanting more.

She ran her hands along his chest and felt his muscles through the denim. Morgan groaned hoping she would unbutton it and put her hands on him. He took her face in his hands again and kissed her deeply. The kiss made Ava throb with pleasure between her legs. She felt wet and needy. She opened Morgan's shirt as they kissed again, and traced her fingertips along his chest and then down to the top of his jeans. Morgan wanted her badly but he had to let her take the lead. He couldn't risk frightening her or taking advantage. His heart was hammering, and all he could think of was if she would take the chance and open his jeans. He wanted her cool fingertips there tracing down to his cock.

Ava took one of his hands and brought it to her breasts. Morgan opened her shirt and cupped her breasts in his hands, moving her bra aside as he kissed her again. They both let out a soft moan, and then to Morgan's surprise Ava began to smile against his lips.

"Morgan, this feels so good. I'd like more. I'd like to make love. I need to. I need you." Her whisper against his lips made his cock stir and his erection began to strain against his jeans.

Ava unzipped his jeans and freed him to her touch. It made Morgan gasp, but he started to unzip her jeans and push them down her hips. He kissed her and whispered to her, "Ava, your kiss is delicious. I only want what you want. I need you too. Let me take your jeans off."

Resting his face against hers, Morgan tried to breathe properly, then helped her take off her jeans kissing her as much as he could. They both pushed Morgan's jeans down so that Ava could straddle him. He didn't let her guide his cock inside her until he had felt her wetness with his fingers. Morgan teased her so that he could feel her throb of pleasure against his fingertips, and he muffled her moans with a kiss as he pushed a finger into her.

"I really need to," he whispered, as he moved his lips to her breasts, and sucked.

Ava thought she might come right then on his fingers with his mouth on her breasts, and so she held his erection and kissed along his neck where she could reach.

She whispered into his ear, "Morgan, I need you inside me. Morgan." Her breath sent sensations coursing down his neck and he brought his head up to kiss her, lifting her with his hands around her hips to ride him.

As she felt his thick, hard erection slide into her slowly until he was completely inside, they breathed against each other's lips, overwhelmed by the feel of it.

They kissed each other softly, lovingly, and then they began to move.

They moved fast and hard, and then slowly and tenderly. They moved so that they each felt as if they would melt with the sexual pleasure that made them gasp and suck on each other's tongue, and neck. Their kisses became deeper and consuming.

Ava felt her orgasm start. She slid slowly on Morgan and kissed him with the tip of her tongue in his mouth as the waves of pleasure made her gasp.

Morgan let himself come. He let himself pump into her, grasping her hips and thrusting hard. It felt so good that Ava had another, deeper orgasm, and it made her grind down on him thrusting her hips. They kissed and held each other tight. They closed their eyes against each other's face and rested.

The rain was making trails of diamonds down the windscreen and the back windows of the Land Rover were a little steamed up.

Morgan held Ava gently. They listened to the rain and soaked up the closeness and tenderness they felt for each other.

When Morgan traced her backbone with his fingertips and felt she was cold, he hugged her.

"I think we should dress, and maybe I can drive you home. It looks as if the rain has set in."

Ava was snuggled against him. She didn't want to let him go, but she leaned back a little to nod her head. "Okay, although I should at least try to do a little of the work I thought about doing today. Even in the rain I could get some shots of trees and plants."

Morgan was interested. "What work, Ava?"

She needed to move off his lap. She kissed him and nudged his nose with hers. It made Morgan seek another kiss and he held her hips to help her off him. Ava couldn't help herself, she had to put her hand between her legs and feel him as he slid from her. Morgan gasped a little at her touch and she quickly kissed him again until they smiled at each other. Ava found her jeans and underwear. She struggled them on and Morgan pulled his jeans up too. They both smiled as they did this, and then leaned to kiss each other again.

"I'm conducting an environmental impact study on the part of the forest that belongs with the smallholding. You probably know it was sold to the chemical company and they want to raze the woods."

Morgan stared at her in shock. "I didn't know. Why didn't I know? They can't do that."

She looked at him and nodded. "I'll try really hard to stop it, Morgan."

His expression softened. "You'll get really wet. What if I come with you and help?"

Ava wanted him with her, and she opened the door of the Land Rover. The rain was teeming down and she glanced back at Morgan.

"The rain is very heavy, maybe I should leave it until tomorrow after all."

Morgan seemed pleased with her decision. He put his arm around her and cuddled her to him.

"Are you hungry? I've got coffee and apples."

Ava smiled as she nestled against him. "Sounds perfect," she said, and lifted her face to be kissed. Morgan bent his head to hers and kissed her. He slowed his kiss prolonging the delicious sensation.

He leaned over the passenger seat and picked up the thermos and a brown paper lunch bag. He took a big red and gold apple from the bag, offering it to Ava. She took it and turned it over in her hands.

"Wow, this is a great apple, Morgan." She bit into it. The apple was very sweet, crisp, and juicy. Ava sighed in appreciation.

Morgan smiled. "It's from my mother's orchards."

They shared the coffee and Morgan put his arm back around Ava's shoulders. He nuzzled against her hair, kissed it, and pulled up a few strands to feel the softness.

"I think it would be better if I drive you home. Come on, it seems as if the weather has brought dusk early." He moved from her and they went to sit in the front seats.

Before he started the engine, he leaned over and kissed her. "I am so very thankful to have met you, Ava."

Chapter Six

Ava directed him to her cottage. The rain was driving down with such force it bounced back from the surface of the road.

The sky was dark with more rain, and Ava looked out of the window as Morgan drove. The windscreen wipers slashed away the water and made an almost hypnotic swish in the silence that had fallen between them.

She was wondering what to do when it came to saying goodbye to Morgan.

He suddenly said, "Ava, it will be hard to just drop you home after this afternoon, after what we shared. May I stay for half an hour? I'd like to know more about you and the work you do."

She turned to him and smiled. "I'd love that, Morgan. Where do you live? Will you have far to go afterwards?"

Morgan glanced at her as he drove. "I live at the edge of the three forests. My family lives there. We share a very big house and have gardens. My mother's orchards are there."

When Morgan said the word 'family', Ava was scared for a moment that he might be married. She decided to ask him right then.

"Morgan you're such a lovely man, very attractive, tender. Are you married or anything?"

Morgan broke into a grin. "Not so far, Ava, and thank you for the compliments. I could ask you the same. You are so pretty and loving, intelligent, and obviously skilled, so are you single?"

"I am single, Morgan," Ava told him happily.

A flood of relief came over him, and he smiled as he drew up at her cottage.

He jumped down from the Land Rover and went around to make sure Ava was okay getting out. She smiled at this, and took his hand to walk down to the front door of the cottage. Morgan held her hand and ran his thumb along her palm. It gave Ava a jolt of sexual feeling that made her stomach flip.

Inside the cottage, Ava made coffee and told Morgan about the environmental impact survey she needed to start.

"I'd love to help you, Ava." Morgan sparkled with excitement. "I know lots about those wild woods. There's a few badger setts. There are squirrels, and the birdlife is very diverse. The trees themselves are old. On the edge of the wood where it meets another private property there is a tree more than five hundred years old." His eyes were bright with enthusiasm, and as Ava put a cup of coffee down on the table in front of him, he caught her hand and pulled her onto his knee.

"I can help with information. Take you straight to the important things in the forest, so that your preliminary is finished, and they will surely call for the full scale assessment." He kissed her, and Ava put her arms around his neck to hold him and kiss him back.

She sighed with pleasure, and closed her eyes to kiss him more until he smiled and whispered, "Ava, I'll need to make love to you again if we keep going. I have some things to take care of for work, and so I'll need to leave very soon." He was fishing in his jeans pocket for his cell phone as Ava broke away from him and stood up.

"Here, put your number into my phone, let's see each other tomorrow." He handed her his phone and Ava added her number. She wanted his number and yet she couldn't ask for it. Morgan looked into her eyes. He read the confusion in them and pulled her into his arms to kiss her again before he left.

"I have to go, Ava."

With Morgan gone, Ava sat on the chair he had used and touched the handle of his coffee cup. She was happy to have met him, happy that he was interested in seeing her, and it was a wrench to have him go. Her kitchen felt empty without Morgan's vibrant presence in it.

She took a shower, and after dressing in clean jeans and shirt, she sat down at her laptop to do some research on the Internet. It was an hour later when her cell phone rang. Morgan wanted to say goodnight and he said she must save his number to her contacts. Ava smiled with delight as he told her softly and sexily that he wished she was with him. They arranged to meet the next morning at the edge of the forest that was under threat.

In bed, Ava hugged a pillow to herself, and thought about making love with Morgan that afternoon. She hoped she would dream about it.

Chapter Seven

When the sun woke Ava as it streamed through her bedroom window the next morning, she stretched, realizing she felt happy. She sang little snatches of favorite songs as she dressed, and checked her bag for the things she would need to get started on her work in the forest.

Ava was still singing as she drove to the smallholding and parked in the yard at the front. The 'For Sale' signs had been partially covered over with stick-on 'Sold' labels in red and white. The former owner of the smallholding had gone as soon as the contracts were exchanged and the place had a sad air about it.

Ava walked down through the fields and the few pens, now empty of chickens and piglets, to the edge of the woods that were under threat.

She was unsure where Morgan might meet her, at this side of the woods or the other side, and so for a short time she took photographs of the oldest oak and ash trees. She looked around. It felt as if someone was watching her, but she could see no one. She took out her small, sharp pruning shears to take a sample of a particular plant. She had placed the cutting in a small, plastic zip-lock bag when she looked around again. Ava was certain someone or something was watching her.

She didn't see or hear anyone and so she wandered further into the wild forest where the trees were growing very close to each other, some covered in ivy. Ava saw mistletoe growing on an old oak and she went towards it, fascinated. The pearly berries were already there, and the plant looked especially healthy and festive amongst the oak leaves that had the slightest hint of gold on the edges.

The hairs rose on Ava's neck as she realized she was not alone. She closed her eyes in fear, but then snapped them open, as she quickly turned to whack the person with her backpack.

It was Morgan, and for a split second, Ava saw him covered in leaves that were green, copper, red, and gold. His eyes, instead of the wonderful blue she knew, appeared bright green.

She stepped back from him, gasping.

"Ava, I'm sorry, did I startle you? You looked so fascinated by the mistletoe I didn't want to call out." Morgan's blue eyes expressed concern. He held out his arms to shelter her within them and chase away the fear he saw in her eyes.

Ava stepped into the circle of his arms and he hugged her to his chest. It was comforting and he had the loveliest fragrance of spruce and cedar about him.

"Morgan," she almost whispered his name. "I've been feeling watched since I got into the forest, and you did startle me a little."

He took her face in his hands to kiss her slowly and tenderly. "Maybe it was the forest sprites, the woodland elves, or maybe squirrels. There are heaps here." He hugged her. "Are you okay?"

She grinned. "Yes, thank you. You very nearly got a whack with my backpack."

Morgan smiled, but didn't comment, and took her hand to lead her further into the forest.

"I'll show you where a rare orchid grows wild."

Ava held his hand tightly. It was so good to feel his skin.

"You'd have degrees and things to do this job, wouldn't you, Ava?" Morgan asked as they walked.

She glanced at him. "I have an Environmental science degree and a post graduate diploma in plant science. I love the countryside too. That makes it easy."

Morgan smiled in appreciation. "Me too, I could never live in the city or even the town. I love trees and plants too much to be away from them. I think I would die away from them."

Ava stopped walking, to turn and look at his face.

"Morgan, that's so heartfelt. I hope you never have to leave them. I understand. I do really. That's why I walk in the forests. The first time I saw you I was walking off the stress of a council meeting about the destruction of this forest."

Morgan looked down into her pretty eyes and saw just what he hoped for; care, affection and understanding.

He smiled and bent his head to hers.

His kiss tasted better than chocolate, sweeter than the apple he had given her the day before. It was gentle and compelling, and Ava felt as if she was drifting away in a satin mist of sensation. She wasn't the only one. Morgan was drowning in need, and the strangest feeling of wanting to possess Ava and make her his forever.

They left their faces against each other's for a few seconds after they ended the kiss. Morgan suddenly remembered. "I've brought you presents." He fished in the large patch pockets of the dark green, waxed cotton jacket he wore, and from one brought out a large pear, and from the other a fat red pomegranate. He held them up for Ava. "They're from my mother's orchards. You'll like them. She grows the best fruit ever."

Ava smiled at him and stood on tiptoe to kiss him.

"That's so kind of you. They look lovely. Where are your mother's orchards, Morgan? Are they close by?"

Morgan nodded, but didn't speak. Instead, he stepped away and bent to show her the flower he had brought her to see. It was a strange thing, as many orchids are, and Ava took a photograph of it.

She could hear water. "Morgan, is there a stream in this part of the forest?"

He looked wary for a moment, and then he nodded.

"Yes, just a little further up close to the private property I was telling you about yesterday."

Ava nodded in interest. "I've seen that on the maps and survey documents, but couldn't quite find out what it was. It's almost as if this forest is shielding a secret place."

Morgan's look was enigmatic when he said, "That's very romantic, Ava. It's a house and gardens. The stream runs past the bottom of the gardens and on through the orchards that belong to the house."

Ava took his hand. "Let's go and look. I love these things, streams and woods. I wonder if there is a bridge?"

Morgan held her hand and brought it to his lips. He kissed her fingertips. Ava shivered in pleasure.

Chapter Eight

They reached the edge of the wild forest and Ava gasped in delight. The stream was beautiful. It had banks full of ferns, and trees grew right down so that it looked as if their roots were drinking. The water looked deep where the old wooden bridge crossed it, before growing shallow as it continued its journey, dappled from the sun that filtered through the overhanging tree branches. The forest continued on the other side of the stream, but seemed less wild. Ava thought she glimpsed a circular clearing just a little way in, surrounded by urns of flowers. The light was shifting with the breeze as it moved the leaves and branches.

The old bridge had moss growing on the handrail here and there, with little filigree white flowers on delicate stalks poking their heads up from the dark greenery. The stream flattened out as it went around a bend. A few water flowers and big flat leaves bobbed about. Ava almost ran to this edge of the stream and took out her camera. "Look at this, Morgan. It's so lovely. Do you know if the stream belongs to the house here, or is it part of the smallholding forest? If it is, then it's an extra reason for the forest not to be razed."

Morgan was quiet. Ava turned to look at him. He shrugged.

"It belongs to the house."

He moved to her and put his arms around her.

"Ava, tell me what needs to be here in the forest to stop the company destroying it."

She looked into his blue eyes and put her arms around his waist.

"Some special things. Flora and fauna that are protected, or should be. Things that are not replicated very often in other forests. Endangered things," she listed, as she looked at his lips, wanting them on hers.

Morgan's eyes darkened at her as he realized she wanted his kiss. He crushed her to his body and kissed her hard. Ava molded her body to his, and a little sound of pleasure escaped her as his lips left hers.

Morgan took her hand. "I'll show you more things that might help," he told her, and led her away from the stream.

They spent a half hour gathering little samples of plants and photographing birds, squirrels, and a particular tree that Morgan said butterflies liked. The day grew a little colder, and Ava shivered as they stood next to a huge copper beech tree. Morgan watched as a few leaves floated on the breeze that played in the top branches, before they fell onto Ava's hair. She seemed so beautiful to him then it almost took his breath away, and he stood before her silently watching as she took the leaves from her hair.

"Your hair is almost that color when the light catches it. You are very lovely, Ava." His voice was low and felt like a caress to

Ava. She put the leaves carefully into her backpack. The gesture was not lost on Morgan, and he took a deep breath.

"I don't need to work today. I'd love it if I could spend more time with you. I don't want to stop you working, of course. It's lunchtime. My sister runs a small café in the next village. We could eat and then you could work." He sounded hopeful and Ava was already nodding.

"I'd love that."

Morgan smiled. "I'll give you directions, if you will drive us. My vehicle is quite a way off. Where did you park?"

"In the smallholding yard, so not far," Ava said, and they walked towards the edge of the woods and the smallholding.

Morgan took Ava's hand. He hadn't intended to introduce Ava to any of his family so soon, but he couldn't help himself. He knew already that he was in love with her, and Polly his sister was a good person to start with.

Ava secured her backpack in the back of her car and Morgan put his jacket in there. He was wearing a faded denim shirt and it showed off his muscular body as it moved with him. Ava ran her hand up his back and Morgan turned to her, his eyes betraying his desire.

They moved quickly to kiss each other, and he lifted her against the car, pressing his hips to hers. Ava could feel his erection, and touched her tongue to his gently. Morgan groaned softly and deepened the kiss. They neither wanted to stop, and as Morgan pressed against her, Ava brought her legs up around his thighs. He held her there so that his erection teased her. Ava couldn't think of anything but making love to him.

"Morgan, are you really hungry? I was thinking maybe we could go home, to my place, and…"

He kissed her again and then finished the sentence, "Make love. I don't know if I can actually hold out until we get to your cottage. I think I'll die if I don't feel your skin against mine right now." He lowered her feet to the ground and pulled her T-shirt up. His kiss was wet and gentle on her breasts as he unhooked her bra and moved it aside. He sucked a nipple into his mouth and swirled his tongue around it, as he cupped the other breast in his hand, kneading so that Ava gasped.

She unzipped his jeans and trailed her fingers down over his stomach so that his muscles clenched in anticipation of what she would do next. She dipped her hand into his boxers and touched the firm, velvet head of his erection. She pushed his jeans and underwear together down his thighs, and ran her hands over his hard bottom. Morgan had his tongue in her mouth and he was making tiny sounds of appreciation. She brought her hand around his thighs, took his sac in one hand, and curled her hand around his erection. It felt like heaven to hold him as he kissed her hard and thrust his hips.

They were both moaning, and Morgan had opened Ava's jeans, pulling them down to mid-thigh. He was kneading her bottom, and thrusting against her.

Ava whispered, "I need your fingers in me." He kissed her, licking the side of her mouth before his tongue slid along hers. He pushed two fingers into her and it felt so good, she thrust towards the palm of his hand.

They clung to each other, kissing and touching until Morgan groaned.

"Ava, I'm going to turn you around and lean you over the car a little. I have to make love to you. I have to be inside you." She whispered her agreement, and he turned her, holding her tenderly around her neck, bringing her face to his to kiss her, before he leaned her forward, and thrust into her warm, wet entrance. His thick, hard erection slid along her bud as he thrust, and Ava pushed her bottom back into him to have him go deeper and thrust harder. She was moaning and Morgan held her around her stomach to lift her against his thrust, and then she was coming. She shuddered, gasped, and whispered his name as she thrust back onto his cock, wanting the sensation to last and last. Morgan leaned and placed wet kisses along her spine and then he let himself come. It was so delicious it almost made his legs weak, and he held onto Ava with one hand, and leaned over to the car door with the other.

They stayed like that with their eyes closed for a few moments, and then moved apart. Morgan hugged Ava and kissed her ear.

"Good thing you parked between the hedges." His whisper made her smile, and after she had pulled her jeans up her hips and her T-shirt down over her breasts, she leaned back onto her car and looked at him. Her look was full of love and Morgan soaked it up.

He took her in his arms again, and held her head to whisper in her ear.

"Ava, you mean so much to me already. I want you to know that I…I care for you, and about you. What do you want to do now?"

Ava wasn't quite sure of his question, but settled on it meaning 'did she want to go to the café they had been heading for?'

"I don't know if I can meet your sister right now, after we… Perhaps we could go to my cottage and have a sandwich. Is that okay?"

Morgan hugged her. "It's great."

Chapter Nine

Morgan made coffee, and Ava made sandwiches. She put the plates down on the table in her conservatory, and went back to get the pear and the pomegranate that Morgan had brought her. They sat together to eat, looking out of the big windows onto her garden. The sun had gone, and the afternoon was gloomy. Morgan was thoughtful.

"It will soon be properly autumn, Ava. The village not far from where I live will celebrate the harvest festival. They have an evening fete on the twenty-first, the day of the equinox. It's special and very atmospheric. I'd love it if you would come with me. My family always has a picnic in the afternoon, and then we go to the fete in the evening."

Ava smiled at him. She was cutting the pear in half to give him a piece.

"I'd love to, Morgan."

When Ava bit into the pear, she was amazed by how delicious it was.

Morgan watched her expression. His eyes twinkled with satisfaction at her delight in the pear.

He cut the pomegranate, and scooped out the red pearls for her to eat.

"My mother's name is Pomona. She's magic with the fruit orchards. My sister Polly runs a café, but she's also a musician, and will play with her band at the harvest festival fete. My brother plays the flute with the band. Even my grandmother will be there, bringing the flowers she grows to the little market they always have. Her name is Rose, and she's a goddess when it comes to growing things." As he talked about his family, he seemed to shimmer slightly before Ava's eyes. The pear juice in her mouth was incredibly sweet. She felt almost drugged. Ava gazed at Morgan as he talked, and his eyes became green like new grass. Ava moved back in alarm.

Morgan held out the spoon of pomegranate seeds.

"Taste this Ava, taste this," he said gently, to soothe her, and she let him put the fruit into her mouth. As she ate the pomegranate seeds, she felt her mind become clearer. When her eyes met his again, they were blue like the sky on a bright summer day. She made a murmur of appreciation.

"The fruit really is delicious, Morgan," she told him.

He smiled.

That afternoon, Ava put together her preliminary assessment and called for a full-scale assessment of the wild forest, along with a halting of consent for any plans the chemical company had submitted to the town council.

She constructed a strong case for the forest being left alone, and cited her findings along with the assertion that the loss of the forest would impact negatively on the surrounding woodlands. She wrote that the community would lose some of the oldest trees in the county, which along with the devastating loss of wildlife habitat would mean a degradation of the countryside in general.

Her writing was scientific, but her words as she told Morgan what she had written were full of emotion.

He stayed with her to make her coffee and sit by her as she worked on her laptop, before reading the report himself. He kissed her and told her the council would surely rule to leave the forest alone after reading the report. Ava kissed him and said she hoped so.

As night fell, Morgan didn't want to leave and Ava wanted him to stay. They showered and cuddled together in Ava's bed. The moon, flanked by dark blue clouds, was visible through the window as Ava trailed her fingers over Morgan's chest.

He caught her hand in his and brought it to his lips. He sucked a fingertip and then began to trace her fingers with his own, over each finger, and around her palm. It was soothing and Ava rested her head on his shoulder.

"Morgan, I wonder why 'The Trust' wouldn't have told you about the threat to the forest?" she asked him unexpectedly.

Morgan turned and kissed her forehead.

"Sometimes the administration doesn't tell us things. I work quite independently at times. The jobs are planned according to the tracts of land I look after, and the seasons too. I do have other people on my team and we meet to report on the health of the environment." He stopped talking to kiss her as Ava looked up at him.

She put her hand up to run her fingers over his jaw and hold him to kiss more, before she said, "There was a representative of 'The Trust' at the last meeting. Perhaps they will tell you if my report is unsuccessful."

Morgan had not moved far from her lips and kissed her again before he agreed.

"You're probably right."

He held her close and Ava closed her eyes. She felt so safe with him, and Morgan felt her soft against him. He knew she was falling asleep and he closed his eyes.

Chapter Ten

They had fallen asleep cuddled together not having made love, but just before dawn Ava stirred in Morgan's arms and felt his hard body against hers. She traced the line of his hipbone, and then kissed his chest along the muscles, as her hand drifted further down to run her fingers gently over his cock. She kissed along his neck, but Morgan seemed to be sleeping deeply. Ava stilled, and was taking her hand away from him when he caught her wrist and brought her hand back to his growing erection.

Morgan pulled her over his body and began to kiss her softly at first, and then as she curled her fingers around his erection and began to move them up and down, he kissed her hard. He held her head to his before finding her nipples and sliding the palm of his hands along them. He ran his hand down her back to knead her bottom as he kissed her.

Ava was beginning to move against him, wanting him inside her. She held his erection tight and left his lips to kiss down his body. Ava licked all the way along his erection until she reached the tip, and then she took him into her mouth to suck until Morgan was groaning. She liked the sounds of pleasure he made, and so when he gently pulled her head away she whispered his name.

Morgan brought her to face him and kissed her mouth.

"Ava, sit on me, ride me."

He helped her over his body and Ava guided his erection into her purposely, a little at a time, until they were both desperate to thrust.

They moved slowly, savoring the feel of each other, and then she rocked on him so that he groaned and held her hips. Ava had an orgasm which had her sinking across Morgan's chest to kiss him. Morgan clasped her close, rolling with her and then thrusting hard into her, lifting her hips to his. They came together and hugged, groaning into each other's mouths as they kissed.

They held each other close for a long time, until the sky had lightened, and both of them slept for an hour. Ava's cell phone woke them as her alarm call for work sang out.

She reached for it to shut it off, and Morgan nuzzled her neck before he raised himself on one elbow to speak. "Ava, I have to get going. I need to be in a different part of the county today, but I'll call. I'll call later today, late afternoon. Will you submit your reports today?"

Ava looked up into his eyes and nodded. "I will, and I have a meeting too with a few 'reps' from various groups; bird watchers, the local green group, that sort of thing."

He leaned over her and kissed her. "Good luck with everything. Remember I'll be thinking of you and that I care about you."

He dressed, and Ava pulled on her own jeans and jumper to go downstairs with him.

"Morgan, you have no car with you. How will you get to work? Let me drive you somewhere," she said, as he opened the front door.

Morgan smiled. "No need really. I can walk into the woods easily from here just as you do, and my Land Rover is there."

He kissed her again and walked quickly away. Ava watched him for a few moments and then closed the door.

She ran upstairs to take a shower and dress. Today, she had important work to do.

Morgan reached the edge of the woods quickly. He was thinking about how to make sure those old, wild woods survived. They edged his family's property on the other side of the stream Ava had discovered. The loss of them would open his family's property up to more scrutiny, and he couldn't have that.

He wondered why his family hadn't known about the threat. They knew most things that went on in the town, and in the surrounding countryside, but then again they were busy harvesting the fruit and making wine. Perhaps it had simply slipped by them. These were not the old times when they knew everything. He grinned as he reached his Land Rover, and thought of Ava. She was very special. He wanted her in his life forever.

Once inside the car, he checked his emails on his cell phone and messaged his mother. He wanted to arrange plans to help Ava if need be.

Chapter Eleven

Ava was in a meeting with all the stakeholders in the fight to stop the wild woods being razed. They were allowed to read copies of her preliminary assessment and seemed suitably impressed with her endeavor, especially given the short amount of time she had to do the job. One of the other town council planning officers had joined their meeting. A new element had been added to the struggle. The chemicals company was categorically promising a hundred jobs for the town if their building and expansion plans were passed. They would also upgrade the town leisure center providing a new building for youth groups to use. It was a tempting package, and Ava watched some of the faces of the people at the meeting. The town needed jobs. There used to be a thriving tourist trade in the town, but over the last few years, it had declined considerably.

Ava was not confident that the woods could be saved.

She talked with another senior environmental officer after the meeting and found them resigned to the certainty that the woods would be cleared.

All day Ava quizzed her contacts and pushed to have a meeting with the chemical company officials. Ordinarily the council officials would not have held another town meeting so soon after the first, but she convinced them to conduct another at the end of the week. She posted advertisements in the local papers about it. She quickly designed a handbill and photocopied some.

When Morgan called her, she was about to go around town handing them to shop owners and anyone who would display them for the general public.

"Ava, how are things going?" he asked her, and she sighed downheartedly.

"Morgan, it doesn't look good."

He was concerned. "I'm sorry, Ava. I wanted to see you tonight but I have family stuff going on. I'll call you later to say goodnight. Could we see each other tomorrow night?"

Ava smiled a little. "I'd like that, Morgan." They ended the call, and Ava put on her jacket to go out along the high street.

Many of the business people knew her because of her attendance at various council meetings beyond the scope of her actual job. She was interested in the town and they liked her.

The wind was cold as she walked along the street. It seemed that autumn was upon them. There had been a few meetings and concerns raised for a few weeks when people realized who had bought the smallholding and the woodlands. People had continued either to protest against the planned building and development, or shrug their shoulders resigned to the fact that they probably had no power to stop it. The nights were closing in and people were thinking instead of their warm homes.

When Ava went back to her office in the town council buildings, she was dispirited. More people had begun to question the sense of knocking back a hundred jobs for the town. At least they were happy to display her handbill in their premises.

Ava worked late on her other tasks, and then she left for home.

As she walked around to the car parking lot, she felt drops of rain and hurried to get to her car.

On the drive home, the rain began to pour down. Ava wondered what Morgan was doing, and what time he might call her that night.

It was ten o'clock, and she was sitting in bed reading, when instead of a call he messaged her that he missed her, and would call the next day. Ava was disappointed not to hear Morgan's voice. She went to sleep thinking about the previous night and kissing Morgan.

Chapter Twelve

Morgan was with his family. They were all there, his mother, grandmother, brother, and sister sitting in the huge kitchen in the house they shared.

It had been Rose who came up with the idea of the picnic. Should Ava not win a further assessment of the wild forest and stop the building going ahead, they would help. They had a few times in the year when magic was closer to this world than other times, and the harvest equinox was one of them. The whole week surrounding the twenty-first of September was sacred to them but they could invoke something very special on the day itself.

If Ava was not successful, they would hold a picnic for the company officials, and spin their web of wonder and delight in trees and woodlands to guide the business people gently back to value all forests.

Morgan had already asked his lovely girl to a picnic, and so it would not seem too bizarre for him to extend the invitation to the company executives.

It was arranged. His sister Polly would compose a special piece of music for his brother to play on the pipes. It would beguile the company executives. His mother who had already harvested the most delicious fruit in the world would make wines to soothe their senses, and Morgan would convince them that trees were the one of the most important things on the earth.

Morgan felt happy when he drifted to sleep that night because he knew that his family had accepted Ava even without meeting her. He wished he was with her right then, but he would see her the next day, he reminded himself.

Chapter Thirteen

Morgan took some fruit for Ava as he left his home the next morning. His mother had left two different varieties of apples out for him and they produced a delicious sweetness as he put them into a bag.

He was humming as he drove along to his first stop. He had the job of pollarding a section of the young trees in a forest at the edge of the county. When he got there, he parked as usual in one of the special access lanes. Instead of immediately setting to work, he took out his cell phone and called Ava.

Ava had gone into her office early and caught up with the most senior environmental officer. She knew that the wild forest was already doomed when he had pointed out that nothing within it was not already to be found in the neighboring forests, those that the National Trust held and maintained.

He sighed as he said this, and added, "Were it up to me, of course the trees themselves would hold the greatest significance, but the council is thinking now about the jobs and the promised help with the community leisure center. Sorry, Ava, I know it meant a lot to you."

Ava sat looking at her computer screen and the huge amount of emails in her Inbox that she hadn't started to open. Her cell phone sang the little snatch of music that was her current ring tone, and she picked it up, looking at the screen. It was Morgan, and she smiled despite her melancholy over the forest.

"Ava, has anything happened yet? You expected a swift response to that first assessment didn't you?"

She shook her head as if he was there to see it. "Sadly, I think the final decision is that the chemical company will be allowed to raze the forest and build. I hate it, Morgan." She cried, suddenly angry and frustrated.

Morgan frowned. "Don't be upset, Ava, I have an idea. It might work, and there is no harm in trying." His voice was soothing. "Ask the company executives to come with you to the picnic on Friday. Tell them you simply want to show them the orchids and the beauty of the forest. The weather forecast is good, and the picnic will be at noon. If they decline the invitation, let me know, I'll send them a fruit basket to help change their minds."

Ava smiled at this. "Morgan, you are sweet, but sometimes these business people will not be moved even by a fruit basket. What are you doing today? Where are you?"

She wished he was with her.

Morgan could hear the sadness in her voice, and his heart went out to her. "I'm a few miles away. I wish I was with you right now. Meet me for lunch, Ava. Could you come to the edge of the woods where we met? You know the access road now. I'll be there about one."

"I will, Morgan. I'll be there."

They ended the call. Ava picked up her desk handset to call the chemical company representatives she had met a week previously.

No one was available, so she left a message saying that she was inviting them to lunch on Friday. Ava put down the phone, knowing that if they really wanted the town to be onside they would call back. She emailed her invitation to one of the company reps just to be sure.

Morgan began work, and finished his task in plenty of time to drive to the woods closer to where Ava lived. He drove down the access road and parked the Land Rover. He walked along the well-trodden path and then veered into the wild forest.

He wanted to create a more discernible path from the yard of the smallholding to the orchids and the stream. The business people Ava would bring would need to be able to walk easily. Morgan touched the tree branches and high ferns as he walked and they knew him. His hands became gentle swathes of green and golden leaves. His blue eyes became the color of the dark green foliage around him. What he looked upon felt his intention and parted, making a path. Morgan glided rather than strode, and everywhere he went he blessed the forest.

On reaching the stream, Morgan walked over the bridge to his family's property and looked around the space where they often brought a meal to eat. The urns were still full of late blooming pansies and the trees had lost only a few leaves. Soon the ground in all the surrounding woods would be ankle deep in orange, gold, and red leaves. Morgan looked forward to that. He would take his lovely Ava to walk through the rich carpet and make love to her on a bed of the autumn glory.

Morgan whispered to the forest as he retraced his steps and the forest sang back to him. Rustles and little swishes surrounded him. Morgan smiled.

He got to the Land Rover just before Ava, and although he had changed almost completely so that no leaves were detectable on his hands, a couple of silver leaves remained in his dark hair.

Ava parked her car behind his, and walked towards him, smiling.

Morgan clasped her against his body in a hug.

"Ava, it's so good to see you," he murmured. He held her, his arm around her neck to keep her close, and he kissed her for a long time.

When Ava began to smile between kisses, Morgan loosed his hold on her a little.

"I brought you apples from the family orchards."

He took her by the hand to go back to his car for the bag of fruit from the passenger seat.

Ava looked inside.

"Wow, Morgan, they smell divine," she said. He grinned at her choice of words because that's exactly what they were.

She put them into her own car and Morgan watched her, loving the way she moved and looked. Her auburn hair had fallen out of the clips she had it in as he had kissed her, and now there were tendrils all around her face.

He smiled in appreciation, and leaned against the Land Rover, wondering if he could make love to her right then.

Ava came back to him, and stood between his legs, pressing against him. She traced his lips and then his cheekbones with her fingertips, before taking the silver leaves from his hair.

"Morgan, you are covered in leaves," she said. He experienced a little wave of worry that he had not totally changed back into his human form.

She held the leaves for him to see.

"They're pretty."

Morgan nodded happily. "It's birch."

He kissed her quickly.

"Ava, tell me what's happened about the wild forest. Did you have a chance to contact the company people and ask them to the picnic on Friday?"

Ava cuddled against him and he ran his hands along her back and down to hold her bottom. Ava savored the feeling of his hands on her.

"I did leave a message, and sent an email. I hope they answer this afternoon, Morgan."

Ava reached up to kiss him, and Morgan whispered, "Call me if they say no," before he returned the kiss and took her breath away.

Ava put her hands up inside Morgan's shirt and felt his skin. She wanted him right then.

"Morgan, can I see you tonight?" she asked, breaking away from the kiss.

His eyes were full of love.

"Yes, I'm desperate to see you again soon. What time?"

Morgan would go over to Ava's house about seven. They both had to go back to work, and so they split up.

Ava went back to her office, and took her apples with her.

To her surprise, one of the company representatives was looking over the report she had made. He sat in the boardroom and Ava was asked to join him.

She watched him finish reading her report, but as he looked at her, she knew they had lost.

Ava smiled at him. "I have the most delicious apples from a local orchard."

She opened the brown paper bag and offered the man an apple. He was surprised into taking one. The wonderful aroma had him smiling.

"Smells great," he said, and bit into it.

Ava watched him as she told him about her invitation to lunch on Friday. She would meet them here at the council chambers and go to a local place.

He readily agreed to remind the others, and as he left the building, he continued eating the best apple he had ever tasted.

Chapter Fourteen

That night w Morgan arrived at Ava's cottage they fell into each other's ar Their kisses were hungry, and Morgan lifted Ava up to carry her lay her on the sofa. He undressed her, and kissed where he toud so that Ava felt as if she would melt before he entered her. Ava Morgan's shirt off and gently bit along his stomach as she unzd his jeans. She pushed them down, and trailed her fingers ud down the hard column of his erection until he was thrusti wanting her hands tight around him.

Ava moaned nst his mouth, as he put his fingers into her wetness. Morgan w red to her about what he wanted to do to her; push his fingers her until she was coming on them, lick her nipples until her br ached for his mouth whenever she saw him, kiss her so hard lips were swollen. Then he told her he loved her. Ava did c on his fingers and was gasping against his throat as she held on m. Morgan lifted her hips and thrust into her. He took her hard fast into another orgasm and his own release made him gr against her breasts.

They didn't p nstead they still thrust gently onto each other. Their lips were soft against each other's.

"You told me love me," Ava whispered.

Morgan smiled, but hardly took his mouth from hers. "I do love you. I love you so much."

Ava kissed him. "I love you too," she whispered, and her tongue found his so that they breathed against each other and Morgan's cock grew hard inside her. He smiled he moved her hips.

"I can't get enough of you. I'll never get enough of you. Say you'll be mine forever. Please, Ava?" He thrust her and the sensation made Ava groan with pleasure.

"Yes," she gasped.

Later when they were in Ava's bed, Morgan traced the curve of her hip as he talked.

"I want you in my life always. I do mean it. Tell me how you feel about that."

Ava kissed his chest.

"I'd like that. I want you too, Morgan."

They fell asleep cuddled together.

The next day was busy for Ava as she met up with other work and left the saving of the wild forest to picnic. Morgan was going to meet her in the smallholding yard lead the way to the picnic area. They were not going to see each other until then, and so the day felt a little barren to them both they went about their work.

Morgan {led Ava that night and told her he loved her. It made going to s{p without him easier.

Friday da}ed just as forecast. It was quite bright even though there wa{ cool bite to the air.

Ava coul{ardly wait for the designated time when the company reps w{d arrive. When they did, she ushered them into her car. They wer{ongenial and made polite small talk. They were puzzled when sh{ulled into the smallholding yard and parked her car, but they {intained a professional air, and shook hands with Morgan wh{he introduced himself as a woodsman with the National Trust. A{grinned a little as they followed Morgan through the wood{nd she noticed the way was easier than before. It almost felt as if { trees and ferns were leaning back to let them pass.

At the stre{, the company reps stopped to admire it. Ava watched them wa{ver the bridge with Morgan, and she felt sure she saw a strange {mering mist swirl around them. It was there and then gone, an{e too followed over the bridge.

The picnic {s already in progress and food was laid out on a long trestle table,{ere people sat on benches. Morgan sat the officials down, and{ sister Polly filled their glasses with fruit wine. The food wa{ssed around and soon everyone was happily talking. The atmos{re felt charged with magic to Ava as she sipped her wine. It {ed of cherries and plums. She took a fruit pastry from the ma{organ introduced as his brother when he passed her the plate{d it was so good she felt as if she was eating Faery food, magical{en food. There was music playing, a mix of flute music that add{o the charm.

It was almost a surprise when they found timselves back at Ava's car, the picnic over, and Morgan shaking hals goodbye with the company reps.

Ava felt slightly dreamy, but as soon as shtarted the engine of her car to drive everyone back to the cocil chambers her mind became clear and sharp. All that remained che picnic atmosphere was a feeling of overwhelming happiss.

When the company people had left the cocil building Ava went to sit in her office and call Morgan.

He answered on the first ring. "Did you eyy the picnic, Ava?" He didn't give her time to say anything.

Ava smiled as if he were there with her. "was magical, Morgan, and if they don't at least have more lové forests after that, then I will be surprised." She didn't want tcedict that they would save the wild forest.

Morgan was happy with her answer.

"Don't forget tonight I am taking you to? village fete. I'll drop by about six, it will be fun."

"I'm looking forward to it, Morgan."

"I have a little work to do in the forest, sll see you later," he said, and they ended the call.

It was about three thirty when she got ather call.

"Ms. McCartney, we were so impressed the wild forest, we thought better of our plans. We will not be ting it down.

We're submiting a new proposal to the council. Only the smallholdingwill be developed. We can put a two-story office and small researcl lab there. Thank you for lunch, by the way it, was most enjoyabe."

Ava was stunned.

She satfor two full minutes after the call, amazed at what had happened

She piced up her bag and jacket, and walked through to see the other envimnmental officers. She asked if they had heard the news. They ha. They grinned and applauded as she left the building.

Ava wa going to see Morgan, and after parking her car, she ran through thforest to where she thought he would be working.

He was owhere to be seen. She took out her cell phone and called him.

There wi no answer, and she walked rapidly along towards the stream to chik if he had gone back to the picnic spot. The forest helped her. Brarhes swayed away to let her pass, for here was Morgan's loved ie.

Ava reacld the bridge and she could hear the flute music. She could see pele in the picnic spot. They were laughing and talking. The air bore her eyes wavered and as she crossed the bridge, she felt a ght push as if she had crossed a barrier.

Ava stopp as she came to the picnic table. The people before her were cnged. Their clothes were those from long ago, as if they had steppefrom a Greco-Roman fresco. Morgan's mother and grandmother who had been old were now young, and dancing with men who had not previously been at the picnic. She thought that Morgan's brother had grown horns and fur over his legs. She looked again, and a tall, beautiful man with sandals that had wings adorning them swept Morgan's sister up into the air to dance and kiss.

Afraid, Ava wanted Morgan. Her eyes searched the amazing scene, and then she saw him. He was covered in leaves, green, gold, and some silver. He seemed to be made from them. He had a crown of twisted twigs on his head and from the twigs bloomed red and purple berries. Morgan's eyes were green, and not the blue she loved. Frozen still, Ava stared in astonishment.

Suddenly the picnic was shrouded in mist. Ava felt Morgan's strong arms around her.

"Ava," he said softly, "drink this." He pressed a glass to her lips.

His mother's pomegranate wine would take away what she had seen until he slowly introduced her to his world. He was intent on that. He was going to ask her to marry him, and in his pocket was a ring.

Ava felt compelled to drink and as she did, the mist cleared, and only Morgan, her lovely blue-eyed Morgan stood before her. She did not remember what she had seen, but she knew why she had come to find him.

"I was packing up the picnic things for my family," Morgan told her, and he placed the glass down on a nearby flower urn.

Ava smiled happily.

"I came to tell you the wild woods are saved. The company had a change of heart. Isn't that the best news, Morgan?"

He laughed. "It is. I'm so pleased for you." He hugged her close.

"Ava, I was going to ask you tonight, but now you are here I can't resist. I love you, you do know that?" His voice was low and Ava felt a stir of magic in the leaves of the trees close by.

"I do know, and I love you too," she whispered, before Morgan kissed her.

"Marry me, Ava, please?" He took the ring he had for her from his pocket.

Ava looked at it her eyes wide, as he held it out to her. The huge stone was set in a red gold band. It was the color of yellow autumn leaves and reflected the bronze of the leaves behind her.

"I know you haven't known me long, but I promise you'll not regret it. I'll love you forever." His voice was a whisper and Ava could only gaze at him. Morgan leaned to kiss her. He sighed against her lips disappointed because she had not answered.

Ava started to smile. She put her arms up around his neck and kissed him hard.

She drew back. "I love you, and I will marry you," she said softly, her lips a fraction from his.

Morgan smiled as his heart filled up with love and he put the ring on her finger. It was a perfect fit.

His family who watched from a mist amongst the trees looked at each other in delight.

"Nothing is better than a real love story," Polly whispered to Pomona, and she agreed.

Chapter One

October 25th

"Rebecca! Sit still! You're making me fidgety."

Rolling her eyes at her grinning friend, Rebecca complied and made herself comfortable. It wasn't easy, as she was being made to sit cross-legged in the middle her itchy carpet – but Louisa had said this was the best place to do it.

It was just one week before Samhain, the most important date in the Wiccan calendar. A Wiccan New Year, of sorts. It was also the Parting of the Veil…a time where the dead could freely pass through to the living, and converse with them.

Or so people said, anyway. Rebecca personally had never truly believed that part. She believed it was a day for remembering those who had passed, rituals to remember them by…but talking to them? Come on. She lived in the world of science and mobile phones. If the dead were going to talk to the living, they would probably send an email. Much easier than waiting for some floating curtain to rise.

But Louisa was deeply into all the spiritual aspects. Which is why Rebecca was sat like some yoga-twisted-grasshopper on her carpet, with the entire stock of Yankee Candles spread out around her in a ring. Louisa had this 'amazing' idea to do a past life regression. Not wanting to hurt her friend by the inevitable failure, Rebecca had already done some research on the Middle Ages. She would moan a little, mutter something about wearing velvet clothes, pretend she was in a castle, and that would be that. It wasn't as if she liked lying to her friend, but she remembered the upset of the 2010 Séance Fiasco.

"Okay…now just put your hands out like this…that's right." Louisa leaned over and manipulated her friend's hands into the right position, motioning for her to close her eyes. Rebecca shrugged and closed her eyelids, just opening them enough to peep out at the room. The lighting was soft and dramatic, the flames from the candles quivering in the breeze from the open living room door. It made the shadows from them dance manically on the wall, as if they were truly alive for this one night. It made her shiver, but she was ready to claim it was the breeze from the open passageway if Louisa said anything. The room was silent except for the rumbling of the boiler in the hallway outside, just warming up for the night. Rebecca felt a little silly, a giggle bubbling up inside her chest. She held it back, biting her cheek to subside it.

Louisa swivelled around to find her crystals, which were neatly laid out behind them on a silk cloth. She brought them into the centre of the candle-lit circle, patting the sides of the fabric reverently as she muttered to herself. The sleeves of her satin kimono dress whispered as they were swung about, almost flying into the licking flames. It wasn't Louisa's usual garb, but she had thought it right to wear something special for the occasion. Finally settled, she took a quick glance up at Rebecca, who hastily squeezed her eyes shut.

"Okay. Here we go. Now, I want you to relax. Just take a deep breath, and start to slowly count backwards from ten in your mind. Ten…nine…"

Rebecca curbed the grin once and for all, and inhaled heavily. At the very least, this would be relaxing—more like meditation than anything else. She tried to ignore the noise of the boiler outside, and concentrated on her own mind, chasing away anything other than counting.

Ten…nine…eight…wow, I do feel pretty calm right now…seven…six…maybe this will de-stress me at least…five…four…three…are my hands supposed to start feeling numb?…two…one…

Louisa's intonations floated over to her somewhere inside the bubble of her head. "Now I want you to imagine you are walking into a station. The station is old, but tidy. There is a train on the platform. I want you to slowly walk over to that train…"

I'll just walk over here to it. Hmm…it's green and a steam engine. Who would have thought I'd imagine a train like that? Just put my first foot on the step. Now my other. I'll hold onto the rail as I get into the carriage…wouldn't want to fall out of the imaginary train. And…in we go. Ooh, there's the whistle. Must be heading off soon. How come I'm moving around, but I can't feel my hands? Odd. I'll sit in here. An empty carriage. Perfect. No weirdos offering me tuna and haemorhoid cream sandwiches. It looks gorgeous outside…sunshine, green fields.

"And now the train is moving along…going slowly past those fields. And as it goes along, you can feel your mind slipping back…back into your past. Back into your other lives. The train stops at a small platform, just for you. There is a single door on the platform, waiting for you to open it…"

Okay, so off we get. Glad I didn't have to buy a ticket. Hah! That sun feels gorgeous…so warm. And I can hear birds. Wow, I didn't think my brain was good at imagining things. Everything is so pretty here. Oh, right…the door. It's red…paint peeling off. But it's my door. Apparently. Yes…yes…it feels like my door…

"…and now you're going to step through that door, into your past life…"

Why does Louisa's voice sound so far away? I should go through though. I'll just…there we go…crack the door open. It feels so welcoming. I can't hear Louisa very well, but I'll go through. Maybe I can hear her in there, maybe that's what I'm supposed to do. And…we're in. But…there's nothing here. It's black. And quiet. No, wait! I can see something! It's hard to make out…a tree? Yes, and more than one. But I'm facing the wrong way. I feel like I'm facing the wrong way…

Woah! It's a village! There are shields on a big hut…no, no, a longhouse. And people in old clothes. A chicken running about. I can hear a ringing, like metal…a blacksmith? This must be a…a…Rebecca's brain struggled for the correct term. A Viking village! That's it. This is Viking decoration. Almost as soon as she thought it, another word came to her — Ostmen. Ostmen? I never…but, yes…'Ostmen' sounds right. More so than 'Viking'.

Someone is walking over to me, I can hear them. If I just turn around…oh my GODS! He has to be the hottest man I've ever seen. A real Viking — er, 'Ostmen' warrior. Except for that dark hair. Yum. And he's so tall…oh, he's speaking to me! Something about…why do the words sound like they're coming through water? He...loves me? Wow. My brain sure knows what I like. Gods...his grin! I think I've just gone weak at my metaphorical knees. And there's another man. Yup, also yummy. I think my brain knows I've been on my own for too long. Two Viking warriors at once. I have got to...oh, what? Now he's proclaiming his love for me. Messy. The other dude is not happy.

Wait, where are they going?

There was a blinding flash, and Rebecca blinked, at least in her mind.

Huh? I'm in a room now...my room? Maybe. It looks like a bedroom...ah yes, I'm in bed. Cosy, nice and warm. Even if it does feel like straw underneath me. I wonder if I can get metaphorical hayfever? Hey, I can hear those two men again. In my house? They sure were easy-going about breaking and entering back then...or at least my brain thinks so. Oh, I can hear them coming this way...are they fighting? I'll just stay here and listen. Wait...they're coming in here.

"NO! He's going to kill you, wake up!"

I could hear that. Really clearly. I guess I'll turn over. One of them is behind me, I can hear him. I'll just...gods, this bed is itchy...he's just a shadow. It's not light enough. What was that flash? Is that a dagger? He's...FUCK! HE'S STABBING ME! HELP!

Rebecca jerked, her eyes snapping open to the bright modern ceiling light in her living room. For some reason, the patterns of it etched themselves in her mind with amazing clarity, green lines against the cream ceiling.

"Oh thank goodness! I couldn't wake you up! I thought you had-"

Louisa was babbling. She always babbled when she was worried. Rebecca realised she could feel her limbs again, even if they did feel like they were coming out of cryogenic freezing. She was back…from wherever her mind had been. Her head spun as she gingerly raised herself up into a sitting position. The room was brighter than it had been before, the candles blown out and swept away into their boxes once more. The crystals had vanished as well, and the carpet was clear of spiritual paraphernalia. The feeling of being back in modern life was strange and thrilling, like she had truly been somewhere far away. She hadn't, of course. Rebecca knew it was just her overactive imagination. Closing her eyes for a second to blot out the dizziness, Rebecca opened them again to the sight of Louisa, her face streaked with tears.

"Oh no! What's wrong, Louisa? Why are you crying?"

Louisa gaped at her before shaking her head melodramatically. "Why am I crying? You were crying—that's what set me off! And then it went on for an hour. I couldn't wake you up. You were just laid there, babbling to yourself in a foreign language. Then you started crying. Then you screamed and woke up. Now we're stood here having this conversation and I'm screaming at *you.*"

"I…screamed? I was crying?" Cautiously, Rebecca put her fingers to her face. Shock registered on her features as they came away with salty water. Pawing at her face, she could feel the tell-tale rivulets where tears had cascaded down. "This is…weird."

Louisa threw her arms around her, breathing rapidly to try and regain her composure. Rebecca patted her back, her brow set into a frown. "So…what did I say?"

"I have no idea. You weren't speaking English. What did you see?"

Rebecca shook her head, looking puzzled. "Why wouldn't I speak in English?" In a daze, she reached behind for the arm of the sofa and pulled herself up onto the soft green cushions. She still felt like she had just been woken up from a deep sleep. Plumping herself into the cosiness of the couch, Rebecca looked down into the worried face of her friend, her brown eyes wide with anticipation. "I, er…I guess I saw a village. Like a Viking village. But the word 'Ostmen' kept coming back to me. I don't know why."

Louisa nodded knowingly, her copper hair falling across her shoulders. "Yes, that makes sense. The Vikings called themselves 'Ostmen'. It meant, 'men from the East'."

Rebecca grinned. She could always count on Louisa to know her ancient history. She had been interested in it since they were both children. It was probably where her brain had picked up the word, in another of Louisa's enthusiastic talks. "Anyway, while I was there, two men appeared. They both said they loved me—and they were *hot*, by the way. Then I was in a bedroom…one of them shouted something out about the other one killing me. Then I got stabbed by this shadowy figure. I couldn't see his face. That was it." She clasped her hands together in her lap, and grinned. Settling back into the sofa, she grabbed the remote and pointed it at the TV.

"Hang on just a minute!" Louisa snatched the remote out of her friend's hands and shoved it behind her. "That's it? You just saw your own murder from a past life, and you're going to watch *TV*?"

Rebecca's intense cerulean eyes roamed over her friend's face, considering her answer. "What are you talking about?" There was a moment's pause as Louisa waited for Rebecca to give answer to her own question. Finally glancing away, Rebecca heaved a sigh. "Look, you know I don't believe in this stuff. It was just my imagination. Like a vivid dream, or something."

"Oh, yeah? Then why were you crying as though your heart was breaking? Pretty damn vivid, alright."

"What? You think it was *real*? Oh, come on, Louisa." Rebecca leaned over and caught the remote back up in her hand, clicking the TV into life. The droning comfort of colours and voices washed over her as a comedy appeared. Louisa stared at her in astonishment for a moment, shaking her head in disbelief. Rebecca stared solidly ahead at the screen, blatantly ignoring her friend's attempts to get her attention. Shrugging her shoulders, Louisa jumped up and plonked herself next to Rebecca on the sofa.

"Whatever. I'm telling you, it was real. I watched you. Those men were real, and your murder was real."

Chapter Two

October 26th

The light buzzed and flickered about her head before returning to its static glow. Rebecca gave it a disdainful look, tapping it with one finger. Shaking her head, she returned to brushing her teeth, her tired face reflected in the bathroom mirror. She really needed to rent a new house—the landlord did nothing to fix the faulty electrics. At least it was cheap though.

Laughter floated through from the TV in the bedroom, making her brush faster. She hated missing this program. Rebecca spat out into the sink, running the water to clean off her brush. As she placed it back into its holder carefully, she glanced back up at her face. Her fingers traced the sides of her eyes, where crow's feet were starting to emerge. *Ugh.* Rebecca had always been one of the first ones to say that you should grow old gracefully, but she didn't mean at the young age of twenty-eight. She peered in for a closer look-

What the hell?

Blinking, Rebecca spun around in shock. She had seen a shadow blur past in the landing behind. The blood drained from her body, her limbs going icy with fear. *Someone is in my house!* With the bathroom door wide open, she had a full view of it. Her head darted from side to side as she tried to look for anything that might be a useful weapon, if she needed it. The bathroom was not the best place to find it. *If only I'd had a machete installed along with the bath suite.* Finally settling on her straighteners, she padded out into the landing carpet. They wouldn't have been her first choice, but she was ready to give a good smack with them if she could.

The light in the bathroom buzzed again, flittering on and off as if a moth was caught in its beam. The sound made Rebecca flinch, but she ignored it and slowly tip-toed across the dark landing. She knew better than to shout out, "Who's there?" She had seen enough horror films to know that you never got an answer, and that was usually how you gave away where you were. There was no noise from the spare room where she had seen the shadowy figure run into. The light in the bathroom finally came on full again, but then the landing light came into life.

The hair on the back of Rebecca's neck stood on end as she dared a glance at it. She knew full well it wasn't switched on. It flickered on and off, before finally giving up the ghost and returning to the darkness. A trickle of cold sweat ran down her forehead, making her grip the straighteners even tighter, everything in her body willing her to scream and run away. For a second, Rebecca did think about darting down the stairs, grabbing her mobile to ring the police, and running outside. Really, it shouldn't even be a thought. She should be *doing* it.

A noise from the spare room made her look up in panic. Her chest rose and fell rapidly with the silent breaths that were rushing from her lips. Taking a nervous swallow, Rebecca leaned her arm out to switch the landing light back on, and advanced towards the room. The landing light flickered yet again, but stayed on, bathing the landing in artificial yellow glow. Her lips had never felt so dry. Her heart was pounding against her ribcage so fervently she was sure it would give her away before anything else, the blood from it rushing through her ears louder than the laughter from the TV.

Rebecca's hand trembled as she reached out to push the spare room door open. It slowly swung on its hinges, protesting loudly with a creak. *Great. So much for not letting them know I'm here.* Moving fast so she didn't get surprised herself, Rebecca lurched across for the light switch in the spare room. She snapped it on, bracing herself in the doorway, and turned to find —

Nothing.

No-one was there. With the room fully lit, all she could see were the cardboard boxes from when she had moved in. A layer of dust. The carpet. Nothing else. Even the curtains at the window were still. She nudged the door back on itself, to be sure no-one was hiding behind it. Another scan. No, the room was definitely empty. Rebecca let out a deep breath and lowered the straighteners. She gave a nervous laugh, echoing off the walls.

"See, *this* is why you shouldn't live alone…silly girl," she muttered to herself. A '*ping*' of noise made her look up sharply at the ceiling light. It was swaying. A moment ago it had stood still. *A breeze, perhaps? The windows really need that insulation putting around them.* It continued swinging, and began to flash on and off, as the other lights had done. As if in response, the bathroom light and the landing light began to do the same. Rebecca refused to be worried by it this time. *Damn electrics.* But she couldn't ignore it when she suddenly realised the laughter had stopped coming through from the TV—instead just channelling static.

Whipping her head around, Rebecca saw something that made her body turn to stone—petrified, in every sense of the word. A shadowy figure was indeed in her spare room. But not a physical one. A human shaped figure was moving across her wall, ghostly and dark. It looked straight at her, its red eyes burning into her skull. A sound somewhere between a squeak and a low moan escaped her strangled vocal chords. Then there was silence except for the static as the figure stared...and moved closer.

Rebecca dropped the straighteners like lightening, spinning and racing for the stairs. She nearly slipped on the carpet, righting herself on the bannister at the last moment, her ankle protesting in agony. Half-jumping, half-sprinting, she made her way into the dark hallway below, snatching her mobile off the side table. A blast of icy midnight air slapped her face as she threw the front door wide, and flung herself out onto the sharp gravel of her driveway. With trembling fingers, she looked back up at the erratic light show going on inside her house, and dialled for Louisa.

"Louisa?! Louisa, it's me. I...I have s-something b-bad in my house. Please come quickly! Yes, I'm fine...I'm fine..." her voice dissolved into sobs.

Chapter Three

October 27th

"Will this work?" Rebecca gave a doubtful glance over to the pile of colourful vegetation and crystals Louisa had brought over the previous night. She had also brought a large overnight bag, promising she wasn't going anywhere until she got rid of whatever that shadowy...*thing*...was.

"It should do. I've done it a few times." Turning from brushing the windowsill with a bunch of assorted herbs, Louisa smiled over at her worried friend. "Whatever it is, it won't come back when I've finished. And I'm not leaving until I *know* it's gone."

Rebecca gave a shaky nod, and folded her arms nervously. Chewing her lip, she paced back and forth across the room. "It just...it freaked me out, you know? I've never felt like that before. Like...like I was rooted to the ground."

"Typical of hauntings."

Louisa turned back to the windowsill, and laid a stalk of lavender in the corner. Chanting quietly under her breath, she reached over for a pack of matches, and struck one. It burst warmly into life, leaving the room with the scent of sulphur. A candle flame grew under the match's heat, wavering like a dancer awakening from slumber. Louisa picked the candle up, and held it up to the window, announcing loudly, "This candle is to lead you away from this house to the Summerlands. Follow it and be free."

She turned away from the window, and began to make her way across the room, motioning for Rebecca to follow her. Rebecca remembered this part—they had to 'lead' the ghost away from her house by use of the candle. Going from window to window, they would finally take the candle outside by the front door, and let it go away. She had no idea if this would work, but…she had no valid explanation for what happened in her house the other night. This might work. Unless the ghost was as doubtful of the process as she herself was. The thought of that shadowy figure watching them with curiosity and deciding to stay instead made her shiver.

They made their way through the whole house, the chant sounding ominous and heavy in the silence. The little candle swayed wildly as it was taken from window to window, momentarily breaking a light through the darkness. Rebecca briefly wondered what her neighbours would think if they looked up at her house. Eventually coming to the front door, Louisa prepared to unlock the door—

"Wait!"

A chill rose over both ladies, cold hands clawing their way up across their heads. The voice that had spoken somewhere in the air behind their heads sounded far away and burbling, as though it were coming to them through water, or a thick wall of marshmallow. Louisa grabbed her friend's hand—whether in fear or comfort, she wasn't sure. Rebecca's throat had dried up, leaving her swallowing just to suck life back into her mouth.

"Please look at me. You have nothing to fear from me."

Fearing she would come face to face again with the shadowy nightmare from last night, Rebecca slowly turned to meet the voice, keeping her eyes cast to the ground. Her breaths came out in short huffs as she prepared herself to look up and come face to face with the entity haunting her house.

To her surprise, the sight that met her eyes was not that of the shadowy creature. A very definite man was stood before them, dressed in a long linen tunic to his knees and tied at the waist with a leather strip. He wore muted brown woollen trousers beneath this, and a long cape was thrown around his shoulders, fastened at his throat with a brooch of exquisite detailing. His shoulder-length blond hair was partially plaited and tied back, his pale blue eyes roving the two women's faces with interest. The only hint that he was not a living embodiment of a Viking stood before them was the soft gold glow resonating around his figure.

Louisa let out a sharp gasp. "He's...a Viking. Like the men from your regression!"

Rebecca shook her head. "No. He *is* one of the men from my regression."

"You remember me then, Rebecca? I have missed you...my love."

Dumbly, she nodded in response. "A-are you the one who scared me last night?"

The man looked downwards, his form shuddering as he sighed. *"No. I'm afraid not. That was…him. The other man. He wanted you all those years ago, Rebecca. But you were in love with me. He killed you out of spite…and…I didn't get there in time."* The image wavered once more as his tone grew mournful. *"Every lifetime you've had, he's come back to murder you again. He waits until your twenty-eighth year, the year he betrayed you. The veil grows thin and both of us pass through. But every time I have tried to protect you, you ran from me. Alas, I do not hold my once human form, and it scared you away."*

There was a pregnant pause as Rebecca turned to Louisa. "Is this…is he speaking about me? This can't be real."

"I am real, my love. If only corporeal. And this time I know I will protect you. Let me stay, please. The ritual will only cast me out, not him, for he does not follow the light. He only follows the darkness. Let me stay and save you this time." His voice was as pleading as his soft eyes, holding out his hands in a gesture of helplessness.

A doubtful look was cast between the two women. Louisa shrugged at Rebecca's wide-eyed stare. "I don't know," she hissed. "It's *your* past life's love. You tell me. Should I leave it?"

Frozen to the spot, Rebecca could only stare helplessly as the figure glided across to her. He stopped just short, towering above her with his built frame. An ethereal hand rose to her cheek, gently making a gesture of stroking it. All she could feel on her skin was a prickling sensation, like pins and needles. Her gaze drifted up to his, his tender eyes brimming with unshed tears.

"I love you, Rebecca. Remember me." Before she had a chance to move, her ghostly intruder had lowered his lips to hers, sending

tingling sparks dancing across her mouth. A flash of memory raced through her mind...his lips on hers...laughing with him...running through a forest as he playfully chased her...holding her tightly...the memories somehow didn't feel entirely real, but she put that down to the fact that none of this seemed real.

"I...remember you," she whispered as he pulled away. Her hand unconsciously went to her own lips, to trace where he had just touched her in that strange way. Taking a deep breath, she turned back to Louisa, and motioned for her to bring the candle back in. "Don't do it. I don't know how, but...I think this man was my lover." Turning back to the shimmering image, she narrowed her eyes. "This does not mean I'm happy with all of this. But I don't want that...thing...in my house. If you can get rid of him, I'll be happy."

"Consider it done." The image of the man smiled, and he quivered for just a second more before fading into thin air.

Louisa softly padded over, the candle still in a death grip in her left hand. She laid a hand on Rebecca's arm, making her start in surprise. "Rebecca...I just want you to know...this is weird. Really, really weird."

Chapter Four

October 28th

Dark bags showed beneath Rebecca's eyes. She hadn't slept properly for three nights now, only getting rest in fitful bursts. She rocked herself on her bed, knees drawn up to her chest as she sat upright watching the doorway. The hallway light was on outside, but the bedroom light was off. Louisa had said she just couldn't sleep with it on.

Alright for some, Rebecca thought to herself, smiling gently as she glanced across at Louisa's snoring form. She sighed. Another quick look at the alarm clock by her side. 4:40 am. Nearly morning. Soon she could have a nap.

Her eyelids lowered themselves automatically, and she snapped them wide open again, stretching them as if to keep them open. She didn't dare fall asleep. The thought of that creature creeping up on her in the middle of her room while she slept was just too much. *Maybe I should just have a nap. Only for five minutes.* Her mouth stretched in a gaping yawn, as if in response to her thoughts.

He's unlikely to turn up now, right? Another furtive glance at the clock. 4:43 am. *It's practically daylight.* Rebecca leaned back into her pillows, accepting their welcoming softness with a sigh of contentment. She stared up at the ceiling for a few moments, listening intently. Her eyelids threatened to pull themselves shut again. Another look at the time. 4:47 am.

Rebecca closed her eyes in sweet relief. The darkness behind them was soothing, beckoning her into the arms of sleep. Her quilt had never felt so warm and comfortable. She twisted over and drew it up above her shoulders, taking a deep sigh of satisfaction.

A buzzing sound alerted her. Her heartbeat raced up to lightning speed before her eyes even saw the light in the hallway flashing on and off. Through the crack in her eyelids, she could spy the light swinging wildly about as though it had been caught in a strong wind. A few heartbeats passed before she saw the encroaching figure of the shadow man, arching its way across the hallway wall.

A whimper escaped her throat, and she leaned across to nudge her friend. "Louisa! *Louisa!*" she hissed frantically. But Louisa appeared to have been struck almost into unconsciousness. She didn't even stir when Rebecca anxiously started prodding her sharply. The shadow flickered across the wall outside again, and Rebecca suddenly realised he was the one doing it. He had made sure she was all alone.

What the hell does one even use against a shadow?! Despite no logic flooding her brain in response, she began to desperately search her room with her eyes for some sort of weapon, anything. She remembered what the other ghostly visitor, her lover from another lifetime, had said to both her and Louisa... *'he doesn't follow the light'*.

So perhaps it could chase him away. Her eyes alighted on the torch Louisa had brought in with her. But it was halfway across the room, away from their beds. This meant she would not only have to leave the safety of her bed, but also go closer to the shadowy man outside. Rebecca curled her hands into fists, and tried to calm her breathing, readying herself for the leap out of bed. "Just a second, that's all it will take. Just a second, Rebecca," she murmured to herself. Her voice came out in a squeak, draining her already depleted confidence.

Heart so high in her throat she felt sick, Rebecca whipped off the covers and sprinted towards the torch. Her knees burned from the friction as she skidded down on the carpet. Trying to ignore the flashes of light from the swinging ceiling lamp in the hallway, she threw her hand out towards the torch. Grabbing it, she drew it to her chest and clicked for it to switch on.

Nothing happened.

A whimper fell from Rebecca's mouth as she rapidly clicked and re-clicked the 'on' switch, the torch still refusing to burst into light. A rush of air made her look up with dread, her body growing numb from the fear racing through her veins. *The shadowy man was watching her!*

He stood in the doorway, flickering and dark, those burning eyes searing a hold into Rebecca's head. If she could have taken a guess, Rebecca would have said the rushing, howling sound that filled her ears was the shadowy creature attempting to speak. She had no interest in what he wanted to say though. The shadow man took a slow step forward. He seemed to wait for her response, or perhaps he was judging his position. As Rebecca's body gripped in terror, he came forward a little more, stepping over the metal trim that ran between the two carpets of the hallways and bedroom.

As he moved into the bedroom, no more than two metres away from Rebecca, she tried once more with the torch. As she furiously tried to click it 'on' once more, her fingers fumbling over it, the light finally gave up in the hallway—and went out altogether.

Left in the pitch blackness, with the shadow man so close she could have reached out and touched him, Rebecca let out a piercing scream. It was so high she could feel her own eardrums reverberating with the force of it, ringing in her ears. As she screamed, the torch finally sprang into life. It cut a stream of brilliant white through the darkness like a knife, putting the shadow man's face into sharp relief for a split second.

A face could just be made out, a shape that could have been a nose, a hollow for a mouth—and those glaring red eyes. His mouth fell open into a large chasm in his features, larger than any human mouth should go, and gave a blood-curdling yell that screeched through the air. A second later his face was gone, as he moved away from the light. Terrified, Rebecca swung the torch around madly, seeing only flashes of his eyes as he attempted to dart out of the way of the light.

Just as she had the fearful thought that this might go on all night, there was a blinding white light behind her. It seared into the corner of her eyes, flooding the room with light. Before she could think of what was happening, it grew brighter, and the shadow man could be clearly seen. The shadow man screamed in horror, and disappeared into the darkened hallway so fast it seemed he had been sucked into it.

"You're safe now. I'm sorry I didn't come sooner, Rebecca."

The voice washed over her like a wave of relief. As the torch rolled from her limp hand, the figure of the Viking man who had spoken to her in the hallway appeared. His smiling face was almost too much for Rebecca, and she burst into tears as he glided around to face her.

"Sh, sh…what's wrong? I'm here now, don't cry."

"I'm…I'm sorry…I just…and he was here…and I was so frightened!" Rebecca's words were broken up by breathless sobs, her vision blurred by sudden tears. The figure brushed his hand along her arm, sending prickles spinning across it like sparks. She raised her tear-streaked face to his, feeling more comforted by the second as she looked into his eyes.

"Come. Get back into bed." Although he couldn't help her back up, the ghostly figure gestured towards her bed, cradling his ethereal arm around her. Shoulders racked by the sobs she couldn't prevent, Rebecca gingerly rose from the floor and made her way into her welcoming sheets. Louisa was still fast asleep, stirring a little as Rebecca passed her. She was glad to see that her friend was okay.

As she sank into the pleasurable delight of her mattress, Rebecca leaned back against the headboard. As she went to close her eyes, desperate to stop the flood of tears, she heard the ghostly man speak once more.

"Rebecca, he is afraid of the light. Make sure you keep this by your bedside at all times. If you see him again, simply turn it on. I cannot always pass through the obstacles he puts in my path, but I will always come as fast as I can." He smiled adoringly, and passed his hand over her forehead as if soothing it. Rebecca sighed in contentment, and allowed the calming motion to pass over her.

"What's your name?" she murmured.

The figure's smile faded a little. *"It's not important. The name would mean nothing to you now. Just remember I love you."*

"But why—" Rebecca snapped her eyes open to find he had vanished, and the hallway light had come back on. For a few seconds, she stared at it steadily, daring it to move. Her eyes never left it as she slid down below the covers, torch clutched tightly in one hand…

Chapter Five

October 29th

Louisa swirled the wine in her glass, holding it up to the light. The brilliance of it shone through, ruby-coloured glow falling onto her face. "So, do you think he'll be back tonight?"

Rebecca shuddered. "I damn well hope not." She leaned over and checked the lightbulb in her small desk lamp for the twentieth time. Her whole room looked like Blackpool Illuminations. Deciding not to take any chances this time, she had filled the room with almost every lamp in her house. Several torches were scattered in a small pile between the two women, and there were five lights stuck on the walls that ran off batteries alone. If the shadowy man tried to step foot near her, he would surely be blinded.

Louisa herself looked as though she was blinded by the brilliance of thirty sixty-watt bulbs. It was lucky for her that both women had decided to stay up tonight, so there was no chance of her sleep being disrupted by them. Rebecca leaned back against the bed and sat on the floor next to her friend. She nodded towards the wine bottle. "Can you pass me a glass, please?"

The room fell silent except for the burbling sound of wine pouring. Rebecca took the proffered glass gratefully, smiling and murmuring her thanks. Louisa gave a grim smile back and took a large swallow of the crimson liquid. They both went back to their silent vigil, watching the doorway between the bedroom and the hallway. The room was silent. The house was silent. Even the night outside seemed silent.

The hallway light flickered for a few moments with a buzzing sound, but remained lit. It grew more insistent, then the sound melted away. The room fell hushed once more.

Chapter Six

October 30th

The last two nights had passed without incident. Nothing at all. It was as if the shadow man had truly been frightened away by the stacks of light illuminating the house — or was perhaps afraid of the ghostly Viking who was so kind to Rebecca.

Louisa had left early that morning as she needed to get to work, promising she would be back that evening. There were large black shadows under her eyes, which had made Rebecca feel guilty. She didn't want her friend to have to struggle with anything because of this damn shadow-creature. But at least it was almost over. Tomorrow night would be Samhain, the Parting of the Veil, and he would be unable to cross over after that. She would be safe once more.

As a writer, Rebecca worked from home, so there was no way to leave the house for very long. She had deadlines to meet. But sat in front of her screen, no words would come. She began to type, but stopped herself when she realised she had written utter nonsense. Groaning in annoyance, Rebecca pushed away from her desk on her wheeled chair. She jumped up, grabbing her coffee mug to get her fifth 'inspiration-inducer' of the afternoon.

She rubbed her eyes as she pattered through into her small yet cosy kitchen. It was a typical cottage-style kitchen, charming and covered in pale green, but certainly not modern. The coffee machine thrummed into life as she tapped one of the buttons, leaving her mug underneath to collect the rich nectar it held.

As the liquid burbled into her oversized mug, she hummed a tuneless ditty to herself, checking a few things pinned up to her noticeboard. Already she felt a little calmer about the situation. In the brilliant daylight, shadows and ghosts seemed like a distant dream. Rebecca spun a little to her made-up song, smiling at her own silliness. As the machine clicked to let her know it was almost done, she turned around—

Rebecca froze in horror. She was sure she had just seen a long shadow flit across the kitchen floor. She swallowed, but couldn't seem to make her dry throat work, only succeeding in swallowing so much her jaw ached. Turning away from the kitchen, she looked out of the window until she felt her heartbeat calming down. "It was nothing, Rebecca. It's playing on your mind, that's all." Her eyes roamed over the lit landscape waiting outside. The gentle swaying of the trees, their golden and ruby leaves fluttering down to the ground in a swansong ballet. The weak yet brilliant sunshine that poured through the open window, silently warming the glass. A few birds who were fluffed up against the chilling breeze, merrily singing their admiration for the scene before them. Rebecca let out a heavy sigh, slowly loosening her grip on the kitchen sink where she had dug her fingers into the hard steel.

The room felt somehow colder than it had before however, as she reached over for her coffee cup. Hands still trembling, she took a long sip of the caramel-flavoured macchiato. If her nerves didn't calm down soon, she was going to have to stay somewhere else for a few days—ghosts saving her life be damned. The soothing liquid trickled down her throat, pouring warmth into her fear-cold body.

"Rebecca…"

The coffee cup did not survive the crash as it slipped from Rebecca's shaking fingers, splintering into a hundred different pieces that flew across the kitchen tiles. A strange mewling sound echoed from her lips as her wide eyes took in the figure that stood before her. "He…he…he said you would be afraid of the light. T-That it would chase you away," she whispered. She *had* seen a shadow tilting across the floor.

The six-foot black shadow before her tilted his head, his red eyes looking like two car beams in the dead of night racing towards her. *"Normally, that would be true. But I have braved it for you. To come for you, Rebecca."* His voice sounded as though it were rasping on sandpaper. To her dread, a black hand reached out for her. But it paused, as though he were waiting for her to take it. She shook her head, closing her eyes as tears rolled down from them.

"I see. I see he has got to you once more, and convinced you that he will save you. That I will kill you, yes?"

No answer came from her mute lips.

A scream rose from the shadow's twisted form, rising in pitch until Rebecca had to clamp her hands over her ears. The reverberation rang around the small modern room, chasing itself, echoing over and over. Before she had time to think, the shadow had moved in so it was no more than a few inches away. This close, she could see that tiny parts of the shadow seemed to float away, black cinders rising into an invisible wind.

The shadow's arms wound around Rebecca as he advanced towards her, and her world went dark before she had a chance to utter another word…

☙ ☙ ☙

…"Help!" Rebecca sat upright in a panic, her head darting from side to side. The shadow was gone. But something still wasn't right.

Her hands went to touch the coolness of the kitchen floor, but instead she met simply with the suppleness of animal furs. She dropped them immediately with a horrified face, only then realising her kitchen had vanished altogether, leaving her in an ancient wooden room. It appeared to be sunk into the floor, as if the room had been dug further down than the ground outside. A howling gale could be heard wracking itself against the walls outside, and Rebecca shivered in response. Twisting around, she could see that she rested upon a large wooden bed frame, curved along the headboard so that it vaguely resembled a sleigh. The sides of the bed were decorated with small gold emblems, and the sheets looked as though they had been woven from clean, new threads. Her hands flew up as she felt something move on her head, and Rebecca warily felt along the edges of what resembled a crown, except that flowers and ribbons seemed to be entwined around its many edges.

A giggle came from outside the room, along with much shushing and muttering. Rebecca didn't know whether to stay where she was, or to go and find out about the noise. When another voice—a male voice—sounded out, she decided to stay put for now. The fire crackled in response to her pondering, making her jump and swivel her head sharply to the noise. It was against the far wall, heating the room gently. A few pots sat either side of it, gleaming in the roaring calm of the flames.

"Go on! She's in now, you've all been witnesses. Go back to the feast and enjoy yourselves."

There was more giggling and tittering, but eventually it died away and disappeared as a heavy door boomed shut. The roar of the wind outside whistled in for a split second, before vanishing again to its subdued banging inside the strange house. Just as Rebecca was about to call out, the door into the room opened, and a tall, dark-haired man strode in.

He was easily six-foot or more, and dressed in a simple tunic and cloak. The cloak was fixed at his shoulder by a gleaming blue topaz brooch, matching the clarity and colour of his eyes. It was a direct contrast to the short black hair he sported, light stubble growing through on his chin. The man's lips curled in a soft smile as he saw Rebecca's frightened expression.

"Please, don't be frightened, Rebecca. You're quite safe here."

Shaking her head, she replied, "W-What's going on? I was in my kitchen, and then there was a shadow, and then—"

"Rebecca, don't you recognise me? *I'm* the shadow man from your house."

There was a split pause as she digested this information, before she made as though to leap from the bed and out of the door. The man grabbed her wrist as she moved across, pulling her back towards him. Because she twisted as she went back to him, Rebecca managed to position herself right in front of him, so close she could have brushed his lips with hers. The thought that this was the shadow man was nearly swept from her mind as her breathing sped up in response to his woody scent. "How can you be? You're a normal man!"

The stranger grinned, and looked away for a second. "This…" he swept an arm across the room. "This is not real, Rebecca. Think of it like watching a film you've seen before, but haven't watched for a while. We're not in the past, but it's a memory of the past. A memory of…our wedding night." A deep sigh escaped his lips, and his fingers fiddled with a loose thread on the edge of the blanket.

"Our…" Rebecca's repetition of his sentence floated away as she frowned. "But I don't even remember your name. And if you're the shadow man, why do you look like this? Why are we here? You are trying to kill me. The other Viking told me so."

Another shake of his head. "No…you've…you've got it the wrong way around. Why would I harm you? I had loved you since we were children. When our parents agreed to our union, it was the happiest day of my life. Radormr was always jealous that you loved me in return and not him, no matter what he offered you for your hand. To punish us both, he first killed you, and then me. Every lifetime we've had since, he's tricked you into believing I will harm you. Then when you've managed to keep me away, he kills you all over again. He plants untrue memories in your head to make you believe you loved him, but they are never as strong as this."

"Radormr..." Rebecca rolled the name around her tongue like an exotic fruit. "It...it sounds familiar. But what was your name?"

His lips curled into a confidently sexy grin. Despite the conversation, her stomach did a leaping flip at that grin. It was as though her body truly was yearning to have him as her own. "My name is Hafgrímr. It means 'the sea'. Your name in this life was Sigrior."

"Hafgrímr and Sigrior. I...yes..." Rebecca's voice trailed away as flashes of memory came back to her, dancing around her mind like wisps of smoke almost too intangible to grab and hold onto. This man and herself standing before a large crowd of people, first trying a ribbon around their wrists, then exchanging rings from a sword. A great feast, people laughing and joking. Before then, as young children, running through the woods. As teenagers, whispering to one another about the day they would have a child of their own. Feeling overwhelmed by the thoughts flooding her mind, Rebecca groaned and pressed the heels of her palms into her eyes.

Hafgrímr wrapped his large hands around hers and stroked them tenderly. "I'll make them stop, Rebecca. But I need you to see just one more memory. Just one."

"No! I have no idea what's happening! And you're the one who is *trying to kill me!*"

Hafgrímr winced at that, and hid his eyes from her. Through gritted teeth, he muttered, "I would *never* kill you! I would never harm you in any way. Radormr killed you, and killed me...then every lifetime when I tried to save you, he came and convinced you I would kill you. It's not true!" Without another word, he pulled Rebecca's hands away from her eyes. As he did so, a flame leapt from the hearth of the large fireplace, and danced along his arm before circling itself around Rebecca's head.

As though she were watching someone else, Rebecca could look through the spinning flame to a scene unfolding in this very room. She lay asleep under the covers, peacefully cuddled next to Hafgrímr. It was then she noticed the third presence in the room — a golden-haired man. He was crying a torch of an oiled rag around a stick, fully ablaze and yet small enough not to disturb the sleeping couple. There were only a few heartbeats as he darted across the floor, slid a dagger from his sleeve, and plunged it into Rebecca's — or Sigrior's — chest. Rebecca cried out as her mirror image in the bed stirred, only to start screaming. Blood pooled from her in a terrifying rush, the wound making her collapse back onto the bed on feeble limbs.

Hafgrímr woke up at the screams, leaping from the bed in one swoop. It took only a few seconds of him looking from Radormr to Sigrior to work out what had just occurred. As Sigrior's eyes grew glassy and he realised she was dying, he let out a howl more akin to an animal than a man, falling to the floor in horror. The next events seemed to swirl in slow motion. Hafgrímr reached for his side, to pull out his sword. As the metal sang with deadly intent from the sheath, Radormr ran forwards, throwing his arm back. The sword swung free, swiping towards Radormr. He moved out of the way, stepping neatly to the side. Hafgrímr prepared to swing again, but Radormr threw his arm forwards and let go of the torch.

Rebecca watched with sick horror as it sailed through the air, alighting on Hafgrímr himself. He yelled out in pain, but simply carried on advancing towards Radormr, his sword whistling as he arced it through the air. His whole body was now aflame, a living embodiment of the fire itself. But there was little he could do as it ate away at him hungrily. As Radormr watched in silent vigil, Hafgrímr's body sank to the floor, his hand still moulded to the hilt of his weapon. As he burned until he turned black, Radormr gave him a kick with the toe of his boot, and spat on him.

The image faded, leaving Rebecca with a dizzy feeling of having been somewhere else. She was still sat in the room with Hafgrímr, but even this wasn't real, as he had told her. Seeing her pain and confusion, Hafgrímr wrapped his arms around her, tucking her head in under his chin.

Before she could stop herself, Rebecca found her shoulders shaking from tears. They racked her; a flood of emotion for the life and love she had lost not once, but many times over. All because of one jealous man. Hafgrímr said nothing, simply holding her close to his chest, squeezing his own eyes shut.

Eventually she broke free of his hold, her eyes streaked red from the salty water. Taking a shuddering breath, she asked, "Why was he lit up then? And you were a black shadow!"

"He is lit up, because he was the one who carried the torch. And I have always been black and shadowy because of my burnt body. I suppose the fates intended for these to be triggers for you to remember us both, but unfortunately you always saw him as the good man because of the light."

"But...you're suggesting this has happened many times over?"

"Yes."

"Why haven't you done this before, then? Why haven't you shown me what you have shown me now?"

Hafgrímr looked deeply into her eyes. Rebecca gasped as she not only saw, but almost felt the intent in them. "I haven't been strong enough. Every lifetime I came to see you, he weakened me by shining light on me. It repeats the agony of the light of those flames so long ago, and leaves me powerless to help you. He keeps me trapped in the darkness, so I can only sneak away a few times to find you. I finally figured out that the only way to save you was to reach you through the worst light of all for me. Daylight. It burned, but I would do it a thousand times over if it would save you."

Finally convinced, Rebecca gingerly laid a hand on Hafgrímr's arm. He looked down at it as if he were amazed by her gentle caress. His breathing sped up as he continued to stare, but he said nothing. Rebecca leaned forwards and whispered, "Thank you."

"Please, don't thank me. I...I should have woke up that night. I should have stopped him before he murdered you. I should—"

"Ssh. You did everything you could. It wasn't your fault."

Hafgrímr raised his eyes to meet Rebecca's, his jaw set in determination. "Rebecca, you must go back now. Then this time I can try to save you."

She looked around herself mournfully, still stroking his arm absent-mindedly. "Must I go right now? Even if this isn't real, I…I want to know more about you. I want to know what kind of man you were. Or are."

"Are." Hafgrímr assented. "I still exist, if not in the form I once had. I wish…" His voice trailed away, and his crystalline eyes grew dark. "I wish I could make you remember the times you could feel me in person, know me in person. But this is as close as I dare."

Rebecca's brow creased into a frown. "What do you mean?"

A tongue dabbed nervously out over his lips. "Rebecca…even in the ethereal form I hold now, when I see you…Gods, I want to touch your skin, to breathe you into the very essence of my being. To taste you, and have you linger about my lips. To touch you in such a way that my name rings out from your throat."

The breath left her lips as she listened to Hafgrímr's heartfelt words. An ache, long since forgotten until now, seemed to stir within her soul. A burning need for him, that could only be sated by a true love lost over centuries ago. "Why can't you show me now?"

A flash from those wickedly handsome eyes again. Hafgrímr shook his head. "You don't understand. None of this is here. I've woven this image of your memory around you, of our wedding night. But it's not really here. You are still in the kitchen, and you're sat talking to a shadow man with fearful red eyes. Although it's still me…I can't ask you to look at me in that way. This is how I was once. What if the image faltered? Would you want to look upon the face of your lost love in the ghostly form he now takes?"

To his surprise, Rebecca responded, "Yes. I don't care about that. You loved me once. And I loved you. Any man who would come back again and again for me, to try and save me, despite the fact I have rejected you every time…you must be a wonderful man." The end of her sentence trailed away in the heavy silence. Before he had a chance to react, Rebecca leaned over and planted her lips against his in a chaste kiss. "Let me remember your touch," she whispered.

Hafgrímr groaned at her words, his eyelids sliding shut. Almost as though he were in a trance, his left hand went to her cheek, stroking the silky skin. Rebecca trailed her lips over his strong jaw and down the side of his throat. Hafgrímr grabbed both of her shoulders at that, pulling her away from him. His face was a mixture of confusion and lust—no, stronger than lust, Rebecca reasoned. She had never seen the purity of desire for her from any other man that he now held in his eyes.

For a second, he looked as though he were going to stand firm on his decision not to allow her to do this to them both, before Rebecca could see he relented in his own mind. As though he wanted to drown in her, Hafgrímr pulled her back towards him and slanted his mouth over hers, enveloping it in heat. Rebecca moaned, sinking into his firm hold. He wrapped his arm tightly around her shoulders, trapping her against his chest and entwining them both in a tangle of two bodies melting into one. Her hands came up to grip his hair, her silent signal that she wanted more.

Leaning her back against the bed, he pulled the crown from her head, an exact mirroring of what happened on their lost wedding night so long ago. The ancient ritual of 'deflowering' his new wife. Rebecca felt a tingle along her spine, a strange déjà vu of having done this before with Hafgrímr. He gripped her nape tightly, taking her mouth in a relentless kiss, leaving her gasping for air as he bruised her lips. Rebecca responded by using her hands to trace along his features, his jaw, his powerful lips, his elegant nose, those devastating eyes. It was like touching a man she had known for years. Everything was familiar to her, every movement of his body already embedded in her soul.

Wordlessly locked in this strange memory with Rebecca, Hafgrímr gently pulled back her soft brunette locks, revealing her slim white neck. He leaned down and fluttered butterfly kisses across her neck down to her décolletage, sucking and nipping. Rebecca writhed beneath him, head rolling back on the furs of the bed in pleasure. "Gods...I've missed you so much, Sigrior...I never want to leave you again." His murmured words in her ear brought equal tears and need. She blinked the tears away, and reached up for the clasp of the brooch holding his cloak. It came away easily, the fabric of the cloak disappearing over his right shoulder with a whisper. He rose himself up on his elbows to look down at her face, manoeuvring himself with practised ease. Rebecca almost let out a whimper. There was a look of pure desire written across his features, a promise that he would give her no allowance for tears now. Without saying a word, he sat up and pulled off his tunic in one fell stroke, leaving his torso bare for her to see.

Rebecca bit her lip, hands eagerly flying forward to touch him. His chest was covered with a light dusting of dark hairs, and muscles curved and moved under his skin. Not the muscles people got from going to the gym, but true muscle; gained through a life of hard outdoor work and battles. Two long scars were struck across his stomach, raised out from the rest of his body. Rebecca glanced up at him, and he nodded a silent assent that they were gained through a fight he had won but was permanently etched by. Her hands worked their way over him, taking in every inch in detail. Hafgrímr's brow knitted together in frustration, letting her take her time. But it was evident that he needed to pin her down, to do things to her that she wouldn't forget in any of her lives, to suck her down into his very soul.

Rebecca relented and laid back, pulling her own strange apron dress over her head. Hafgrímr let out a curse that was not in English, the ancient syllables sounding desperately erotic when rolled across his deep tones. She arched up towards him, offering herself. But he was agonisingly slow, holding back. Clearly he wanted her to remember this. His rough palms fell to her warm breasts, kneading them until she whimpered her satisfaction. Her nerves became a tangle of her nipples rolled against his touch, of his rough legs pushing her thighs open in an unspoken command, of her hands skimming his lean back and carving around his taut figure.

His lips across her skin once more drove her into a frenzy, wrapping her legs around his narrow waist as if to urge him where she needed him. The prominent bulge against the front of his roughhewn trousers pressed into her folds, and she cried out with want. He smirked against her nipple and ran his teeth across it, lapping with his tongue to soothe the sharp shock from it.

"Hafgrímr…Hafgrímr…more, I need more! It's…I've never…" Rebecca's words were lost in the jumbled thoughts in her head. She ceased to have conscious thought, her mind becoming one of electricity tingling over her body, of *his* hands, her *lover's* hands, *Hafgrímr's* hands on her. Her own hand slid down between their warm bodies, firmly wrapping itself around his hard length.

Hafgrímr hissed through gritted teeth at the touch, as though she were pouring cool water on hot metal. Without a second thought, he ripped his trousers off, throwing them to the floor in abandon. Rebecca gasped and shivered in delight at the feel of skin on skin, the pad of her thumb gently circling the velvet hood of his cock. It felt hard as rock, and her hips moved of their own accord as she tried to imagine how it would feel sinking against her warmth.

Her hand stroked up and down firmly, demanding, stoking the fire burning within Hafgrímr. Keeping his lips firmly latched on her soft breasts, his fingers dipped lower until he found the small mound within her folds. Rebecca let out a sharp inhale as he touched it, the jolts of ecstasy from it almost enough on their own to tip her crumbling over the edge. He smirked with masculine pride as she writhed beneath him, her eyes wide and aching with lust. Over and over, his fingers circled, sending her spinning higher. The room ceased to be, the fire was a distant murmur under the sounds of their breathing and movements…Rebecca had never had a sexual encounter like this. She felt as though she were floating in some other place, one that only existed for Hafgrímr and her.

"I need you, Sigrior," he murmured, shifting so that he was facing her, propped up on his elbows either side of her face. His hands came down to stroke her face, his thumbs leisurely grazing over her flushed cheeks, pausing at her parted lips. Their eyes met, sapphires gazing into blue topaz. Rebecca let out a shuddering sigh.

"I need you too, Hafgrímr."

Something in the air changed. The passion continued to build between both of them until it felt as though the fire in the room poured from their very bodies, but there was a bittersweet edge to it as though they had just realised this would never happen again. Hafgrímr leaned down to kiss Rebecca, deep with intent, but softer this time. He delved his tongue into her mouth, sealing them with his lips. Rebecca moaned behind his kiss, and let her tongue meet his, entwining and exploring with abandon. Her arms snaked around his back, and her hands met the firmness of his buttocks. Hafgrímr gave a laden grunt, and eased his body closer so that the steel-hard head of his length pushed against the top of her channel.

Rebecca let out a desperate cry, and arched herself, sending his cock sliding along her. Hafgrímr stilled for a second, relishing the exquisite contact. The tension in the room built as he stared down at Rebecca and sank himself into her, groaning eagerly. Her hands curled into claws against his backside as she urged him closer, further, more. Gritting his teeth, Hafgrímr slid out, only to pound into her a second later. The intensity of that one movement made Rebecca fraught for him. Her head thrashed on the pillow as she moved her hips up to meet him. He picked up his speed, joining the two of them perfectly with every thrust. Driven to see her tumble over that precarious edge, he matched her movements like a glove to a hand, thrusting harder with every sound she made.

Rebecca's moans and cries grew louder and more urgent as he lifted his body to fit her, pounding forcefully into her giving body. One final thrust sent her spinning into oblivion. Her head jerked back, her eyes slamming shut from the power of her orgasm. Every nerve in her body lit up, arching her spine and throwing her hips open to Hafgrímr's relentless pace. Her body throbbed from the pleasure echoing in her body, the only comprehensible fact that Hafgrímr was close with her.

Her throaty scream was the signal to him to let go what he had been holding back. Hafgrímr's body tensed as it built to his own orgasm, his cock straining as it buried deep inside Rebecca's warmth. For a split second it felt tense almost to the point of being painful, and then came the light-headed release she demanded from him, light fingers sparking along his spine. Yelling to the ceiling of the small room, Hafgrímr gave himself over to Rebecca, pumping his warm seed into her with unrestrained need. "Sigrior, I…I love you!"

Rebecca, still clinging to him from the force of her own desires, let out an unexpected sob at that. As their bodies sank into an easy softness, he looked down sharply. Tears rolled freely down her cheeks, but she was smiling. He understood. Without moving himself from inside her, Hafgrímr pressed his lips desperately against hers once more. A goodbye kiss. A kiss that he wanted to demonstrate all the love and need he had held for her for over ten centuries. Rebecca pulled him closer to her, as if pinning him to her would keep him by her side. With his kiss, she remembered everything they had shared in her past life, every joy they had together, every promise they had made to one another until they were ripped apart.

Afraid to see him gone, Rebecca cautiously prised her eyes open. The warmth of the Viking longhouse had dissipated, and she was laid out on her kitchen floor. The illusion had vanished. Night had fallen, casting the kitchen into near darkness, except for the glow of the TV in the next room. The clock on the cooker read '1 AM'. But above her, was Hafgrímr. His human visage had gone, and her arms were wrapped tightly around the charred, ghostly remains of her lover. His red eyes held grief, watering with their own tears. Instead of pulling away, Rebecca smiled through her tears and whispered, "I love you too, Hafgrímr."

A choked grunt came from the shadowy figure of Hafgrímr, and she leant up to kiss him once more. Nothing more tangible than sparks and tingles passed over her lips, but she could feel him kissing her back. Their lips parted, and a silence weighed over them as they stared into each other's faces.

"Well, this is cosy...isn't it?"

Chapter Seven

October 31st—Samhain

Hafgrímr jumped up from Rebecca, pulling her up off the floor and behind him in one swift movement.

Standing before them, his face twisted into rage, was Radormr. His hands were balled into fists, and Rebecca realised that the kitchen was lit up from the golden glow he gave off. It was brighter than ever—but she now knew it was from the deathly fire he had produced so long ago. Hafgrímr stepped forwards, his eyes spewing scarlet hatred.

Radormr took a quick glance from Hafgrímr to Rebecca, and shook his head. *"I see now there is no point in trying to convince you he killed you. Yes, it was I that murdered you. Stupid little girl, wanting him over me. He may have loved you, but I could have given you anything. I had money, riches…I would have showered you with precious jewels and houses so large they rivalled the longhouse of the Chieftain."*

Rebecca's heart pounded with fear as she stared back at him blankly. "But I didn't love you. Hafgrímr had my heart, and he would have done anything for me. I didn't want jewels. I wanted what I want in this life…my soulmate. And you took him away from me." Her voice shook as she spoke, but her chin jutted proudly towards the evil ghost.

Hafgrímr's smile of pride for her pluck was lost in the black shadows of his face. Advancing until he was only a few feet in front of Radormr, he growled, *"You will never harm her again. This ends now. Even with the lost years between us, even with you ripping us apart, we still love each other. That will never change. And I know that now. I've seen it in her face. So once again, I'll sacrifice myself for her."*

"What?" The shocked utterance from Rebecca made Hafgrímr spin around. He held out a hand to her, clasping it to show she had always been in his heart. The gesture made her choke back a cry as she looked into his face, trying to read what was there.

Hafgrímr rasped, *"I'm sorry, Rebecca. I know we have just found each other again, but…this will never stop. He'll keep returning, intent on breaking us apart once more. I had hoped that one day I would be reincarnated to be by your side. But I see now that will never happen. I must end this. I must end Radormr, so that you may have peace. And hope that I see you again one day in Bilskirnir or Valhalla, wherever the gods see fit to let me rest. My heart aches for you, my love."*

"Hafgrímr! STOP!" Rebecca rushed forwards, not knowing what he was planning but determined to stop it. Radormr grinned wickedly, flashing a dagger at her in a threatening movement. It was clear now that his punishment from the gods for murdering someone had driven him crazy. Years of loneliness had eaten away at whatever blackened soul he had already held, turning him further against the young couple he had destroyed.

As she ran headlong, she was met with a strange force that stopped her short, sending her flying back towards the ground with a heavy thump. As she picked herself up again swiftly, Hafgrímr looked over at her despondently before turning back to face Radormr. Rebecca looked up, and she could see that there was a thin black wall preventing her from entering. With a cold shiver across her spine, she realised this was *the Veil*. The physical embodiment of the membrane that kept the spirit world and the living world apart. It grew at its thinnest on Samhain night, allowing ancestors to pass through and visit the living to watch over them. But somehow Hafgrímr had closed it over, preventing her from entering or passing it.

As she watched in desperation, Radormr moved closer to her ancient lover, pointing the sharp blade to his chest. *"So, this is how it ends, Hafgrímr? What are you planning to do? You know that both of us will return again and again. You made a promise as you lay dying, to allow the gods to let you watch over her in every lifetime. Of course you didn't mean like this, but it cursed us both. Both cursed to carry out the same tragedy again, and again. To kill me, you must kill yourself."*

Hafgrímr bent his head. A sound halfway between a sigh and a growl escaped his charred features. *"I know this. So I will."*

Radormr's eyes widened in fearful astonishment. Ignoring the look on his face, Hafgrímr raised his face to the heavens, and called out, *"Gods! If you be merciful, I ask you to release the curse that has been held over our lives for so long. I understand now. I can only protect Sigrior...Rebecca...by not being with her. Please release us. Please...let her live."*

"No, Hafgrímr, *no!*" Rebecca rushed onwards again, slamming her palms against the Veil, her body racked with sobs. It was being repeated all over again, her heart ripping in half. He turned to face her, silently placing his palms flat against hers, joining them for the last time.

Radormr's eyes burned with fury, and he ran for a final thrust, raising his arm back in an arc. Just as the blade was about to tear into the shadows of Hafgrímr's body, the blade fell away as though it had been sharply knocked from his hand. Radormr let out a howl of anger. The howl of anger rose in pitch to a terrified scream as his form began to falter and fade, floating away on a roaring wind that came from nowhere. Screeching figures soared down from the wind, clawing out at Radormr with vicious hands. He gave one last yell, one last panic-stricken look over at Hafgrímr and Rebecca, before the creatures pulled him away. They spun into a dizzying whirlwind, their cries ringing out over his voice as they ripped into him. Pieces of his body spattered around the whirlwind, painting it red with blood. The whirlwind eddied a few times, and vanished through the ceiling as fast as it had come, taking Radormr and the creatures with it.

Rebecca stared at Hafgrímr, her brain blank with the words she needed to say. *So much, and I have no time.* Gradually, the black flakes that always hovered around his body started to float upwards. She pressed her forehead against the Veil, as if seeking to break through, to get closer to him. Hafgrímr came to her, pressing his forehead against hers and whispering soothingly. Rebecca stayed silent, but her vision blurred as it filled with tears. More and more of him began to float away, black flakes disappearing into the invisible hold of the Otherworld. His arms and head waned as more of him passed over. Rebecca's hands clawed as she watched. Hafgrímr sighed deeply, a tortured sigh. *"I love you,"* he mouthed as the last of the ghastly body he had been trapped in for centuries went peacefully to its grave. Then he was gone.

The film of the Veil dissolved beneath her touch, and left her swaying uncertainly on her feet. Her cheeks felt scorched by the salty water running down them. As her eyes cleared and she looked across the room, she was met by the worried gaze of Louisa.

"I loved him too," she murmured before falling to her knees.

Louisa ran over, the Veil now gone, dropping her handbag hastily into a corner. "Rebecca! What the *hell* happened?" Rebecca's eyes stared listlessly past her, to the spot where Hafgrímr had remained in some form only a few seconds ago. Louisa wrapped her arms around her friend, pulling her closer in a bear hug. She rocked her to and fro, shushing her as Rebecca burst into heart-rending sobs…

Chapter Eight

A Year Later — Samhain Night

Louisa glanced over at Rebecca. Rebecca gave her a weak smile and a shaky thumbs-up, but it faltered. Louisa smiled back brightly, but it felt forced. As her friend turned back to her task, Louisa's smile fell.

Rebecca had never been the same since last year. At first, Louisa hadn't known whether to believe her or not, but the way that Rebecca had talked about her 'Hafgrímr' had convinced her. Her friend was not one to make up wild stories — and they had both seen this 'Radormr'. Louisa tensed up at the thought of standing not more than a few feet away from a ghost, one who had the full intention of killing her best friend. It gave her chills just to remember it. And it broke her heart to learn that the shadow man had in fact been trying to protect Rebecca. Not just her lover...her soulmate.

Rebecca dejectedly placed one of the plates onto the dining table. Louisa had suggested having a so-called 'Silent Supper'. It was a Wiccan tradition, where you laid out plates and food for loved ones who had passed, in the hope that they would join you as you ate your meal. Not a word was spoken during the meal, which suited Rebecca fine. But if it gave her a chance of seeing Hafgrímr again, if only for a second...she would cherish that second as though it was years.

It wasn't as though she had tried to mire herself further into sadness, quite the opposite. It had taken days after Hafgrímr had vanished for her to stop crying and hurting. In a way, it felt ridiculous to her. She had known him only a few days in this life, and most of those were in pointless fear of him. But in that beautiful vision he had given her, she had known him. Everything about him, everything she loved. So when he vanished that night...it was as though he had died all over again. Rebecca had, with Louisa's encouragement, thrown herself into other tasks. She had joined local clubs for drama and dance, she had taken up sports and flung herself headfirst into churning out books—which of course, her publisher was delighted by.

But every time she came to write about a young couple in love, her fingers would halt over the keyboard. The same feelings would settle in once more. And her couple inevitably ended up careering towards a tragic end. Her books no longer held happy endings, but there seemed to be a market for them. She hid it well from everyone, but whenever she saw something that reminded her of Hafgrímr, her soul broke again. The only person she couldn't hide it from was Louisa. That woman had known her since they were children, and knew her better than she knew herself.

Rebecca knew Louisa was worried about her, so she tried to show how she was coping with it. Inviting her to go out for lunch, going over for Christmas and Yule...even this. Rebecca didn't want to make Louisa worried. But neither could she shake off how she felt. It clung to her, no matter how much she tried to carry on. She had to admit it; she needed Hafgrímr. The idea of an eternity of lives stretching into the future, one after the other, with all of them empty without her soulmate was something that haunted her nightmares.

"Rebecca, honey, would you pass those spoons? Thank you." The metal clattered as it was handed over, Louisa taking it gently from her hands. Rebecca let out a deep sigh, lost again in her own thoughts. Louisa was about to say something when a strange light over her shoulder stopped her.

"Rebecca? Sigrior?"

In shock, the two women slowly spun around. Behind the dining table, as if it had always been there, was the Veil. It shimmered like frost on spiders' webs, gleaming and glittering with the promise of the beyond. Rebecca froze as she took in the figure standing behind it.

In a small wooden room, with a warm fire blazing behind him, stood Hafgrímr. Not as he had been in his shadow form, but as he had been in life. Tall, strong, with a brazen grin stretched over his features. His eyes twinkled at her, full of love.

"Hafgrímr," Rebecca breathed. Louisa simply gawped in surprise.

"I've been allowed to visit you. Not for long, but…long enough to see your face once more."

Louisa felt her heart warm as Rebecca's face broke into a huge smile. She hadn't seen that smile on her friend for over a year. This man truly was meant to be hers. He glanced over at Louisa, and nodded at her. She nearly laughed with nervousness, before shyly raising a hand to wave at him.

Rebecca moved forwards, raising her own hand to place against Hafgrímr's in a mirror image. He did the same, intending for their hands to meet on the shimmering film of the Veil. To both their shock, Rebecca's hand passed through, sinking into it as though it were made of nothing more substantial than water. She gave a small shriek before jumping back, pulling her hand away as though it had been burnt.

Louisa placed a hand on her arm, rushing over. "Are you okay, Rebecca? What the hell was that?"

"I'm…I'm fine. I don't know." Both women raised their gaze questioningly at Hafgrímr. He shook his head, then something akin to recognition flitted across his face. Swallowing hard, he looked up again at Rebecca.

"*Sigrior…they are letting you through. To stay with me, if you wish. To be by my side once more. But I don't think you will be able to come back.*" He gave a worried glance at Louisa. "*You cannot leave your friends for me. It wouldn't be right.*"

Rebecca bit her lip, holding back her anguish, and nodded smartly. "I know," she whispered.

"No, no, no!" She looked up in shock as Louisa shouted at her. To her astonishment, Louisa steered her back towards the Veil. "Of course you must go. You have to. You were meant to be with him."

Rebecca twisted around, grabbing her best friend's arm tightly. "No, Louisa! I can't leave you, either! You're my best friend! We've been together ever since we met in playschool, and we both—"

"No," Louisa repeated firmly. "That's *why* you can go. We will always be best friends. Always. But you need your soulmate. It would be selfish of me to keep you from him, just like that bastard Radormr did so many years ago." Louisa gave a wavering smile. "And we'll meet again. This is proof, if nothing else, that we'll meet once more in the afterlife. I can wait. I still have to find my soulmate." Her smile broke into a huge grin, although she gritted her teeth to prevent herself from releasing the lump she could feel in her throat.

Rebecca stared at her for a long moment before throwing her arms tightly around her, squeezing Louisa so hard she gasped for air. "I love you too, Louisa. You're like my sister. And when you come to meet me, I'll be waiting for you." She glanced over at Hafgrímr's beaming smile. "We both will."

Louisa pulled away, and gave Rebecca's hand one last squeeze. "I don't doubt it! Now go! Go on…I'll find you both again. Go and be happy."

Both of them smiled tearfully at one another, before Rebecca nodded and turned to face Hafgrímr. He held out his hand for her, his face etched with elation. Rebecca raised her chin, and pushed her hand through the Veil. It met his, firm and warm, and he gripped it tightly as though he would never let go. Taking a deep breath, she closed her eyes and stepped through the shimmering glass of the membrane between them.

Louisa watched as Rebecca stepped through into the warm room beyond, her clothes metamorphosing from modern into Viking wear. She looked radiant, her face lit up with happiness. Louisa felt her heart soar as she saw her friend so elated. Yes, she could wait. They would see each other again. They were sisters in friendship. And Louisa would have her own soulmate by her side, she knew it.

Rebecca and Hafgrímr kissed, a passionate, aching kiss that spoke of centuries of love rekindled and re-joined once more. An unbroken love. They both turned to face Louisa once more, waving at her through the gleaming Veil. She blew them a kiss, waving happily as the image wavered and faded into the thin air. Then…they were gone. The wall of the dining room looked as it had before.

Louisa stood for a moment in the quiet calm of the dining room, too happy to even cry. Her finger trailed over the edge of the metal spoon her friend had held a moment ago. It still felt warm. But something seemed right, as though time had somehow been out of kilter, and now it had been placed back. Her phone beeped with a text message, a high-pitched sound in the silence that made her jump hard enough to send the spoon clattering to the floor.

Hey Louisa. It's Colin. I feel nervous asking you out on a date, I know you're at your friend's house, but…want to come for a drink?"

A brilliant grin broke over Louisa's lips. *I might find that soulmate sooner than I thought.* She had wanted to ask Colin out for weeks, but she hadn't felt right leaving Rebecca to her sorrows. With one last touch against the wall where the veil had stood, she strode across the dining room, grabbing her bag and tapping furiously into her mobile with one thumb. She passed through into the hallway, and opened the door to the cool autumn night. The sounds of children trick-or-treating could be heard, and an owl called out somewhere distant.

Louisa beamed happily to herself, and clicked off the lights. She took one long last gaze around, before sailing through the open door and shutting it firmly behind herself. Her footsteps could be heard crunching over the gravel outside, followed the slamming of a car door. A moment later, headlights flashed through the windows of the house, an engine growled, and she was gone.

The only sounds left were the clock still ticking in the hallway, and the distant splatter of dripping water from the kitchen tap. Then there was a strange moan that drifted through the empty house, a wind almost so quiet that human ears would have strained to hear it. The moan carried through the rooms, and the landing light buzzed for a second as they met, flickering on and off erratically. The light grew stronger, wildly flashing back and forth, before dying abruptly.

It fell silent once more. The house stood still in the darkness, the very shadows seeming to come to life…

Chapter One

<u>Victoria</u>

As I begin my Winter Solstice prayers, it is appropriate to think about the events that have transpired over the past few years, and the changes that have manifested in my life. I remember my dear grandmother, Anne O'Briant, and how she was insistent that I be taught the old ways.

I am the only daughter of the seventh son. My father was named Thomas simply because by the time he was born, all the old family names had been taken by his brothers. My own mother had died giving birth to me, so maybe that was why Father and Grandmother gave me such special attention. Grandmother and I looked remarkably alike - both being of average height, but athletic, with piercing pale blue eyes and the golden hair, which was the family trademark. We also shared the strong, independent nature that some Southern women have made legendary. I am even named after her, Victoria Anne. Maybe that was another reason she was so protective and attentive to me.

Grandmother was insistent on teaching me the rituals and ceremonies that had been brought by her ancestors from the old country, centuries ago. Those traditions had been passed from mother to daughter for generations – from their homeland in the British Isles, through the settlement in Virginia, and into what is now, and has been for over two hundred years, the family farm in the mountains of Tennessee. The ceremonies and rituals were timeless. Besides imparting the rituals of each of the eight holy days of the Wiccan calendar, I could also divine water with a forked branch from an ash tree and plant a garden by the astrological signs. The birds and animals gave meanings to weather changes and changes in our lives. Signs and omens were valued and honored. No detail of the old ways had been overlooked in my grandmother's teachings.

Father and his brothers had shortened the family name to Bryant before I was born. Years ago, I had moved to Atlanta, Georgia from Tennessee to attend school at Emory University. However, my roots stayed firmly in Tennessee. I practiced the traditions taught by my grandmother in private, from a condo in Midtown Atlanta now, not in an oak grove on the family farm. Except for Yuletide – Yule, the Winter Solstice, was always our special ceremony. I always traveled home for the Winter Solstice to complete the birth of the sun with my grandmother.

We would gather the holly and mistletoe that symbolized the promise of life to come as the longest night of the year passed and we looked forward to the return of the sun. We used the recipe that Grandmother had learned from her mother to anoint the candles.

We would take a few moments to remember what it was like for our ancestors at this time of year. The harvest had been brought in, and they knew that in a few months, their stockpiles of food would be running low. It was the season of Death, the time when the Earth went dormant once more, sleeping until the spring returned. Our ancestors knew that despite the darkness of this night, soon the light would return to the Earth, bringing life with it.

This night, the Winter Solstice, welcomes back the Sun the ultimate giver of light.

We would cast the circle. We cast a circle in order to create an energetic temple that is appropriate for interaction with the Elementals and the Goddess. We cast the circle every time we interact with our altar, generally for Sabbats and Esbats. This circle, this esoteric temple, protects us and enables our energy work. Due to the teachings and from Grandmother, I had reached the third level of elevation of the old religion.

In order to purify the sanctified area of our ritual space, Grandmother brushed the ground with a pine branch. Before prayers, we would light our candles, then begin our ritual.

Tonight is the night of the Solstice,

the longest night of the year.

As the Wheel turns once more, I know that tomorrow,

the Sun will begin its journey back to us.

With it, new life will begin,

A blessing from Earth to her children.

Going back to the family farm in the mountains of Tennessee for Grandmother O'Briant's funeral a few weeks ago had been very difficult. It had happened almost two years ago, however the pain of loss remains with me. She had taught me enough to know that the passing of the old signaled the birth of the new. My father had taken her loss very hard. I will never forget the cold wind that blew through the valley on that barren, early winter day as we stood at the graveside and watched her being buried. Old traditions have meaning in this part of the world. It was very difficult leaving Father in Tennessee and returning to Atlanta.

My career sounds very exciting. However, the truth is that marketing and public relations is exhausting work. Any involvement with the public is very difficult. Throw in demanding customers and it makes for an even larger challenge. I work as an executive director for the international public relations firm Humphrey & Land, in the US headquarters based in Atlanta. However, George Humphrey and Susan Land have offices across the globe. H & L, as we call the company, pride ourselves on developing and maintaining relationships with the client base. I have been with them fifteen years since my days as an intern from Emory, so I know the company and most of the employees, as well as personally knowing the majority of the key client accounts representatives.

A week or so following that sad visit to Tennessee, H & L hosted an international event in Atlanta for the company's executives. Even though I wasn't in much of a mood for celebrating, George, Susan, and the rest of the team were buzzing because James Wellington planned on attending a corporate event for the first time. James was the hot shot Director of Sales in the United Kingdom, one of H & L's largest markets. His name made me laugh – James Arthur Wellington II. How English could one guy possibly get? James had a reputation as a closer – there was no deal that walked away from him. Wellington was our go-to guy for any client that needed special attention.

James and I had discussed a few key accounts over the phone and swapped a few emails in the three years that he was employed by H & L. However, we had never met in person. I really didn't know what to expect, although I loved to hear his clipped English accent during our telephone calls, absolutely loved his sense of humor, and knew from our Skype conversations that he was a very nice looking guy. He was educated at Eton and Oxford and came from a very wealthy background.

Susan had told me once in a hushed tone over cocktails, as if she was speaking of a dignitary or a rock star, "H & L is fortunate to have someone of his caliber on the team."

From what George said, James was the type of man that would change a flat tire for you in the rain, but would then go do whatever he wanted to do instead of ensuring you made it safely to your destination. Guess that was George's nice way of saying James was nice but had a ruthless side. Of course, a certain amount of competitive ruthlessness was required in the position James had at H & L. It was all very interesting to a small town girl from Tennessee. Even if I didn't understand all of George and Susan's innuendoes, it was good information to have. However, nothing could have prepared me for the force that was James Wellington.

Chapter Two

<u>Victoria Meets James</u>

We were hosting a cocktail party at the W Hotel Downtown to accommodate everyone from around the globe – employees and clients would be in attendance. This was the largest international event H & L had ever sponsored and George and Susan were emphatic that our guests know the full extent of southern hospitality.

George and Susan had rented the largest corporate room at the W Downtown. No expense had been spared in preparing for the party. Four tables of food ranging from seafood to roast beef were arranged for the guests. Four bars were set up in the corners of the room and all drinks were free. The red, green, and gold Christmas velvets and tinsels danced dreamily with the blue and silver Hanukkah decorations. The candles placed on the tables throughout the room flickered and beckoned the attendees to enter the enchantment of the room, have a drink and something to eat, and stay for a while—get to know their colleagues and clients. A beautiful ice sculpture of an angel stood at the entryway, which only added to the magical, festive quality of the decor.

An hour before the party began, Susan found me.

"Victoria, why don't you go to your room and freshen up before the guests arrive? I can handle everything for an hour. Let's get ready to party. This is going to be a party we will never forget. You have to go get prepared. Get out of here right now and at least go freshen up your makeup and put on some high heels."

"Oh, thanks, Susan. If you have it under control, I will run upstairs for a few minutes. Thanks for the offer."

Looking at my Cartier watch as I entered the elevator, I realized that there was only an hour to get myself prepared and to say my Yule prayers. Keeping this in mind, I quickly showered and placed very little make-up on my face – there just wasn't time. Before leaving my condo, I had strung juniper berries in order to attract love into my life. The holly, mistletoe, and pine had all been carefully arranged. I had brought small amounts with me to the hotel in order to build a small Yule altar in the hotel room.

Finally, I had time and anointed the candles, using the recipe from Grandmother. I began the prayers by drawing down the circle, lighting the first candle, and completing the first prayer.

Next, I lit the second candle, and said:

It is the season of the Winter Goddess.

Tonight I celebrate the festival of the winter solstice,

The rebirth of the Sun, and the return of light to the Earth.

As the Wheel of the Year turns once more,

I honor the eternal cycle of birth, life, death, and rebirth.

The remaining candles were lit and I finished the prayers, alone for the first time in my life. Before, I had always been with my dear Grandmother.

Following the rite, there wasn't much time, so I decided to wear a black Hugo Boss suit and blue Oxford shirt. I brushed my long blonde hair and placed it in a ponytail that hung down my back. It was a very corporate look. The cocktail dress could wait until another party. I placed lotion on my legs to make them shine and stepped into a pair of simple yet elegant black pumps. I placed my grandmother's single-strand pearl necklace around my neck and matched it with a pair of pearl earrings. Then, with a bit of lipstick added, I was on the elevator and on my way to see what this night would bring. At the last minute, I walked to the altar, plucked a sprig of mistletoe, and placed it in my pocket. Maybe that would be fun and flirty later in the evening.

Our guests were beginning to fill the room by the time I returned. There were already maybe two hundred guests mingling, drinking, and some meeting for the first time. It was easy to work the room when I knew most of the attendees, and it was fun to spend time with them when we weren't working. Susan was getting agitated because James was late. Honestly, that was my pet peeve as well. It just seems rude to arrive late, especially for corporate events.

As I told you, nothing could ever have prepared me for the force that was James Wellington. When I saw him, my heart sank to my stomach. He was the most gorgeous and magnetic man I had ever seen. The entire room was electrified when he walked through the door. He was the type of man that made other men walk up and shake his hand as he entered the room. The women? They were all like me, completely mesmerized by his looks and elegance.

James was tall with dark hair and eyes, which I expected. I was tall in heels, but James was taller, maybe six feet two, maybe even six foot three. It was refreshing to look up at someone for a change. However, James was much more handsome in person than I had expected. His face was classic movie star handsome. He even had a cleft chin like Clark Gable did.

His clothes were impeccable. The Armani suit looked as if it had been made just for him. The textures of the crisp white cotton shirt against the black wool suit made you want to reach out and touch the fabric. Well, all that and the silk Zegna tie certainly added to the entire picture. The perfect shirt James wore had tailored French cuffs with silver cufflinks. No detail had been overlooked by his stylist. James Wellington was flawless. It was as if James Bond himself walked into the room. I hadn't expected the full extent of his charm and looks. He was even wearing assassin gloves, the latest hot new accessory for men.

Did he just look at me from across the room? I actually felt my knees get weak when Susan took my arm and said, "Let's go, Victoria. You need to meet James Wellington."

Why had I worn this plain black suit with a blue Oxford cloth shirt? What was wrong with me? My long hair was in a ponytail. Really, I should have dressed in a cocktail dress. At least I had on a skirt to show off my legs. James had caught me completely off guard and had shaken my usually confident demeanor.

"James Wellington, it is so nice having you finally visit Atlanta. I want you to meet our Victoria Bryant. She's in charge of executive sales in the Atlanta office. I believe you two have worked together on a few accounts, and it is time you met in person," Susan Land said.

"Oh yes, Victoria. It is so lovely to finally meet you. Maybe we can have a drink later and go over a few of the key accounts," James replied.

Oh, that velvety smooth English accent did something to me. James Wellington – now I understood why he was known as the Velvet Hammer.

Did one of Susan's eyebrows actually move upward when she looked at me? Oh yes, I needed to say something now. The twinkle in his eyes as he spoke; did everyone see that or was it just for me?

"Of course, James, just let me know. Welcome to Atlanta."

Did I say something that completely idiotic? What had happened to me? Who was this new me that swooned just because a good-looking Englishman walked in the room? The rest of the event was spent in a haze. It seemed that every time I looked, James was glancing in my direction. Maybe that was because I was always looking at him.

As the event ended, one of my colleagues came up to me and said, "A few of us are going downstairs for drinks, Victoria. Why don't you join us?"

An hour or more was spent in the bar with everyone wishing each other well on another good year at H & L. There was definitely an air of festivity and holiday cordiality in the air. Eventually, our co-workers left the bar, and James and I were left sitting at the table.

"Let's have another drink, and get to know each other better, Vix," James said as he turned toward me. "It is okay if I call you 'Vix'? With legs like yours, you should be called Vix, for vixen, not a name as stodgy as Victoria," James whispered and winked. "Now that it's just the two of us, we can be ourselves, don't you believe?"

"Oh yes, James, I believe."

He was so close I almost believed he was going to put his arm around me and pull me closer. His expensive cologne only added to his allure. I felt as nervous as a teenage girl. Yes, this was what was known, once upon a time, as a swoon. I needed to have that drink and get myself together, because James and I would be working together consistently over the next few years, if all went according to corporate plans. I couldn't allow a sudden schoolgirl type crush interfere with corporate affairs.

James signaled the waiter, ordered a Scotch for himself, and a glass of Merlot for me. Before the night ended, I knew all about his life, his career, and his longtime girlfriend.

In turn, I told James everything about my family, my career at H & L, and my sometime-boyfriend. I shared with James that my career was too busy to commit to someone because I didn't have time for a full time relationship. It was difficult to think how much I was sharing with someone that I had just met. James and I confided secrets as if we were long lost friends, reunited. I even told James about my grandmother and that I practiced the old ways in private.

As James paid the waiter for our drinks, I knew that I had too much to drink when I removed the sprig of mistletoe from my pocket and placed it between us. I looked at him and said, "If you ever break up with your girlfriend, let me know. If you call me, you'll never regret it."

James looked me straight in the eyes as he finished his Scotch. "Let's go," was all he whispered as he placed his arm behind my back and motioned with the other hand for me to stand.

We walked from the bar; James never removed his hand from my back. To anyone watching us, we appeared as friends walking to the elevator following a few holiday drinks, nothing more.

We entered the elevator and James placed the card for his penthouse in the slot. By the time the elevator door closed, James had pulled me into his arms and loosened the ponytail. He pushed me against the mirrored elevator wall and kissed me passionately. All I could do was put my arms around his neck and draw him closer. He was so muscular and tall. I felt the hardness of his body as my own body gave in to him. There was no way I could deny the desire I felt. I could tell he felt the same. One of his hands unbuttoned my blouse. No words were spoken as we glided upward toward his penthouse suite. The acceleration of the elevator was only matched by our hot, heightened passion.

As the elevator door opened to his room, all I could think was this was beyond all imagination. We were business colleagues and this was against all the rules. He had a girlfriend and I had a friend with whom I was very comfortable spending time.

His kisses were soft yet forceful. His touch set my body ablaze. The consequences of our actions hadn't been thought out – only our intense burning for each other mattered at that time. There was no way either of us could deny the passion – the fire and desire. James and I were much like a train with no brakes.

Chapter Three

Fire and Desire

As James unbuttoned my blouse, there was no more thinking that this was wrong, that we worked for the same company and that we had only met for the first time. There was only his touch and the way my body responded to his.

As I thought, *this is out of character for me. I never act this way,* James said, "This is out of character for me, Vix. I never act this way. We don't have a physical attraction, Vix, we have a chemical reaction to each other," James whispered to me in his velvet-toned voice, now husky with lust.

We couldn't get our clothes off fast enough. I remember laughing as we stumbled through his suite, finding our way in the darkness to his bedroom. He unbuttoned my blouse to reveal the black lace camisole underneath. I felt his body shudder as he touched the outline of my body and then placed one hand under my skirt. I was so ready for his touch. I had never wanted a man the way I wanted James. My blouse and jacket were tossed mindlessly to the floor with James' jacket. James tore off his own tie and shirt to reveal the most perfect chest I had ever seen. James Wellington was as physically perfect as he was charming. He pulled me down with him as we fell laughing onto his king-sized bed.

Before I could say *this is wrong*, James had pulled my mouth to his again. His naked body moved onto me. The first time we made love we were so hungry for each other that he pushed the skirt up - it was around my waist, my bra was still on, and he couldn't wait to get inside me.

His hand reached between my legs as he murmured, "Victoria, you are so very sexy. You really want me, don't you?"

All I could do was nod yes, as my head cradled against his chest.

James had used his powerful body weight to turn me onto my back, slowly kissing me and biting my neck, so hot was our passion. I matched his intensity with my white hot desire – feeling his strong back tense under the touch of my nails running along his sides then up his spine. He pressed his lips to my nipple. How was it possible that such a single physical motion could create such an explosive reaction? A swirl of sensations ebbed throughout my body. I moved against him rhythmically, my hands sliding along his toned back until my nails scraped into the muscles of his shoulders.

He rested gently on me before his knees spread my legs apart to accommodate the width of his body. The sensations were consuming, and my mind blurred as every inch of skin he touched became enflamed with desire.

He moved my panties to one side so he could enter. His hand felt the wetness between my legs and he easily slipped inside me. We moved naturally together. My legs wrapped around him tightly. There was nowhere else on Earth I wanted to be.

He slipped inside me as easily as if I had placed him there with my hand. I moaned and my body shuddered at the way he filled me. My fingers dug into his shoulders. The kiss got deeper. James gripped my hair and the back of my neck, holding my body to him while he made slow, passionate love to me. My entire body shook. The bed shook. The world moved.

I forced my eyes to open – to pay attention to every detail of this exquisite moment in time. I wanted to watch his face as he made sweet, languid love to me. James was looking into my eyes until the very last moment when pleasure overtook him and we were both lost into the ecstasy of our lovemaking.

James came as he whispered my name. A moment after that, James sighed a soft groan. He gave himself to me completely, and I to him.

I felt his heart beating against mine as we held each other, spent from the passion. Never in my life had I experienced such pleasure. I had given my body and soul to this man.

That was only the beginning.

Chapter Four

James Departs

James and I spent a passionate night together. All I can truly remember is taste, touch, and sensation. Yet in some type of way, I remember every nuance, every touch, every sound he made...every sound we made. The way his skin felt when it touched mine, the salty taste of his skin, the very magic of the air around us...it all takes on a dreamlike, surreal quality as I look back. Until that night, I had never known passion. I was swept away, helplessly and hopelessly, by the enchantment of James Wellington.

The next morning I opened my eyes, only to think, *I had too much to drink*, followed by the soft breathing of James as he licked my neck.

"Vix, I have heard of southern hospitality. However, I must say that I am very pleased at the extent southerners will go to in order to please their guests."

This made us laugh in unison. As I laughed, he pulled me close. To my surprise, he dropped two Altoids in my mouth. He whispered, "Let's see if we are as good this morning as we were last night." With those words, I moved onto his beautiful, long body and mounted him. The arousal and lovemaking we shared was as intense as it had been the night before.

We exhausted ourselves and briefly fell asleep in each other's arms. James woke up first and gently shook me in order to bring me to consciousness.

"Vix, time to wake up. Why don't you shower and I'll order lunch? After that, I have to leave for London."

"Lunch? Oh no! What am I going to tell Susan? What will she and George think? I'm never late."

"Vix, you're going to let them know that you and I have been working on a few new strategies. That should satisfy them. God knows it has satisfied me." He winked as he said it. "Actually, if you would like, please make any calls from here today. Take a late checkout and give yourself a Spa Day as well. I'll treat you to a massage, manicure, pedicure – whatever you want, Vix."

"What will George and Susan think about me charging a Spa Day to the H & L expense account?"

"Oh, don't worry about that. The room is in my name, not the company's name. This will be our little secret. Everyone needs a secret, don't they, Vix?" His large hands caressing my body drove me crazy with desire.

James picked me up and carried me into the luxurious bath. Still kissing me, he turned the shower on, full blast. The touch of warm liquid streaming down my face and body as James held me and made slow languid love to me was as intoxicating as last night's drinking.

"I love you."

There was no answer to my declaration as we finished the shower. James was as passionate and generous a lover as any woman would ever desire. He never gave me an answer in reply.

As we finished the shower, James went into the dressing area to prepare for his flight back to London. I sat in front of the bathroom vanity, wrapped only in a towel when he emerged. He was as elegant and breathtaking as the first moment I saw him. Today, he wore a gray checked three-piece suit, a green gingham plaid shirt, and a pink and green paisley tie. The assassin gloves were once again in evidence. He definitely had the look that kills.

James picked up his briefcase and luggage. Before walking to the door, he set them down and turned toward me. I impetuously ran into his arms for one more kiss.

"James, I love you. I mean it with all my heart. Even if we have just met, I know, James, I know. We are meant to be together."

He kissed me with all the passion and hunger that had consumed us last night and again this morning.

"Vix," he said, looking into my eyes. "As I told you last night, we have a chemical reaction toward one another. Yes, I have an attraction toward you, but I have a girlfriend and you have a friend. We live on separate parts of the globe. We must work together. We can't change anything. Understood?"

"Do you have feelings toward me at all?"

"Yes, yes I do, Vix. Look at yourself – you're beautiful. You are also a very intelligent and successful woman. Those are powerful aphrodisiacs for a man like me. Vix, how could any man experience what we did last night and not feel anything? But, you must understand that doesn't change anything."

With that, he turned me loose, took his belongings, and walked to the door.

"James, I never say good-bye, I always say *see you later*."

He turned before walking out the door, smiled and said, "Catch y'all later, then."

Chapter Five

James Leaves

James and I continued to work together in the new year. His weekly calls began coming later in the day, after 5:00 p.m. Before we met, his calls came in earlier, sometimes right as I came into work. I was noticing a pattern.

"James, are you calling me late because you think everyone has left the office?"

There was a pause, then he said simply, "Yes, I believe that is exactly what I am doing, Vix. I am...I wanted to talk to you and find out how you are doing."

Now the pause was on my end of the phone line.

"Aren't you the one who said we couldn't change anything, James? That we had to work together?"

"Well, yes, Vix, I know that. However, I want to talk to you sometimes, to hear your voice. I also wanted to let you know that I will be in Atlanta again a few weeks' time. I'm scheduled to arrive in March. Looking at my calendar, it appears that I will be in your city 23rd March until 25th March. Is there a chance we can meet for a drink?"

"It really depends on your intentions, James. Is this drink to discuss work, or are you inviting me to meet you for a drink after work?"

A chair squeaked in the background and James lowered his voice. "I have to see you again. It doesn't matter if it's only for a drink. We can go to dinner. We can do whatever you want to do. I just need to see you again."

He made me so confused. Every time he said something, my heart would break a little. What could I do?

"James, you are going to have to admit that you're in love with me. How can you want to see me so badly if you don't have feelings for me? Until you admit it, and since we work together, I can only agree to see you in a professional setting. It's not appropriate for us to be alone." Why did my heart break a little more as I said those words?

"I'll take that as a 'yes,' then, Vix. Cheers until then."

With that, the phone line disconnected. He really wouldn't take "no" for an answer. It made me curious. Would he so openly, almost desperately, want to see me to tell me something? Would it be the words I wanted to hear?

James was gorgeous at the meeting in March. H & L held a reception afterwards for the executives and a few select clients. It was like being at a party in a movie. Everyone was beautiful, everyone was having a great time. James walked up to me at one point and I remember saying, "After this, you need to take some time off and do something really special. You have charmed the entire client list."

He placed his hand under my jacket, and in the most sensual way, ran his hand down my back. Then he leaned over and purred in my ear, "Forget them. I want to go somewhere and do something fun with you."

Later, after the reception, George and Susan took a group of us to dinner. I received a call from a client at one point and excused myself from the table. In order to get a bit of privacy, I walked to the bar and entrance area. James suddenly appeared and whispered in my right ear, "Follow me. I want to show you something upstairs."

"James, this is your first time in this restaurant. How can you possibly know what is upstairs?"

"Vix, it helps greatly if you tip the maitre'd a hundred dollars or so. Now hurry - we don't have long."

He walked ahead and I followed. We left the restaurant foyer, walked up a flight of stairs, and into a small room off the corridor. James closed the door. The minute the door closed, he took me in his arms and we embraced as passionately as before. The desire between us was as strong, possibly even stronger, than the first time we met.

After a kiss that took my breath away, James and I looked into each other's eyes. We had a sense of knowingness. The expression on James' face made me wonder if he was thinking the very same thought.

"James, we have to get back to dinner. Susan and George will notice we are gone at the same time. This isn't the right thing to do." I distanced myself slowly away from him.

Simply knowing that a man could desire me with such intensity filled me with a pleasure I had never experienced, yet once again, James broke my heart a bit more.

"Victoria, we *do* have something between us that I have never experienced before. Please understand that there is nothing I can do about it. Nothing can change."

"James, love changes everything. You only have to open your heart and the universe will give you what you desire. All you have to do is let the change happen."

"It's too late, Victoria. There are events in place we haven't discussed yet. Please know that I hadn't planned on you entering my life or things could possibly be different."

We returned to dinner and nothing was said about the upstairs encounter, not that evening or ever.

After March, I felt as if I could fly. Then, one day in late April, I noticed that James stopped calling. There were no more emails; not even business emails. I remember waking up one day knowing that he didn't love me anymore. It's a day I will never forget as long as I live. It was over. I could feel it. He didn't love me or want me anymore. In some way I could accept that, but what about our business relationship? Was he running the risk of destroying that?

Around Midsummer Solstice, Susan and George called a brief meeting with the executive staff in our office before we left work for the day. I remember it being Midsummer because that morning, I had said my prayers before going into the office.

As I walked into the conference room, I could sense something was wrong. Had George and Susan sold the company? Had we lost a major client? As everyone gathered around the conference table, George stood up and said, "Susan and I received a phone call from James Wellington today. He has decided to leave H & L in order to take a position as CEO with another company. Our loss is their gain. James has agreed to work with us on the transitions over the next few weeks." There was a hesitation on George's part, then he continued. "We must all congratulate James for the advancements he made on the global efforts of H & L, but also for another reason. James let us know that he is officially engaged to his longtime girlfriend. That's really why he is leaving because he wants to concentrate his efforts on his new life with his soon-to-be new wife."

With that, there were well wishes all around. Knowing that James was leaving on good terms for a good reason seemed to please the H & L team. Susan brought in two bottles of champagne, which I believe she said had been sent to the team from James. I attempted to act happy, but I was stunned. Completely stunned. This time he had really done it – James Wellington had completely broken my heart.

Chapter Six

<u>Memphis</u>

The remainder of the year had been spent in a fairly useless haze. My career at H & L became my life. I completely stopped socializing unless it was work related. The brief, intense affair with James and his sudden departure from my life had left me shattered emotionally, and I stopped dating completely – anything except work was just too draining.

George and Susan never mentioned James after he left. They apparently didn't want to lose such a valuable member of the H & L team. However, they seemed pleased with his reasons for leaving, wishing him well. Instead of replacing him, they had brought in two new executives – one for the UK operations, the other for European operations. This was an excellent sign of growth for the company.

My business grew during the rest of the year. I cultivated new clients as well as preserving and growing my previous customer base. Summer turned to autumn, and the wheel of the year slowly began turning toward winter.

Late in November, George called me into his office.

"Victoria, one of my largest clients wants to meet with me in Memphis a few days before Christmas. Since your family is in Tennessee, why don't you attend the meeting in my place? Take an extended holiday visit with your family and friends in Tennessee."

"Of course, George. It's no problem. Is everything okay with you?"

"Victoria, you are a valuable member of the team here at H & L and you have done a great deal of work in growing our business in the last year. Thank you for doing this for me. Think of it as a favor. This way, I can stay with my family here in Atlanta during the holiday season."

"That sounds like fun, George. I love Memphis. It's nice of you to trust me with one of your accounts. It is also very thoughtful of you to let me take a few days to visit the family. Do you have the date for the appointment yet? That way I can get my schedule arranged."

"Yes, Victoria, the meeting is scheduled for December 22nd. Plan on flying into Memphis on December 21st. Why don't you stay in Memphis both nights, then take your holiday break? H & L will take care of your expenses."

"Thanks, George! Let's schedule a meeting a few days before I leave. In the meantime, please send me any pertinent information about the account as soon as possible. That way I can begin reviewing their history and chart our future plans for the account growth."

"That's what I wanted to hear. Now, get back to work," he said as he peered at me from above his glasses.

Memphis. I loved Memphis. It had been a long time, too long, since I had visited. This would be the first time something exciting had happened to me since James broke my heart in June. I finally had something to be excited about. Of course, it would be December 21st. That was the date for Yule this year. Funny thing, this would be the second year in a row I would spend Yule in a hotel.

The next few weeks went past in a flurry of activity. Between work commitments and corporate festivities, I barely had any time to think about my complete lack of a personal life. Before I knew it, I was on a plane on the way to Memphis.

I walked into the Peabody Hotel and loved the holiday décor. The tree was magnificent, standing two stories tall in the open lobby. Not just during the holidays, but any time of year, there was that certain something about the Peabody that no other hotel on Earth had. In Tennessee, we called it that certain *"je neus se quoi"* — that certain indefinable something.

Plus, it has live ducks in the fountain in the Lobby Bar. Ducks that are paraded daily into the Lobby Fountain in the morning, and then paraded out of the Lobby Fountain in the evening, a tradition from long ago when the Peabody's manager was asked to return from a duck-hunting weekend due to an emergency at the hotel. In his haste, he brought the live decoys back to the hotel and placed them in the fountain in the lobby. Hence, a new tradition was born. Those ducks were treated like royalty. I miss the value that Tennesseans place on tradition. When I checked in, I was a bit surprised that I had been upgraded to a suite. What a welcome relief it would be to unpack, freshen up, and join the always festive Lobby Bar. I just couldn't wait to get upstairs and get unpacked.

The suite was exquisite and had Christmas decorations - even a tree had been placed in the main room. The concierge carefully unloaded my bags in the bedroom while I removed the contents of my briefcase, mainly the folders for tomorrow's meeting, organizing the items on the desk in the main room. Once the concierge left, I could unpack my Yuletide candles and items and begin my prayers.

Funny, why did James cross my mind? He never crossed my mind anymore. After the pain of losing him and the numbness of never seeing him again, I was finally getting over him. To say I was hurt was an understatement. I truly believed he would remain the love of my life. However, life has certain paths we are to walk. Apparently James and I were meant to only cross paths, not walk together. It made me sad. However, the experience of loving James – knowing that my heart, body, and spirit could love so fully, was a gift from the Goddess and I would acknowledge that during the Yule prayers before I went out for a drink tonight.

Once the bags were unpacked, I freshened up and arranged my Yule altar. As I reflected on the past, there was a sudden sense of loss that overtook me as I realized that in just a little more than one year's time, I had lost my beloved grandmother, and a few months later lost the man I believed I would love forever. However, this was the season of renewal, of new beginnings. This was the time of year when the Wiccan wheel turned and brought with it the birth of the Sun.

I concentrated on the prayers while lighting the candles, the holly and mistletoe arranged as I had been taught. The spell cast by the incense made my mind roam to happier times in the past and what should be happier moments of the future. I lifted my arms as I faced the Christmas tree that had been placed in the room and I began my meditations. One stanza in particular resonated within me:

Today I honor the god of the forest,

The King of nature, who rules the season.

I give my thanks to the beautiful goddess,

Whose blessings bring new life to the Earth.

This gift I offer you tonight,

Sending my prayers to you upon the air.

For some reason, I put on a skin-tight black cocktail dress with a plunging neckline. It was time to feel sexy and fun again. At the last minute, I put on my black Louboutins and wound a long string of pearls around my neck, which provocatively covered enough of my cleavage to make my chest look even that much more alluring. Time for a drink!

The Lobby Bar in Memphis was the best place in town, maybe one of the best places in the world. It was not only packed with Peabody guests, it was always packed with people from

Memphis. I walked in and found a seat at the bar. This was going to be one fun night; I could sense it. There was something magical in the air. That's what it was – there was a magic in Memphis.

New people in a comfortable place, and I knew the conversations would all be enjoyable. Southerners always had fun, lively conversations and were good at small talk. I was in my element. Instead of having a beer, which I always had in public, I decided to order a glass of Merlot. I rarely drank wine in public, but why not? Red wine was the drink of the Goddess on Yule as She awaited the Oak King and together they welcomed the rebirth of the Sun.

The wine arrived. I had no idea my Yule rituals and prayers were about to be answered until I heard James' clipped English accent say from behind me, "I'll have another."

Was it possible? James was here - in Memphis? Standing right behind me, so close I could feel his breath on my neck? I turned around and there James was. That look of fire and desire was in his eyes. He looked good, dressed in a dark, tailored grey suit with a red tie. An amused smile appeared on his face. Did he know that I was going to be here, or was this divine intervention?

"Well, hello, Vix. Mind if I join you for a drink?"

"You can have a drink with me, James, but only if you introduce me to your wife first."

James looked at his feet, such a disarming maneuver from him and his usual confident demeanor. There was an almost awkward pause until he said, "Oh, I didn't get married, Vix. I have apparently fallen under the spell of a beautiful Tennessee witch."

"What are you saying, James?" By this point, I could barely breathe or think.

"I'm saying that I'm in love with you, Victoria, and love makes men do things they wouldn't normally do, such as shake up the status quo. It makes men intrepid. We will travel halfway around the world just for the chance of having a drink with the woman we love and to ask for forgiveness."

This came as such a shock. I set the wine glass on the bar, pausing momentarily before saying, "James, are you calling me a witch?"

"Oh, Vix, you told me about your Goddess and your religion the first night we met. The phrase 'beautiful Tennessee Wiccan' just doesn't have the same romantic notion I wished to conjure up for you."

With that being said, we both laughed, that beautiful, spontaneous laugh we both enjoyed.

As we looked into each other's eyes, we each knew this was going to be a magical Yule to be remembered forever.

Who could ask for anything more in life?

Chapter Seven

Yule

The last two years had been spent in hotels at Yuletide. This was the first time in three years that I wasn't in a hotel at Yuletide – I was at home.. Two years ago, Grandmother passed away and I met James at the H &L international corporate event a few weeks later . Last year was the fateful meeting in Memphis that brought James back. I was in my own condo and could perform the prayers and ritual in solitude.

Someday, I will return to the family farm in Tennessee and perform them in the oak grove where Grandmother taught me the old ways, but not this year. This year, I set up the altar in the condo in Midtown. There was no fireplace for a Yule Log, so the Christmas tree served as the Yule Tree.

As always, I reflected on the past. Yule is the time of the Winter Solstice. It is again time to say goodbye to the old, and welcome the new. As the Sun returns to the Earth, life begins once more. Yule is deeply rooted in the cycle of the year – the wheel of the year. Yule is the seedtime of year - the longest night and the shortest day, where the Goddess once again becomes the Great Mother and gives birth to the new Sun King. The Winter Solstice, the rebirth of the Sun, is an important turning point in the wheel of the year.

The holly, mistletoe, pinecones, and a few oak leaves were carefully arranged on the altar: Holly, the symbol of death and rebirth, so important for Winter Solstice rituals; Juniper for visions and for attracting love into our lives; Mistletoe, the most sacred of all the Greens because of its protective powers.

The frankincense, cinnamon, and myrrh incenses were secured and placed throughout the altar on the table in front of the tree, but not lit until the candles were arranged. The tall taper candles are so important to the ritual because Yule is a celebration of light. The candles are a powerful symbol of a universal truth - the light comes into the darkness, and the darkness cannot overcome it. They had all been properly blessed and anointed at the correct moon phase before Yule and arranged around the altar. Green for the north, for Earth. Yellow for the east, for air. Red for the south, for fire. Blue for the west, representing water. The center candle is gold and taller than the other candles because it represents the Sun.

After taking a cleansing bath as keeps with the traditions, I returned to the altar and cast a circle to enable the energy of the prayers and rituals to manifest in the journey throughout the remaining cycle of the year.

To begin the ritual, I sat on the floor near the altar, once again taking a few moments to remember what it was like for our ancestors at this time of year. It was the season of Death, the time when the Earth went dormant once more, sleeping until the spring returned. Our ancestors knew that despite the darkness of this night, soon the light would return to the Earth, bringing with it life.

This night, the Winter Solstice, welcomes back the Sun, the ultimate giver of light.

Tonight is the night of the Solstice,

the longest night of the year.

As the Wheel turns once more, I know that tomorrow,

the Sun will begin its journey back to us.

With it, new life will begin,

a blessing from Earth to her children.

It is the season of the Winter Goddess.

Tonight I celebrate the festival of the Winter Solstice,

The rebirth of the Sun, and the return of light to the Earth.

As the Wheel of the Year turns once more,

I honor the eternal cycle of birth, life, death, and rebirth.

Today I honor the god of the forest,

the King of nature, who rules the season.

I give my thanks to the beautiful Goddess,

whose blessings bring new life to the Earth.

This gift I offer you tonight,

sending my prayers to you upon the air.

Then, I began the Blessing of the Greens, which were on the altar.

Oh Mother Goddess, Father God, we ask that you send your spirit down upon these branches taken from your creation. May you bestow upon them a special Yule blessing and may these greens be a symbol of your unchanging presence in our lives. Blessed be.

May our prayers voiced here this night manifest into our physical world. As above, so below. Blessed be.

Soon, our nights grow shorter and our days grow long. We look once more on these earthly symbols – firelight and evergreens – and embrace the glow of hope.

That Light and Life will return once again to the Earth.

The people who lived in darkness have seen a great light, and we have beheld its glory.

The Life-Light blazed out of the darkness and the darkness could not put it out.

Light, generous from the inside out, true from start to finish, full of grace, full of truth.

Let our intention be that we will shine with the Light of understanding and truth. Let our Light awaken what is best in our human family and help us to restore wisdom, honor, balance, beauty, and good will among all beings. Let the Light guide our hearts and hands to act for the healing of our Mother Earth.

I light this first candle in honor of Earth. Today I honor the stability of Mother Earth, the strength of Her love for us, the comfort of home that the starkness of the season highlights by contrast. Mother Earth, help me to bring this comfort to more of your creatures. Let it be so.

I light this second candle in honor of Air. Today I honor the knowledge that has been given to me, the desire to learn more, and the music that weaves through the past and the future. Let my spoken words and the words of our country's leaders lead to peace. Let it be so.

I light this third candle for Fire. Today, I give thanks for the passion and enthusiasm in my life in so many forms. May courage, drive, and creativity be mine this season. Let it be so.

I light this fourth candle for Water. May we trust our intuition and embrace our feelings and those of others this season. Let it be so.

I light this fifth candle for Spirit. May the power of the elements infuse my spirit so that I may manifest a positive influence in the world. Let Spirit combine the elements, to be more than the sum of its parts. Let it be so!

After the candles and prayers were completed, I lit the incense. As the smoke of the incense rose, I made an offering of food – the sweet Jam Cake, made from the recipe of my grandmother and her female ancestors. I meditated on what changes I would like to see before the next Sabbat - reflecting upon the time of the season. Although winter was here, life lay dormant beneath the soil. What new things will the wheel of the year bring to fruition for loved ones and for me when the planting season returns? How will everything change as the wheel turns into the new year?

Chapter Eight

Birth of the Sun

After the ritual and prayers, I let the candles burn for a while. The lights from the tree continued to sparkle and shine. The fragrance of the candles, incense, and pine filled the entire condo. The condo was packed with gifts and Christmas cards from family and friends. Every inch of the great room was filled with presents, well wishes sent in the form of cards or poinsettias. Some friends and family had sent exquisite Christmas arrangements of holly, mistletoe and amaryllis. My home had a lovely, festive feel. The holiday spirit was in the air and it intermingled with the feeling of hope. I adored this condo and I was very thankful for what my life had become.

For a moment, I opened the glass door that lead to the balcony which overlooked Peachtree Street. Stepping out onto the balcony, I looked down at the lights and elegant decorations that lined Atlanta's most famous street. The crisp, cool winter night air made it appear as if you could practically reach down from the nineteenth floor balcony and touch the decorations, or possibly even look up and touch a twinkling star. That was the promise of the night air as it mingled with my hopes and desires for the wheel of the next year. Nights like this were magical and made you believe all things were possible,

It was chilly on the balcony, so I moved back inside the condo, securing the glass door to keep the winter chill outside. I wanted to remember this night - every sparkly light, every leaf and berry on the holly - all the feelings I was experiencing. *Please dear Goddess, let me remember them forever.*

I thought about the past, about James and unexpectedly spending the last two years with him at Yuletide. The first Yule we spent at the W Hotel Downtown Atlanta following the H & L corporate event. Then it was this time last year I had spent the night with James at the Peabody Hotel in Memphis. Both meetings had been unplanned on my part but had such a tremendous impact on my life now. Taking the time to look back, I know that I had been in love with James since the night we met. The thought of James was never far from my conscious mind. My dreams, my subconscious, were also filled with James. How quickly these last few years had gone by, and how much my life had changed in a short span of time. As if to wake me from the dreaming, I heard keys in the door.

"Vix? Hello, darling." James' clipped English accent pleasantly filled my ears. His voice still made my heart melt when I heard him speak. "Traffic was terrible tonight, but I'm home safely. Are you ready to go?"

As he walked in the door, I moved toward him, and he said with a lowered voice, "Yule truly is our special day of celebration, isn't it?" By the time he uttered the words, I was in his arms.

He dropped his briefcase and keys to the floor and pulled me close to him, saying, "Thank the Goddess and you for giving me the best year of my life. This last year spent with you has made all my dreams come true Vix."

He pulled me toward him, kissing me softly yet passionately, curling my hair around his fingers as we kissed. I kissed him in return with matching intensity.

We stood entwined in each other's arms and caught in the moment. After a sweet, short pause, James kissed me on the forehead and placed his hands on my shoulders as we gazed into each other' eyes. I saw the overnight case I had placed by the door earlier.

"Dr. Smith is waiting for us, James," I whispered.

James kissed my right hand and held it to his lips for a second longer than he should have. The romantic notion did not escape me and it suited the evening, and James, as well. " Are your rituals completed?" He picked up the case, and took my hand in his.

"Yes, sweetheart, everything is completed." We briefly kissed again. James held my hand as we walked out the door and took the elevator downstairs to to our car. We drove silently but with great anticipation to the Emory Hospital where I gave birth to our son that night. James Arthur Bryant Wellington was born just before midnight, on Yule, Winter Solstice. As James, the baby, and I were together in my hospital room following the birth, I remember James kissing me, as I faded into a dream, my mind recalling the last chant of the ancient prayer.

Today I honor the god of the forest,

The King of nature, who rules the season.

I give my thanks to the beautiful Goddess,

Whose blessings bring new life to the Earth.

This gift I offer you tonight,

Sending my prayers to you upon the air.

Two years later following the birth of our son, our daughter was conceived at Yuletide. She was born the following September. In order to return to the old ways, James and I named her Anne O'Briant, the name of my grandmother. Yule forever remains a special time in our lives. We will never forget the magic in Memphis that finally brought us together and opened our hearts to the love that changed our lives forever.

As above, so below. Blessed Be.

Chapter One

River Christofel tapped his fingers against his desk and glared at his computer monitor. The blank screen was mocking him. For that matter, so was his own reflection. The dark eyes and serious face that stared back at him appeared almost accusing. He had sat there for two hours, and the only thing he'd accomplished was getting caught up in a political war on one of his social networks and winning a few rounds of virtual solitaire. His new manuscript, however, was nothing more than his name and the words "Chapter One" typed out in two dozen various fonts. He had started writing a real story more than once, but every time he got past the first page he found himself hitting the delete key and starting over. It just wasn't quality work, and River was nothing if not a perfectionist.

The whole situation was just plain aggravating. Sure, his first book might still be on the best sellers list, but that was no consolation when his recent novel was being ripped to pieces by the critics and he was in a slump in regards to new material. He was officially River Christofel, the one hit wonder, and it seemed like that was all he was ever going to be.

River pulled off his wireframe glasses and pressed his fingers against his eyes, hoping to rub away the headache that was just beginning. He was so busy feeling sorry for himself; he didn't notice that his girlfriend, Brie, had come into the room until she was peering over his shoulder.

"Working hard again, I see?"

River lifted his head just in time to see her roll her emerald eyes. With a grunt of frustration he slammed the laptop shut and ran his hands through his short brown hair. He knew it was just good-natured teasing. After all, his monitor had been opened to a game of *Minesweep* since he had already conquered solitaire. Yet, for some reason the light comment that was meant to be playful really grated on his nerves. Maybe it was because the last thing he needed was yet another reminder of his failure to get anything accomplished. Even Brie's sweet smile as she adjusted the beret that covered her hair didn't stop his harsh reply.

"What would *you* know about work?" He huffed. "Haven't I been supporting you the last few years?"

River regretted the words almost as soon as they spilled out of his mouth. Brie had given up her own promising career in advertisement to become his personal assistant as soon as his book started to take off. She probably worked ten times harder than he did making travel arrangements for book signings, handling their finances, answering fan mail, and even working as an unofficial editor. She took care of all the menial tasks so he would be able to concentrate on his writing. Originally they thought his success would leave the door open for her to pursue her own dreams of singing fulltime on the stage, but his hectic schedule and cross country tours had left her little time for her own desires. She never complained and had never been anything but supportive, but despite her sweet and loving disposition, she also had a quick Irish temper. River saw her eyes narrow and her lips press into a tight frown. He knew she certainly wasn't going to stand for his insults when she knew quite well she had done nothing to justify them.

"Humph." She put her hands on her shapely hips and glared at him. "Weren't you living in your mother's basement when we met? Who did the supporting back then, huh? And who was the one who stole your first manuscript and sent it into that agent when you didn't have the nerve to do it yourself? You wouldn't even be here without me!"

"Here we go with that old line again." River snorted and gave her a dirty look. "The acknowledgements page just wasn't enough for you, was it? I guess now you want your name listed on the cover? Or better yet, maybe I should just sign over half my royalties!"

"That isn't what I meant and you know it!" she argued, her emerald eyes flashing. "I couldn't care less about getting any credit and I'm happy about your success. I love that your dreams were realized. I just wish you weren't so...so *moody* all the time." She sighed, and relented a little. "I know you've been struggling with the new novel but—"

"Don't you dare play the sympathy card with me!" River snapped. "I don't want your pity!"

"Aghhh! You're impossible when you're like this!" Brie spat back. "Really, do you have to play the role of the temperamental artist all the time? I can't even be nice to you without you jumping down my throat. Seriously, you were a lot more fun before you were famous!"

"The money doesn't seem to bother you too much." He gestured to the *Louie Vitton* bag she was clutching. "Looks like another designer handbag you've got hanging on your arm."

He knew he had pushed her too far when he saw her close her eyes. He could almost hear her counting to ten in her mind, but when she finally spoke her voice had lost the angry edge and she only sounded disheartened. "I don't know what's happening between us, River, but I really hate this. I don't want to fight with you anymore. I'm so tired of fighting..."

"If you're so tired of me, then why do you keep hanging around?"

She shook her head, defeated. "I guess I *won't* hang around since my presence here seems to bring out the worst in you. I have plans anyway. Maybe I'll come back tonight. Maybe I won't."

River sat at his desk and scowled as Brie pulled her jacket from the closet and disappeared around a corner without another word. A few seconds later, the door to their penthouse slammed shut with so much force the paintings on the wall rattled. River should have shouted something nasty to her retreating back. Something that would have made her feel miserable and guilty about making silly threats he knew she didn't mean. Apparently his writer's block was spreading and he had commentary block as well because he couldn't come up with anything that was even remotely witty.

Afterwards, River hoped and even expected that she would come back. Brie did that a lot when they had arguments. Despite her quick temper, she was one of those people who not only hated to go to bed angry, but also hated to walk away from any argument that was unresolved. This time, he must have pushed her too far. When she didn't reappear, he peeked out the window and looked down into the city streets. He caught a glimpse of her far below, hailing a cab with one hand while her other was holding down her beret so it wouldn't blow off in the wind. He turned away before she even got into the vehicle, realizing that this time, Brie wasn't coming back.

The moment River knew she was really gone, he instantly regretted their argument. For a second, he thought about following her and apologizing, but he knew it wouldn't make any difference. Even if they patched things up tonight, there would just be another argument later. Things just weren't the same between them. Sometimes he longed for the old days, even if it would mean giving up his newfound wealth and fame. Back before he was consumed with deadlines and interviews, it had seemed like he and Brie were the only two people in the world. That was the happiest time in his life and the time when he had done his best work.

The thing he missed the most was spending his evenings watching Brie perform on the stage in a little jazz bar called *The Rusty Nail*. It was a small club that was lucky to have ten patrons on a busy night. The few people that were regulars there were all collecting social security, but River had never been a socialite and he preferred the company of elders to people his own age.

River treasured the memories of that little bar with its high stools and candlelit tables. He loved watching Brie sitting on top of the grand piano in her little black dress, belting out jazz standards alongside a sax player who was old enough to be her grandfather. Every time he heard her sing, it would stir his own artistic drive. It was her exotic voice that had inspired his first novel, *The Siren's Call*. And it was her insatiable love making that had turned a simple fantasy into an exotic phenomenon that had housewives all over the country dusting off their vibrators. It was just a shame their own bed had turned to ice. River knew it was mostly his own fault. His lack of inspiration left him in a foul mood and Brie's fiery temper made her less than sympathetic to his plight. The clash led to a lot of fireworks and not the good kind.

River banged his head against his keyboard and groaned. He was such an ungrateful, undeserving idiot. Brie was beautiful, talented, and energetic. She could have any man she wanted. River knew she was getting tired of his artistic melancholy. She was spending more and more nights out on the town with her friends, and he was usually asleep by the time she came home. He couldn't remember the last time they had made love. Sometimes he had to wonder if she was really out with the girls at all or she had found a new love to warm her bed.

To River, it seemed like his whole life was plummeting out of control. His career was going down the toilet right along with his love life. He should never have let his agent coerce him into changing his last story to suit what they thought the people wanted. He should have stayed true to his vision instead of selling out for a larger advance. But he was paying the price for his foolishness. Soon he would be a washed-up author whose books would only be sold on the discarded quarter shelf at the library and he knew he didn't deserve any better.

Eventually, being alone in the huge penthouse with nothing but his inactive imagination and negative thoughts became too much to bear. River threw his laptop and a notebook into his briefcase, grabbed his winter coat, and headed out. He hoped maybe a change of scenery would help get his creative juices flowing, but he wasn't prepared for the bitter cold wind and icy hale that slapped against his bare cheeks when he stepped through the door. Immediately his glasses fogged up from the sudden temperature change, making it hard for him to see where he was going. Things were even more out of focus when he took them off and tried to wipe them down. Endless hours of staring at a computer monitor hadn't helped improve his already poor eyesight. He would probably be legally blind before he reached forty. Just one more thing for him to be depressed about.

Once his glasses were back in place, River walked with his head downcast and did his best not to make eye contact with any of the passers by. Sometimes people recognized him as the famous author of *The Siren's Call*, and he always felt overwhelmed when fans gushed about how wonderful he was, especially when they knew nothing about him. He had only made it a few blocks when his teeth started chattering. He probably should have checked the forecast before stumbling out into the city streets. It had to be ten below in New York City, which was hardly surprising for the first day in February. Piles of soot stained snow were heaped up two feet high on the corners, remnants from their last snowstorm. The overcast sky promised yet another winter squall was on the way. It was already starting to flurry pretty heavily. Not many pedestrians were brave enough to face the harsh weather, making the city street seem strangely barren, despite the late hour.

River shoved his hands deeper into his pockets and wished he occasionally remembered everyday things like gloves and hats. It seemed that even in his creative slump, his artistic mind still pushed the necessities to the side when he was in writer mode. The work was often so all-consuming he would sometimes forget to eat or use the bathroom for hours at a time. He was certainly paying the price for his absentmindedness that day. His cheeks were chaffed and his fingers were numb when he finally pulled open the door of his favorite coffee house. He stomped the snow from his metal-tipped boots and stumbled through the door. He hoped the large coffee he ordered would warm him up a bit, but his hands were shaking so badly that he splashed creamer all over the counter when he tried to pour some into his cup.

As he wiped up the mess, River noticed a couple walking together just outside the window. They were snuggled up close to brace themselves against the harsh gusts, but still laughing and holding hands. His thoughts again turned to Brie. Back in their home state of Vermont, they had faced much colder nights than this one, but it hadn't seemed nearly as uncomfortable with her warm body beside him. He wondered if they would ever get back to that place or if his heart had turned as cold as the frosty February night.

Frustrated with his own depressing thoughts, River tossed his dirty napkin toward the trash bin. Of course, he missed his intended target and it landed on the floor. He bent down to pick it up and told himself that he wasn't doing anyone any good by dwelling on the past. What he had with Brie had changed. Maybe it had died right along with his artistic drive. Maybe in real life there were no happy endings.

River sighed over his heavy thoughts as he squeezed into a corner booth. He was determined to put his personal issues aside for at least a little while and concentrate on his work. The table he had chosen was big enough for four, but he liked to have room to spread out his papers. There was also a large fire burning in the flue not too far away and the flames added a little extra warmth to the chilly air. He was grateful for the heat it emitted which was finally thawing out his frostbitten fingers. The combination of the fireplace and the hot coffee restored a little of his energy and he decided he wasn't going to spend the whole night sulking. He pulled out his laptop and hooked into the coffee house Wi-Fi.

If he couldn't think of anything interesting to write, River decided he could at least do some basic research. His genre was fantasy, but his work was loosely based on ancient mythology and legends. He didn't have much of a plot charted out yet, but he knew he wanted his hero to be a despondent human who had lost his home, his family, and his hope. His love interest had to be something more—a divine female with the power to heal the grief stricken heart of his protagonist and give him the strength he needed to face whatever perils might lie in his path. River wasn't sure what type of creature would realistically fill that role. He only knew she had to be something unique and beautiful.

River concentrated for quite a while but nothing was coming to him. It was ludicrous that he couldn't even establish his basic characters without drawing a blank. If he couldn't get that far, he might as well admit to himself now that it was hopeless and move on to a more mundane career choice, because he was never going to make it as a professional writer. He was just about to slam the laptop closed when the flickering lights of the fireplace caught his eye. River watched the flames dance and twist with a life of their own, and a small seed started to sprout somewhere in the deepest recesses of his mind. As he studied the radiant blaze, he at last had a spark of inspiration. He knew what type of female his hero would encounter. She would be a goddess—a goddess who had control over the element of fire.

Feeling a twinge of excitement for the first time in days, River typed the words "fire goddess" into the search engine. Instantly, dozens of fabulous images popped up onto the screen. There were humanoid women, their naked bodies consumed by the blaze yet untouched by its fury. Some wore gowns woven from flames as they waltzed in the heavens among the stars. There were also elemental creatures that were made entirely from fire with hair that sizzled down their backs in a red-orange glow. Some of the women wore vicious expressions and seemed bent on destruction as they welded swords of fire towards unseen enemies. Others appeared peaceful and serene with deep set eyes that held the wisdom of the ages.

They were all divinely beautiful, but one image stood out from all the others. River found himself instantly captivated by a beautiful woman with auburn tresses that spun down her back, in a blanket of curls that reached nearly to her ankles. She wore a rich gown of green velvet embroidered throughout with Celtic insignia that was sewn in delicate silver threads. A golden crown with a solitary emerald sat upon her brow and beads and feathers were braided into her hair, making her appear to be of royal lineage. Yet, despite her majestic beauty and vivid finery, a small calf stood by her side which made her seem somehow much more approachable. She could have been human if not for her inhuman perfection and the flame that she cradled in the palm of her hand.

It was strange how that image called to him. As a virile man, he should have been more intrigued by the less modest images of naked she-devils with perky breasts and welcoming, seductive stances. Yet somehow, the loving grace he saw mirrored in that woman's eyes appealed to him on a much deeper level than those primordial urges. It was as though her outstretched hands were beseeching him. Instantly smitten with her, and hungry to learn who and what she was, River clicked his mouse on the image. He was brought to a website dedicated to Celtic myths and legends. At the top of the page was an odd symbol he had never seen before. It had a woven square at its center and four radials that jutted out from all four corners. It was called Brigid's Cross and apparently it was the symbol of the flame haired woman he admired. River sipped his coffee as he scanned through the website and learned her story.

"The Goddess Brigid," he read aloud. "Also known as Bride and Brigitania, Brigid is the patron goddess of poetry, childbearing, and hmmm, smith craft. That's an interesting combination. Then again, they do all require hard work and labor before the final project is complete, so maybe it makes sense after all."

River muttered his thoughts out loud, forgetting where he was. Luckily there weren't any other people desperate or foolish enough to face the elements for a late night latte, so no one overheard him mumbling to himself. Even the lone worker was too busy texting on her cell phone to notice him talking to himself.

River went back to reading, this time silently so the counter girl didn't take notice. He learned that Brigid was also the goddess of creativity and inspiration, which may be why he felt so drawn to her. He was certainly in need of a little heavenly motivation. Still, it was more than just that trait that made her the perfect fit for his story. Of all the goddesses he had studied, none seemed quite as personable as Brigid. She really cared for her people and walked among them in their time of need. It was believed that in the heart of the winter the Goddess Brigid would come with her undying flame to warm their hearths, bringing with her healing and the life saving energy of the sun. This tradition was celebrated each year of the sacred night of Imbolc. A day when despite the bleak cold, the people would give thanks for the new life that was beginning to stir beneath the earth. People made corn dolls, had candlelit vigils, and honored the seeds that were churning with life beneath the soil. The feast of Imbolc or Candlemas, River discovered, was still celebrated to this day in many cultures on the first of February.

River jerked back in surprise when he read that date. Then he had to double check his virtual calendar because it seemed like too much of a coincidence, but it was indeed February first. He realized that it *had* to be divine intervention. Obviously, River had found his fire goddess. He continued to page through dozens of different websites on Brigid and he studied images of her in all her aspects. He jotted down a ton of notes, but as enticing as her tale was, it wasn't stimulating his own work. He stared down at the blank word document where his story should be coming to life, and he wondered if he would ever write again.

River grunted in frustration and looked up from his monitor just in time to see that the brunette at the register had put away her cell phone and was giving him dirty looks. He couldn't blame her. He wasn't looking forward to the trek home in what was quickly blossoming into a full-fledged blizzard. He was certain the idea was even less appealing to someone who was pouring coffee for minimum wage. River noticed that so far she had only accumulated a few pennies and one quarter in her tip jar. Luckily for her, the royalties were still pouring in from his best seller and he could afford to be generous. After he packed up his computer and drained the last of his latte, he reached into his pocket and pulled out a hundred dollar bill that was crumbled almost beyond recognition. He tossed it in amongst the change, and headed toward the exit without another word. He would be well on his way before she unfolded it and realized how much it was, which saved them both from any embarrassing displays of gratitude. Like most authors, River was introverted. He had never been very good with people and avoided confrontations with them whenever possible. Brie was the only one he had ever really been able to talk to. Of course, even that seemed to be a thing of the past.

River pulled his jacket tightly around himself as he stepped out into the freezing cold night. He was sure the temperature had dropped at least another twenty degrees, and the walk home seemed to take a lot longer than usual. When he finally arrived, he peeled off his damp clothes, pulled on a pair of sweatpants and a t-shirt, and wondered if he would ever thaw out. A part of him had hoped to find Brie waiting for him, but the penthouse was empty. River found himself alone once again. He wondered where Brie was, what she was doing, and who she was doing it with. He couldn't even blame her if she *was* cheating on him. Did he deserve any less after the way he had treated her?

Chapter Two

It was close to midnight when River finished changing, and he realized that he was in for a long and lonely night. He considered turning in early, but the late night coffee had given him an energy jolt he wasn't quite sure what to do with. Since he still felt chilled straight through to his bones from his walk home in the snow, he started by turning on the gas powered fireplace. It wasn't quite as satisfying as building one the old fashioned way, but at least it added some warmth to the bedroom. However, even with the blaze roaring River didn't feel any warmer and he still found himself shivering. He tried both watching television and reading a book under his down comforter, but he couldn't concentrate on either. Like a smitten school boy, he found his mind kept wandering back to Brigid, and he wondered what magic the fire goddess would use to drive the cold away.

River decided to put his fantasies to good use. He climbed out from under the blankets and pulled his handwritten notes from his briefcase. As he looked them over, it finally dawned on him. Brigid wasn't just the answer to his hero's fictional dilemmas. She could be the solution to his writer's block as well. In ancient times, the bards had called on Brigid to inspire their work and even today there were chants and spells designed to conjure her aid. His eyes strayed across the room to the little altar that Brie, who was a long time Wiccan, had constructed in the corner. It was a just a wooden table, painted in the center with a large silver pentacle, but to Brie it was a temple. At each corner there were colored triangles in yellow, red, blue and green. Each one faced a different direction to represent the elements of air, fire, water, and earth. Brie often retreated to that quiet corner to mediate and, he presumed, to work magic.

River had never been the most spiritual person, but he had always listened to Brie talk about her chosen path with interest. At first, it was just the typical observance of an author looking for inspiration in everyday life. But the more he learned about things like pagan deities, spell work, and reincarnation, the more familiar it seemed. If he was called to any religion, it would be the pagan path and Brigid was a part of that tradition. Brie's incantations always seemed to get the results she desired. Why couldn't the same thing work for River? Why couldn't he invoke Brigid, the goddess of creativity, on her most sacred night and ask for her help? He figured it couldn't hurt. At best, the novel whose fleeting glimpses had been teasing him for weeks would finally come to fruition. At worst, he'd have an embarrassing tale to share with Brie when she got home.

Determined to give it a shot, River set to work planning a mini ceremony. He had been to enough public rituals with Brie to know the basics. He would begin by smudging beforehand with a bundle of sage to remove any negative energies and then calling in the Guardian elements. After that, it was going to be a little more difficult, but he figured he could wing it. He searched through the little chest Brie kept beside their bed. It was filled to the brim with her various witchy supplies, but he wasn't sure how to use the athames, cauldrons, and wands. He had the feeling they were more for symbolism than a necessity, so he hoped Brigid wouldn't be offended if he left them where they were. There were also dozens of different sachets of herbs, but unless he was supposed to pull out his rolling paper and smoke lavender or mugwort, he wasn't quite sure what to do with those either.

River shrugged, put the confusing tools away, and settled for a single candle tinged a yellow-orange color that was reminiscent of the flame Brigid carried in her palm. As an afterthought, he also pulled out a few sticks of sandalwood incense to help set the mood. He turned down the artificial lights so that the fireplace and his candle would provide the only illumination in the room. Then he pulled out an invocation to Brigid that he had come across during his internet search. He had only jotted it down because he had enjoyed the meter and rhyme. Little did he know there was a deeper purpose behind that random act.

River felt a little nervous as he called in the elements and lit his lone candle. He remembered Brie telling him that intention was the most important part of any conjuring, so he tried to concentrate on his purpose and to do so with the utmost respect for the deity he was summoning. The smell of the incense made his eyes water at first and he had to take off his glasses, but after a while the calming scent seemed to chase away the last of his nervous jitters. He breathed in deeply and evenly, allowing the smoke to encircle him. He repeated the process several times until he felt himself drifting away from the physical world. His eyes began to dilate as he stared into the bright red flame. The floor beneath him became less substantial. The sound of traffic and heavy winds outside his window faded into the background. The circle he cast and the work he was doing became his only reality. He had to strain his eyes to read his own sloppy handwriting without his glasses on, but before long he had the words memorized and he started to whisper the short chant from memory.

"Brigid I call you on this sacred night.

I summon your flame. I invoke your might.

The words will come. My mind will soar.

My strength and confidence will endure.

Goddess Brigid, fill me with creativity.

As I will it, so mote it be."

He repeated the words once, twice, three times, each time his voice rose in volume until his whispers morphed into thunderous plea. Still, nothing happened except for the slight dizziness that came from the unaccustomed heavy breathing. River wasn't sure what he expected, but he was strangely disappointed. Feeling disillusioned, he leaned over, prepared to snuff out the candle with his fingers, when something caught his eye. The flame seemed to twist and bend at an odd angle, almost as though it were dancing away from the wick and becoming its own entity. It only lasted for a millisecond before settling back down to its original location, but River felt his heart pound with exhilaration. He felt a peculiar presence in the room with him, and he knew he was no longer alone. The thought didn't frighten him. Instead, it made him tremble with excitement. He instantly started up the chant again, speaking louder and faster this time, so that his words kept pace with his accelerated heartbeat.

"Brigid I call you on this sacred night.

I summon your flame. I invoke your might.

The words will come. My mind will soar.

My strength and confidence will endure.

Goddess Brigid, fill me with creativity.

As I will it, so mote it be."

Again and again he repeated the verse. His voice quickened and rose in crescendo with each chorus, until it became an almost frenzied mantra. His whole body seemed to tingle with the building energy around him until it was an almost tangible thing. The verse flowed naturally now. He no longer needed to look at his cheat sheet because the words were engraved on his mind and his soul. He even found himself improving and adding his own words to the chant as long dormant knowledge from a time and place far from this life was awoken within him. As he chanted, his eyes never strayed from the flame. He felt as though that tiny light wrapped his whole body in its embrace, warming him inside and out. The last of the icy chill seemed to melt away from his skin, even though his arms were bare.

As he continued to chant, he started to sway in time to the music of his own voice. His body tingled from head to toe. Eventually the energy reached its peak. River finally allowed himself to stop reciting and catch his breath. He almost collapsed against the altar in exhaustion from the intensity of the ritual, but the energy flow was already beginning to dwindle back down. He felt a little shaky and heady from the lingering scent of the incense, but there was no burst of creativity—no rush of ideas that sent him running for his notebook.

Again, River felt disappointed, even despondent. The magic had felt so intense. He was so certain he had sensed something — some higher power inching its way closer as the invocation had intensified. He still felt the energy crackling around him. Maybe the results weren't meant to be instantaneous or maybe he had just failed at spell casting the same way he seemed to be failing at everything else these days. Either way, nothing had happened. River assumed it was his lack of experience, and feeling defeated, decided he had fooled around with magic enough for one evening.

Novice or not, he still knew better than to offend the spirits, so he thanked them and the elements before releasing them back to their mystical realms. He was about to extinguish the orange candle and go to bed, but when he leaned in to snuff the flames, he felt a strange sense of vertigo. Again the flame began its bizarre, magical waltz. It lifted high above the candle, growing larger, glowing brighter, while River watched with wide, frightened eyes. This time the fire's erotic dance didn't end above the wick. The flame rose higher above the wax, and flew over his head toward the back of the room, leaving the remaining stub sitting in a pool of melted wax.

Strangely enough, his first thought was concern that the flying flame might have set the curtains on fire and he wondered how he would explain that to Brie. Then it hit him that something extraordinary had just happened. River had to blink a few times to make sure he wasn't dreaming. He tried to tell himself it was just the wind that had blown out the flame because it couldn't possibly have detached itself from the candle and flown away like a firefly. Except that there was no wind inside the penthouse. His heart started beating faster, and he prayed this was real and that he was about to witness his own personal miracle. His body was tingling again, this time with a power that was almost sexual, and he wasn't ready for that feeling to end. He wanted to believe and embrace the magic. Feeling a little shaky, unsure of what power he might have unleashed, River turned his head to see where the flame had ventured off to.

It was then that he first saw her. She stood in his bedroom doorway, in all her naked perfection, her lips pulled back in a seductive smile. River's jaw dropped and his mouth stayed open so long, he wondered if it was possible for it to get stuck that way. He had to grip the dresser with both hands to keep his legs from buckling beneath him. Though he was certain that he had sensed her presence even before that first breathtaking glance, it was still a shock to see her standing there—a gorgeous auburn haired woman. Even without his glasses on, he could clearly see that she holding the inextinguishable flame that had flown from his candle neatly in the palm of her outstretched hand.

"Wh..what? Wh..who..."

River stuttered and couldn't even finish the sentence. The woman seemed to find his inability to articulate humorous and she laughed lightly as she took a step further into the bedroom. Of course, she didn't need to answer his question. He already knew who she was, and she was certainly not of this world. Even without the flame in her hands that would have been obvious. She was too perfect, too spectacular, to be anything less than divine. Though the dim lights provided by the fireplace cast her features in shadows and the whole room was a little blurry without his glasses, he still recognized her from the portraits he had admired online just hours earlier. This was Brigid. The Goddess of poetry, creativity, and inspiration had answered his prayers in a way that even an author of fantasy novels had never imagined.

Brigid was beautiful. Ravishing. Even without the velvet gown and other finery she had worn in the drawings, it was still clear that she was something far grander than royalty. She was the most glorious creature he had ever seen. As stunned as he was to see her there, in all her divine perfection, he still felt the instant stirring of desire as he studied her bare anatomy. Her auburn tresses hung to her waist, just shielding her breasts from his view. He dared not look any lower, despite the desperate urge to do just that, afraid she would think him brazen and disrespectful. Overshadowing the primal need that every man felt when he saw a beautiful woman was the instinct to show her the esteem and honor she deserved. Yet, at the same time, he wanted to take her into his arms and offer her the pleasure her thick lips and naked body seemed to beckon.

She gave him a teasing smile, as though she understood his inner struggle. She inched a little closer to him, opening her arms in invitation. "Come to me, River," she whispered, her voice as calming as the roaring fire. "Let us see if my flame can't kindle the passion within you."

The goddess gestured him closer with her free hand. River instantly felt his body's response to the sweet chime of her voice which was somehow a soft, seductive whisper and a booming demand all in the same breath. He longed to rush into her arms, but though the area between his legs instantly rose to attention and throbbed with a yearning that was almost painful, his feet seemed glued to the floor.

Brigid giggled and looked him over like he was nothing more than a virginal school boy, which was an adequate description of how he felt at that moment. When she realized he was unable to comply with her request to come to her, she moved toward him, still holding the living flame in her palm. With her free hand, she gently coaxed him out of his corner and out of the sweat pants and t-shirt which were the only clothing he wore. He raised his arms as she lifted the shirt over his head, stopping to kiss his bare chest and stroke the fine layer of hair. He had to shut his eyes and try to still his pounding heart as with her help his pants slid to the floor. Stepping out of them, River found himself as naked as she was. He wasn't sure if the flush that came to his cheeks was from modesty or the heat that radiated from her skin — skin which glowed with a supernatural hue.

The goddess licked her lips seductively as she looked him over from head to toe and nodded her head in obvious approval. Her scrutiny wasn't as intimidating as he expected. In fact, it put them on even turf and he finally felt free to study her perfect body as well. The beauty before him was almost incomprehensible. It made his heart stop for just a moment, and he took in a sharp breath. When he finally exhaled again, his heart hammered.

Her face still seemed cloaked in shadows from the incense smoke that clouded around her, but every crevice and curve of her body was crystal clear despite his bad vision. Centered between her shapely hips he saw a tuft of fire red pubic hair perfectly trimmed and calling him like a moth to the tempting flame. Her firm pink breasts were taut, their nipples erect. Not from cold, since heat radiated from her, but from pure and intense arousal. His own naked body wasn't standing up to the cold quite as well. His skin was peppered with gooseflesh, which the fire woman noticed instantly. Again she beckoned River forward. He took a step closer, but he had no idea how he dared to touch her. River was afraid the apparition would vanish or that he might be smitten on the spot for daring to think he was the equal to her majesty. Yet, when she lifted her finger in a come-hither gesture, River could no longer deny his goddess's call.

"Come into my arms, my love. Let me warm you with my flame."

It was a request that River could not ignore. He yearned for her touch, to feel her hot hands against his icy skin. This time there was no resistance and no inhibitions. Yet, it was not lust that steered him forward but an adoration that bordered on unadulterated love. With unbridled passion, he wrapped his arms around her waist and pressed his mouth against hers, allowing his tongue to explore her mouth. River was immersed in invisible flames as soon as their bodies collided. Every inch of his flesh burned hot and feverish with desire and yearning. The heat even poured from her full lips, which smothered his own with an equal desperation and wanting, leaving them both panting and gasping for breath when they finally pulled apart. His skin burned, but instead of draining him, the heat instantly invigorated him and set his loins on fire. He felt the skin of his manhood stretch tighter as his erection grew, and he knew he had to take her soon.

River brushed her long red locks to the side, and took one of her succulent breasts into his mouth. He was amazed at how hot, almost feverish her bare skin felt, despite the cold February night. She was practically sizzling and yet there was not one bead of moisture to mar her perfection, though already River felt the sweat dripping from his own brow. He almost expected to see steam rise as he gently ran his cool tongue in circling motions along her nipple, tickling and teasing until she moaned and pressed her body harder against his. The other bosom he cupped with one hand, exalting in the firm feel of it because it was proof that she was real and not just a figment of his imagination.

Brigid tired of the playful teasing quickly and pulled River toward the bed with demanding need. She pushed him onto the down comforter, and fell to her knees in front of him. With an almost wicked smile, she took the whole of his engorged member into the warmth of her mouth while her long fingers gently massaged his tender pouch. The whole time her eyes stayed on his, watching for every tremor and moan as the ecstasy took him in waves, enjoying the control she had over him.

It was almost embarrassing how swiftly he exploded from the pleasure of her erotic kiss. She didn't seem to mind his quick release. She greedily sucked every last drop of his essence until River shuddered and collapsed back against the sheets, feeling as though he had been drained by the most beautiful of succubae. She didn't give his trembling body long to recover before accosting him once again. She threw her milky white figure down on the bed beside him and opened her legs. Throughout the whole of the encounter, she somehow still managed to hold her eternal flame high above her head in the palm of her right hand.

"Come taste my fire," she told him.

It was an invitation she didn't have to make twice. River turned so that he was on his belly and buried his face into her moist folds. He exalted in the sweet taste of her and the feel of the velvet soft patch of pubic hair that was nestled at the center of her most sacred space. She arched her back, bit down on her lower lip, and ran the fingers of her free hand roughly through his dark hair as he began his tentative exploration. His tongue discovered the deepest recesses of her cavern before finally coming back around to frolic on the small mound whose sensitivity almost instantly brought her to a breathtaking orgasm. When he knew she was reaching her peak, his thrust his fingers inside her even while his tongue continued its teasing probe. Her cries shattered the silence as she screamed out her intense pleasure. Even as her legs convulsed and snared his neck, he did not release her, but continued to lick and suckle until once again her body shuttered and peaked. The flood of warm juices that rushed into his mouth was sweeter than fruit and hot against his throat.

The multiple climaxes still did not sate her sexual appetite. Seconds after River sat up and wiped his mouth, Brigid was already demanding more. She pulled him toward her, pressing her lips roughly against his. He was beginning to worry that as a mere human, he might not be able to satisfy her immortal hunger. But the second her free hand stroked him, he felt himself harden so tight it was almost painful. When she opened her legs for his embrace, he never faltered before pounding into her with an all-consuming yearning unlike anything he had ever known.

Even as she wrapped her arms around him and guided him inside of her, the flame she carried was not extinguished. Instead, it was as though River took the fire into himself even as Brigid took every inch of his manhood into her tight grotto. He plummeted into her again and again, and being inside of her was like being enveloped in endless miracles. Each joust sent spasms of ecstasy coursing through every inch of his body, and a thousand mini orgasms racked his frame with a pleasure that was almost unbearable. She cried out with a craving that matched his own and arched her back high to meet his every penetrating thrust. Her hands, now finally free from the fire he had ingested, raked down his back before attempting to pull him even deeper inside of her warm, wet nether region.

As their love making intensified, River at last found the muse he had sought for so long. In her arms, his story, *their* story was unraveling, playing out like a movie in his mind. Every heartfelt moan was another chapter unfolding. Every shuddering mini climax filled him with new inspiration until finally the full novel was clear. In the arms of the Goddess Brigid, River found an uninhibited passion he had never known and had never even imagined existed. It was a rush as sensual as the joining itself to know that his creativity has been restored. His pleasure became more intense. He hardly noticed the strain of his muscles or the sweat that dripped from his brow. He was bordering on his peak and holding back until he was certain she had reached her own.

River watched with masculine pride as the goddess of inspiration thrashed in his arms. Finally she cried out and dug her nails deep into his skin. She had probably drawn blood but he didn't care. River's seed stirred and burst forth within her in one final rapturous eruption, just as the seeds were stirring below the earth on Imbolc night. At the same time the seeds of his new novel sprouted, thrived, and grew to fruition.

Perhaps Brigid could have continued that way for eternity, but River was only human. After two more rounds of mind blowing sex, he fell exhausted against the pillows. He was spent, and all he wanted was to close his eyes and rest for just a few minutes. Yet, he was afraid that if he took even that brief reprieve, if he turned his eyes away from his beautiful goddess for just one moment, she would vanish forever—that the whole night and all its wonders would have been nothing more than a dream or an illusion.

Forcing back a yawn, River sat up in the bed and picked up the extra pair of glasses he kept on the nightstand. He leaned over to study her, wanting to memorize every detail and hoping to at least get a clear view of the face that had somehow stayed hidden in shadows throughout their night of passion. Still, he found he couldn't see because her long red hair was blocking his view—hair whose sweet vanilla and jasmine scent suddenly seemed strangely familiar. Even as he brushed the curls aside, the last of the fog fell from his eyes. He finally saw everything clearly and he gasped from the shock of it.

"Brie?"

She yawned and giggled a little as she turned to meet his questioning gaze. "Were you expecting someone else?"

River smiled too, and looking down at the woman he adored, he felt his heart swell. "Of course not," he whispered. "You have always been my goddess."

"Well, that *was* some damn good sex, but I wouldn't go so far as too call me a goddess," she teased. Then she turned more serious. "Really, I'm not sure what came over me. When I came in, I just had this undeniable urge to find you and…well, you know." River thought it was charming the way her cheeks turned almost as red as her hair. "They do say that make up sex is the best, and I did feel really bad about the fight we had before I left. I didn't mean the things I said. You're an amazing writer and you would have sent in that manuscript eventually, with or without me. I wanted to make it up to you and—"

"Shhhh." He smiled and entwined his fingers with hers. "It's okay. We both said things we didn't mean, but it was all my fault. I was the one being a jerk, but it's all good now. I think this was just what we needed. It was a...a rekindling of sorts."

"I've been rekindling a lot of old passions today," she told him seriously. "I didn't want to say anything until I was sure, but I landed a gig with a little Jazz trio. I was out at the tryouts tonight. They group plays every Friday and Saturday night at this little bar called *The Common Ground* over on Sixth Street. It's just like *The Rusty Nail*, except there are actually some people there." Her lips pulled back into a conspirative grin. "Maybe it was my excitement over getting to sing again that made me so...insatiable tonight. It always was our love of art that drew us together."

"Whatever it was, I hope it happens again...and again...and *again*," River teased. Brie laughed, and to River it seemed like she was glowing again, but this time it was just with happiness and not with that supernatural hue she had earlier. "When is your first show?" he asked. "I want to come hear you sing."

"I'd really like that, River. Having you in the audience always gives me more confidence. When you're out there, I'm not nearly as nervous."

"Well, I am your number one fan," he said with a playful wink.

"And I'm yours." She almost leapt back into his arms to kiss him again. He could taste her familiar kiwi-strawberry lip gloss and wondered how it hadn't noticed it before. "I always have been and I always will be your biggest fan, no matter what the critiques say. You just write what's in your heart. What makes *you* happy. Don't worry about the rest of the world."

"And what about you?" River asked. "Can I worry about what makes you happy?"

Brie waved her hand in dismissal. "You don't have to worry about that because just being with you makes me happy. I know we've been having a bit of a rough patch lately, but you do know how much I love you, don't you, River?"

River was so overcome with sudden emotion; he had to clear his throat before he could speak again. "Of course I do. I love you too, Brie. More than anything."

He pulled Brie against his bare chest, exalting in the feel of her familiar touch and the sweet scent of her hair. The two of them laid there for a while, listening to the crackling of the fireplace and the sound of their hearts beating in time. A few minutes later, River heard the gentle even breath that signaled Brie had fallen asleep. Again, he studied her familiar features from the shocking mane of red hair to her rose petal skin, and it was as though he was seeing her beauty with fresh eyes. He started to realize the true gift the goddess had given him, and it was more than a new story and some hot and heavy love making. Brigid had reminded him that Brie had always been the embodiment of the goddess to him. At the height of their passion, she had literally taken on that form, but it had always been Brie that he longed for. Brigid had answered his prayer by rekindling that flame that had always been there between them. Her eternal fire had thawed the icy layer he had allowed to grow over his heart. Now that heart swelled with love for the woman he knew was his soul mate. Brie was his goddess as she had always been. Brie was his inspiration.

"I love you," he whispered, and stroked her fire red hair as she slept.

Even in the mist of her dreams, River knew she heard him, because her eyes fluttered and her lips turned up into a pleasant smile. She rolled over, and he tucked her in under the heavy blankets. River kissed her check before hauling himself up from the bed. He wrapped a robe around his naked body, pulled out his laptop, and sat down at his desk. It was the wee hours of the morning, but sleep could wait. His mind was racing with ideas and he wanted to document them while they were still fresh in his mind. With more excitement and enthusiasm than he had felt in weeks, River started to pen his next fantasy novel. It was an epic tale of love and passion that would be titled, *Brigid's Flame*.

THE END

Enjoyed this book? Take a look at Moon Rose Publishing to find more of our stories and authors!

www.moonrosepublishing.com

Publishing what you *really* want to read.

Made in the USA
Charleston, SC
16 March 2013